Jane M H Bigelow
June 10, 2006

Talisman

JANE M. H. BIGELOW

ANTELIOS

www.pronghornpress.org

For Robert and Mother

1

*D*ark true green, heavy in my hand, the emerald called to me. I was too mesmerized by its beauty to hear the footsteps coming up the hall, too fascinated to escape over the rooftops.

The temple-woman gave a screech fit to break glass when she saw me standing there. That broke the spell, if spell it was, and I'd moved out the window and half-way across the tiles before she'd drawn breath to scream again.

I ran barefoot, and the cracks between the smooth green tiles gave footing sure enough for me. Across that roof, on to the next, a little drop to the one after that; it's like a dance. You must set your feet just so, with no hard thumps or uncontrolled slides.

A tree grew near one of their fine mosaic walls, just near enough—a good quick spring, a slither down its most obliging branches, and I touched ground. So far, contrary to what most people believe about Sarinsat's eye, the temple had not collapsed.

Behind me, the temple guards rushed towards the screams and lamentations of the devout. Need I mention that they were also rushing away from me?

My woman-clothes were as I'd left them, hidden behind a water jug under a bench by the well. It took only a moment to put on the plain, dark wool caftan and headscarf. In place of a gem thief there stood someone's plain sister, someone else's third or fourth wife. The poor creature filled her water jug and walked towards home in the dawn light.

Even so downtrodden a woman would look up when the

temple gates were flung open, and well for me that it's so. The gallant temple guards nearly trampled me in their rush. I survived unharmed, but the water jug was less lucky.

There went a good part of my disguise! With it, I had an obvious reason for being out so early. Without it, I'd surely have to explain myself to someone.

"Best leave it, little sister. There's no mending that one." A woman's voice, low-pitched and half-laughing, startled me into a most unprofessional jump. She was indeed a good bit taller than I, and probably somewhat older, though the braided edging of her headscarf hid the color of her hair. Aside from that, she dressed plainly for this quarter; someone's housekeeper, perhaps. It's shameful how even the servants of the rich have time to stand around.

"No, even the handle's in several pieces," I agreed sadly. Oh, but it was hard to hide my laughter behind a worried frown! "I wonder what all that was about so early in the morning."

"Someone's robbed the temple, I think. I wonder who'd be so bold? And what was taken?" She looked at me strangely then, or so it seemed.

"I don't know, but I do know what's waiting for me if I don't get back soon, especially since I'll get there without water or pitcher. Wish me luck!" And I turned to go.

"I wish you the best of luck, little sister. I believe you'll need it." The voice was amused again. I do not like being laughed at, or being addressed familiarly by those who are no kin of mine, but I murmured my thanks and left.

The temple was new, and the streets around it wide; I breathed more easily when I'd reached my own tangle of narrow ways. They were crowded already with provident folk who meant to get most of their work done before the day's heat began. My work was done for awhile now. I needed to wait a few days before trying to find a buyer for the emerald; the temple guards would have put the fear of the entire pantheon into all the jewelers.

I had a small room at the back of the house of two widowed sisters. They liked quiet tenants, and asked no questions so long as that one requirement was met. A woman alone was a scandal, but they'd overlooked that for a little extra rent.

I'd made myself comfortable there with fat cushions and stolen silks. (The cushions I bought, just like an honest woman. Try running while holding a cushion in your arms.) Someday, of course, I hoped for better. That night's work had brought someday a great deal closer. I'll say this much for my unlamented teacher: he taught thoroughly.

Yes, and one lesson he taught by example. No thief goes uncaught forever. Bad luck, enemies, or age itself if you live that long, will take you out unless you take yourself out. Someday, before my joints hurt after a night spent roof-running, I meant to find safer ways of thieving.

It proved no great sacrifice to stay quiet for the next several days. There were far too many temple guards around, too many priests asking too many questions. I waited, mending my clothes and studying the emerald.

May the gods bless my father for letting me watch him at his jeweler's work. Thanks to him, I can recognize most false jewels from several feet away, and know just how to present a flawed jewel to hide that flaw. In his memory, I've never yet robbed a jeweler.

This gem had no flaw. Emeralds that large are rare enough, even when flawed; unblemished, it was almost unbelievable.

It was also almost unsalable. I went to Old Parata to handle it; he has a number of foreign clients and a strict conscience about protecting his sources. I trust no one, but it's impossible to sell something without at least admitting that you know where it can be found. Of course, I didn't tell him I had it in a pouch tied snugly against my stomach. I needn't have been quite so cautious in what I told him—he wanted nothing to do with it.

"Surely some of your distinguished clients are more concerned with beauty than details of provenance?" I asked.

"Some are, indeed," he agreed. Before I could continue my argument, he continued his. "But that beauty's unmistakable, and word of its loss has been sent as far as Issrandar. It'll be a year before I'd dare even hint that I might have it. Not to mention the fact that not everyone is as refreshingly free from superstition as you are. In a year, if we've no famine or flood and if the priests quiet down, I might be able to try. Maybe. Sarinsat's priests are after vengeance as much as the emerald, you know. This whole thing has Kossinli's faithful stirred up again, claiming that Sarinsat's eye wanted to be back where it properly belonged. They say that the thief was only a tool of Kossinli."

I snorted. The things some people will believe! I know what inspired me to rob Sarinsat's new house, and it had nothing to do with deities. Still, the religious quarrel might help keep Parata from deciding that the emerald would be safer with him than with me. He'd always dealt fairly, but this was more temptation than I'd offered before.

He expressed his regrets, and his hopes that I'd bring other business to him, "Especially if you manage to acquire rubies, or even garnets. I think the young must be showing how brave they are; I've had several inquiries lately."

I expressed my thanks, and assured him that I would come to him if I had such good fortune. Since many in Charransar still consider them unchancy, rubies are rare here. Then I left to consider the problem of dinner. I'd dug up some of my savings for last night's lentils, and I hated to make a habit of that.

Back in my room after taking a long and indirect route to get there, I fished the emerald out of its hiding place. "So, you want to be somewhere else, do you?" I asked it. "Fine with me. Just give me a way to do it that'll give me some payment for my efforts. And while you're at it, you might do something about the dinner I can't afford to buy." I slipped it back into its pouch, drank a little

water from my new pitcher, and settled in to sleep through the day's heat.

When I woke, I was hungrier than ever. The moon was up, which at least spared me the expense of a lamp. I went to get another drink of water and kicked something that rang against the uneven floor. Something that proved, when I picked it up, to be a coin.

This warranted lighting the lamp. A silver piece, unclipped, gleamed in its smoky light. When one has as few coins as I have, it's no great burden to keep track of them, and I knew that coin had not been there before.

"Thank you," I whispered. As I sat wondering what to do next, my stomach rumbled. I could think at least as well over dinner as I could sitting here.

I had meat with my dinner for the first time in a week that night, and couldn't truly enjoy the guilty pleasure. Nothing is free, nothing. What would the price for that silver coin be? At the same time, I couldn't quite help wondering what else I could have for the asking.

Two men watched me from the corners of their eyes as I sat alone in the tavern. Had they seen me pay with silver in spite of all my care? I'd best decide later, and elsewhere, how to test the powers of the stone. I could live off what I had for a day or two.

I could have, but I didn't. Curiosity as much as greed led me to use the emerald again. It, or the being to whom it truly belonged, had an odd way of doing things.

One morning when I'd dreamed of journeying far away, to a land of cool gardens and adoring men, I woke to find a donkey in my room. Unfortunately, he also woke the two sisters. Such cries of consternation and threats of eviction! My arguing that it must be a joke gained me grudging permission to stay after all, and comments on the sort of company I must be keeping.

Fortunately, I did manage to sell the donkey. My other possessions certainly wouldn't bring much: I owned two threadbare cushions, some crumpled silks, a small hoard of smaller coins, a little chipped pottery, and a magic gem with a perverse sense of humor. I began to lose sleep, wondering which offhand wish of mine the emerald would decide to answer, and how it would decide to do it.

At least my landladies couldn't blame me for the Joy-of-Princes tree that appeared in their tidy scrap of garden, or rather, they didn't know they could have. Really, I would have been satisfied with a few—all right, several—of the delicate pale green fruits that I'd seen being delivered to the grain broker's house. There was no need to send a whole tree.

Once, I caught myself almost wishing to be back with my husband and our kin in Nahouendar. He never meant to be cruel. Even his other wives were kind enough so long as I made no trouble. Perhaps there were worse things than boredom and hurt pride. I'd at least had someone to talk to when things puzzled me, even if they laughed.

"I don't mean that!" I said aloud. I fished the stone out of its pouch. "I don't mean it at all. I was only tired and worried. I don't mean it!"

That night I hardly slept at all lest I wake to find myself back in Nahouendar. Clearly, I needed to get rid of this gem. Kossinli's faithful might not pay well for it—fanatics tend to offer blessings in lieu of money—but they would take it off my hands, and I didn't know who else would.

The big problem would be coming safely away from the encounter. The first problem would be making contact at all.

Trying the obvious first, I went to Old Parata. If he knew where to contact the source of his rumors, he concealed his knowledge well. Obviously, I felt reluctant to press the matter; I didn't want anyone knowing quite how badly I needed to find a buyer for my prize.

Reluctantly, I turned to the emerald itself. "I need to find Kossinli's faithful," I whispered to it that night. "Please, don't mock me this time. I'm asking you seriously. Please answer me seriously."

For a change I slept well, but there was no answer when I woke. I sighed a little and went out to the baker's for something to break my fast. Really, I must have been dazed by all that lost sleep to think that praying to the source of my problems could solve them.

The bakery faces a little square with a fountain in the middle, all shaded by an enormous jacaranda. It's free pleasure to sit there and eat, if you're content with the edge of the fountain for a seat. I sat there feeling sorry for myself, a foolish luxury for one like me. It meant I didn't notice the woman's approach until she spoke to me.

"Greetings, little sister." It was the tall woman, wearing a different fringed headscarf. She smiled gently. "Do you not remember me?"

"Forgive me, of course I do. It's only that I was surprised to see you here, in such a humble part of town." And why in the name of all the deities and djinns are you here, I thought. She smiled again.

"Why surprised? You asked me to come."

I detest that sort of ostentatiously mystical answer. For a moment I was too angry to realize that this time I knew the answer to the riddle.

She had been waiting patiently for me to understand. She could tell when I did, too. "Will you come with me to my own house? This square is lovely, but not the best place for the sort of conversation we need to have."

Oh, yes, and be buried tidily in your garden, I thought. "I'd prefer to go to the shop of a jeweler I know." Old Parata would demand a cut, but better his sort than a slit throat. "It's humble, but more convenient to where what you want lies hidden."

"Do you think I carry that much money on my person?" she asked. "I haven't your skills." When I still didn't agree, she frowned. "Layla,"—So she knew my name, too!—

"If we'd intended to kill you and take what we seek, we could have done so any time during this last week that you've been...wishing. And I know you have it with you. That's how I found you. I might mention that I am trusting you in taking you to my own house." She smiled as she whispered, and so did I; two women gossiping in the cool morning.

They probably could have killed me. I'm strong for my size, and quick, but I'd been too bewildered and weary the last few days to be as alert as I usually am. Perhaps they'd continue to be so peaceable. Not everyone would. I needed to be free of that emerald, whatever deity claimed it.

"I would be honored to go with you to your home, Madame," I said. "However, it's quite safe to tell me here how much you're willing to pay for the gem."

"I'm called Firousi," she said. "As for price...my family is not wealthy..."

There are times when I could wish it wasn't always necessary to haggle.

"But I have help in this matter from those who share my interests. Shall we say, an even hundred lirials?"

I did not gasp. I was silent for awhile as I tried to decide whether or not to go through the motions of haggling over a price that was better than I'd dared hope. Even the best of my previous efforts had never brought me a tenth that sum. Money had been scant since a certain bright-eyed man left at midnight with my savings. I'd planned to burgle some truly ugly bridal jewelry later that night (the girl would be better off without it) and my ex-lover made sure I wouldn't follow him by alerting the householder. Bribing my way out of prison before they could remove a hand kept me very busy, and very poor.

I wanted that money, but I wondered whether I should simply run. Perhaps she made such a splendid offer because she'd no expectation of actually paying? People talk of the old town as dangerous, but if I wanted to cause someone to disappear quietly, the high-walled houses of the rich would serve as well.

Running would leave me still stuck with the emerald, unless I simply threw it away, and all that risk and effort with it. Also, for all the strange things one hears about Kossinli's faithful, Firousi didn't have the look of a murderess.

Ah well. If I'd wanted a long quiet life, I could have stayed home in Nahouendar.

"Your offer is a reasonable one, Firousi. I'll not ask any more of your patience by haggling now."

Together we walked back out of the old town, but not out to Sarinsat's quarter. "I told you we were not wealthy," Firousi said when I hesitated. "It isn't far now."

Nor was it. The house had been splendid, once; the outer wall was faced with marble all the way up to spikes which had once been gilded. Most of the gilt was long gone, and the intricately patterned tiles of the courtyard were cracked. Were a hundred lirials going to come out of here?

It might be so. Whatever they'd lost, the courtyard was still filled with flowers and cooled by a fountain. A stocky, gray-haired woman shuffled in with sharba in silver cups that would have kept me for six months. As the cool sweetness slid down my throat, I began to believe that Firousi truly meant to pay that handsome price.

It was a disappointment, then, to hear her say, "There's one other offer I would like to make you, Layla."

"Oh?" I said.

"I want you to consider it carefully before you answer. It could affect the rest of your life."

There was no good way out of that flowery box. Oh, there were several doors, but I only knew where one of them led. I could hear people moving around in the rest of the house. Though I'm quick with my knife when I must be, my reluctance to use it has kept me from becoming expert.

"Layla, it's all right. You're safe here, whatever you

decide." Firousi frowned slightly. "I only meant that this is a serious offer, which could bring you much more than a hundred lirials in time."

By all the gold in Issrandar, what did she want me to do? Were there more sacred jewels to be stolen? Thank you, no. I've had enough of temple treasure. I waited for her to continue.

"You obviously have a talent for magic. Did the emerald ever do any miracles for Sarinsat? No, because no one with talent worships there. Also, they've confused the means and the end—but I doubt that theology interests you."

"I fear not." Would she ever come to the point?

"Would you like to learn to control the sort of thing you did with the emerald?" she asked.

"What's the price?" I asked quickly, before my own visions of wealth swept me away.

"Oh, Layla..."

"There's always a price. Always. You can call it whatever sort of divinely-ordered balance you like, but nothing's free in this world, and I don't think the gods give anything away either. So I ask you, what price?" Crude, perhaps, but she had that intent look that believers get before they tell you how much good it would do you in the next world to do well by them in this one.

She sighed. "There is no cost in money. You may keep the entire hundred lirials, if you like."

If I liked! With much effort, I kept silent.

"But you must agree to be guided by us in matters of magic. Consider the trouble these few small attempts have brought you, working blind. Please believe me—you must learn to see."

"That sounds reasonable." Remarkably reasonable for one of Kossinli's faithful. I waited for the rest of the conditions.

"Forgive me, but there is one other thing. You must also be guided by us in your thieving. There are people to be left in peace, and there are other...objects that do not properly belong where they are."

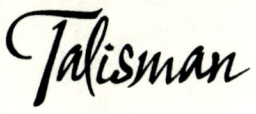

So. All they really wanted, then, was to control my every move, in return for which they might be able to teach me something about what had just happened to me. And she sat there looking as if she'd just offered me something wonderful! It's best to be gentle with the mad.

"Thank you, Firousi, but I've been working alone for too long now to welcome working under direction again. I can accept only your first offer."

"We don't compel anyone," she said, and called the servant. She brought a small bag with her this time, and in it were my hundred lirials. It's a tiny coin to be worth so much, but then, it is gold.

Even though the emerald had lain snug against my body all day, it felt cool in my hand as I fished it from its pouch. After one last look at its flawless green glow, I handed it to Firousi.

"If you ever change your mind, the second offer will still be open," Firousi said. She looked almost sad. "Take care of yourself, little sister."

"I always do," I assured her.

What I did then still surprises me. I gave her back five coins and asked her to thank Kossinli for me. For a moment I thought she wasn't going to take them, but then she smiled and handed them to the servant.

She was still smiling as if at some private joke when I left. It is funny, I suppose, to see a temple robber turn religious even for a moment. I've no intention of doing that again.

I have been trying very hard to be careful about my wishes, but this morning there was another donkey.

2

*L*ife had been hard enough even before that happened. For once in my life I had money, and I dared not spend it! It was day-old bread and red-twig tea again for me most mornings, while enough gold for an entire almond grove made a cold hard lump against my middle. Ah well, my middle would have worse to complain of if Sarinsat's priests ever found me.

I dreamed sometimes that they had. The other night I dreamed of being carried into His temple, wrapped round and round with a rainbow of embroidery wool until I could neither struggle nor scream, nor even breathe.

It had begun as such a nice little dream, too. I'd been strolling by a stream, wearing boy's clothes like those I wear for thieving but made of silk, plucking strands of bright silk floss that hung from the willows with a jewel at the end of each strand. I was talking to someone—who had it been? She'd fled suddenly, and the willows turned to thorn-trees, the silk, coarse wool.

Wool was smothering me, in truth, though I lay safe in my own garret. Hanks and piles of raw wool covered me, my sleeping mat, and most of the floor. Here under the roof tiles, the sun was already drawing a ripe smell from it.

"Not fair, Kossinli," I muttered as I flailed my way free. "Dreams don't count. Not real, sleeping dreams, those don't count as wishes. Why are You still listening, anyway? I sold You out, Lady of Mirth. I took money instead of a chance to learn more of You, remember?" Some goddesses just can't take a hint.

Ah well. The wool could have been a herd of sheep. At

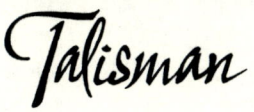

least wool doesn't make noise, or messes. It doesn't upset the landladies. This room may be always too hot or too cold, but it's private, cheap, and well placed for quiet roof-running. I'd truly hate to have to leave.

I spat out a wisp of wool and began stuffing the rest into a half-embroidered cushion cover that was turning out poorly, anyway. With Sarinsat's priests still prowling around even this humble neighborhood, I'd had to do some of the embroidery by which I supposedly earned my living.

Fortunately, I actually like embroidery. During the years of my marriage it was my only relief from boredom, and the shame of never quickening. Such tangles of leaves and flowers, such fantastical beasts as I devised while I sat in the ordered geometry of the women's gardens!

I sighed, remembering, and sneezed violently three times as wool floated down onto my nose. If ever I am ruler over anything, and someone offends me, I shall sentence that person to clear a room that has been filled half full of top quality, well-carded wool. There will be no need at all to call in the royal torturer. Making the offender work on an empty stomach, as I was doing, would be too cruel.

Was it boredom that weakened my wits? I'd barely left my room since Harat's uncle's funeral two days ago. Bless Harat for smuggling me in as a cousin of sorts! Harat, his uncle and I all followed the same trade, but Harat's wife pretended she didn't know just what that was.

I'd stuffed wool into another cushion cover and an old set of trousers I'd been keeping for patching my others before it occurred to me that I was going to have to see Firousi about this.

She'd said I could keep all that lovely money, but what good was it doing me? Maybe a nice fat donation to Kossinli's worship would do the trick; I could give a handsome amount and still have some left. It didn't mean I had to take her up on that other offer. I didn't want to control this contact with a goddess.

I wanted to end it.

The wool I kindly gave to a neighbor with twelve children and lots of discretion. When I told her the wool was a gift from Heaven, she rolled her eyes and laughed. Sad, isn't it, how often people won't believe the truth?

The best almond rolls in Charransar are found at Marana's bakeshop. How fortunate that it lay in the same direction as Firousi's house! I'd need my strength for the journey.

It's well that I did stop there, for I got no refreshment at Firousi's. The courtyard doors were shut, and no gatekeeper answered my knock. I tried twice more. After all, would not a friend try more than once? In this quiet quarter, I would have heard if anyone approached the gate from inside. Was Firousi gone, or just not receiving visitors?

The rich take their deliveries at the back door, thank you. By now it was mid-day; only the most urgent order would bring anyone along the unshaded cart-road. At least, I hoped so. You can't climb walls in women's clothes without hoisting your skirts to a shocking level.

There, at least, luck was with me. The back wall hadn't been mudded in some time, giving lots of toe-holds, and no one came by. The climbing roses did put a rip two handspans long in my skirt as I slithered along the wall and over to the inner courtyard.

The pretty flowers were all half-dead; the windows, shuttered. Dry leaves rustled across the tiles in the courtyard below. I would find neither help nor answers here.

My perch was too prickly to stay puzzling there long. Back along garden wall, then, and down the hot bricks of the outer wall. Still, I could not help wondering how long Firousi had been gone, and why she'd left so suddenly. She'd meant to come back, or else why bother with the shutters? If Sarinsat's men suspected she had that emerald, and she'd managed to learn of their suspicions, that would explain it. Suddenly I was glad she'd gone; it made it that much more difficult for Sarinsat's men to find me.

It was good to leave those open streets with their blank walls for the chaos of my own quarter. Neither of my landladies returned my cheerful greeting as I went up to eat my spiced chickpeas. I'd indulged in some cucumber salad as well. With my stomach full, it was easy to sleep through the heat of the day.

It did mean I needed cash again. As usual, I went through Brilliant Street on my way to Oven Square. It's convenient for before-breakfast business, and the times that I didn't stop at Old Parata's helped conceal the times that I did. There's nothing like a fresh hot almond roll on a cool morning, after working up an appetite with a night's clambering after carefully-chosen gems.

By late afternoon it's usually so crowded that it's hard to tell accidental pushes from attempts on a poor widow's purse. That day there was room enough to walk at whatever pace I chose, even in the narrows where the old Skandarian Gate used to be. The two old men who beg by the fountain had fallen asleep in the dappled shade of the locust trees.

It seemed to me that the few people I saw looked at me strangely when they didn't keep their eyes firmly on the ground. None of the jewelers acknowledged that they saw me, not by the lift of an eyebrow or a glance towards a side door. Even one-handed Mata turned to sweeping out his shop, the broom wedged between his arm and his skinny ribs. Ingrates. I never steal from jewelers, and I could.

Old Parata stood blocking the door to his shop, gazing through me. I stared back reproachfully. It's a fine thing to be snubbed by my banker when I'm completely caught up with my payments!

Then, with as much of a bow as his back allows, he waved me through the outer shop, making his usual loud lament for the miserable state of the second-hand jewelry market. His son gave me an even sourer look than usual.

"You'd best peddle some of those embroideries," Old

Parata said after he'd poured us some mint tea. "It's too hard to explain having lirials in the till; I'm just a humble second-hand jewelry dealer."

Yes, and I'm a widow living by my needle. "Parata, old friend, you're not refusing to exchange anything today?" He was silent for long enough to scare me before grudgingly acknowledging that he could manage to oblige me one more time. We haggled awhile, and I eventually got one lirial changed for rather fewer sekals than last month. He looked away politely while I fished it out of the waist-pouch I wear cinched tight under my robes.

Indeed, he was working hard at not staring at me. "Have you started spinning as well as embroidering?"

That explained some of those odd looks I'd gotten. "No, why? Oh plague! Am I covered with wool?" I'd worked so hard at getting the last wisps out of my room, too.

"Not quite. If you'll allow an old man?" I nodded, and he plucked several wisps. "Another kind attention from Kossinli, I take it?" He rolled the wisps into a neat little bundle. I told him the latest verse of that song, and he agreed that I was lucky She hadn't sent me the whole sheep, live and baaing.

"And if She sends you any other livestock, you're on your own! Finding a buyer for that donkey was bad enough. I know you're too stubborn to go to whoever was brave enough to buy the emerald and offer money back to get the curse taken off—"

"You're wrong there, old friend. I've tried. The house is closed, not even a caretaker left to guard it."

"Forgive unrequested advice from a man old enough to be your father. But lirials travel well. Why not do just that? Go somewhere that isn't crawling with men asking questions every time more than three sekals change hands? I've seen you eyeing my shop. Unless you let someone cheat you badly, the price of that emerald ought to set you up."

Plague. Must've been a lot more obvious than I thought.

"Why not set up shop far enough away that no one will ask too closely about your departed husband, and sleep soundly at night? You'll have to give up roof-running someday."

Gods, did he see me as such competition? "Someday, when my knees hurt and my eyes won't judge the gap between roofs, and you're drinking sharba in the shade, I might try a shop like yours. You could advise me to your heart's content! But I like it here. I know this city, or at least my part of it. Why go where I'll have to discover all over again who I can trust, and convince them to trust me? Where else would I find such a good—ah—banker? And you know they'll never suspect a mere female of stealing the gem from over Sarinsat's own nose. So long as I'm discreet about what I spend, I'm as safe as I ever was."

I do like it here, though it isn't my birthplace, and I've had to look sharp to keep it from being my grave. How should I not like the place where I found my freedom? If I could also find a way to eat regularly without risking my own skin I'd like the town even better. Something like Old Parata has would do nicely, once he himself hands the business over to his son. I won't do it sooner; it would be both unkind and unwise to go into competition with him. But his worthy and honest heir has tried several times to get his father to give up the...*irregular* side of his trade. The skills I learned from my father would be useful again; reset the stolen gems, and who's to say where they were before?

"You're only just past the best time for finding a caravan to join. My cousin Isradan's heading back to Liriat soon. We'd dinner last night with a mine-owner from the Ngarra who'll be heading home next week, or I can introduce you to the widow of an old friend in the wool trade. She and her clan are journeying to Tzakende—"

"Tzakende? The city with more gods than rats? Incense makes my head hurt. Forget the Ngarra, too. Even the little children carry knives, and I'm a peaceable sort." Parata didn't ask why I wouldn't travel with Isradan; it may be that he suspected in just what way Isradan had tried to persuade me to join his household at the start of his visit. And him with four wives already, not to mention several children older than I am. That near-rape may not have been Kossinli's doing, though I had been daydreaming about taking a lover. Daydreaming's about all I do these days, alas. Celibacy gets tiresome, but not so tiresome as wondering whether someone's hand is after my body or my take. Plague take Harat's wife for being the jealous sort.

"Tzakende's peaceable enough, and Mother Rissa tells me she's always treated well there. The journey would cramp your usual style, but I'm told there are wonders to be seen along the way."

"Sorry, my friend. The last thing I need is more priests."

We drank the last of the mint tea in silence. Old Parata grimaced, though it was as sweet as it always was. No stinginess with the sugar here.

"Then what will you do, Layla? Wait until Sarinsat's men are watching your house and you have to bolt wherever you can, with whoever will take you?"

How should I answer this? We'd worked out an unspoken agreement long ago, Parata and I; I let him try to tell me what I should do, and he let me ignore him.

"Parata, my friend, this isn't like you. You've always said..."

"Never mind what I've always said. You're an affront to the proper order of things, and may the little godlings of the Wastes seize my poor old hide for a waterskin if I know why I care if you get yourself killed, but I do—at least, at the hands of Sarinsat's priests." He sighed heavily. "Don't gawp, girl. Maybe I just get tired of dealing with people who can't tell gemstones from dyed rocks, or think I can't. Take care."

A lean, lemon-faced man watched me all the way to the next turning of the half-deserted street, and for once I was glad of my robe and headscarf, faded to almost the same yellow-brown as the walls. By the huddle of buildings that surrounded Sarinsat's temple, I finally encountered enough crowds to feel almost comfortable. One of the Servants of Duty stood by, overseeing the efforts of three sweating acolytes to keep the square swept clear of dung. Sunlight flashed half-blindingly on his silver Manacle of Devotion and drew my eye as he pointed out fragments they had missed. Sarinsat is the cleanest of the Gracious Ones.

As I skirted the chief temple, I was nearly run down by one of the Rememberers Guild. Not stopping even to curse me, he raced up the steep steps of the western door and tried to push past the guard there. He was still arguing when two priests, bearing a body between them, came out the same way. There was very little blood on the corpse, but it sagged bonelessly between its bearers.

I'd let the crowd hem me in; the corpse-bearers drew closer. I could see more than I wished already, yet I couldn't look away. I knew that man. It was Harat.

Behind me, his wife's voice shrieked incoherent curses. The Rememberer rent his outer robe from neck to hem, ripping through its rows of gold braid as if they were cheap cotton. The crowds retreated as if from a plague victim.

I wedged myself into one group and let it carry me around the corner, invisible as one stick in a flooding river. There I sat down on the ledge around a fountain until my knees stopped shaking. From the temple steps, a fine sonorous voice cursed the Rememberer for taking so long finding a will that his stupidity had caused the Servants of Duty to question an innocent man on his sudden prosperity.

The Servants of Duty had killed before; there is no respect without fear, they claim. But it had always been planned before. Now they had killed poor Harat, who never neglected the flowers for the end of the Dry Times, and always put a pinch of incense on the altar of whichever god's turn it was. A most dutiful thief, and leaving thievery entirely now that he'd become rich. He'd've known how to keep his riches, too. Poor Harat. I could even think, "poor Harat's wife," though she always looked down her nose at me. Who'd steal for her now?

Our Prince does not meddle in religious matters, a wise policy which I wish I had continued to imitate. He concerns himself with the security of our borders and that of his coffers. Surely, though, a little official disapproval of this sort of thing would not be interfering too much.

No, I didn't mean that. Please, Kossinli, I do not want two groups of spies snooping around here.

For the next week, I led a life that would have won the approval of my husband's second wife. Lady Massara would have been pleased to see how well I remembered the embroidery skills she taught me. Besides the money I got, the detailed work numbed my mind to making careless wishes. Except to go to the dressmaker and the linen-draper who sold my work, I seldom left the house until nightfall, and that not often. Only my roof-running kept me sane. Sanity was about all the good I got of that; Old Parata's prices were worse than ever.

I did keep the cloudfleece cloth. I'd seen a light-green length of it draped over the robe-stand in one fine Lady's dressing-room, and left with it and the tourmalines lying nearby. What did she want with it, that respectable merchant's wife? I could practically see my skin through it.

Poor Harat. He had none of the good of my theft, but he'd paid for it. I never meant it so! May the silent god of thieves witness, I've never set up anyone to take the cut for me. Yet I had no wish to pay myself for a theft that had done me so little good. Some nights I simply ran the roofs without taking anything, only for the sweet oblivion of sleep that followed.

Perhaps I should set up as a physician, and recommend this method of curing insomnia. It leaves no hangovers and costs nothing—well, the roof-running itself—no. It would be so crowded up on my roofs then, with bankers and slavers and others who certainly should be having trouble sleeping, all scampering along!

I was on my way back from the baker's when I saw the

lemon-faced man in animated conversation with a ruddy-faced man as round as the lemon-faced one was lean. "What business have you here?" both hissed at each other as I passed. It was suddenly crowded near the wall as several people tried to look as though they hadn't just seen two such important men speaking like a comic chorus.

"His Majesty empowers me," said the ruddy-faced man.

"The Servants of Duty require answers of you," said the lemon-faced man at nearly the same time.

I left at a discreetly hurried pace; behind me, I could hear each man calling out for help in bringing this miscreant to his particular authorities. It was all I could do to get back to my room before I collapsed with nervous giggles. All that effort, and they'd never find the man responsible. With luck, they'd keep each other busy for a good long time.

And without luck? Would I like Kossinli's next joke as well as this one? I settled myself more comfortably, wedging cushions behind my back so that I could see out the low window.

Not that there was much to see; there are few gardens in my quarter, and fewer people with money for the water to keep them green this far into summer. Buildings leaned against each other as if they too had wilted. Perhaps Old Parata had been right.

But would Kossinli's jokes be any less dangerous in a strange city? Not likely. And Parata always came through when we'd drunk tea together awhile. All this sitting and waiting was getting on my nerves, that was my problem. Whenever I wasn't actually terrified I was more bored than I'd been since my days as the third wife of a minor noble (never mind who; the poor man's suffered enough). I should go out roof-running again tonight; those gathering clouds that were making such a fiery sunset would give just the sort of shifting shadows that help thieves.

Was it only thinking of theft that made me glance out my window just then? What had moved down there on that scrap of a street that led nowhere but the fallen-in ruins of a long-dry fountain? Well, even a poor widow may gaze out at the sky. With my head up but my eyes down, I saw a shadow shift when there was no wind. Normal skullduggery, or someone watching the house?

We impoverished widows have to make use of all the sunlight we get. I unwrapped the sash I was embroidering and sat by my window, stitching industriously, thinking furiously, and resting my eyes now and then by gazing at the street below. As the sun shifted, I indulged myself by lighting the smaller of my two lamps. I could afford a little good-quality lamp oil now, and it was the sort of small luxury that doesn't attract attention.

What was I going to do if Kossinli continued to insist on "helping" me? It wouldn't take much to attract unwanted attention just now, as Harat's death showed. Why hadn't selling Her eye closed Her regard for me? I'd been so sure that it would! Her priestess Firousi had said otherwise, but then, Firousi'd been so eager to acquire an expert gem thief as Kossinli's servant that I still doubted her word.

Well, it made no difference now. I hoped Firousi was still alive. There's so little laughter in the world that even infuriating know-it-alls should be allowed to tend its sources.

I pinched the wick of my lamp and waited. The moon was descending again when a bit of shadow I'd been watching slid away from a doorway and down the street. Prince's man, or priests'? And whichever one it was, why not simply haul whoever they suspected in for questioning? Could he be working alone, hoping to sell information to prince and priests alike?

For whatever reason he came, he was leaving. Or was he? How far away would he go? If he was truly leaving, would he go east to Sarinsat's temple or north to the palace of the prince's men? I rose and scrambled into my boy's clothes. I'd only need to follow him a little way; no need to fuss with hauling my woman's clothing with me. The same weather that helps thieves could help a spy as well, and I'd a mind to steal some knowledge.

The only nasty part of getting from my window to the roof above is the moment when I must lean backwards over the alley wall, getting a good grip on the roof tiles. One good push and I was up and running from shadow to shadow, the tiles pleasantly cool underfoot.

Below me, the shadow-man slid from doorway to doorway, never stopping long. He never once looked up. Oh, the sweet night wind and the hastening clouds! Would I truly let someone else do the roof-running while I sat in a shop, even if I could?

A loose tile slid beneath my foot. The noise of that was loud enough; the crash when it hit the street not five steps from my spy was louder still. I dived for the shadow of a dovecote.

Fool. Amateur. I knew better than to give my mind to anything but the theft at hand. I lay flat and motionless as a tree-rat on a branch, hoping that the cat will go soon.

Face to the tiles, I lay listening for departing footsteps. I would have given several of those damned lirials for a good look at the street below, but with the moon behind me I dared not risk it. As I waited with a broken tile digging into one leg, I realized why someone had posted a watcher outside my house instead of hauling all within it away for questioning. Just as I had followed him, he was watching for someone he could follow to the emerald. No thief would do such a thing, of course, but a worshiper might. A worshiper creeping back to take that emerald from its safe hiding place to some altar where it could be openly used, or going to worship in secret, but going to it in either case. A priestly spy, then. So much the worse for me. A prince's servants are so much likelier to grow weary, or bored, and of course the prince may die.

Ah, Kossinli. I don't know where your eye may be now, but could I ever convince the Servants of Duty of that?

Finally, as the wind rattled the seed pods of the trees, I heard a scurry of footsteps. A quick peek over the edge of the roof showed me the spy hurrying almost silently down the street. As he left, he looked up. It was surely the moonlight that made his face look so much like a skull. At the year's turn the storytellers whisper of glowing eyes and fangs; an ordinary human face will frighten well enough, I find. Childishly, I closed my eyes. When I opened them he was gone.

And so would I have to be, soon. The moon was sinking. How far would I need to go? Did I dare go back to my room? Certainly, nothing there was so valuable that I couldn't replace it. I could just wait here in the wind until I could slip around to Parata's and get him to set me up with his friends in the caravan business.

Right. Dressed as a boy. Unfortunately I cannot pass as a boy, not in daylight. I would simply have to be very careful getting back to my room, and waste no time with wishing.

Being careful takes time. The sky was beginning to pale with the false dawn by the time I reached my own roof. Well, at least it made it easy to see that there was no one at all in the street below. No window overlooks my room; that's one reason I rented it. I slid down into the room and curled up among my cushions, trying hard to think of nothing at all as I went to sleep.

It was the whuffling that told me I was not alone when I finally wakened in the late afternoon. The previous donkey had brayed, but this one just wanted to eat my hair. "Kossinli! You did this once already," I complained.

Actually, this donkey was half again as large as the first. It was also piebald. A dark splotch over one eye gave it a quizzical expression. I'd better get out of town before Kossinli worked Her way up to camels.

Gathering up my belongings didn't take long. My boy's clothes, my other set of women's clothes, and my smaller oil lamp took little space. I left the cooking pots, but took a bowl and a plate, and my silver spoon. I stuffed my embroidery work into a corner of the bundle beside the cloudfleece. How could so little be so large? Two long sash-pieces pulled back out of the bundle tied it and my longest cushion to the donkey's back. He stood all this better than I'd expected; he only tried to kick me twice.

Would any of the caravans Old Parata had mentioned still

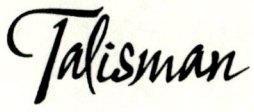

be there? Surely at least one would. It had only been yesterday, after all! Isradan, oh ye imps of sour water, not Isradan. Priests or knives, priests or knives?

I really don't like knives. Oh, I won't deny I've used one when I must, but only when I must. With all the priests, priestesses, and scryers there are in Tzakende, there must be someone who really does have some explanations for the whims of the Divine. And if not, they weren't likely to mind one more divinely pestered resident. They might not even notice.

Donkeys are nimbler than horses, but getting this one down to the courtyard required coaxing it down stairs just barely wide enough for its hooves; its middle brushed the wall on one side and hung out into space on the other. Donkeys are also brighter than horses. This one understood that I was asking it to do things which no rational donkey should consider.

My landladies heard us long before I got the beast down the stairs. "You slut, you wretched, miserable creature, leave our house immediately!" was only the beginning of the scold. Most of the rest of it was incoherent. Rossalena, the elder sister, gave up on speech entirely and set after us with her broom.

"Nay, Lady, she must be mad. We must not harm a madwoman!" cried their maid. Rossalena swatted at her with the broom.

The lemon-faced man was waiting as I staggered out of their courtyard gate, dragging the donkey, Imchi, behind me. Suddenly there was a thump and a bray and Imchi was dragging me; Rossalena's broom had connected. How angry she'd be to know that she'd saved my life! For the lemon-faced man was too helpless with laughter to do more than lean against the wall and bray like a donkey himself. The combined noise made it impossible for any of us to hear what Rossalena was saying as I fled.

Don't ask me how I got to Old Parata's without disaster. I remember dodging a stack of chickens in cages, but most of the rest is a blur. "Silently as a thief, our hero slipped from the city of his enemies," the old songs say. Heros must lead such simple lives.

Plump old Parata is much stronger than I had ever supposed. He whisked me and the donkey through his back door and shut it so quickly that he had to open it again to let me get the hem of my robe in with me.

"What do you need, Layla?"

"An introduction to one of your honest caravan leaders. You were right after, all about, the house being watched." He mimed fainting from astonishment; I ignored him. "Right now one spy's laughing too hard to suspect me of anything except idiocy, but I don't believe I'll count on that continuing. Is the wool-merchant clan still here?"

"Mother Rissa's? Yes, surely. But I thought Tzakende was the last place you wanted to go."

"No, the third-from-last. Sell me a few trinkets for trade, my friend; I'm going to be an honest merchant." He cast his eyes and his hands to the heavens, or at least the ceiling, but he did as I asked. I was in such a hurry that I didn't notice until much later, halfway across the Wastes, that he'd sold me back two sets of ear-cuffs and a trio of braid-clasps that I'd originally sold him. High rent for a night in his stable with Imchi!

He demanded more than money of me. As he was choosing what to sell to me, he stopped and put his hand on my arm. "You'll be an honest merchant, Layla," he said. "I want your promise."

"I'll be as honest as you are yourself," I assured him.

"More so. Layla, you'll be out there a long time. If you steal from Mother Rissa's clan she'll catch you, and if she catches you, she'll leave you out there. If you steal from someone else and draw trouble down on them, you won't escape that trouble. Promise me, or I won't take you to her."

"Well, this is a fine time to talk like that! You're the one who wanted me to do this in the first place."

He rubbed his forehead, right where his eyebrows almost met. "Layla, I did warn you that you couldn't live the way you do here. I can't send you to Mother Rissa without your promise."

I could see the wisdom of not stealing from the people I was traveling with, but not to steal at all seemed stupid. Who knew what opportunities there might be out there? For that matter, who knew but what I still might need to give back Kossinli's money? For once there was no persuading Old Parata to give me a better deal. Finally, reluctantly, I agreed.

Mother Rissa had clever eyes, bright in their nets of wrinkles. They were almost all that I could see of her, for she was draped in multicolored layers of shimmering cloudfleece. Elegant protection against the dust of the gateway!

"That's a memorable donkey," she said as she stared at Imchi and the clumsy bundle he carried. That thought had crossed my mind, too. "Well, no matter; it's been very dry here lately." Before I could ask what that had to do with anything, she continued, "Let's get you a proper packsaddle, dear, you'll never get past the outer gates without dropping something and even if you do, that arrangement will rub his back raw before the end of the day. I'm guessing you don't mind leaving today? We wouldn't normally go as far as Tzakende this late in the year, but we've a commission from a breeder there that makes it worth the extra trouble."

Indeed not. One night in Old Parata's stable was enough; my sneezes had kept me awake half the night. The packsaddle was provided, at what I suspected was an outrageous price. My bundles were rearranged, and Imchi and I were tucked into the middle of a crowd of wagons, other donkeys, oxen and children. There were even two camels, which I thought would please Kossinli. They're definitely someone's perverse idea of a joke.

Then, having rushed through a bewildering series of

commands from Mother Rissa, we waited. The fine yellow dust billowed up from the trampled ground and settled over us. Now I understood why Imchi's unusual pattern didn't matter; he could have been striped under all that dust without anyone's knowing it.

The gates used to be wider once, and decorated with carving that the clumsy infill had broken. Bits of a smiling woman looked out from the remains of a formal garden; the broken edges made her seem to wink as we inched our way past and onto the open road.

3

*F*irousi peered through the fine netting that covered the windows of her wagon. So far as she could tell, the scenery was unchanged from the last time she'd looked. At least the speed of her horses spared her the dust of anyone except the caravan guards.

She settled back into her corner, pushing the cushions into something like comfort. Really, there was not even room to stretch one's legs in this crate! Those cushions must have been around since the days when the Illyini still ruled. Where had Roshana gotten them, the attics of the Charransar house? Ah well, at least the sale of that termite-infested warren had brought enough money to smooth a few of the bumps on the journey. There would be trouble over that! Well, let those who complained find the money for buying stolen goods and rushing off just ahead of the Priests of Order. Done was done, and no one could deny that the house had been hers to dispose of.

"Roshana?" she said softly.

The figure curled in the diagonally opposite corner opened her eyes. "My Lady?" She sounded wide awake.

"Ah, good, you weren't really asleep. Find us the cards and let's ignore the journey as best we may." The wagon hit a bump just then; her voice rose comically on the last word. Both women laughed. "And set up the card-holder," Firousi continued, "or we'll have to play Scrambled Eggs instead of Kings."

In spite of the wagon's irregular swaying, Roshana managed to fasten the wooden card-box between the ties that ran to the roof and floor. She slid the box's lid back; at Firousi's gesture she shuffled the cards. Firousi dealt them each seven, then placed the rest securely in the box.

"What stakes, my Lady?"

"On a trip this long? A sequin a point, or you'll own the wagon and all that's in it by the time we arrive."

Roshana smiled thinly and shook her head. "Well, my Lady, I have been playing a few more years! You've learned caution, at least."

Both ladies took their cards too seriously to talk much while they played. Not even the most dedicated players can go on forever, though; by the time the caravan stopped for the night they had already closed the card-box.

With the netting thrust back from the door, Firousi sat dangling her legs over the edge of the wagon. Roshana soon had some of the thorny brushwood snapping in a cook-fire. Firousi knew better than to protest when their two guards crouched for a game of knucklebones; after three throws one man cursed and rose to keep watch. Once the driver had hobbled the horses, he took that man's place at the game. Even the brackish water from the hooded well smelled sweet. Deepening shadows spared her the sight of the road worn straight across the plains.

Soon enough Roshana called her. "I'm sorry the meal's so plain, my Lady. There's not much to be done cooking in one pot over a campfire, I fear." Roshana handed the bread basket to Firousi. "Come, have a little of this before it goes hard; we'll get little enough fresh bread in the next weeks."

Firousi broke off a small piece. "Don't fuss, Roshana. The meal's well enough." She nibbled at the bread. "I never have much appetite when I'm traveling, you know that. Still, it's good to be out of that oven of a city. No wonder the family never used to live there in summer!"

Roshana sighed and helped herself to bread, then divided what remained among the men. Firousi smiled at the dance of the guards trading round for a turn at the meal.

The driver touched his forehead in silent thanks and mopped the last of Roshana's stew from his bowl, then ate the remainder of the bread in three bites. "Sleep safe," he said, as he took his bedroll from the back of the wagon. The man on watch touched his sword-hilt and grinned.

"Sleep safe," said Roshana. Firousi sat gazing into the fire. Roshana clicked her tongue against her teeth. "Now, then, what would Kossinli say to a face like that?"

"How should I know? She's barely spoken to me, or to any of us, since the conquest. I'm doing all I can! Haven't I traveled the Wastes four times, even going to the swamps of Kribas trying to find the pieces of Her statue that those barbarians scattered? Didn't I offer both wealth and knowledge to that miserable little thief who found the Laughing One's eye in the Temple of Sarinsat? And I would have taught her, too, if she'd let me!"

"Hmph. Let you!" Roshana tugged the seats of the wagon towards each other more vigorously than was needed.

"The Lady of Mirth has no slaves," said Firousi. Roshana said nothing to that, as Firousi had expected. How could she argue with the doctrine that had freed her when Firousi was a toddler?

"The gift unasked, and she wants to refuse it," Firousi muttered. She sighed and rose to her feet. As lifelong priestess of Kossinli, she ought to be able to see the humor in yet another journey across the Wastes, shuttling back and forth like a demented sand-beetle. Maybe it would become clear to her later. She walked a little ways, stretching and enjoying the cooler air.

In the distance, the campfires of some other late season travelers flickered. Firousi could hear the clanking of pots and one loud laugh carrying across the open ground. Looking like shadow puppets, people passed back and forth getting ready for sleep. They would travel at first light. This late in the year it would not be necessary to travel by moonlight to avoid the heat.

"Kossinli, your loyal sand-beetle is here," Firousi murmured. A breeze rattled the branches of the thorn trees. She wondered if Kossinli was angry at how long it was taking to repair Her statue. "Kossinli, did she come back, the little thief? She almost took the offer of teaching."

It would serve her well if she had come back to find the house empty. But Kossinli never responded to anger; Firousi made herself think instead of the night she'd met with the few followers of Kossinli in Charransar who'd still admit their allegiance. Some of them had actually envied her. She was to bear such a glorious role in restoring the Lady of Mirth, and would doubtless have such adventures doing it! Firousi wouldn't have called it that herself.

We're never content, are we? Kossinli, I pray You send me some mirth on this journey. And when You find me a thief in Tzakende, make that thief someone who will be guided by me.

As Firousi lay trying to convince herself that the prickling of her skin was only the dry air, and not sand fleas that had decided to have an all-night revel, she began making a series of verses in the linked three-part rhyme scheme of Nahouendar. The verses turned on the fact that the man who'd bought her house, thus financing her flight across the Wastes, worshiped Sarinsat.

4

I felt like a bug on a tile. When I hitched a ride on one of the wool-carts, I could see all of us bugs straggling across a yellow-brown plain which seemed to stretch to the edge of the world.

That couldn't be true, of course. Tzakende is obviously nearer than the edge of the world, and I couldn't see it. Even if I couldn't see Tzakende for the dust we were raising, I'd surely have been able to see the mountains beyond it, so we couldn't really be going anywhere near the edge.

I knew a woman once who held that there is no world's edge, that it is round as an orange. She explained it all to me at one of the family feasts, she and I being equally left out of things for our various reasons. It made sense when she explained it. I wished I could believe it while journeying across this cracked plate. By the end of the first day, I wondered how I was going to endure the weeks that our journey would surely take. By the end of the second, I was almost sure I couldn't. The hooves of our animals powdered the dry earth; the smell of them seemed almost as hard to breathe as the dust.

And always, I was surrounded by people. I'd chosen to travel with a caravan for the same reasons every sane person does not choose to try crossing the Wastes alone: I didn't want to get lost, and I didn't want to be murdered by bandits. None of the travelers' tales mention that this means the caravan-traveler will be surrounded by other travelers every moment. Even when I needed to go behind a bush, I was supposed to go with others.

"Surely I'd see any danger miles away!" I protested when one of Mother Rissa's daughters told me off for going away by myself.

That was when there were still a few bushes. Later on, I came to be glad of the shelter of other women's skirts as we took our turns in the center of the circle. Well, I came to be glad of the shelter once I learned to do my business in public.

The bush had proved a very thorny bush, but better than the sword-leafed plants that bordered the road like some mad gardener's idea of a hedge. Nearly man-height, their long, pointed leaves had spines all down the edges. The children said they were the swords of demons who hated travelers, and would spring up from their burrows to kill and eat anyone who strayed from the caravan. That's a useful tale to tell children.

"Don't be so certain of what you see," Mother Rissa's daughter said. "You were able to hide, weren't you? Also, there are a lot of strangers on this journey, people none of us know to be trustworthy."

Including young widows of no known family, I thought. Myself, I'd not have said that there were a lot of us of any sort, whether strangers or friends since birth. If we'd had a few more in our company, I'd have felt happier.

"You'll journey easiest if you teach yourself now to stay with others. It's wet enough here to keep down the dust a little even in high summer, but later there'll be the risk of dust storms. When those strike, you may lose sight of us within a few feet and be led astray by the calling of the demons. However, please yourself." She turned her horse's head and rode on up the line.

This was wet country? There wasn't much dust here? Perhaps she'd only been trying to frighten me. I'd already heard tales of the demons who called for help or sang of love, of course; children have been frightening each other with those stories since the world was young. Just in case there might be some truth in them, I'd bought Imchi a blue bead to wear as protection.

Although all Charransar was crowded, nowhere more so than my own humble quarter, I'd been able to ignore most of those people most of the time. Sharing a tent with five other women, three of whom had little children, I had no choice but to pay attention. You'd have thought it was my fault I tripped over Mayra's brat! I did manage not to fall on the child, a trick that should have gotten more thanks than it did. She was the smallest and the fastest child in our tent, and the most reckless. Well, if I'd had to ride most of the day in a basket slung from a pack-mule, I'd have been a little crazy by evening myself.

It had been years since I'd had to listen to anyone else's snores. Now I discovered that a dainty-looking young woman could have a louder snore than my former husband with his seasonal sneezing fits upon him. Getting to sleep and staying asleep became as challenging as getting over the glass-topped walls of the wealthy.

By the fourth night of our journey, I was weary enough to slip into sleep with less struggle. I was dreaming of a garden much like Firousi's, only cooler, when loud shouts jolted me awake.

Shrieks soon filled the tent, for I'd leaped to my feet and drawn my dagger from under my pillow before my eyes were well open.

"Elassara help us, the barbarian's run mad!" This from a woman with a ring through her nose. I couldn't hear what was going on outside for the noise from inside. Hauling on an over-robe, I left to find out.

Outside was now much quieter than inside. A chilly breeze washed the anger from me, leaving only curiosity. The moon was only a fingernail-paring wide; no one saw me slip through camp to the torches burning at one edge. Several of our young men ringed a dozen or so half-dressed people and two donkeys. Though several of the men wore weapons, none seemed eager to use them.

"Who are you that creep up to our caravan in the dark?" Mother Rissa demanded as she arrived, followed by two other women. The amiable grandmother I'd met was gone; in the light of the torches she looked like one of those fierce goddesses whose statues men are not allowed to see.

A woman in the group cast herself at Mother Rissa's feet. "Lady, we mean no harm! Indeed, harm has been done to us. We went to sleep in our own camp, with our guides and guards about us, a day's journey outside of Nahouendar; we awoke to find ourselves alone in the Wastes. Have pity, Lady, and give us shelter!"

Nahouendar lies a week's journey from Charransar, in the other direction from Tzakende. Magic was at work here. Magic? Or the work of a certain goddess? I sat down suddenly as I remembered wishing that there were more people in our caravan. Why had I never even wondered where Kossinli's gifts came from?

A coin or a heap of wool, a donkey or an entire family of travelers, where had they come from? Nothing comes from nothing. Certainly, these poor folk had their own lives before Kossinli interrupted them. I clapped both hands over my mouth to smother a laugh. Why, the goddess was as much a thief as I was!

"Where were you going, and why?" asked Mother Rissa. The woman who had spoken before settled back on her heels and looked over her shoulder.

"Lady, we journey to the wedding of my youngest sister," said a tall, gray-haired man. "It will be in Istkana, two days from now."

There was silence for awhile. One of the women near Mother Rissa murmured something in a clear, high-pitched voice, just too softly for me to hear it. "You're certain, Linna?" Another murmur. Mother Rissa looked back at the strangers warily.

"Linna tells me your strange tale is true. Who have you offended, to be treated so? We're four days west of Charransar. You will miss that wedding, I fear."

There were agitated murmurs from the strangers as they huddled even closer to each other. The man who had spoken before put one hand on the kneeling woman's shoulder and lowered himself into a kneeling position.

"Lady, we know of no one in all the realms between the seas, or above them or below them, that we have offended so much. Lady, do not abandon us here to die!"

Mother Rissa raised her hand for silence. People and animals obliged except for one camel. Then, "Who shall say how luck falls? It's ill luck to abandon injured travelers on this road, and you may be just that. You may journey with us as far as Meerat, if you wish. There you should be able to hire guides."

They accepted with thanks. Well, what else could they do? I went back to my tent, but not before Linna saw me. She stood between me and the torches; only her posture, and the fact that there was nothing else behind me to look at, told me that she looked at me at all. She said nothing. The questions I got when I returned to the tent made up for that.

On I traveled, constantly breathing dust and surrounded by people who regarded me with suspicion when they bothered to regard me at all. Sometimes we passed places where other tracks joined us, bare worn patterns on the ground with no buildings near and seldom any other travelers in sight. One day a sheep poked its nose out of one of the carts, looked down at me, and snorted.

"Same to you, and the horse you rode in on," I told it. Oh gods. First I talked to a donkey and now a sheep. What next? Would I reach Tzakende babbling to one of the geese? "And why do you get to ride?"

"She's prize breeding stock, bound for the Lord of Malakandra's flocks," said a voice from the front of the cart. "Also she's pregnant." Mayra? Yes, when I pushed forward I could see her sitting up there out of the dust. "You can join us, if you don't mind the smell of sheep," she added.

Well! I'd evidently been forgiven for my clumsiness. Sheep-smell would at least be a change from droppings dust. I thanked her and went to tether Imchi to the wagon-gate. He and Madame Sheep could sneer at each other.

Before I could get the rein looped through, I was nearly

knocked under the cart as the entire mob tried to pack into the same narrow strip of road without impaling themselves on the sword-leaves. Someone shouted in my ear, "Get over!" which seemed like a good idea except that there wasn't any room to do it. Oh, I could see open ground enough, but there was a solid mass of people between me and it. Someone important must be overtaking us, I supposed. I tried and failed to bury myself in the middle of the crowd. Alone, I could have slipped away; with Imchi and my bundles, I needed more room, particularly since Imchi was following close behind me like a dog. A very large dog.

Sometimes I hate it when I'm right. Several men on dark gray horses thundered closer, setting our beasts braying, honking (for several wagons bore geese in cages) or lowing. Babies wailed as their snug carry-baskets were jostled in the crush.

One voice carried over the rest. "We are cursed!"

And so was I, with deafness after that shriek in my ear. As if they thought Imchi and I could give them some special protection, several sheep rushed into our part of the road. Someone trod on my foot. Imchi bit him.

We inched forward; someone leading a tiny donkey laden with clanking bottles was squeezed out of the crowd and stood between me and the galloping horses. Past his shoulder, I could see pennants stitched with the symbols of Sarinsat whipping in the wind of their passage. How had they followed me here? My stomach twisted as I wondered what they'd done to Harat. I slipped my knives loose; even if I couldn't kill any of them, I could at least die quickly myself.

Silver glinted on their horses' bridles as the Priests of Sarinsat pulled even with Mother Rissa's wagon. They rode so close together that it was hard to see how the horses didn't trip each other. That rider in the center must be an important man, to rate such a bodyguard!

Even the choking dust couldn't stop me from letting my mouth fall open when they passed the caravan by. I stood motionless, the statue of a fool, while the rest of the caravan sorted itself out around me.

"They won't usually bother us," said the voice that had yelled at me earlier. "Not so long as we get out of their way."

The voice belonged to a young man well worth looking at as well as listening to, with tightly-curling dark brown hair and eyes like Barinian amber. Alas, I was busy trying to calm Imchi. The stupid animal seemed to want to race.

"Are they always in such a hurry?" I asked, while hauling back on Imchi's halter.

The man laughed. "Best when they are. Otherwise they get bored and have to think up something to do." He was checking his goods as he spoke; evidently all the bottles had survived. "Leather-wrapped, most of them," he said when he saw me watching. "Got enough sheep-cures here, all simmered down and bottled up, to keep every sheep from here to Tzakende in perfect health if I can just convince folk to buy them. Oh, I'm called Issimante." He waited politely.

"And I am called Layla." How fortunate that he'd given no clan name! I had none any more, which can be awkward to explain or to leave unexplained. "I've less fragile cargo, myself. Braid clasps and ear cuffs, pretties for someone who'll never see Charransar and know what the really good work looks like."

"You're the mysterious stranger, then! We're mostly cousins here, you know, one way or another."

It must be a large family.

"Do you mind being the stranger? You're a brave woman to travel so far from your kin. Oh, not that kin won't fight, but when you know you're going to cross the Wastes with the same group of people many times, it does make you think twice about causing trouble. And of course, we all know that our guides won't betray us."

I wasn't too sure about that.

"There's no future in it. I did hear of one man, angry at

his caravan-leader because she wouldn't let him marry his double first cousin, who went to the Tasri and offered to silence the sentries one night. The bandit leader had him torn between horses as an example to the other bandits of what happens to traitors. That was after the Tasri'd taken the caravan, of course."

It did make me wonder what they did to thieves. Not that I'd planned to try thievery while I traveled; there were too many obvious problems in addition to my promise. Where would I hide my take? How long would I have to hide it? Also, I never had been very good at picking pockets, and these people mostly wore their wealth.

"Are you all right? You've gone so quiet. I'm sorry! We've all heard such tales since we rode in baskets, but to a city-sheltered woman they must be grisly fare. Zada's told me before I don't know when to shut up. Come, eat by our fire tonight. Let the best cook in the family make up for my turning your stomach."

"Oh, there's no need for apologies; I'm not so delicate a flower. I will accept, though, if I may bring something to the feast." What, though? I'd some dried apricots, maybe enough to give a taste to—how many? I'd left in such a plague-stricken hurry that I'd brought nothing except for the apricots and a few sugared almonds grabbed on my way out. I'd just plunked down Mother Rissa's standard fee for journey-food and hoped it wouldn't be too disgusting.

"You're kind to offer, but there's no need. I'd better go tell Zada. She says it's a wife's right to be warned, though there's always plenty and it's always good."

He jogged off happily with that easy-seeming pace that even their children have, leaving me to curse softly. Well, who had I thought Zada was, his aged mother? He'd been flirting, no doubt about that, and in town I might have taken him up on it. Not here, though. Men may tell you otherwise, but I've known very few wives who were happy to see their husbands get interested in someone else. I was getting enough dagger-looks as it was. Damn.

I started walking again, though not at an easy jog. Before I began this journey, I'd thought myself well-hardened to performing feats of strength. I was discovering that walking all day is different from making a sudden dash across the rooftops; that caring for a donkey taxes the body in ways that my tumbler's tricks of wall-climbing did not. No doubt I'd harden to this, too, in time. That time hadn't come yet. Ah well, better to be walking with sore feet than staring at a prison wall, always assuming I'd still have had eyes to stare with by now.

I never understood how Mother Rissa's people could put up their sprawling tents so quickly, nor was it ever clear to me why those tents stayed up. There were only a few poles and some ropes strung here and there to hold the heavy wool in place, all of it looking more like windblown leaves than shelter, but it worked.

Issimante's family had set theirs up in a sort of hollow triangle. Scrawny, twisted bushes grew in the dry wash we'd camped beside; they made a hot, sweet-scented fire. One crackled busily in the open center when I arrived.

Over goat stew cooked with dried vegetables, which the amazing Zada had managed to make quite tasty, I raised the subject of Tzakende's mystics. Issimante laughed and shook his head.

"Ah, soul-cures! Sheep-cures are my line. Linna may be able to say." He nodded to a lanky woman whose skirts were nearly every color of the rainbow, and whose tunic made up what few colors her skirts lacked. When she spoke, I recognized her as Mother Rissa's advisor. That soft, clear voice could have made directions to the nearest bakery sound like dangerous secrets.

"There are more of them than there are stripes in my clothes," she answered, smiling straight at me. "There are followers of every Power that's worshiped between the two seas there, and others there are who will not name the ones they serve. Fortune-tellers cluster beside the temples or place themselves up on the hills that ring Tzakende to show their importance. It does little good to say, 'Be careful,' yet must I say it. Buy advice as carefully as you'd buy gems, or more so! You'll mostly encounter nothing worse than greed and fraud, but there are always some who truly do seek darkness. They change their names, or I'd give you better warning. I think your wits are sharp enough to cut some tangles." With that, she went back to popping little balls of chewed-up goat and vegetables into her baby's mouth.

The tent was very full of children. By the way Zada's stomach had just jumped, it would soon become fuller. "Take warning by us," she said when she saw me looking, and slid her eyes over towards Linna, "If you think to lie down with our Simi!"

I truly could not think of one thing to say. It was certainly a unique way of warning off a rival.

"Don't scare her off!" Linna protested. "I've just got this one almost weaned."

Simi groaned and pulled two handfuls of his curls almost straight. "Ungrateful wives! Will you please stop embarrassing our guest? I'm past being embarrassed by them," he added, turning to face me.

Even in the smoky firelight, his eyes gleamed amber. There was certainly no embarrassment in them! Mischief, yes, and a certain hunter's gleam. Why not risk it? I'd no need to fear getting pregnant. May the Mother witness, I'd tried hard enough when I was married, and hadn't always been careful later.

Ah, but what of the rest of the journey? Zada and Linna seemed to like each other much better than my husband's wives had, but that didn't mean they'd welcome a third woman even for the rest of the journey. There was no getting away from anyone here while we traveled. No, I'd been third woman before. It had been bad enough in a town mansion where you didn't have to see too much of each other, or the man.

It had gotten quiet in the space between the tents. The children had all curled up by twos and threes in the blankets piled at the tents' edges, and Issimante and his wives

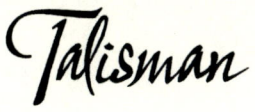

all gazed silently at me.

"I'm seldom left speechless." Was that the best I could manage? But what else was there? Flee screaming? Ask for time to consider, like a shop owner with a dubious offer? Lunge wordlessly at Issimante right there in front of wives and children?

Linna's baby squirmed and whimpered just then. "Sleep safe," she said, and vanished with him into one of the tents. "Sleep safe," I called after her, seizing the opportunity to thank Zada for dinner and make my escape. After a little argument, I managed to leave without Issimante's escort. I wanted to think this through, and I didn't think he'd give me much chance of that if we walked through the desert night together.

The moonlight turned the fine dust white, and the tents cast black shadows. It had been so long, and he was so handsome! Why was I dithering like some sheltered virgin? It would certainly ease the tedium of the journey. As I walked to my tent, it occurred to me that there was going to be one real problem to lying with Issimante: neither one of us had anywhere private to go.

As I stood still a moment to consider that problem, I realized that I had a more urgent problem yet. Someone was following me.

I worked my larger dagger loose in its sheath on my hip and walked on as if unaware. The footsteps continued, keeping about the same distance. "Issimante?" I called softly. There was no answer. Why would anybody else be following me? No one hated me enough to kill me. I was neither young enough nor fair enough to be worth the risk of stealing me away for the slave markets. I was fairly sure Mother Rissa wouldn't approve of that anyway, and absolutely sure that not much happened in her caravan without her approval.

I walked on, and the sounds followed. Dust-muffled almost to silence, they landed without hesitation or hurry. I feigned a shrug. The tent I shared lay towards the center of the encampment; if I just kept clear of tent-ropes on my way in, I should be safe from rape or kidnaping. If someone did try, well, I'd two knives with me.

I was near my tent now. Spaces between tents were narrower; if there were to be an ambush, it would be here. Just who was following me now? Damn it, wasn't being pursued by vengeful priests for a gem I no longer owned, and being spied on by men I hoped worked for the Prince, trouble enough for one woman?

Turn in the same footprints, then, run quickly back toward my pursuer, pulling the dagger from its hiding place and surprise—

"Layla!" It was only a whisper, but I somehow knew it was his.

"Issimante," I whispered back, fumbling a little as I sheathed my dagger. "What in the name—" but I didn't want to call on the demons of sour water here, we were too close. "What did you think you were doing?" I might have killed him. By the way he still stood well away from me, he'd realized that, too. Brave of him, then, to have whispered rather than shouted.

"I only wanted to see you safe to your tent. I see I need not have concerned myself." What light there was came from behind him; I couldn't see his face. He sounded annoyed.

"I told you I'd be all right. What danger did you think there'd be, here in the middle of camp?"

"You thought there was some," he answered.

"Once I heard someone sneaking along behind me, yes."

"And just where do the widows of Charransar learn night-stalking and knife-fighting?"

"This one learnt it because she had to, alone in a world of men who'll sneak up behind a woman who thought she'd found a friend!" Now, would he realize I hadn't answered his question, or would he take the bait and defend himself?

Someone peered out from behind a tent flap. "If you wake my baby, I'll kill you, whoever you are," said a woman's voice.

"Let's argue a little farther away," I suggested.

"I don't see a need for argument. I wanted to be sure you got safely to your tent, and I've done that." Issimante strode away. What eyes the man must have, to walk so fast in the dark without tripping! And what a fine belief in his own importance. Seen me safe to my tent, had he?

At least I managed to creep in among the other women without waking anyone. I ground my pillow between my teeth, and regretted that immediately. It tasted strongly of my own sweat, and the dust rasped my teeth. Plague take all handsome men. No, I didn't mean that. Kossinli, that was not a wish! Some otherwise reasonable men do get jumpy around a woman who knows how to use knives. I doubted he'd repeat the story of my unusual skills.

5

*T*he air felt peculiar all the next day. In Nahouendar, even in Charransar, I would have said it was about to rain. Our route led down a dry river-bed; finally I grew nervous enough to go to Mother Rissa.

She sat alone on the cushioned driving-bench of her wagon. At her invitation, I tethered Imchi to one of the bright green posts that held up its turquoise roof and clambered up beside her.

"Forgive me if I'm being impertinent," I began. She looked at me sidelong, but said nothing. Oh well. "I can't help but notice two things: One is that we're traveling over a dry riverbed, and the other is that—well, in any other place I'd say that it feels like rain."

"Ah, you can feel it, can you?" She actually looked straight at me then, a thing she seldom did with anyone. Just as well, too. The full force of those sharp black eyes was hard to bear. "Don't worry so much, girl! That's my job. We won't be drowned, though there may be a dust storm coming. D'you remember what to do?"

"Huddle together with several other people, wherever I am," I began. My habit of wandering from place to place in the caravan had become accepted, if not liked. "Cover my face with my veil, hang onto Imchi's halter so he doesn't run off, cover his nose if he'll allow, and don't listen to anything I may think I hear."

She gave me a friendly wallop that nearly knocked me from my perch. "Good girl! The last's 'specially important for someone like you, who hears things that not everyone does." She laughed,

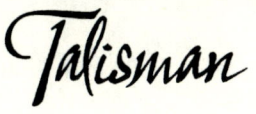

not unkindly, at my expression. "Do you think I could run a caravan like this, letting strangers travel with my kin, if I couldn't tell lots about people in a short time? I'm not asking any questions about just what you hear. I can take care of my own, and if I thought you'd be a problem, I'd've left you in Charransar. I tell you, girl, you worry too much. It'll give you wrinkles." She called out a greeting to Linna and I jumped down, my audience at an end. Imchi complicated the task of untying his lead from the wagon by nuzzling hopefully at my skirt-pocket.

"Greetings of the day, Mother Rissa. And to you, Lah-ee-la!" Linna's rainbow skirts rippled as she walked towards us. "Worried about the storm?"

"Am I the last to figure it out?"

"No, they," she cast her eyes towards the strangers, "probably haven't figured it out yet."

The little group trudged along in the middle of our larger one, blank-faced except for two young men and one half-grown girl who were scowling ferociously. "But why?" One young man demanded. "No one hates us enough to buy a curse like this!"

"Are you sure?" the girl asked. "What about the bakery-woman's kin, my brother?" She gave a yelp then, and started running.

Not your curse, I thought, but mine.

Quarrels were breaking out all up and down the road. The dust churned even more than usual as quarrelers forced their way ahead or dropped back to demand Mother Rissa's support. Neither Linna nor Mother Rissa objected when I let Imchi slow his pace to drop us back a way. Hills lay blue in the distance ahead, much too far away to give us shelter.

When the storm came I'd stopped to get a stone out of Imchi's hoof. I was only a little way behind Issimante; he'd halted to wait for us when suddenly the wind came in from all directions at once. I'd time to yank my veil up and grab the chin-strap of Imchi's halter, no more, before Simi and all the rest disappeared.

A sense of direction and of balance are essential to a thief.
I can walk through unfamiliar streets during the dark of the moon,
with detours along the tops of walls and the edges of roofs, just
once and retrace the route. I can find my way back out again if
some new obstacle forces me to change direction. Yet when I tried
to move forward to catch up to the group, I found that I wasn't
sure which way that was, and I stumbled and fell hard to my knees
in trying.

Imchi brayed behind me, pulling hard against my hold. I
promised him sugar, I promised him jennets, I promised him I'd
take his hide off myself if he didn't stand still. After lifting me half
off my feet trying to rear, he gave up and lay down. I sat down
beside him rather suddenly.

The veil over my face felt as though it would smother me,
but when I took it off the dust scoured my face and packed into my
nostrils. I clawed the veil back into place and fastened Imchi's
empty feed-bag over his nose. "Just once, don't fight me," I hissed
into one hairy ear. I think he grumbled; I could feel his throat
move. The air had become almost solid. I was able to get just
enough, filtered through the veil, to keep from fainting.

Over his noise and mine, over the howling of the storm, I
ought not to have been able to hear the demons at all, but demons
don't follow ordinary rules any more than goddesses do. As I had
done with Imchi, they promised and threatened, but I huddled
against my companion and concentrated on breathing through
donkey hair, dust and the heaviest gauze in the world.

No one had warned me it would go on so long. I tried to
move, and could not for the sand that had piled up around me.
Imchi must have felt my panic. He had been lying absolutely still
with his head down; suddenly he floundered to his feet. My hand
was cramped so firmly around that chin-strap that he pulled me to
my feet as well. Once I got my head up above Imchi's back, I heard
the voice.

"Layla! Layla, are you still here? Come to my voice, I've lost everybody! Come, we can shelter together." The wind rose again. Poor gallant Issimante and his dog-sized donkey! He'd halted to wait for me in spite of our quarrel. How could I not try to help him? I may be a cold-hearted, unnatural woman—I've been told so more than once—but I am not utterly heartless, and he sounded utterly desperate. Still clutching Imchi's bridle, I struggled forward. Issimante must be close for me to have heard him over all this noise.

Damn this wind! I could hear Issimante so clearly, but each time he called out his voice seemed to come from another direction. Surely he wasn't moving, too? "Stay where you are!" I called out. "Let me come to you, Imchi's big enough to help me get through this." I was desperate enough to think of praying, but I didn't want to find out what Kossinli would consider helpful under these circumstances.

"Oh, really, Layla." The woman's voice carried easily over the roar of the wind and Simi's faint call. I knew that voice well, but it belonged to no one on this journey. "Must you always be chasing men?" Attar of roses overwhelmed the dung-scented sand.

The Lady Massara, my husband's second wife, stood on a hillock of sand and stared at me with the same pained expression as she had worn when we shared a husband and a house. She'd always insisted that I'd somehow entrapped our mutual husband, since otherwise he could not possibly have contemplated more than the briefest liaison with someone like me.

"I knew all the time you were sneaking out to meet the gardener's boy, but have you no sense of occasion?" Her headscarf was pleated into the same prickly frame I remembered her adopting just before I left, and her trailing sleeves hung in perfect loops from wrist to elbow.

In this wind? Attar of roses, or any scent at all, persisting in this whirlwind? Elegant, indolent Lady Massara, wearing the same styles after all this time? Besides, the idea of her bothering to come out into these inelegant surroundings even for the pleasure of scolding me was so absurd that I had to laugh. The image shivered and shredded; all I could hear was the wind. I trembled, wondering how far I'd wandered.

When the wind stopped, Imchi and I stood in a bowl of sand. I still couldn't see. I chose the gentlest slope of the dunes and began to struggle up it. For once, Imchi didn't fight me. We both had enough to fight in the sand that slipped away underfoot, carrying me back downhill at least as much as I'd climbed. Once I slid back so fast that I landed up against Imchi's head. His indignant toss of his head got me going again.

I stopped trying to go in a straight line and zigzagged up the side of our bowl. Gods, but I was thirsty! We reached a spot where the sands lay a little more level, and I dug out my water bag. There wasn't much. I gave Imchi a little in the palm of my hand. When he finished, the donkey slobber dried before I could wipe it off on the end of my scarf. How long had we been out here? The shadows were growing. The caravan often traveled during the evening to make use of the cooler–or at least less hot–time.

Kossinli, surely You didn't rescue me to let me die of thirst out here? I didn't speak aloud. The next time I opened my mouth, I wanted water pouring into it. There was only one way that was going to happen. Stumbling, sliding, we forced our way on up the shifting slope. Imchi followed me willingly, but I had to struggle against the weariness that whined to rest, protesting that someone would come looking for me. Sand and sweat blurred my vision.

I didn't find the top so much as fall over it. When I picked myself up and rasped a little of the dust from my eyes, I could see the rest of the caravan not so very far away.

Not far at all, once we reached firmer ground. "Here's the last," someone called out as Imchi and I rejoined the group. People were bathing cuts and soothing children all around, but even all the sheep seemed to have survived. My kidnap victims looked almost calm; perhaps when you've been mysteriously transported by a goddess, little else alarms you.

Mother Rissa looked us both over. "You're luckier than you deserve," she said. I had to agree. Considering my endless complaints about her, the Lady of Mirth had been most gracious in rescuing me.

The chai that night was muddy with sand, and tasted wonderful. Every bite of dinner gritted between my teeth, but I was so ravenous that I didn't chew much anyway. I did hope we'd get to Tzakende before I became a toothless old woman.

After the storm, the journey grew easier. In part, I had learned a few of the tricks that make caravan life less troublesome: I could roll my blankets so that they gathered almost no dust during the day's travel, and I learned how to hobble Imchi so that I could catch him without a long chase and the help of several children. I grew used to walking most of the day. Even the chatter of my tentmates bothered me less, though I think it annoyed them that I often didn't hear them the first time they spoke to me.

Also, we began to come upon towns now and then. They were poor little dust-colored things, generally smelling of dung fires and hardly ever having a good bathhouse, but they were places to trade and rest for a day or two.

It was strange to me that the people were so different when their towns were so much alike. One village threw a feast for us; another herded us into a space just within the town walls and kept apart from us as if we might have plague. It was hard to leave Mirsande and its dancers. I was glad when we left high Kirastha. It may well be true that in such wind it's wise to go veiled, but two days of dealing with people whose eyes I could never see was plenty for me. Even the market seemed veiled by its maze of walls. The open sky that had made me so uneasy was welcome after that.

I found myself buying as well as selling, for cleverness with metals and gems showed in surprising places. In one village barely bigger than our caravan, a woman was making rings and necklets all of tiny beads of animal bones and hooves. I traded her a few of my smaller jewels for a number of the more strongly patterned ones, and thought it a pity that I'd not see what she did with real gems.

"Why did you do that?" Mayra asked. "Where do you think you'll sell that upland trash?" She touched her new braid-clasps as if to be sure they were still securely fastened; their bright chipstones glinted. They were dyed, but there was no point in telling her that now.

"Take it far enough away, and it'll be exotic," I answered. "I find it intriguing; so may others." Mayra shrugged.

We were walking uphill now most of the time, which did at least help to fight the increasing cold at morning and evening. At night I was glad of the warmth of my companions in spite of their snores.

6

*T*here were tufts of true dark green in the distance, startling against the gray-greens and greenish-browns of the Wastes. When Imchi snorted and broke into a trot, I had no choice but to do likewise. The dull headache I'd had for the last several days throbbed with each footfall.

"He smells the sweet grass!" called one of Mother Rissa's granddaughters as I hauled back on his lead. "Make him slow down, save his strength. It'll take us the rest of the day to get there."

Right. After all these weeks of trying to control Imchi, I'd be ready to pull myself up onto the steepest roof in the Empire if I ever did return to thieving. It was good to know we were going someplace with water, though. It must be a true town to show so clearly from a day's journey away. We'd sleep within real walls! I'd have a bath, and sleep in a bed that didn't smell of dung and dust. I'd be warm enough again, too; as we came down into the valley we left the cold behind us.

What was I going to do about Issimante? He'd avoided me ever since that night I'd nearly stabbed him, but his eyes followed me still. I know, because I looked at him often. Men. Maybe the whole sex is another of Kossinli's jokes. Yes, and the fact that we women are fools enough to want them around anyway just improves the jest.

By midday, I could see high walls and the roofs of houses that half-filled the valley. Our road led through fields now, glowing green against the red and yellow mountains. So much green, in such close neat rows! It made me blink.

Tired though we all were, no one was quiet as we passed the open ground separating fields from town. By the standards of The Wastes, this was a city. It had permanent markets, several bathhouses, and luxurious inns where no more than two or three need share a room. I couldn't help glancing back to where Issimante and his family walked, all except Linna talking at once, even the children. If he saw me he gave no sign.

I arranged for a room with three of the five women whose tent I'd been sharing. We were used to each other by now; the other two would be returning to their families and taking most of the babies with them. Why pay for a private room if all I'd do there was sleep? It was still in my mind that I might be able to slip my tie to Kossinli by returning the money Her priestess had given me. I'd managed to sell trinkets at what passed for markets in the Wastes; if Tzakende bought as eagerly I'd more than pay for my journey.

The sentries all knew Mother Rissa's clan; we were soon sorting ourselves out in front of our caravanserai.

"Here, let me take care of your donkey," Issimante offered. "He'll need to be given less grass than he wants, after so long on journey rations. I already know the mix."

Well, I must be back in his good graces if he was volunteering for extra work on my behalf. He must surely be as eager for a bath as I was. If he wanted to show off his expertise, that was fine with me.

If it was really his idea. It might be, of course; then again...Kossinli, I thought, please let me manage my own love life.

This admirable town had a huge bathhouse solely for travelers, with separate halves for men and women. No waiting for certain days of the week here! For a price, you could even get some clothes washed while you bathed. I'd have called the bath and laundry prices outrageous, but what price a good soak in clean water in the middle of the Wastes? I'd economize somewhere else.

The water was clean; even the dirt of our journey fouled it

only for a few moments. Then it swirled away in a rush of clean water to show the bright fish mosaics clearly again. The children were fascinated with the currents of the water; several had to be carried firmly back into the shallow part when they pursued the boxes of soap or bottles of scented oils they'd set sailing.

In spite of the squeals of the children, I could feel the headache easing. I stood up to my neck in water until Linna, laughing, told me I'd be late for dinner if I didn't hurry.

"Don't worry," I called, and splashed up the stairs into the misty air. Most of the bathers had already left; it was easy to find a solitary corner to dry and oil myself.

It wasn't quite solitary enough. Mayra's brat let out a shriek that bounced off every wall. "Lady hurt!"

In the sunset light, the scar on my side did look almost like a fresh wound. The woman who had given me the scar had been trying to slash my face; thanks to my clumsy efforts to fight her off, she nearly killed me. The scar's worst just below the collarbone, where the knife thrust deepest and first.

I hauled my towel around me. "No, I'm not hurt," I assured her. "It was a long time ago. It's ugly, but it doesn't hurt."

She stared at me wide-eyed. "Long time?"

"Before you were born. It's all better now."

Her mother pulled her away as if she thought scars might be catching. "Let's go see if our clothes are dry," the woman said. "Sorry," she mumbled as she pulled the child away.

I let the rest of them go on ahead. The two women brought by Kossinli kept looking slantwise under their eyelashes as they left; the Traveler women ignored me. Only Linna stopped beside me. "The child was afraid for you, not of you," she said gently.

I nodded. "It's all right," I managed. "I'll just finish drying off." Stupid, not to have thought how that scar would look to children, or for that matter to most adults. So many of the women in the Old Quarter bathhouse had scars of some sort that I'd forgotten to be self-conscious about it soon after the wound had

healed. Granted, most of theirs were from beatings. No one had
beaten me in several years now.

Linna was still there. "What, are you wondering, too, how
I got it?"

She stared at me. "Yes, of course! But you don't want to
talk of it, so I wasn't going to ask."

I had to laugh. "Oh, Linna, it's a story of stupidity and
luck, not much worth telling. I was alone in a part of Charransar
I'd no business being in at all, and escaped with my life but little
else." All of which was true as far as it went. Linna had the sense
not to press for more, and left me with a smile.

The slap of her bare feet echoed in the empty room. I was
dry enough already, but I toweled off again, feeling the hard
welt of the scar. I'd been running then, too, running from my
good marriage.

It was a big step up for a gemcutter's daughter,
everyone had said so. My Lord had seen me first in my father's
workshop. Father had given me some semi-precious stones; I was
fashioning them into flowers for a wreath when a stranger's voice
said, "A flower playing with flowers," and my father looked at me
in a new way.

The wife of a noble had had no business at all in that part
of Charransar. Had I been paying attention, I'd never have gone
there, out at the edge of town where a few steps would put you
beyond the walls completely.

I'd thought to return to my parents when I crept out of the
house that day. Certainly my husband was unlikely to demand my
return. After four years with no sign of a baby, he'd found a fourth
wife even younger than I had been when we married. That had
given his first two wives someone else to fight with!

I could be useful to my parents, I'd thought. Had my
father not sighed to lose my skills with gems? Mother had been

proud to see me wed so well, but she'd wept when the gilded bride-chair came.

Among all the ladies we saw and gossiped with, there had been one who was kind to me. Lady Myrrha had even spoken approvingly of one woman who'd gone back to her parents, saying it was a woman's right to return if her husband misused her. She would surely help me.

"Layla, no! Ah, poor child, your friend's lord beat her cruelly. What have you to complain of? Remember, you yourself were the new bride once." She'd patted my head gently.

"I don't care about him not sleeping with me. No, really, I don't! But Myrrha, am I supposed to just go on like this until I'm too old to care? He doesn't want me. I could help my parents, I'd have something to do with my life!"

"What, slaving away in that little river town? Layla, sweeting, I doubt you could go back now. Besides, it's your duty to stay. It would cast shame on your parents and your lord, to leave for no more reason than jealousy and boredom. Here, I'll send you home in my own chair. No one need know."

Some would say I had betrayed her. I still hold that she had betrayed me. Was I to go meekly in one of those airless boxes, to be returned like a strayed marmoset? I ran.

I had seen no more of the streets of Charransar at that time than can be seen through the strip of grillwork on a lady's sedan chair. I'd had no clear idea of where I was going, and I was weeping. When my eyes cleared, I was standing on a rutted street that stank of garbage and cheap incense. A lean dog had trotted by, grinning. The men there had been grinning, too; the women were scowling.

Naive though I was, I had been able to tell what those women were. I had never known that anyone followed that trade openly, though! Temple prostitution was, of course, fully honorable. Those who practiced it worshiped the life-force. I had actually believed then that anyone who offered herself only for money would be punished by the Goddess.

One of the whores had minced toward me, wobbling on pattens that kept her out of the dirt of the street. "You, out! This is ours."

I had certainly been willing to go. I'd turned, and almost run into a man in a greasy robe. He was too tall for me to see more than that.

"Don't be so unfriendly, Cartha. Maybe the Lady wantsa stay awhile."

"No, thanks, I'd better get home." I'd moved to one side; so had he.

"I want her outa here," Cartha'd whined.

"Who gives a fuck what you want?" He'd grabbed my arm. Cartha had shrieked something I couldn't understand. I'd pulled away as hard as I could, wriggling to free my wrist of that hard grip. My shoulder had felt as if it would pull apart. Just as I felt my hand slide free, I saw a flash of light come past his arm.

Was I always intended to live outside the law? No gently reared girl should have been able to dodge that knife, even as awkwardly as I did. It had nicked his arm as it came; he'd sworn and turned to fight Cartha. Then there had been fire all along one side of my ribcage and I was running again, ripping my long overrobe with its trailing sleeves and narrow skirts to run faster.

Cartha's friends had cornered me easily, herding me into a byway where the rubble of a half-fallen house blocked the road. I'd felt the blood flowing down my side. Up, I'd scrambled up, bricks sliding and turning under my feet. The mob had kept pace below as I ran along the ridge of rubble. One slipper was gone; I'd felt something sharp jab my heel. There'd been an open window just a little way out of reach. If I jumped—could I? Better find out.

I'd grabbed the edge, but that was all. Below me, the crowd had jeered. Someone threw a stone. I knew I was going to die.

Obviously enough, I'd been wrong. Suddenly I'd felt

hands grasp my wrists. I'd screamed at the pain as they pulled me upwards; somehow I'd managed to get my feet against the wall and make it over the sill to fall forward onto my rescuer.

For several days after that, he told me later, I was unconscious or delirious. He'd kept me clean (farewell, modesty!) and made me drink broth or tea whenever he could. He'd trusted none of his band with my care, which was doubtless wise. Thieves welcome competition no more than whores do.

Hunger brought me back to the present and to the bathhouse. My clothes were waiting, clean and dry. They'd picked up a scent from the twice-blooming roses I could see growing against the walls of the drying-yard beyond. The quiet of the robing room, empty of everything but the shimmer of reflections from the baths, was sweet enough to keep me from hurrying to what everyone said would be a feast.

Dinner cured me of my sadness. Who can brood over mistakes made so long ago when she's full of fried fish, fresh greens and sweet ripe fruit? Besides, clumsy and naive though I was all those years ago, I survived.

Somewhere nearby, a voice I didn't recognize was singing in a language I didn't understand. So many doorways pierced the courtyard walls that they could hardly be called walls at all. Did none of these people need to watch their backs? In the courtyard I'd at least have room to slip away from any trouble, and I'd hear the music better.

I had barely stepped out of the light from our eating-hall's doorway when a soft sliding sound made me jump. What a fool I felt when I turned to confront a large, trumpet-shaped flower! The speed of its opening had set it swinging.

"Ah, Layla, will you defend yourself against the flowers?" Why did it have to be Issimante who saw me, hand to my knife before a flowering bush? He came closer. All around us the trumpets were opening.

"Noisy damn flowers they have here!" I answered.

He smiled, and answered in that gentle voice that some men use with unreasonable women. "They have little time before winter; they must hurry. We need not. Here's a seat. Enjoy the moon-gardens, even if you won't enjoy me."

"Have you no shame, Issimante?" I wasn't sure I wanted to point out that he'd been avoiding me since that night he'd nearly gotten himself knifed trying to protect me.

"If the Powers chose to put a beautiful woman, a beautiful garden and a full moon in my life all at once, why should I feel shame?"

Why, indeed? And when was I going to have another chance to let someone nibble on my ear while I listened to flowers opening? Moths the size of sparrows were hovering around them, their antennae visible in the moonlight, their wings marked with black and silver. I took the triangular seat Issimante had pointed out. The solid stone at my back was comforting.

"Ah, Layla, sweet shy Layla," he murmured as he nuzzled my neck. The almond-flower oil seemed to please.

I like compliments as well as most women do, but they should be somewhat believable. I couldn't help laughing. "Do you know some other Layla? Sweet and shy?" He was pouting. "I'm sorry, Issimante, but really!"

"But you are shy, Layla, in your own way. You're shy as a girl child of twelve about letting anyone know you like a man. You deserve a fine quiet chamber, with no prying eyes nearby and no ears listening. Tonight I can give you that."

"And tomorrow we'll be away again, you with your wives and me with a tentful of women and babies."

He stopped nuzzling my ear. "That's it, isn't it? You're afraid I'll give you a baby. I'll be careful, I promise, and even if you should start one Mother Rissa can stop it."

That wasn't it, of course. After all those barren years of

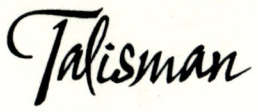

marriage, and two lovers after that, I knew I'd never have to worry about an unwanted baby. I'd certainly tried enough potions and positions trying to catch one, without success. I had my mouth open to tell Issimante that babies weren't the problem when I realized how much easier it would be to let him think they were. Why bother trying to convince this charmer that I'd rather keep the friendship of his wives, especially Linna, than lie down with him?

"Is it Linna and Zada? They told you themselves they don't mind. Mother Rissa arranged my marriages well. Or is it that you mind my not offering to marry you? I wish I could, Layla, but—"

"I've been married once, thank you; that was enough. And I think you have two very smart wives who know clever ways of warning away any other women. Aren't two women enough for you, Issimante? Go let Linna and Zada toss a coin to see who's lucky tonight." He had wit enough to notice that I hadn't said whether luck would mean getting him or not, and courage enough to laugh. It would almost be worth the complications—no. It would not. Besides, remembering my marriage didn't excite me.

There was music coming from one of the courtyards I'd come through earlier; a boy was doing a dance with torches to the wail of mizmar and rebab. It was pleasant to have enough coins that I need not slink away before the end of the performance. The tumblers who followed were almost as good, but when a woman began to sing a song of lost love, I slipped away to the room of my tentmates.

Issrandar's markets would have comforted a grieving widow, or at least taken her mind off her troubles. There were food stalls enough to sample for a year, though I did decline the peppered locusts. In the lane one over from Mother Rissa's caravanserai, swathes of cloudfleece floated pale blue, green, and yellow on the breeze. The jeweler's street had works in every style I'd seen and some I had never seen before. One shop's counter held silver brooches covered in tiny golden beads so as to make pictures, with fierce animals holding the clasps.

My fingers itched. I'd have to steal two, one to sell and one to study. It was all ill-guarded. The fool who owned the shop had set up his displays so that he couldn't possibly watch them all at once, and there was a fine crowded square nearby where I could hide among the crowd. We'd be gone tomorrow. Damn Old Parata for forcing that promise from me. Still, how would he ever know?

"Layla, greetings!" It was Linna. "Come, sleepy-head, we've saved you a little space. I'm off to the herb-sellers myself; do you need anything?"

I grudged the time I had to spend selling my own wares, but a trader must trade. As the sun rose higher, the tent roof trapped its heat without giving much relief from its brilliance. It was a relief to find that no one seemed much interested in my offerings. Oh, a serving girl bought three braid-clasps, and a young man with buck teeth bought the bracelet with stones of five different colors, all false. I yawned, and rearranged the goods.

"You'll do better with those in Tzakende," Mother Rissa said kindly. "Issrandar's right on the lapis route." She didn't ask why someone trying to make a living in the gem trade didn't know that. She'd given me an excuse to pack up my bits and pieces, so I did, and strolled over to the lapis sellers.

Carved wooden screens jutted out over their shops to meet in the middle of the lane; it would have been worth coming here just for the coolness. There was also plenty there to make my fingers itch. Lumps of lapis the size of my fist were offered for sale, along with intricately carved amulets. My father didn't know that art; I could only wonder how it was done. There was one piece with an Issrandaran trumpet-tree and bird-moth carved on it, all on a stone that would have fit easily into my hand. Lest anyone grow bored with such perfection, some merchants carried jade as well in all its shades of green and white.

I stepped back and smiled at the man behind the counter.

That didn't calm him, or cause him to take his hand from the heavily-carved hilt of his knife. Really, did the man think I was fool enough to try grab-and-run in broad daylight in a crowded market? "That's beautiful work," I said. He smiled back and named a price that would have paid my way to Tzakende and back. Sometimes there's just no point in haggling.

"May it find a worthy owner," I said, and moved on. He settled back on his silk-embroidered cushions. I had to move well down the row into humbler territory before merchants stopped staring at me.

They must have been staring because one of their number made it clear he suspected me; there were far stranger-looking people than I wandering through the cool streets. The merchants themselves were as varied as their goods; pale as white jade, yellow as gold, dark as iron-wood, and clothed as if to show how many different ways there are for people to shelter their bodies from sun and stares.

The roofs of Issrandar are flat, and the houses lie close together. No doubt the houses of the lapis traders were well guarded, but what of those who bought from them? Had I known the city, or had Linna not appeared again, the temptation might have overcome my sense and my promise. I was beginning to think it was a very good thing I hadn't lain with Issimante. This journey was trouble enough without adding an angry sorceress to my troubles, especially one who seemed to know far too much about me.

I did manage to trade an interlaced silver necklace for two small lapis pebbles of middling quality and some copper wire to net them in. It would give me something to do for amusement at each day's end, but it had been a long time since I made rather than stole. This late in the day I'd no time to buy the tools I'd need for anything more sophisticated than twisted wire work; I couldn't pretend the earrings would be anything special. Besides, it would have been so much more fun to slip in and take what I wanted!

The moneychangers were bigger thieves than I've ever been, but I changed a few lirials into smaller coins even so. I was far enough from home to enjoy this money a little bit without drawing unwanted attention. Most of the coins remained strapped to my middle in case I did need to return them to Kossinli.

I dreamed of thievery that night, in a city unlike any I'd ever seen. In the dream I knew its rounded houses and sloping streets as I ran alone, silently, and climbed walls with a speed even I've never managed.

It was both a shock and a relief to wake to snores and the close air of other people's breathing. Before Kossinli, I'd have assumed that I'd wake up in the same place as I went to sleep. Now, especially after she added those poor travelers to our caravan, I didn't dare.

We still had one gate to pass through on our way out when Imchi balked by a flower-seller. Hitting Imchi doesn't work; he just goes from stubbornness to kicking and biting. I was yanking on his lead when I noticed something odd about his luck bead. Scratching the base of one ear to calm him, I slid the bead up where I could see it better. The clay bead was now a smooth egg of lapis. It was more the size of a songbird's egg than a hen's, but even a little piece of lapis so clear of inclusions was precious.

Calmly, or so I hoped it looked, I pretended to adjust Imchi's halter. No one would ever believe I hadn't stolen it. What did they do to thieves here? Some people chop off the right hands of thieves; some hang them. Some sell them into service for however long it takes to repay the value of the stolen goods. I'd be about, oh, a hundred and thirty when I paid off that lapis.

What had I ever done to Kossinli? The jokes were getting too damn rough, and too frequent! One of Her jokes was still standing motionless except for stretching his neck out towards the flower-seller, who'd prudently stepped back.

"I'll sell thee to a follower of Sarinsat," I threatened. He brayed and came along.

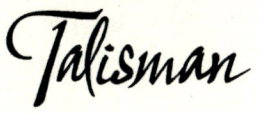

People were staring as we rejoined the caravan. My apologies got nothing but shrugs and suggestions that I keep that donkey moving now that I'd finally gotten him going. Now I would just ever-so-casually work my way into the middle of our muddle and plod on through the gate as if everything were perfectly normal, "Oh, sorry, didn't mean to bump you, I think Imchi'll keep walking better in the middle of the group." Maybe it was a good thing I was living mostly honestly these days. This seemed to be one of those days when I could throw a stone at the ground and miss.

The guard at the gate was staring at me. Hum-ti-tum, just a clumsy woman with a stubborn donkey, nothing interesting here. Plague take all guards, why wasn't he watching out for bandits or something? He couldn't possibly see Imchi's luck bead from where he stood anyway.

Come to think of it, why had I bought that animal a luck bead in the first place? He had all the luck he needed. Kossinli had doubtless whisked him away from his former owner just before whoever it was turned him into donkey kabobs.

Issimante was staring at me, and that was not love-light in his eyes. Had both his wives refused him? He'd been cheerful enough when we parted. There was another of Kossinli's charming gifts. I could have had a nice helpful friendship with that man if Kossinli hadn't "helped" me again. I couldn't go along not wishing for anything!

Wise men have warned about anger, but it has its advantages. My foul mood left no room in my heart for fear, and kept me too busy to mourn Issimante's refusal to walk within twenty paces of me.

Would that Mayra's brat had felt the same. Instead of putting her in a carry-basket or in the cart she drove, Mayra'd let her walk for awhile, "Like a big girl." I tried to tell her that big girls don't annoy donkeys by trying to play with their luck-beads, but she stuck her tongue out at me. When Imchi tried to bite her,

Mayra yelled at me!

The guards were staring at us again. No doubt it was only because they were bored with trying to keep the morning flood of travelers moving. Still, I wished they wouldn't.

Was it Kossinli's doing that two cart-drivers locked wheels just then? She owed me a little help! By the time they'd done cursing each other and untangled their vehicles, we'd left the city.

7

There was nothing to do with that lapis but leave it hanging from the loop on Imchi's halter. I had no other luck beads, and no hope of buying one unobserved. I'd no doubt I could steal one, but I'd had my fill of meddling with anything that might annoy even a minor Power. A luck bead ought not to cause nearly as much trouble as that emerald had, but who could say? Maybe no one would notice that one donkey's bead had an unusually fine color. They would notice and worry if he had none.

Issimante wouldn't notice. He never got anywhere near me. That took some effort on his part; we were a much smaller group since Issrandar. Aside from myself, the only person who wasn't part of Mother Rissa's clan was a spare, balding man who had not said one word the whole journey. He didn't even eat with the rest of us, keeping to his own tent and cooking fire whenever we stopped and keeping to the back of the line when we traveled. He was going all the way to Tzakende.

The land rose sharply out of Issrandar. I traveled the first three days cheerfully enough, convinced that these were the foothills of the Tzakendi mountains. We were climbing steadily after all, and people spoke as if the journey would soon be over.

Everyone in the tent fell silent when I wondered when we'd start seeing the forests of Tzakende. The songs all mentioned their shade and sweet scent. The children stared from the center where they lay snuggled together in a kitten-heap against the cold of the high desert night. All at once, they giggled.

Mayra hushed them. "We have these mountains,

then Cloudfleece Valley, the Sarayan Slope and the Flats to cross first, Layla."

I suppose the lack of so much as a small bush, never mind trees, should have warned me. Feeling like a complete fool, I crawled into my own blankets.

"It really isn't so very far," said Mayra's daughter as I fell asleep. I made myself thank her.

"An' we get to see the vegetable lambs," the girl said sleepily. "We can't pet them though, 'cause they bite."

Oh, come on! I was ignorant, but not stupid. The child looked perfectly serious, though, and Mayra and her sister each held a finger to her lips. Vegetable lambs were a tale for children; well, this was a child. It did seem unkind to let even a brat like that one build up false hopes of seeing fabulous creatures.

We journeyed on. Soon enough, Imchi's lapis showed scratches where it had fallen against the rocks as he grazed. He'd been plodding along for days, grumbling and sighing, when he suddenly went into a brisk trot late one afternoon. Our trail narrowed to edge its way around a cliff just there; my left arm was nearly out of its socket by the time I got him to slow down. We didn't quite run into the wagon ahead.

"You're learning," said Mother Rissa from her wagon. "He must know we've a surprise for you both! Don't worry, it's nothing dangerous."

The land opened out; the trail widened. Imchi was pulling hard, and his ears were forward like a curious cat's. I yanked hard on his lead and he slowed after nearly deafening me with his bray. Aside from some strange-looking plants, it was a valley like several others we'd passed. A small dun-colored village sat at one edge.

The plants shifted as if a wind blew through them, but the air was still. "Mother Rissa," I began to ask, but she held up her hand.

"Wait. You'll see soon." Everyone else was smiling knowingly; even the silent man allowed a faint smile to appear.

We came down into the valley, and I saw that each of the plants had a neat circle around it where the grass was short and even. It was as precise as the ordered gardens of my husband; a strange thing for what must be fields of some crop.

The crops were definitely moving. I stopped (over Imchi's braying protest) and stared to be sure of what I was seeing. From partway up each plant, just under a brushy umbrella of leaves, came two long drooping branches. At the end of each was a small green sheep. They nibbled greedily at the grass, each stretching as far as its branch would reach. A woman passed me bent almost double under a load of some plant with blue flowers. The lambs leaned towards her eagerly, but she went past them to a farther field whose lambs gleamed a soft blue-green.

Mother Rissa smiled proudly. "Everyone's heard the tale of the vegetable lamb, and no one believes it! The secret of cloudfleece is hidden in plain sight." Did her eyes stray to Imchi's lapis?

"Come, ride for awhile. It's flat enough here." One didn't refuse such an invitation. We rode in silence for a time through the multicolored fields. Water flowed between the rows of lambs, and men and women moved among them with flowers and pruning shears. It was the most peaceful place I'd ever seen; there were not even any walls around the village.

"That's lapis hanging from Imchi's halter," said Mother Rissa.

"I didn't steal it!"

"Who says you did? Though it would be no care of mine if you did, so long as no one came after us because of it. Linna says that lapis has the smell of magic."

I sat silent, motionless, though I knew this threat wouldn't pass on if I waited. This was not Charransar, and there were no shadows to hide in.

"I knew you weren't exactly what you claimed when I met you; respectable widows don't leave town in such a hurry that they haven't even a pack saddle for the donkey. Parata said you'd do nothing to cause trouble on the trip, and so far as I can tell you haven't. But neither he nor you said anything about divine involvement. All honor to the Powers, of course!" She touched forehead and heart quickly. "But I don't like Them taking too close an interest in my doings."

I smothered a laugh, not quite completely, and the look I got would have made the Emperor himself babble. "Oh, Mother Rissa, how thoroughly I agree with you! It's why I'm going to Tzakende. Please don't ask me to tell you the whole story, I hate looking that stupid. I promise you that I'll do nothing to endanger you or your clan."

Mother Rissa grunted. "But can you promise for whatever Goddess this is?"

My face told the answer. "You're—you're not going to leave me here, are you?" Oh, what a pitiful little voice. Before Kossinli, I'd gone years without having to ask a favor from anyone. Now all I seemed to do was beg.

"I couldn't if I wanted to. The Goshthari don't allow strangers to remain in their valley, and if I left you here to find your own way out it'd be the last time we drank from their wells. You're safe for the moment."

I managed to thank her. When one of the cousins came up with a question, I hopped down from the wagon without waiting to be asked.

I had cause to be glad that Mother Rissa couldn't abandon me in that valley. Imchi tried to eat one small lamb, and got his nose nipped for the effort. The Goshthar who hurried over to defend the lamb spoke a strange half-singing language unlike any I'd ever heard before, but the meaning was clear enough. Issimante managed to help me rig a muzzle for Imchi without once letting his hands touch mine.

A shred of raw cloudfleece blew across my headscarf and stuck. "No, keep it!" Mother Rissa commanded when I would have tossed it back among the trees. "It is gross discourtesy to cast off any fleece that the gods of the grove give you. Save it! No one will accuse you of stealing." Obediently, I twisted the soft, faintly blue mass into a thread of sorts and tucked it into my belt pouch. I didn't ask Mother Rissa why she thought that I thought that someone might accuse me of theft.

There is a shelter by Strangers' Well there, made of stripped branches planted in the earth and bound together along a spine of twisted reeds. I'd have thought they grudged spending money on foreigners, but what I could see of the village beyond looked little better.

"Some say it's all fine tapestries and cloudfleece pillows within the houses," Mayra commented. "Don't ask me how anyone knows. They'll trade with us, but even Mother Rissa's never been offered so much as a cup of tea in the outermost room of anyone's house. We have to watch the children, for the Goshthari will kill even a little child that gets into a village house." Her determination to educate me got on my nerves sometimes, but right then I was glad of company that asked no questions.

Evidently strangers couldn't even stay overnight here. We were soon on our way again, leaving dull but sturdy wool in exchange for a few bolts of cloudfleece.

Please, Kossinli, I thought as I slid and stumbled down the scree, please don't do anything more for me, at least for a little while. I won't even ask You to do something about Imchi. If they throw me out here I'll die in the wilderness. That wouldn't be funny, would it? Please let me get to Tzakende. Once I'm there I'll find out what to do. If there's something You want from me still, I'll do it. Just let me get to Tzakende.

Then my heart sank. What was I promising?

8

I had become respectable! How could it not be so? The Guardian of the Gate, Servant of the Emperor, had banged his seal twice, precisely as a brass-maker's hammer, on my permits to trade here among the mystics and merchants. Imchi had his own permit to be there, though I doubted that any number of seals would make him respectable.

The wind sang softly along the wandering walls of Tzakende as I said farewell to Mother Rissa and her clan. For just a moment I regretted turning down her offer of lodging. She's a hard woman to lie to, though, and curious as a little child. She and her clan wouldn't be in Tzakende long enough, anyway. They'd need to leave again almost immediately to return to Issrandar before winter. Why had they even bothered to come to Tzakende? Money, Mother Rissa said cheerfully.

"Remember, don't let them give you a stall on the southwest side of Strangers' Square! You can't see the tanner's quarter from there, but when the wind's right the stench would gag Imchi."

Houses and temples and all their surrounding walls were built in rounded, irregular shapes like the hills that ring the city. Sounds carried strangely; twice Imchi shied violently at porters' warning shouts that must have come from some other street, and once I would have sworn that I heard someone calling on Sarinsat, whose worship I thought I'd left far behind me. I suppose it may be so; they say every deity worshiped between the two seas has a temple somewhere in this city. Yet I found no temple for Kossinli.

Gods-haunted Tzakende, wails every tea-house singer. Certainly I saw temples enough, each ringed with fortune-tellers and amulet-sellers. Where some talk of lovers and some of gold, and some of the price of wool, Tzakende talks of the Beyond. They're fortunate none of the deities has smashed their city flat just for a little quiet. Someone here would surely be willing to sell me the answers I needed to rid myself of Kossinli's kindness.

It was a relief to come out of the tangle of streets into the open Strangers' Square, although it was no more square than anything else here. In spite of the confusion, it was still easy enough to find the official in charge of stall space. His building lay behind the largest and most motley crowd of all.

I wasn't even the only woman. I was halfway through my poor widow story before I realized that nobody cared why I was alone. The same official who gave me a stall-space permit (and quietly accepted a bribe to change me to one not so close to the tanneries) named me several innkeepers who still had rooms.

One had a quiet room up under the eaves. Below its window, a tiled roof sloped to within a few feet of the ground, with a little round bake-oven like a footstool set just beyond the roof-edge. There were sturdy shutters just in case I wasn't the only thief in town. I didn't even mind too much paying the innkeeper for the flowers that Imchi ate from the vines at the front.

I'd always thought that you needed dirt to grow things, but so far as I could see these grew straight up out of the cobblestones. The flowers were star-shaped, striped purple and blue, and as large as my hand; they and the ferny leaves gave off a sweet scent even as Imchi chewed blissfully. Ah well, I was in Tzakende; maybe these were magic flowers. The innkeeper priced them dear enough.

By the end of the first week, I began to think that I had chosen my booth site too well, or else that Kossinli had decided to "help" me again. People kept thronging in to look at my jeweled braidclasps (a very good use for the tiny stones most gem dealers

will sell by the bag, like lentils) my bracelets, and my ear-cuffs.
Some of them even bought something. That I should deal in such
trash, who have owned a flawless emerald the size of a goose's egg!
But few will bother to steal such trifles, and fewer will do murder
for them. That's a consideration for any merchant working alone
among strangers.

When the selling was done, there were the accounts to be
kept lest the Tzakendi tax collectors do it for me. They are very
ready to assist strangers in this, as I discovered when I was foolish
enough to wish that someone would come and explain these damn
rules to me. Well, it was late and I was tired. It was so hard to be
careful all the time, especially when Kossinli didn't answer every
single wish—for which mercy, I thanked Her.

"Never mind!" I cried as soon as I'd thought it, but a man
showed up next day anyway. I'm not sure that was Kossinli's doing;
Yrantza at the next stall said they often dropped by the newcomers'
stalls, "Just to make sure you're not overlooking anything."

Yrantza really was helpful. Born outside the city walls,
unrelated to anyone within them, she was forever a "stranger" by
Tzakendi law. She'd been trading there since she helped her auntie
by stringing beads, though, and what she didn't know about
Tzakendi feuds and alliances didn't matter. Besides, she laughed at
my jokes.

There was little time to gossip, and almost none to go
visiting the numerous Seers whom Yrantza or my clients
recommended. Choosing among those Seers was a challenge.
Some paid special devotion to one deity, some to many, and some
to their own prosperity.

Just finding the different Seers was trouble enough. It cost
me time every day, and once nearly gave me a seizure. There, where
I'd expected to find a cluster of Free Visioners (strange even by
fortune-teller standards, Yrantza'd warned me, but more honest
than most) was a squat, square-edged temple of Sarinsat. It was
only a little one, but I still needed three horn-of-plenty pastries and

a large pot of tea before I felt well enough to go on.

From the supposed servants of various deities I heard, "We know pearls of wisdom, Lady, oh yes, but before we show you any of them you must give us your trust." (They generally wanted money as well. Some of the temples could certainly have used some fresh plaster.) "Be guided by us, and when we have decided you are ready, we will tell you what we think you need to know." Feh. I could have had that bargain without traveling for weeks across the desert, surrounded all the way by the smell of wool and camels.

"Oh, Imchi, why can't I find someone who can say something that doesn't involve tall handsome strangers or pious courses of study?" I grumbled one evening. I made time to check on him frequently; no stable-owner can take the same interest in an animal as the animal's owner. Besides, Imchi was at least as good company as most of the people I met. He brayed rather than spoke, but that isn't necessarily a disadvantage.

"It's all right for you to laugh! Here I am, working hard at a respectable trade and spending most of my free time in temples. A woman can actually go alone to tea-houses here without having to fight off some damn man, and can I find the time? Not often! Only yesterday I heard Ana, the innkeeper, holding me up to his daughter as a good, hardworking businesswoman. This is not what I had in mind when I ran from my good marriage, Imchi." He made a rude noise.

"Not, you understand, that I'm demanding that life get more interesting. No, no, no. Not at all." Donkeys do not have eyebrows, but something about his face gave the impression that he raised one.

The next Seer I consulted shuffled her cards back together after one glance. She was one of the pale Tzakendi, green-eyed and red-brown-haired, with those odd little sprinkles of cinnamon color across the nose and cheekbones. She had just gone paler still.

"I do not meddle with the Immortals, Lady, or those they have chosen," she said. She must have meant it; my fee lay untouched before her.

I denied being chosen by anyone for anything.

She smiled thinly across her bundle of cards. "To be sure, my Lady. Forgive my clumsiness. I pray you, take back your silver in earnest of my apology."

Did she think the coins were contaminated? Perhaps she did. I had never even heard of a Seer offering to give a client's money back, let alone seen it happen. What had she really seen, to make her so eager to be rid of me?

When I made no move to pick up the coins, she spoke again. "I have done nothing for you, Mistress. Take up your coin and go." She rose and opened her door so briskly that it bounced off the wall behind it.

Well enough! I went, feeling both angry and frightened. How dare she not tell me what she'd seen? It was my future we were discussing, after all! Just shoving a coin back across the table didn't clear our accounts, but I didn't see what I could do about it.

The one after that said, quite casually, "I see no more hasty departures for a little while."

No more hasty departures? I'd left home quickly enough to be a little touchy on that subject. I tried to sound amused as I pointed out that indeed, I must depart Tzakende soon. "My permits expire with the moon, and besides, the passes will soon fill with snow."

"Soon is not the same as hasty, gentle Lady. Oh, I mean no insult! The silver bowl has not shown me your reason for fleeing your city, but I have no doubt it was honorable. Perhaps you were pursued by admirers until you could bear it no longer. No, now, don't shake your head at me!" And she returned to the fortune-teller's refuge of romance.

She'd given me a warning about the future, even so. It takes a special permit for a foreign trader to remain in Tzakende through the winter, and peddlers of cheap jewelry don't get one. If I didn't want another scrambling departure, I'd better find Mother

Rissa. Issimante might have forgiven me by now. Even if he hadn't, Mother Rissa might've decided that our safe arrival meant I wasn't bad luck. If she wasn't willing to have me join them again, then I'd need the time to find someone else who would.

It took me long enough to find Mother Rissa's clan that I began to fear that they'd already left, or else were unwilling to have me find them. Finally, one wizened carpet-maker squinted at me dubiously and asked if I sought Larissa, Mother of Larinalanla, who led two caravans safely through the Great Storm of the Old King's second reign.

They'd filled a small caravanserai only a few minutes' walk away, but off on its own stub of a street. If I lived here as long as I lived in Charransar, I would never get used to these pocket-streets with one way in and no other way out! Only the tile walled courtyard kept this one from looking like a burrow dug into the adobe walls. Half a dozen of the children playing there left their game and ran up to me, laughing and asking after Imchi. Over their chatter, I heard Rissa calling out to bring me to her. Iskara, her great-niece I think, claimed the honor.

Rissa made me welcome with mint tea and walnut cakes, and laughed when I told her what name had finally found her. "I hadn't heard that one myself in many a year! It was a vicious storm, my dear; may you never see its like." She drank deeply of her tea. "Are you thinking of joining us again? Perhaps I'll tell the whole story on the journey; the old songs of it wander farther from the truth with every new singer."

She was willing to have me join them, then! In my relief I neglected to keep an eye on young Iskara, who nabbed the last of my walnut cakes. That girl showed promise, but she'd have to learn not to giggle.

"I was indeed, if you're not departing immediately. I've a few things to tidy up first." Such as getting free of a Goddess; I still hoped that might be possible.

"As do I, and more than a few! Issimante has gotten

himself in another knife fight, and I want him healthy before we leave. Sand's murder in a half-healed wound. If that boy weren't such a good fighter when I need one, I'd leave him here for the winter, to learn patience. I hope it doesn't pain you for me to talk of him?"

I assured her that it didn't.

She set her teacup down with a small click. "Yes, I didn't think you were merely playing coy on the journey. You've a little time yet to sort out your bundles; we'll not leave before the new moon, if then." She smiled reassuringly.

I smiled back while I thought fast. How seriously did the Tzakendi take those permits? I couldn't really believe that an official was going to show up the day after the new moon, checking permits; for one thing, I'd seldom seen any officials except tax-collectors since I got past the gates. On the other hand, Yrantza excepted, I wasn't wildly popular with my fellow merchants. It's sad, really. Here I was, bringing life—and customers—into a part of Strangers' Square that held few strangers and fewer new items, and was anybody grateful? They were likelier to betray me.

"Then I must ask you another question, Mother Rissa. Who needs to be sweetened if I'm here past my permitted term, and how do I sweeten him?"

She clicked her tongue against the roof of her mouth. "That's right, I'd forgotten they'd gotten so strict about that with strangers! We've been coming here since before the second set of walls was built, so they don't concern themselves much about us. Still, this year's harvest was good. Probably no one will mind. Just make sure your final tax payment's a little generous. They let plenty of those pestilential pilgrims stay, with their holy poverty and their religious arguments; I don't see why they'd object to you. Will you be all right for lodging? Maranla's got room..."

"I'll be fine, really. No need to inconvenience your niece, though the thought is kind." No need to mention, either, that I'd bed down with Imchi before I'd share a room with Maranla, her

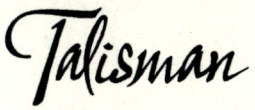

five whining children, and Maranla's own wistful reminiscences of her beloved departed husband. I was still not certain whether the husband was dead, or just gone.

9

*T*he bells were ringing in the temple of Cos, a high sweet sound that is very pleasant for the first few minutes, when I saw a shifting boy-sized shape silhouetted against the sunshade of my stall. They've no technique, these upland thieves, I thought. But this shadow caster slipped suddenly around the side and crouched beside me.

"Lady Layla?" Now, I have no right to be called Lady, but I thought it might balance out some other names I've been given, so I nodded. "Lady Layla of Kossinli?"

"Kossinli? Where is that?" Some of my alarm must have shown; the child backed out of arm's reach while still crouching.

"I dunno. If you dunno neither, ne'min'." He half-rose to go, looking over his shoulder at me while his left hand grabbed two ear-cuffs from my display behind him. I made a long arm; for my height I can reach surprisingly far. His hair was no cleaner than the rest of him looked to be, but long enough to give me a good hold.

I took back the ear-cuffs. "I'll just keep those. And I'll know who's got me confused with some other Layla. Keep still, unless you want the crowd to notice," I told him, with a tug at his hair. He sighed.

"I dunno a name, truth! Y' think they tell someone like me a name?" He'd learned already to murmur, not whisper, when he wanted to speak without attracting attention. "This other Layla, they just wanta talk at her. But I guess you don' care, since you're somen else." He smirked at me.

"Oh, yes I do care! Maybe they won't believe me any more than you do, brat. If trouble's looking for me, you bet I want to know about it."

"Then get Arakante to read yer leaves, other-Layla. Don' ask a hill-brat. Hey, you got a customer comin'." And he was gone, leaving a few hairs behind. He lied about the customer.

He'd also lied when he said he didn't know the names of any of the people who were interested in finding me. This Arakante might be only a finder—a good office for a Seer—but she'd been hired by someone.

All the rest of that week, I dithered while I sold down my stock. Did I want to find this Arakante, or did I want to disappear into Mother Rissa's caravan? Ah, but what then? Back to Charransar with the tie to Kossinli as strong as ever? It would be good to see Old Parata, but not so good to see the Priests of Sarinsat.

The selling-down got grim. The handful of coins that remained after I'd paid stall-rent seemed little reward for all my work; I've had better money for one good night's thieving. More fun, too.

I had to do the final count thrice before I could believe the total. There were fewer than when I'd fled Charransar! Of course, all that visiting Seers hadn't come free. Both my lodging and Imchi's were more expensive than I'd expected. Then there were those few tea-house evenings; plates of little fried things and tips to the performers do add up. If I continued respectability, would I have to buy an abacus and learn to use it? The thought made me shiver.

This indecision was ridiculous. There was a simple lot-casting tool here on my table. The lirial landed chariot-up: go ahead.

Arakante turned out to live and work in a most inconvenient place. Why would anyone with a choice want to live up there, where the streets are so steep that many have stairs cut into them, and some of the tall houses have doors to the outside on all three floors?

Arakante's own house stood where five streets met, flowing uphill so that its second story was wider than its first, and the third was wider yet. The windows were ringed in soft blue and green, a welcome relief from the dazzle of whitewashed plaster. A pretty floral decoration arched over the door. A child giggled somewhere, and someone was frying onions.

This was not how I had pictured the house of a learned Seer, but the doorkeeper assured me that it was indeed the house of Arakante. He also apologized for their sign being somewhat worn. (So much for the floral decoration. Ah well, I never claimed to be a scholar.) The Seer was with a client, but if I would care to wait? He must warn me that, without an appointment, the wait might be long.

My, oh my, appointments! I had come up in the world in more ways than one here, it would seem. I would wait. If I could avoid climbing all those steps a second time, I would. Respectability saps the stamina. The servant didn't ask my name, nor did I offer it. Perhaps giving it would shorten my wait, and perhaps it would shorten my life.

The interior court was cool and uncluttered; one of its benches had a clear view of both doors. While I waited, Tzakende addressed its guardians with chimes, with horns, and a brass-lunged tenor. Even so, time did pass, and the servant returned.

Arakante's fortune-telling room was as spare as the courtyard, with no furniture except a table and two chairs, and a rosewood chest under its one deep-silled window. A three-colored cat drowsed there, forepaws curled in. A young man sat watching me from behind the table.

As I hesitated in the doorway, he smiled. "Good day to you, Lady," he said in a deeper voice than I would have expected from so slight a man. "I am Arakante; what have you come to discover?"

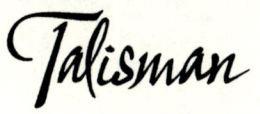

He gestured to a chair. I sat, though I cannot claim that I was graceful. Why would anyone choose to perch on a platform that is always, in my brief experience, either too high or too low? Either situation is not only uncomfortable, but also awkward if you want to leave quickly. I hadn't needed to leave a place quickly in several weeks now, but you never know.

Damn the slurred Tzakendi dialect, damn working blind in a strange town, damn me—for I surely should have considered the chance of a Seer being male. Many of the mystics of Tzakende are above noticing whether those around them are male or female, or so they pretend. Save for clothing-sellers, the merchants only care about the contents of your purse. Still, a man as fortune-teller, when they must be alone with those who seek their advice! Such a young man, too, with eyelashes many women would envy.

Enough of that! I tucked my toes back under the chair lest they dangle, and began.

"You have, I'm told, the true sight. Why then do you need to ask me what I seek?"

"If you're a skeptic, Madame, why come all this way? I'm no temple-pika, to be visited on a whim for tales of romance and inheritance. Of course, I do have my limits," and he made the sign to avert jealousy thrice: demons, humankind, gods. He waited then, perfectly still. I could hear a procession winding its way between the houses below, flutes and bells echoing from the walls.

"What I seek concerns the Immortals. Shall I continue?"

He smiled slowly. "Surely, most especially if it concerns the Sight of one of them."

The damned chair creaked as I tried to edge back. "It seems you do know something of what I seek."

"Lady Layla." He nodded gracefully. "She who wore the eye of a goddess tucked into her navel for a full three weeks—did no one warn you about that? Well, no matter. I think, Lady Layla, that you and I may be able to help each other."

In fact, I had not worn it tucked into my navel; it was much too large. I did wear it in a waist-pouch, cinched snugly next to my skin, which was uncomfortable enough without any dancing-girl tricks. I hoped he wasn't adept enough to know about the promise I'd made out in the desert—better not to think of it now. Better to bargain as though I had a choice. "And have you seen how this may be, Arakante?"

"Laughter can't see clearly with only one eye, far-traveler. When She can, She will see that you need no more from Her."

Really, you'd think a straight business proposition was somehow indecent. Why couldn't he simply say that he wanted me to steal Kossinli's other eye?

The sounds of the procession staggered past. Pity flute players in hills like these!

Arakante continued, "The task is but begun, Lady Layla. When it is finished, the Smiling Sister will grant the wish of your heart. Please believe me, I know that the task is not easy, but I also know that it can be done by...one sufficiently skilled, and quick."

A good enough thief, that meant. I had been once, but I was out of practice now. "You're asking me to take a great deal of risk," I said to fill the silence.

"More than you now experience each day?"

"In the short run, yes. Kossinli," Arakante frowned; was I not supposed to name Her directly, then? I somehow couldn't feel formal dread of a goddess who sends donkeys to someone living in one rented room. "Kossinli isn't actually trying to kill me. I assume this treasure isn't unguarded."

"Yet the reward is also considerable. We're not concerned with other items in the place where the eye is..." He let the statement trail as if he were dangling a string for the cat in the window.

Could I trick some information out of him? I had no idea who else might be involved, but I'd like to. "Who's 'we'?"

Arakante smiled and lowered his eyes. "No one who wishes you harm."

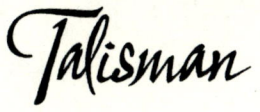

Well, people will sometimes answer a sudden question like that. Not often, but sometimes. If they do, it's almost always the truth.

He looked puzzled. "Do you not wish to be free to think your own thoughts undisturbed?"

"That's why I'm here." Arakante and whoever else was in this might betray me afterwards. They also might have me killed if I refused. Plague take this dithering! I never used to have any trouble deciding what I wanted. Of course, that was before I attracted the attention of a goddess given to granting wishes in Her own humorous fashion. Somehow I had to rid myself of Her, and what other alternatives had I?

"Yes, I'll get it for you. There's the matter of payment."

He blinked. "But is not freedom a gift beyond all others?"

"Freedom's one of those intangible benefits, my friend. My donkey doesn't eat intangibles and neither do I, nor will they pay my caravan fees. I'll have no time afterwards for peddling items of dubious origin, so don't suggest I take your fee from someone else's treasure." We haggled amiably enough until I settled for fifty lirials.

Arakante rose. "Come, you must be hungry. I can tell you what you need to know over a dinner of chicken with lemon and olives at least as well as here."

Well, well! I might be going into unknown amounts of risk for uncertain reward (Never count your coin until you have it in your hand, and then watch for clipped edges!) but I would certainly get an excellent dinner first. Perhaps being a psychic had some practical benefits. Had Arakante counted on my agreeing, or did he always have his cook prepare for guests?

"I would have offered you dinner in any case."

I turned to stare at him. I had said nothing. This damned little Tzakendi card-reader had just burgled my mind as easily as I'd burgled the houses of the complacent. What business had he with my thoughts? He stepped back and touched my hand once, very lightly. "Please excuse me. I was a little insulted that you would think otherwise, and you were thinking very loudly."

I was at a loss for words, no common thing with me. How does one think quietly? Well, at least he probably wouldn't know everything I'd been thinking. Had his talents told him before we even met that chicken would please me more than meat? We'd never eaten flesh of any kind at home; marrying me to a meat-eater had caused my father some qualms of conscience, especially after Mother told him what she thought of it. At first I'd found eating animals to be a more difficult change than accepting my husband's attentions. His tastes were moderate, and I'd known for years what men and women do.

Arakante was still waiting quietly for whatever I might say. Should I apologize, too? "You're very gracious," I managed, finally.

Both the dinner and the garden we ate in deserved more attention than I gave them. Whoever made the couscous had an inspired hand for the tiny grains, and the lemon and olives perfumed the whole room. Civilized persons do not go straight to business, I know. I've sometimes feared that my former husband's second wife was right, and there is no hope of my ever becoming civilized. But then, properly civilized women don't steal things.

"Where is the emerald?"

Arakante looked odd and cleared his throat. "The Scented Garden."

I nearly choked on my couscous. "You want me to go thieving in a whorehouse? A very expensive, well-guarded whorehouse? I'll have to do it in daylight, too."

He nodded.

"But no one's likely to see you, you know. The street's very nearly deserted during the day."

A deserted street, where I'd be conspicuous as a camel in court, and a strictly commercial whorehouse. Sarinsat's temple folk had been so shocked that someone would actually steal from their god that they hadn't moved quickly. I'd bet that nothing had

shocked anyone at the Scented Garden in a long time. I pointed
this out to Arakante. He offered to accompany me.

My expression must have spoken while I was still trying to
find words, or perhaps I was thinking loudly again. "I have heard
of such arrangements, where one person, ah, finds the object and
the other discourages pursuit or guards the doors," he said with
some annoyance.

"Exactly—you've heard of them. A successful thief is
anonymous. I work alone." Perhaps his occult skills showed him
what the end of the argument would be. He sighed and shrugged.

"As you will. Can you work fast? Lissandra's putting
away her mirror. Going to serve the Huntress, if you'll believe it!
Who knows where that emerald will be this time next week?"

"Religion's great for messing up plans, isn't it?" His frown
deepened. "Don't worry. This time next week the emerald will be
wherever you've put it. I expect they'll give her a large and
splendid good-by party?"

Arakante nodded, smiling. "Tomorrow night," he said.

"Perfect. That will give me time to meet with the leader of
the caravan I'll join later this week." Actually, it made timing more
critical than I'd like. The best thing would probably be to move
Imchi and myself to Mother Rissa's right away; I'd be invisible as
one of that mob of travelers, and I wouldn't need to worry about
keeping in touch with Rissa about when they were moving on.

"It would be helpful to know where in the Scented Garden
this emerald is," I said.

"It is in the parlor of that same Lissandra, most renowned
professional," here his eyebrows rose slightly, "of the house. I'm
told it's set in the navel of a goddess who presides over her bed, but
no doubt you will recognize it. It is of course a twin to the other."

With great effort, I smothered a laugh. Kossinli, did you
arrange this misappropriation of your eye?

We talked awhile longer of details of the guards and
barriers of the house. Arakante's occult skills had some very

practical applications. As befitted her fame (and earning power, no doubt) Lissandra's quarters were on the first level above the gardens. Fortunately, Tzakende shares with more mundane places the delusion that thieves never rise early. Also fortunately, even the wealthy here build their walls of mud, though theirs are higher than those of the poor and nicely whitewashed. On the day I can't scale a mud-brick wall I deserve retirement or death, whichever comes first.

The moon was full that night; I journeyed back to my inn well-lit by its beams and well-guarded by one of Arakante's men. To tell the truth, I was glad of his stolid presence. Here at the turning of the year, Tzakende was full of strange sounds and shifting shadows. Perhaps I felt uneasy only because I still hadn't learned to distinguish normal, peaceful Tzakendi noises from those that sent a warning. Yes, no doubt that was it, but I was still glad to reach the inn, with its slightly grimy tables and the muffled snores of poor travelers sleeping rolled in blankets by the firepit.

Ah, but it was good to walk out of the inn the next morning without hurrying to my stall! How did Old Parata do it, year after year? At least Mother Rissa had some change of scenery, though the route was much the same each time.

The city was emptying out for winter; the innkeeper showed no surprise when I paid my reckoning. The roads were filled with travelers hurried along by a wind that wandered like a Tzakendi street. Cloaked against the raw chill, we were all vague wooly shapes in the first light. Imchi's coat was beaded with dew by the time I left him at the caravanserai.

Hurrying traders had driven the children to the edges of the courtyard. People paraded through with questions and tallies and bundles of the subtle Tzakendi weavings whose dyes are a secret even to most Tzakendi. No time for tea and walnut cookies this time! No time for questions, either.

Hurry now, hurry, but only so much as any other honest woman with much to do. The clouds were drifting down out of the

hills to mingle with the rising smoke of the morning's cooking fires. Shadows still lay along the western wall surrounding the Scented Garden, helping to pick out the shapes of the adobe bricks under their covering mud plaster.

Then it was off with my cloak and woman's robe and up the wall with no time to shiver. The gardens were littered with signs that the farewell party had indeed been memorable. A heap of clothing beside the path turned out to have a sleeping body inside it. A hand reached out and gripped my ankle. "Kick a man when he's down?" said a furry voice.

"Terribly sorry, sir." Go back to sleep, damn you. Sleep on the nice soft grass. Sleep. And let go of my ankle.

"Nice ankle," said the voice. "Boy or girl?" The hand not grasping my ankle shoved the remains of a party wreath away from his eyes. "Well, which are you? Makes a difference, at least to me." He squinted at me in some annoyance. "You kitchen staff or some such? Waifs're out of fashion."

Now, which would he not be interested in? A wrong guess would be disastrous. "Sir, please, I've got to get back to the kitchen. They're brewing hangover remedies." Well, if they weren't they should be.

The grip on my ankle relaxed. "Oh, yes. Yes. Bring me one, boygirl. No offense, but I'm not much on an—angodry— boygirls. You bring me one of Mirra's cures."

"Yes, sir, I'll do that." This time he let me detach his hand. I walked away briskly in what I hoped was the direction of the kitchens until a bed of Autumn Damasks gave me a little cover, then veered over to what ought to be Lissandra's window. Looking backwards, I saw that the man with the party wreath had gone back to imitating a heap of discarded clothing.

The house itself was built of the same mud brick as its outer wall, but carved into patterns. There were large latticed windows at even the first-story level. It might have been designed to help me; there were even some flowering vines climbing the wall there.

Too frail for even my weight, they still gave me cover for my climb. Lissandra, heroine of a dozen bawdy songs and several quite romantic ones, lay snoring in her silken bed. Clearly, she had bidden good-bye to her old life with enthusiasm. Beside her bed, in a niche whose top was shaped like a nomad's bow, stood a golden statue of a dancing woman fully three feet tall. Her navel held the emerald.

At home, most floors are of wood. Walking across that without waking someone in the room is a true challenge of skill! This was almost too easy.

When I reached the statue I regretted that complaint. There are different ways of setting gems, but most of them involve either prongs or twists of wire, easily enough pried loose. How they'd managed this setting puzzled me greatly. The gold flowed smoothly as flesh around the edges of the stone.

I could not even swear aloud, though it's just as well Arakante wasn't there to hear my thoughts. Without much hope, I tried to slide my smallest pick between the emerald and the gold. No such luck. If that statue was solid metal—I lifted it gently. No, it must be hollow. It was still awkward.

Horribly awkward. One upraised hand grated against the top of the arch as I tried to maneuver it out. Lissandra stirred and muttered querulously in her sleep. I froze where I was.

"What's that noise?" Tzakende's highest-priced courtesan demanded in a voice like an angry cat's. "Damn it, I need my beauty sleep." One slender hand groped for the edge of the coverlet.

"Sorry, Madame," I murmured in what I hoped was a servile voice. The arm dropped back over her eyes.

"So thirsty. Girl, bring me water!"

A double-walled Brinantan ewer glimmered on the bedside table. Quickly, I walked over and filled the goblet beside it. Lissandra swallowed drily. If ever I needed heavenly intervention! Just let her keep her eyes closed, or be too lazy to look around.

Standing a little behind her, I murmured, "Here you are,

Madame." She raised herself on one elbow to take it from me, but never bothered to turn to see who served her.

"Aah. Here." She waved the nearly-empty goblet vaguely; I took it before she dropped the pretty thing. "Oh gods. I'll start serving the Huntress tomorrow." The last word was almost lost in a yawn, and snores followed soon after.

Back now behind the bed. Carefully, so slowly that my shoulders ached and trembled, I moved the statue out of its niche.

Wonderful. Now all I had to do was get myself and it back down that wall. Well, it was that or dance blithely down the stairs with what was probably the most valuable single object in the house. If no servants were up yet, they would be soon. Even in a whorehouse, people have to eat, and they certainly have to bathe.

Scarves and dance-veils cluttered the table before the mirrors that Lissandra would soon abandon. I don't normally stoop to stealing clothing, but there are exceptions to all rules.

With the statue bound to my back, I came down the wall faster than I would have preferred. Its arms and feet tangled in the pretty, fragrant vines only to pull free suddenly and unexpectedly. I landed with a hard thump and stood gasping, only for a few seconds, but long enough to attract the attention of an overly-industrious early-rising servant.

My soft heart will cause me grief yet. The poor fool was old, and even smaller than I am. I tipped him into an ornamental pond while he was still making up his mind to shout, then left him to fight the water-lilies while I ran as fast as I could down a gravel path with the statue's sharp little toes kicking me in the back.

The wall was in sight now, but I could never climb over it with the entire statue on my back. There was a hedge of something, I could hide behind that—roses, to guess by the thorns. I hacked through the scarves where the thorns hadn't already ripped them and tried again to pry loose the emerald without damaging it.

"Kossinli, if they catch me, it won't be funny," I hissed.

The jewel dropped into my hand.

"Thank you," I muttered. It is never wise to waste a gift of the gods; I reached the wall and scaled it faster than I would have thought possible. Quickly, quickly I hauled dress and cloak on over my men's garb and walked off up the road.

Arakante was waiting at the door when I arrived. He announced happily that he'd had the slaves get the bath ready. "For your poor ribs," he explained.

"Oh, you saw." I haven't blushed in years, but I did then. It must have been as good as a puppet show for children! Besides, what else had he seen? Never mind. There were more pressing questions than that to consider.

"The bath's a kind thought, but I'd best be on my way once we've finished our business." We were going to do that without problems, weren't we?

"This late in the day?" Arakante looked honestly surprised.

"Tell me, do you ever read your own future? I never said I'd stay. I'll still have time to rejoin the caravan I came with if I leave now, and I'll be dirtier than this before I'm home." Best, surely, to let him think I was leaving the city.

"You think I'll steal the emerald from you!"

He looked shocked. I think he really was. I found myself apologizing, denying perfectly reasonable concerns. "No, no, it's just that I never hang around afterward. Nothing personal, it's just..." Plague take the man, he looked hurt. No, I didn't mean that, I didn't mean it at all, I didn't! Or did I still need to worry about Kossinli? How would I know? Was I ever going to be able to lock this door behind me?

Jewel theft used to be such a simple living. I'd wander through disguised as someone's third wife or upper servant (Not that there's that much difference) listen to fountain-gossip until I found a good prospect, and come back after dark. So many wealthy people sleep so soundly! It's all that rich food, no doubt.

Mind you, I have my scruples. No jewelers, in memory of

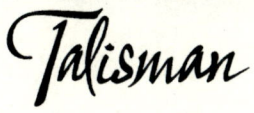

my father. Besides, they tend to have guards with long swords and short tempers. No new mothers, in memory of Mirit, who was so kind to me when I first married her husband. That scruple has cost me! New mothers have typically gotten some nice presents, and when they do sleep you could walk off with everything except the baby without waking them. Well, I've made a few exceptions on that one, but only when the woman talked more about the presents than the baby. No temple thefts, until the rumors of that first emerald overcame my teacher's warnings.

Selling could be a problem; even Old Parata never gave me nearly what the things were worth. At least I didn't have that problem here. Or did I? Arakante had finally given up trying to argue with me, and had decided to try the big sad eyes routine. He couldn't be that eager for my company. I wanted to tell him that looking pitiful is a trick for small children, but I couldn't. For one thing, we still hadn't finished our business. What was I going to have to do? Surely he knew that it's for the buyer to show the money first.

The strangest laugh I'd ever heard sounded from somewhere in the house. Arakante jumped as if he had been asleep and muttered something about noisy damned birds. "Here." He took a small purse from his belt and handed it to me. I counted it— I always do, and since he was already in a snit I didn't need to worry about angering him. All present.

"And here." I pulled the emerald from its pouch and held it out. How many times did I hear my father say of some gem he was trying to sell, that it seemed to glow of its own light? I had heard the same phrase later, from less reputable men. Well, these things that everyone says are sometimes true. It glowed like leaves in a garden at sunset. What would it look like, set with its twin in Kossinli's statue?

I thrust the gem at Arakante, but he ignored it. "What did you see?" he asked.

"I see that I must leave now if I'm to join my friends. Will you take what you've paid for?"   I was starting to get the same feeling that I sometimes got when out thieving, the feeling that says go with what you've got—while you can.   It's saved my skin more than once.

He took the gem then, smiling.   "You know, you're not poor any more.   You can afford a horse in addition to a donkey. Why not buy one tomorrow and catch up to your friends then? Surely it's safer to travel well-rested."

"What do you mean, safer?   Are you looking into my future without my asking it?   If you've a warning for me, give it plainly."

Arakante drew himself up to his full height in order to look down on me.   "When I see for people, I'm well paid for it!   It takes no art to see danger in your future, Layla."

I'd offended his professional pride, clearly.   Clumsy of me. And oh, but it would be good to relax a little while.   Traveling across the Wastes may be many things, but never relaxing.

"My lord, I'd be happy to accept your gracious offer."

10

A good hot bath, especially when your muscles ache with cold and strain, must be the purest pleasure that there is. Scented oils are a pleasant extra. I slid down into the steaming water, resolving not to worry about anything at all until my fingers and toes were as wrinkled as last year's figs.

When I was third wife, I found it tedious to bathe and dress and go to dinner; but then, I had so little else to do. It had seemed stupid to spend hours grooming myself for someone who'd first seen me wearing my older brother's castoffs, squinting at the wire loops and coils that go into making a Trembling Wreath headdress. There was jeweler's rouge on my fingers, and (I later found) a smear of it on my nose.

Yes, well! I was not in Nahouendar any longer, but in Tzakende, and I was certainly not thirteen years old. I was also not bored by having a long, gentle soak in scented water, not after several years of Charransar's public baths, which were too hot in the summer, too cold in the winter and always slippery with someone else's spilled oil. Here, the bath-slave gave me sweet oils and several towels, then curled up on the bench beside the door.

Steam rose from the water, swirling up to the ceiling where it obscured the intricate geometries of the tiles. From time to time, the gentlest of breezes drifted through the room just strongly enough to keep the moist heat from becoming stifling. Hunger finally broke my half-trance; I rinsed my hair one last time and groped for a towel. When someone handed me one, I rose from the water like a startled duck.

"Oh dear, I'm sorry."

I knew that silvery voice, but from where? Charransar? Firousi? All the way from Charransar? How had whoever it was gotten in here? Why had the bath attendant said nothing? More important, what did Lady Silver Voice mean to do? I'd brought no weapons with me. My wet hair glued itself to my arms and back, and fought my efforts to shove it back out of my eyes. Gods, hadn't I lived by my wits too long to trust a wistful smile? Trapped in the baths...I crabbed my way away from the edge of the bath, oh ye gods and little hookfishes, let me not be drowned in the bath like an unwanted kitten in a pond! I got my hair shoved out of my eyes, only to be half-blinded by water dripping from it.

"I didn't mean to alarm you. I should have announced myself." The source of the silvery voice hadn't moved.

Well, if she'd meant to kill me I'd be dead by now, so she must have other plans, whoever she was. "It's customary," I managed to say with a reasonably steady voice.

I got my hair wrapped in the towel and the water out of my eyes and stared indignantly at Firousi. "I might have known." A bath sheet lay on the nearest bench; I wrapped it around me quickly. Being naked before Firousi in her meticulously-draped robe and scarves made me feel like a delinquent slave-girl caught using the mistress' bath.

"You're Arakante's mysterious partner, I take it?"

Firousi nodded. "I did want to thank you for retrieving Kossinli's other eye, and Arakante said that you'd talked of leaving almost immediately." She smiled, gracious and calm as always.

"There seems little reason to linger here now. After all, I came here to find some way to, ah, persuade Kossinli that She'd done enough for me already, and Arakante said She'd see that when She had both Her eyes."

"Yes, that is my cousin's theory." The silvery voice was even cooler now. Was this some feud with the cousin, or did she disagree?

"He said it was so!" I've had some experience in telling when people are lying, and he hadn't had that look about him.

"Oh, it's assuredly what he believes."

But not what she believed. Well, it was no problem of mine. It was another argument for leaving.

I could feel the bath sheet sliding lower. Oh, this was ridiculous! Slippery arguments, slippery draperies, probably a slippery floor, too. What was I waiting for, permission to leave? I hitched the wrap higher and took a step towards the door.

Firousi continued, "I'm sure Kossinli is quite grateful for all your service. Not only did you retrieve Her eye—"

"I stole it."

Firousi made a slight grimace of distaste. If people want me to be gracious, they shouldn't come sneaking up on me when I'm naked.

"But you did so in such an amusing way. Our Lady of Mirth does appreciate these artistic touches. You can tell us more about it at dinner—we couldn't quite see some of your performance."

My what? Kossinli, if You're still listening, could You please arrange for some small accident to happen to this woman? Nothing major, just some silly little thing?

"And surely you're not going to try to leave tonight, alone?"

"No." I took a deep breath, and nearly lost my towel in the process. "Firousi, my Lady, please, please make your Lady understand that She owes me nothing! I've been amply paid! I neither deserve nor want anything more." I'd even give up my plea for an accident to humble Firousi. "Arakante swore that getting both eyes would make Her see that."

Firousi smiled gently. "It may be so. The girl will show you to a room where you can prepare for dinner."

She rose, shook out her skirts, and glided away. It would have been more impressive if one scarf, its hem heavy with spilled bath-water, had not half-throttled her by sticking to the floor. She stepped back, and one elegant narrow sandal hit a pool of bath water. Her reflexes were remarkable for a sheltered priestess; she actually managed to keep her feet. I'm sure that laugh was supposed to sound nonchalant. The long, suspicious stare she gave me certainly was not.

"I believe dinner should be served soon," she said as she strolled away.

The slave led me to a small room with a mural of ducks and ducklings, with a large tawny cat crouched to spring on a duck that was just turning its head to look back. On clothes-tees beside a screen were a heavily embroidered caftan and a set of boy's clothes, none of them mine.

The clothes did look as though they'd fit. Certainly, someone had studied my taste. The boy's clothes were dark green, almost black, with indigo embroidery. I could go a-thieving in them, if I ever wanted to wear silk to do it. It was long since I'd owned anything so fine as the women's turquoise caftan, all spangled with tiny mirrors embroidered on with tinier stitches. It reminded me of home so much that I felt as though I'd seen it before.

Then I felt dimmer than a beggar's lamp. Of course I had, in the pleasant beginning of my nightmare of capture by Sarinsat's Priests. Were hunger and bath oil fumes fogging my brain that I hadn't seen it at once? If I'd still had any doubts as to whether my connection with Kossinli had been severed, I had none now.

Hungry or not, I had to think about this awhile. Kossinli had now embarrassed Her own priestess in order to grant me a wish. She had also, at about the same time, given me something I'd forgotten I even wanted. Didn't that mean that my connection to Her must be stronger than before?

I was going to have to have a few words with Arakante. He had told me—yes, and I had trusted him. He had seemed so honest. I can do that myself, look honest. Or did he really believe what he'd said, as Firousi said he did?

Firousi might also be honest, in her own incredibly arrogant way. Had I just done that tavern-comedy of a gem theft, in an effort to evade the one person who'd been both truthful and able to help me?

Had even my flight from Charransar been a fool's errand? Firousi could probably have kept me safely hidden if I'd agreed to her terms when she'd offered them. She'd certainly disappeared quickly and completely when she wished. I could have just stayed home. None of this was needed.

Yes, and I could have just stayed married in Charransar. That would have been perfectly safe.

Was Kossinli as bored now as I was then? That was a truly frightening thought. What might a bored goddess do to enliven Her existence? To be sure, this gift was more convenient than donkeys or raw wool. Perhaps these things were goodbye gifts? My stomach rumbled. Perhaps I could wait until after dinner to question Arakante and Firousi?

Indeed I could. When someone goes to the trouble to arrange for fish, all fragrant with cilantro and something sweeter, not to mention seven-vegetable couscous and dishes of delicious little fried things, it would be rude to harass that person about what might have been an honest mistake. I could do that later.

Firousi came in after I did, escorted by a sour-faced woman I remembered from Charransar. The woman made sure that every fold of Firousi's robes was elegantly arranged, tucked her trailing sleeves up into jeweled arm-bands, and waited in stiff-backed silence.

"Thank you, Roshana," Firousi said. The woman bowed to Firousi, glared at me, and left.

No evil looks could have damaged my pleasure in that meal. Yet every time I reached out and took another bite of the wonderful food, the heavy silk of my mysterious new caftan rustled. Firousi kept sneaking sideways looks at it, frowning slightly.

Arakante chattered frantically until our short answers defeated him. Then he sat silent, regarding the fragments of dinner as though he could read them like tea-leaves. Perhaps he could.

Finally the mint tea steamed before us, warm and sweet. I sipped mine in a fair imitation of Firousi's elegant manner and set the crystal cup down carefully. I was going to have to say some harsh things to this gentle man; no need to go breaking the dishes as well.

"My thanks for the feast," I began.

"My thanks for your presence," said Firousi and Arakante in chorus, and glared at each other.

Someone laughed. All three of us jumped, for none of us recognized the voice. We accused each other, though I think we all knew that was wishful thinking. Someone upset the table as we all scrambled to our feet.

"Oh, spare yourselves the effort," said Firousi as Arakante and I checked behind the screen that hid the slaves' coming and going, the silken embroideries that hung on the walls, and the tiny space behind the chests of linens. Thanks to someone's (Firousi's?) fondness for tapestries and small decorative objects (Yes, my fingers itched; no, I didn't take anything. I have my standards, also some sense.) that searching took some time. After several long, shaky breaths, Firousi said softly, "She's gone now."

"Is She ever really gone?" My voice sounded much louder than I'd intended. "Well, is She? How can you tell? You," I turned to Arakante, "told me this theft would end it, that She'd let me alone! Both of you listen to me. I've worked with some pretty strange people in my life, and I'll put up with a lot, but I won't be made a fool of. I've had stinking heaps of raw wool instead of the clothes I needed, and I've had money I couldn't spend for fear of priests or Prince's men asking where I got it. Imchi damn near got me killed, and he did cost me my home. What's the catch to the clothes, and when do I find that out? Mysterious gifts are bad enough without hearing Divine laughter.

What do I do if She decides to laugh, or talk to me, when I'm halfway through someone's window?"

"What makes you think She'd talk to you?" Firousi snapped.

Sand devils and sour water, did I have to deal with jealousy here, too? I took a step towards the door and stopped. If Firousi was jealous, I wouldn't have to worry about whether she'd really try to help me break my connection with Kossinli. She might think I was insanely ungrateful for refusing something she valued so highly, but she'd help.

Two of the slaves entered and began tidying up. Soon they had the table righted and the remains of dinner removed. All three crystal cups had somehow survived. The slaves replaced them with goblets, set down a red-ware decanter of date wine, and left as silently as they came.

Firousi put one hand on my arm; a light touch, but one that didn't go away when I moved. "Neither of us is trying to make a fool of you, Layla. Ari truly believed what he told you, and I hoped that it might be true. I want no unwilling students. But surely now you see the wisdom of taking the time to learn to control your connection with Kossinli? You've been trying not to think certain thoughts at all. Surely you've heard the story of the great mystic prince who offered one of his courtiers a famous racing camel, if the courtier could but keep from thinking of the camel's saddle for as long as it took the shadow of a pillar to move from one tile to another? Only saints can live without desires, Layla. Let me show you another way."

I have never aspired to sainthood. "How long will it take, this other way? I've made arrangements with a caravan to travel back to Charransar—"

"Ugh, winter travel across the Wastes? Why?"

"That's Tzakende's choice, not mine! My permits expired several days ago, but Mother Rissa's group seems to be on a longer leash. They'll have to leave soon, though." That ought to give a nice, firm end to this argument that kept springing up again like

Missanla the Many-Headed.

"Oh, don't worry about the pen-pushers. Ari can buy them off, and get a message to this Mother Rissa at the same time. Then we can really settle into teaching you what you need to know. Trust me, little sister, winter in Tzakende's an excellent time for study. There's little enough else to occupy the mind! There isn't much call for Ari's scrying, either, so he can help us find what we need."

She smiled happily at us both while I stood wondering which part of this plan to object to first. Ari recovered faster than I did.

"Does either Layla or I get any say in this?"

"Ari, dear—"

"And don't call me Ari!"

"Very well then, Lord Arakante, Seer and guide. What do you see happening if she goes off alone to find her own way, still untrained, but still thinking she can snap the chain of a goddess' whims?"

Had they forgotten I was even in the room, to talk of me so? "Oh, no, I know better than that! We're still linked, your Goddess and I. Wonder who's more sick of it?"

I turned to Arakante. "Why did you lie to me? You're not Kossinli's servant! What did you stand to gain from conning me into taking risks to get me more tangled up in this monkey-weaving than ever?"

"I thought it would free you. It should have." He stared gloomily at his hands, then back at me. "I'm a Seer, Layla, not a mystic or a priest. When Firousi began pestering me to get involved—"

"Pestering!" The silver voice was showing a little brass.

He ignored it. "I consulted every omen I know. The one thing they all agreed on was that Kossinli couldn't see clearly with only one eye. Believe me, I tried to 'see' what She'd do when She could, but it's harder with a goddess, even a minor one—"

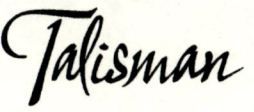

"Minor! Little cousin, I'll feed you to Her ducks for that." The pleats of Firousi's shawl slid into ruin as she leaped from her chair.

"Try it. I'm not so little as I once was, and you're so dignified these days you probably couldn't run fast enough to—"

"Try me and find out! What do you think will happen if that minor goddess, the Lady of Laughter, the Tricksey One, works no more surprises? If life goes on forever the same, is it life?"

Neither Arakante nor I tried to answer that one. She twisted around to face me.

"What do you mean, you already know you're still linked to Kossinli?"

"I know," I said, and shrugged. Well, enigmatic answers worked for Seers and mystics; why not for me?

"Layla, I truly am concerned for you." Firousi's voice was suddenly low and sweet again. I was beginning to feel a little dizzy from all the leaps from one mood to another.

Arakante made a startling vulgar noise. "Oh, stop the bullshit!"

Well, well! I hadn't known he knew such words.

"You don't give a sequin what happens to her. You want someone to help you gather all the other bits and pieces of that damn statue, and since you, my elegant Lady, damn well aren't going to go grubbing around in brothels or risking your delicate skin on the rooftops, she—"

"Wait a minute, both of you! This is my delicate skin we're talking about risking. And what does he mean, Firousi, all the other bits and pieces of what statue?" They both sat and gaped at me. "Don't gape at me as if one of the slaves had spoken. I have a right to know." I might not be trained in arcane arts, but I could tell when I need to ask questions. Where was the mysterious statue, and how much was missing?

Firousi sighed. "There was a statue, back before the conquest, of the Lady of Laughter in Her glory. How lovely She must have been, before Charransar's fall!" She gazed out into the gathering dusk. "Please forgive both Arakante and me; we were raised as brother and sister, and still quarrel like children sometimes."

Very nicely done, that apology, but I still meant to find out more about this statue. I also wondered how Firousi and Arakante had come to be raised together, when and how she'd come to be in Charransar at all.

"We're a complicated family," was all she'd say when I asked. Arakante's expression suggested that was quite an understatement.

"Ah. Well, my Lady, perhaps you would tell me your terms if I should decide to study with you?" I can be formal, too, at need.

"Surely. I will teach you how to guide your contact with Kossinli—I'll be honest with you, Layla." Never trust someone who mentions honesty. "I'm not certain I can completely sever the cord that binds you to Her, though when She is stronger you will be both freer and safer. In return, you will obtain two missing items of Kossinli's for me."

"What do you mean, 'safer'?" I thought I'd taken care of myself by rushing off across the Wastes.

Firousi shrugged. "There's danger in having strength that you don't know how to use, and there's danger for any mortal being tied so closely to one of the Great Ones. A trained priestess would be at some risk in your situation, Layla. For your own safety, you must—"

"Yes, but how will you teach me? And how long will it take?"

Firousi drew a long breath before she answered. "How can I possibly answer either of those questions? I won't know until we've begun how easily you learn the discipline I have to teach you. And it simply isn't anything that I can describe in a few well-chosen words. I really do have your best interests at heart—"

"Thank you, I've heard that one before!" My father said

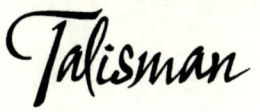

that, and probably believed it, when he married me to a man thrice my age who already had two wives. My husband said it when he asked his senior wife to teach me how to be a Lady (what my mother had taught me wasn't enough, it seemed) and both of his other wives said it more times than I care to remember.

"It was doubtless true sometimes; it is so now. I don't need to force my instruction on you. That's fortunate, since Kossinli forbids me to compel. We keep no slaves, Layla. We treat our servants kindly; they can leave if they wish."

She took a hefty swallow of the date wine. "We have both the eyes of Kossinli now. The rest will be easier with your help, but I can manage without you if I must! I tell you again, I hoped that stealing the second eye might free you." She had hidden her hands in her trailing sleeves, but I could tell from the tension in her arms that her fists were clenched.

"Oh, did you? Your need to get yourself back in power didn't have a thing to do with it?"

The look on her face made me edge nearer the door. Her quiet voice had an edge like broken glass. "I have power, given me by Kossinli and by those who worship her. You little roof-rat, do you think I like having my Lady, the source of light and laughter and song, tangled in your tacky little dreams?"

What did she know of my dreams? How much had she and Arakante uncovered about me? "I'm sure they don't look like much to you. What does Kossinli say? Have you forgotten who's the goddess and who's the priestess? Pardon me, Priestess! I'll take my tacky little body somewhere else."

Clumsy with fury, I stumbled on the slight rise between rooms. Firousi, the woman I'd just insulted, put out her hand and steadied me. It was worse than if she'd let me fall.

If I didn't really need this woman's help...but I did. I swallowed hard. "I'm sorry, Lady Firousi. I was rude. Tell me, please, how you teach? If I ask questions, will they be answered?"

"I'll admit to you that I've never taught anyone before

who was not going to be a priestess. I myself was taught from birth, simply by being the daughter of a household completely devoted to the Laughing One. I was more mirthful then! I will answer your questions as best I may. More than that, I cannot promise."

Fair enough. "Nor can anyone, Lady Firousi. Thank you. But I'm still puzzled by part of this." She looked pointedly at the clepsydra. No doubt she was unaccustomed to the sort of late hours I keep! I'd better go carefully here; the gates between quarters would be shut by now, and while I was pretty sure I could get back to Mother Rissa's if I wanted to, I was truly sure that I'd rather not have to try.

"With all due respect, I think I may be able to judge the risk of a theft better than either of you. How should honest folk know such things, after all? So I must ask what you want me to steal, and what sort of place it's in."

"Forgive me, but if I tell you that, what's to keep you from simply stealing the treasures?"

"The fact that I need your help to control this unwanted gift your Lady has given me." She shrugged, but said nothing. "Lady Firousi, why take the risk at all? Why not simply buy whatever these missing pieces are?"

Now she looked really uncomfortable. "Because the people who have them can't admit to having them."

"The Emperor issued several edicts against exciting unrest among the conquered by interfering with their religion," explained Arakante. "Officially, so long as we pay our taxes and throw a pinch of incense on the right altars now and then, the Empire won't meddle."

Well, that was news to me! I don't suppose anyone had ever thought to mention it to a child or a wife.

Firousi frowned. "How would this be, Layla? I'll teach you for a month, and if you think you've learned something of value, then you'll go get the first item. Then we'll discuss where to go from there."

She was still not telling me what it was, or the barest hint of what sort of place it might be found. I don't mind people not trusting me to be honest with them; old Parata's one of the few I ever found who understood that my own self-interest forbade me to try silly tricks with him. He was also one of the few who thought me bright enough to have figured that out.

Perhaps Firousi simply loved mystery and deviousness. Back in Charransar, she'd also wanted me to steal something for her. I wondered what that had been. Why didn't she need it any more? Had it been there in Charransar at all? I rose so quickly that my chair tipped over.

"Layla? What's wrong?" Arakante asked.

Firousi came and slid one hand under my elbow. "Do you feel ill? It's this way." She tried to guide me through the door.

"Don't worry, I'm not going to throw up." I turned to her. "Did I have any choice at all? Were you planning all along to get me here somehow, never mind how?"

"Layla," Firousi said in a careful, patient voice, "I—"

"How did you do it? Demons of sour water, wouldn't it twist that priest's balls to know he helped drive me where you wanted me. But how'd you make sure I'd wind up here? There were three choices! How did you do it? And why am I so important?"

"She didn't," Arakante said when sheer lack of breath forced me to stop. "Nor did I," he added hastily. "Indeed, we were trying to decide how to go on without you when I...became aware of your presence here in Tzakende."

I laughed. "So it was chance alone that brought me here?"

"Oh, no." said Firousi. "But no compulsion either, or at least none of mine. Layla, truly, truly it is not allowed me! If it were, I would have compelled you to study with me back in Charransar, for my ends, yes, but also for your own safety."

"And if I had, when did you plan to tell me that my service to you and your Lady required me to journey halfway to the world's edge?" Interesting; I would have thought Firousi past the age to blush. "Since you did not, it doesn't matter."

I have seldom been able to sustain anger. It is a serious weakness, and one that has left me prey to those who can. Firousi and I looked at each other under our eyelashes.

Arakante leaned forward and offered the last of the baklava around. He and I divided it, Firousi claiming that she couldn't possibly eat more. It would have been more polite for me to do so also, but it was wonderful baklava.

We were rising to go to our rest when Firousi asked, "Layla. Did you realize it in the bath? That you and Kossinli are still bound?"

Startled, I laughed aloud as I remembered the scene. How strong had that wine been? It hadn't tasted any stronger than date wine, but I couldn't seem to stop laughing even though Firousi's expression said that would be wise.

"What?" demanded Arakante.

Oh, well. I deserved some payback for being scared half out of my wits, didn't I? I told him about the episode with the veil.

"She's got good balance for someone who's never had to depend on it," I added at the end. Firousi really looked as if she might explode. What if she ran and complained to Kossinli of me? "Most people would have fallen flat."

My attempted compliment didn't seem to have done much good. Now Arakante began to laugh, the gleeful bray of a younger brother who's seen his older sister do something stupid. Firousi sat as if she herself were a copper-gilt statue.

She began to tremble, and made a small choking sound. No seizures, oh please, all ye little gods of sour water! It had been so long since I had to help someone through one of those that I wasn't sure I remembered what to do.

Firousi laughed. Once she began, she went on for some minutes, setting Arakante and me off again. The slaves cast nervous glances at each other.

Finally, "Ah well. I suppose we who serve Mirth must be prepared to find that the joke's on us sometimes," said Firousi. Arakante and I both nodded.

11

I woke late the next morning, with no memory of my dreams. Bright sunlight filtered in through a high window. My mind was full of questions, and one certainty: I wasn't going to be able to force answers to any of them right away. Well, I could answer one question. Was there anything left of whatever had sent such good smells up the stairs?

It seldom takes me more than once to learn my way through a maze, but seldom is not never. Rooms opened one into another in places, and what corridors there were wound three steps up and four steps down with never a straight wall for more than a few paces. I began to wonder if my starved corpse would be found by some slave years later. I assumed it would be years later; certainly I saw no one on my wandering way.

Eventually I found the eating-room, and Arakante. He sat alone except for an array of breads and three different bowls of berries. He smiled and waved me to a chair, keeping hold of a roll that left a trail of cardamom scent behind it.

"Good morning," he said when he'd finished chewing whatever it was. "Please break your fast with me. Firousi gets up before dawn, a very unmirthful habit if you ask me, so we don't usually have a set table."

I assured him that I didn't mind. It was comfortable here in this warm corner of the larger room. I might almost have been eating with one of my brothers, back before they grew old enough for the men's quarters. There were seats below the windows; I indulged myself by taking my breakfast over to one of those to sit in civilized fashion again. Now in daylight I saw that not one of the windows had a grill over it. Who'd thieve from the house of a well-known Seer? Well, who'd thieve from a temple of a war-god? Perhaps the house of a Seer had other defenses.

"Firousi seems to have a lot of unmirthful habits," I said when I'd loaded my plate with berries and soft, mild cheese, and a couple of different breads. "I mean, forgive me if I'm being rude, but it seems strange."

Arakante smiled gently. "For a Priestess of Mirth, you mean? Firousi's gift is organization."

"A useful gift, though not much respected." Firousi swept into the room, gathered her own small assortment of food, and seated herself with the sun at her back.

For an honest woman, she certainly moved quietly. So much for finding out a few things before I committed myself! Ah well, Arakante probably wouldn't have told me much anyway.

Over her shoulder, I could see men and women raking and weeding. My husband had a painting like that scene, with figures precisely placed up a slope decorated with impossibly sinuous trees. But none of them had been running!

A familiar bray interrupted the birds' song. I climbed halfway through the window to see that, yes, Imchi had arrived. "Fool of a donkey, I'd have come after you!" I cried out.

Hurried footsteps came up behind me, and the window was suddenly full as Arakante tried to peer past me. "My Flame-of-Passion!"

I thought he was trying not to swear until I saw that Imchi was eating the new leaves and cinnabar-colored blossoms of a large bush. It was only a short drop to the ground, so rather than try to push back inside past Arakante and Firousi, I left through the window. Such cries of alarm! Had they forgotten how I live? I took long enough to give them a flourishing rope-dancer's bow before I ran to rescue the Flame-of-Passion.

Near Imchi, a knot of people gathered around someone

cursing on the ground. "Ware, he kicks," someone called helpfully as I ran past.

A few feet away, I slowed to a walk. "Imchi," I said firmly and quietly. "Imchi, I'm certain Mother Rissa's people fed you. Leave the flowers alone." For he was picking the flowers off without touching the long hooked thorns that surrounded them, well-nigh ignoring the fine fleshy leaves.

He rolled one eye at me and went on eating. When I reached for the dangling strap of his halter, he trotted away a few steps and began again on the other side of the tree. We repeated this dance routine several times.

"Somebody come at him from the other side!" I cried, but no one would. Bored with the Flame-of-Passion, Imchi trotted over to an equally large yellow-flowered bush.

Finally, Arakante came out. "Layla," he called, "Can you herd him this way?" There was a low hedge to one side of him which I guessed might slow Imchi down a little. Flapping my arms, I tried to get Imchi to move. Only when I got close enough to make a grab for that halter-strap did he leave the wonderful yellow flowers.

"Oh, master, no!" Some fool chose then to jump in and try to help. Imchi snorted and rushed him. The man and all his fellow-gardeners ran. Arakante was laughing too hard to stop Imchi as he ran around the corner of the hedge.

Then things really became confused. If there was any more mysterious laughter, it was lost among the brays, shouts, and thunder of hooves, not to mention the treble shrieks of the youngest gardener. Eventually, Arakante and I managed to trap Imchi between us and I managed to grab his headstall.

"You pestilential ass," I said, and Imchi brayed in protest. Then he stood quietly, looking as if he couldn't imagine what the fuss was about.

With Arakante's help, I got Imchi to a stableyard tastefully hidden behind a hedge of roses. Two stablemen approached warily; they'd undoubtedly been watching the fun from a safe distance. At Arakante's command, they shut Imchi into the paddock.

I was covered with dust and leaves, and sweating disgracefully. I'd cheerfully have sold Imchi to the least of Mother Rissa's clan just then, but what would Kossinli send me next?

Ah yes, Kossinli. I took long enough to wash what shows and dust myself off a bit, and rejoined Firousi in the eating room. Arakante had gotten there ahead of me. "Lady Firousi, when can we begin these studies?"

She smiled at me. "Why, the sooner the better. I expect you'll want to move your belongings here from the caravanserai today, but tomorrow we could begin to work. Yes, that would be better, when we're both fresh."

Oh, no. No, I could manage to be polite for a few hours each day, but all day long, for unknown weeks? Maybe months? With someone who thought nothing of moving me in without asking either me or the owner of the house?

"I'm afraid I'm too used to living solitary to make a good houseguest, my Lady. Mother Rissa will know of an inn where they'll not ask for documents. Thank you, though." Well, I hoped she would.

Perhaps Firousi had discussed this with Arakante, for he showed no surprise. "You needn't fear intrusion! It's a large house, as you've only begun to discover. Believe me, you won't want to walk up that hill in the winter."

So, it was going to take months. Gods, could I afford to be independent? Probably, if I ate here part of the time, though it was going to put my nice little pawnshop back into hopes-and-dreams again.

"It will also be easier to sweeten the necessary rulemakers if you're not making yourself conspicuous by staying on in a strangers' inn after most strangers have left." Arakante paused, frowning. "There will be no shame to you in living here; Firousi's presence will make it all respectable."

I had to laugh. "I'm not a respectable person anyway, my friend! But she may—might—preserve your reputation, if I stayed here, which I am not going to do. Doesn't it bother you that you're taking a known thief to live in the same house with those elegant earrings?" Firousi was wearing a fine pair of pearl dangles.

Firousi sighed. "Oh please, Layla, we're none of us stupid people. You need my help too badly to risk stealing from me. Besides, you don't have anyplace here to sell anything that you did steal, and you're surely not going to risk taking off across the Wastes alone this late in the year. My earrings are probably safer than they've ever been before—you'll take care to warn me if you see any signs that any of the servants are pilfering small objects, I'm sure, or if you see any way that a thief could get into the house. That's more likely; we freed most of the servants ourselves and they're loyal to us."

"I don't think she'd steal from us anyway," Arakante said gently while I tried to think what to say next. "But Layla, is my house so terrible a place to live?"

Poor man, it was clear that his cousin didn't respect him much, and now he was being flouted by a common thief! Well, perhaps an uncommon thief; the common sort would have avoided this mess.

"No, no, of course not! Your house is beautiful, and you've been so generous and kind that I feel like an absolute fool turning you down—"

"Then don't do it," said Firousi.

I threw up my hands. Yes, I really did; it seemed better than throwing crockery, and I had to relieve my feelings somehow.

"Thank you both, then. Imchi and I will be happy to accept your gracious offer."

Rissa clearly thought I must have lost my mind when I told her I was staying in Tzakende for the winter.

"Those mysterious loose ends of yours, I suppose," she grumbled. Her expression said she thought some of my mental bundles weren't tied on too tightly. I thought she might well be right.

She turned so that her better eye faced me. "Or is it some man? Listen, my girl, Tzakendi don't marry outside the city. I tell you this for your own good."

There was that phrase again. "I've been married, thank you!" And then I felt childish and unkind. "It's nothing to do with a man. I wish I could explain it all to you." Oddly enough, that was true.

"Nonsense, girl, it's your own tangle and no snarl for me to unknot. In fact, I think I'd rather not know."

Neither one of us believed that!

"I do wonder what you're going to do with that donkey here all winter. Sure you won't sell him? We'd take good care of him. He's a good strong beast, for all his odd ways."

"Oh, that's another of my loose ends, I'm afraid," was all I could think of to say. Mother Rissa snorted.

12

*T*he gardens of Arakante's house climbed the hillside behind it in a series of terraces and half-hidden groves. Instead of formal fountains, springs bubbled up to fill small pools. Strange ducks with iridescent green heads and raucous quacks like the laughter of a bridegroom's drunken friends swam there.

It was hard to be sure how large those gardens were. Like the house itself, their paths wandered and wound back on themselves. A stream divided and rejoined itself. Two of its channels fed ponds where ducks swam among water lilies. Things became truly confusing as you went uphill. What looked from a distance like a boundary wall turned out to be a trellis for vines, or the retaining wall for yet another terrace. Just as we seated ourselves in the shade of a plane tree, one of the ducks let out a raucous laughing quack; Firousi smiled as though she knew what the joke was.

"Now," she began, "One of the great mysteries of the Mirthful One is that in order to understand Her, we must turn away from laughter for a time. The underlying organization of laughter, the nerves and sinews that make the laughing dance possible, are very complex. Indeed, we'll only go into the most general sort of theory here, for all we're striving for is to teach you to control your own gift, not to make a true priestess of you."

Well, that was a cause for rejoicing.

"The most essential thing to remember is that the mirth must match the time and the place. Even those times when the joke seems to lie in the juxtaposition of incongruous things."

"Such as donkeys and garrets?"

"Yes, just so." She frowned slightly. "This only shows how little we truly understand. Because our minds are so limited, the Powers are sometimes kind enough to express themselves in ways that we can grasp. True divine humor is too strong for us, and often seems bitter." Was it the shivering of the sycamore leaves, or did a shadow of pain cross her face?

She brushed an invisible stray hair back into place. "Now then. The categories of appropriateness are: audience, subject, and occasion or situation. In each of these, we must consider vocabulary, sight jokes, illusions, allusions, music, dance and mimetic movements, which some theologians subdivide, and that form of physical humor miscalled the practical joke." She paused significantly.

I had the feeling that I was supposed to say something here, but couldn't figure out what. After a while, Firousi continued speaking.

The Tzakendi wind had dropped to a gentle breeze. Two of the ducks had tucked their heads under their wings. It seemed like a good idea, except that I lacked wings. Too bad, they'd be useful to a thief...

Oh, plague, how much had I missed? It'd be just my luck to miss something genuinely useful. Oh, and please, Kossinli, I don't really want wings, or anything like them.

Firousi noticed that I'd been elsewhere. I flinched at her raised hand, but instead of slapping me for disrespect she patted my hand gently.

"Don't worry if you can't remember all this right now," she said kindly. "We'll go over it again later. I'm just trying to let you see some of how the smaller pieces we'll study fit together."

Oh, gods. How long did she think I could stay in this house, listening to her talk and now and then running out to steal some bit of Kossinli when she figured out where it was? How much of this relentless patience could I stand?

"Firousi, forgive me, but do I really need all this theory? You said yourself that you're not trying to teach me how to be a priestess."

She smiled. "Layla, there's no simple way to give you the ability to control your contact with Kossinli. Be patient, little sister. You will need these teachings more than you've needed any—"

"I am not your little sister!" Damn Firousi, anyway; I'd had years of learning to control my temper, but she could make me forget all those hard-learned lessons with one condescending phrase. She didn't even have the decency to take my anger seriously this time.

"I think you must be tired, and perhaps hungry."

A quick peek at the sun told me that I must have been asleep with my eyes open, or at least I hoped they had been open, for half the morning.

Firousi continued, "I suppose you've not been much accustomed to this sort of study?"

"No, thieves' training is a good bit less abstract."

Firousi raised one delicate brow. "No doubt. Well, perhaps this will help your studies: If you remember all these tedious categories, you won't have to consider other criteria, such as ease of escape."

"Escape? What from?"

She laughed. "Why, from the consequences of the jest! How else should you delight the Lady of Mirth, but with jests?"

Wonderful. All my life people had been frowning down my funniest stories, and now I was supposed to amuse a Goddess?

"Firousi, what if Kossinli doesn't think I'm funny?"

"She will when you've finished your training," said Firousi with perfectly disgusting cheerfulness.

We had a nice little lunch, suitable for ladies, brought to us in the same pavilion where we studied. It was exquisite, beautifully served, and just about enough to keep my stomach from grumbling too loudly. After a brief pause for digestion, Firousi shed two layers of draperies and began to teach me Kossinli's dances.

Now I understood that startlingly good sense of balance she'd shown in the baths. Only a Goddess of Mirth could devise some of those positions. Mortal knees were never intended to point in two opposite directions at once, at least not when the mortal is attempting to use them to stand up at the time. It was a pleasant change from categories, even so. At least I had some talent for this sort of study.

Fortunately, dinner was more generous than lunch had been. Perhaps I had a little too much of the mild-tasting drink the Tzakendi make from fruit juice and honey. Perhaps I simply forgot that a student may not direct the course of study. I'd thought I learned that lesson years ago, when first I studied thievery.

"It's like trying to—to eat this entire dinner in five minutes," I waved at the shards of richly spiced stuffed eggplant, which Firousi and Arakante called "little shoes," the crumbs of fragrant rice and the sad remaining tatters of dessert. "I can't do it." Never mind that the lessons were nowhere near as pleasant as that dinner. They were more like lentil soup without onions. Firousi drew in a slow, ostentatiously controlled breath.

"Still trying to tell the entire *Song of the Baskets* in one performance, Cousin?"

Arakante raised one eyebrow as he spoke. How like Firousi that gesture was! I'd never seen a man with such delicately drawn brows. That's not to say that he looked effeminate, you understand. Just then, he looked like a rescuing warrior to me. He also did the raised-eyebrow trick better than she did.

Firousi was not answering either my plea or Arakante's question, at least not in words. The look on her face was enough to drop birds out of the trees.

"It was a beautiful performance," said Arakante. "Just a little..."

Firousi rose nobly above her aggravations. "Long. That's

the word you're looking for, cousin dear." Firousi laughed brightly. "Oh, Arakante, you brat! You weren't even supposed to be there. It was my first solo performance at the *Rites of Rising*," she explained, turning to me, "And little children are generally not allowed to stay for the full ceremony. They cry, or make rude faces at their older sibs. This one," she tossed her head at Arakante, "hid inside a food-hamper after emptying most of it into his stomach.

"Since you've already had a lesson today, I'll spare you the details of the story I was telling, and all the forms I was required to show. Nobody said I had to take the longest legend we have. I was so determined to do it right, and prove that I was indeed old enough to be trusted with such an honor! Ah, well, I got through it all, every mimetic gesture and vocal inflection, and just at the last, the High Priestess let out a resounding snore. Everyone there laughed."

"Oh, no." Little though I liked Firousi, that story made me wince. How could she tell it so merrily?

"Oh, yes," said Arakante and Firousi in chorus. Firousi continued in mock-serious tones, "Well, they had to! You can't very well ignore the Lady of Mirth when She makes a jest at Her own feast."

We all laughed then. If Firousi's laugh was a little forced, well, I couldn't blame her. I tried to think of something soothing to say and failed. Firousi herself ended the awkward silence.

"Ah well, that was all before the Troubles. I doubt anyone but Ari and I remembers now." This time Firousi turned a little more than was necessary, enough that she half-turned her back on Arakante.

He spoke to her left shoulder anyway. "It was one of the great moments of my childhood. You were always being so mean to me." He took another sip of melomel. "I think you were just jealous."

"Well, you always did have much prettier eyelashes." Firousi said, without turning around. She smiled as though she could see him flush.

He did have lovely eyelashes. I'd always taken some pride in mine, but his made a breeze when he raised or lowered his eyes. He was looking down now, eyelashes lying against skin as smooth and fine as polished bronze.

That's enough of that, I told myself. I truly did not want Kossinli deciding to grant any wishes of mine concerning Arakante, whatever subcategories of criteria might be fulfilled by the jest. Something about Arakante said that he'd been the target of more than enough divine humor, at least as interpreted by Firousi.

Come to that, I was weary of it myself. I had felt less tired after a night of scrambling over roofs and through windows than I did then, scratchy-eyed and restive.

We'd had the last of the summer weather. The next day the rains began, and the streets became streams. Tzakende was folding in like a bright-eyes blossom when the sun goes down. Almost all the other strangers had left; shopkeepers kept short hours and closed before the early dusk. Even most of those who kept taverns or singing-houses shut down soon after moonrise.

We continued our lessons indoors. They weren't all as bad as the first one, praise Kossinli! But I felt more certain every day that this was not going to work; that if anything, it was making matters worse. Even Firousi seemed to be losing a little of her self-assurance as the days stumbled by in half-light.

No one forbade me to explore the house, or even hinted against it. Yet when I did, I'd sometimes find myself back where I started even though I'd swear I hadn't walked in a circle.

"It's a very old house," said Arakante when I asked him about it.

Yes, and a wizard's house. Or should it be mage? I'd never needed to know the degrees of politeness for such people. I did want to be polite, so I just called him Arakante. He probably wouldn't have answered my question, even if I'd known the correct title.

Once I'd learned a few of the basics, Firousi included me in the gatherings she held from time to time. It was pleasant to see other people, even if Firousi and I were the youngest ones there. There's something to be said for a goddess whose followers still dance even after they've gone completely grey or bald.

They were an obliging group, too, willing to appear whenever the whim of their Goddess demanded it.

"You've done so much to help Lady Firousi," one man with a splendid gray-and-white striped beard told me. I had? "We'd had no summons to celebrate all this year until you came! Well, part of the year she was traveling, of course, but even when she was here we seldom did more than recite a few stories on the set feast days. We're so glad you've come!"

"You're too kind," I told him. What a rare gem, a statement that's both polite and true! Getting unpredictable invitations to walk through drizzle and blowing rain wasn't my idea of a good thing, but it clearly pleased him.

We met in a curious protrusion of the villa. It looked as if the house had crept uphill like a vine, and the room was the blossom. There was glass in all the windows there, the ripples and bumps of the tiny panes making rainbows whenever we did get some sun. That and the dances were the only part of the ritual that held any lightness of heart. As we turned and leaped, circling and interweaving our lines, I could see a little of what Firousi was trying to show me. While the rebab's drone kept time and the reed flute sang the dance, I had no need to think what I did or why. If I could have only danced, and never tried to take part in the intricate rhyming speech of the "celebration" that followed, then I think I could have followed Kossinli, at least for long enough to persuade Her to find some more worthy recipient of Her favors.

Organizing all this was enough to keep even Firousi busy, but it also made her simply frantic to get Kossinli's statue reassembled. You cannot, it seems, simply recraft the entire statue of a Goddess, oh no! You must retrieve certain individual bits and pieces. We already had both eyes, and Firousi had managed to save her Lady's earrings by putting them in her own ears just before the door of Her temple gave way to the looters. The headdress had been above even Firousi's long reach; her efforts to climb up to it nearly cost her life, sacred earrings and all.

"I scrambled out the window just as the Imperial bandits broke through the door. I could have used some of your skills in my escape, Layla! By Kossinli's intervention, I fell only the few feet from the roof of the kitchen-shed, and the ash-pile cushioned my fall."

Kossinli's mercy must be as peculiar as her laughter. "You must have landed with some skill, if you were able to get up and go on," I said, and meant it. Perhaps Kossinli's dances had helped her, as my thief's training helped me in learning the dances.

Firousi stared at the foggy hills outside. "Proper apologies were made after the first frenzy of conquest was over. The Prince may even have been telling the truth when he swore to my aunt that he could not find the jewels. I doubt that they would have reached us, in any case. And now...well, it is not precisely forbidden to worship Kossinli. It is merely somewhere between unfashionable and ill-advised. No one with ambitions at court would risk pointing out that the remarkably fine emerald in the back of Sarinsat's head—leave it to these barbarians to worship a deformed god!—was also remarkably familiar to anyone old enough to remember the time when Kossinli's people still laughed and danced in Her gardens.

"The statue is a sad remnant still. We have mended the broken limbs, recast and replaced the high-arched feet and the story-telling hands. We have even been able to reproduce the carved carnelian mouth. On and on, poor Lady of Laughter! How can She bring us joy when the cluster of rubies that formed Her heart is still missing?"

"That shouldn't be too hard to find, if nobody's broken it up." I was beginning to feel quite hopeful. Anyone who owned such a thing would surely display it now and then, either as personal jewelry or on another statue.

"Yet neither my rites nor Arakante's scrying can reveal it. And we must have it, Layla. Even if we could find other rubies of such quality, we no longer have anyone who knows the rituals for making it a true link. It's even more important than the Wreath of Laughter, that one of Kossinli's own daughters created by changing mortal flowers into immortal gems."

She had made a fool of me, had been making a fool of me all along. There she sat, smiling thoughtfully as if nothing was wrong.

"You don't know where they are. You don't even know if they're in this city, do you? You're not even trying to help me break my tie with Kossinli!"

Firousi raised her eyebrows. "Layla, I never said I'd do that now. We must maintain it until we've found what's missing. Now, all we're trying to do is control it so that you don't suddenly find yourself with any more donkeys."

"I'm living with one! Why didn't you tell me? If I'd even known what to look for, I could've been listening in the singing-houses! The careless way people talk in this city, I could probably have found out something."

"Oh, really, Layla! If someone's gone to the trouble of constructing a cloaking spell that hides these tokens from Arakante, do you think they'll babble about it in those third-rate steamers you insist on visiting? Even assuming they'd visit such places, which seems most unlikely?"

"Of course not. But their servants might. And what if it isn't deliberate? What if you and Arakante can't find them because nobody's even thinking about them? The rubies ought to attract attention, but if they've been broken up—" Sold, given away, even stolen by some quicker thief, they'd vanish even from second sight.

Yes, and they might have been scattered. I felt tired just thinking about it.

"No." The word came out hard, flat, most unlike Firousi's usual lilt. "I would know. The Lady of Mirth still laughs, though not so often or so clearly. You'd know too, I think. Layla, I wish I knew more. I won't willingly ask you to fight blind."

She didn't look as if either one of them was laughing just then. I felt that tightness at the back of the neck that says Bad Fortune has just stopped in His wanderings and stared at you. What would happen if someone did break up that heart? Well, if Firousi didn't know—and I didn't think she was lying now—I surely wouldn't figure it out.

I was being stupid about this. I'd worked with people I couldn't trust often enough before. I'd just have to watch this one carefully until I could get myself out of this mess.

"I'm sure you would know, but if the rubies are dark ones, someone may think they've just got a garnet trinket." Old Parata'd gloated more than once over similar mistakes.

Firousi stared at me. "That's a very interesting possibility."

Arakante, when she asked him about it, frowned. "I would have thought I'd find some radiance from them in any case. Such things have their own life. No, someone's cloaked them. They've done a good job, too! Listen if you will, Layla, but be careful."

So I did, and I was, but never heard a word of the jewels. There were plenty of tales of someone practicing Dark and Secret Rites; if half of them had been true, there wouldn't be enough servants left in Tzakende to keep the bread baked or the clothes washed. I told all such tales to Arakante, who laughed or groaned as the mood struck him.

The cold mists made lessons seem even vaguer and less real than they had been before. Dutifully, I went through the motions. Perhaps it would begin to work. Besides, where could I go, in the middle of the season that Tzakende keeps for itself alone?

At night the shuttered windows shut out all the air. Firousi

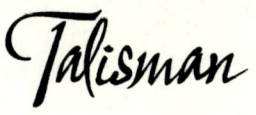

played the lap-harp beautifully, but after the tenth time she practiced some passage that wasn't quite perfect yet, I wanted to strangle her with its strings.

Outside, there was more air than I needed. I had thought the winds made strange sounds earlier; now they seemed almost to speak. Yes, and I could almost understand them.

In time, I asked Firousi if it might be happening because of my attempts at meditation.

"No," she said, giving the word about three syllables. "No, the meditations we've been using shouldn't have that effect. Do you ever actually hear words?" Her gaze was intent.

"No, not quite. It just sounds like a song I can't quite hear, or sometimes like laughter."

"Well, with no more than that to go on...I'll ask Kossinli, of course, but it's probably just the wind." She shrugged, eyebrows raised. "The wind does make strange sounds here, you know; we mustn't seek too eagerly for otherworldly explanations."

"I am not seeking eagerly for anything of the kind! I wish, oh how I wish, that I could hear something that would make you pay attention!"

I swallowed hard then, but the words were out. One look at Firousi's face told me that she knew no more than I did about calling them back.

For several nights thereafter the weather was so bad that I stayed within the house. The days were spent in trying every sort of lesson that Firousi could devise. I tried to imitate Arakante's cat and sleep the remaining empty hours away, with little luck. Arakante himself showed how intelligent he was by spending more and more time in his study. Even Firousi seldom disturbed him there.

One evening when it was neither raining nor clear, I decided to slip out without mentioning it. Not proper guest behavior, true, but I was not a proper guest. I was a thief; either Firousi or Arakante would have turned me over to the axe-man if they hadn't needed me. I wanted to see if I'd lost all my skills at roof-running.

I had not. The Tzakendi tiles are polished by rain into smooth ripples that, if you land just right, are even better than the rougher glaze of Charransar for giving a sure grip. A series of small roofs ran beneath my window, each capping a separate level of Arakante's house. They gleamed slickly in the moonlight. Gods, but the tiles of Charransar roofs were never so cold beneath my feet!

There was no one out on what little I could see of the streets. Well for me that the wall wasn't high; I broke only a fingernail. No, I was not bemoaning my manicure. Fingernails are a useful set of tools for small prying, and no one asks why you have them with you. The Nadarine Stairs were another challenge, their uneven cobbles glazed by the fog. The gritty dirt of the lower stairs was a welcome improvement underfoot.

Warmth seeped from the crowded buildings. I had company now, dim cowled figures in the foggy Tzakendi night. What a place for a thief this city would be! Not too much later, I felt a feather-light flutter at the edge of my cloak. There's always a stone in the lentils somewhere! Those layers of clothing would make life rough for a pickpocket. I drew my cloak closer around me and slipped into a singing-house nearby.

The fire smoked; fried onions and the fiery Tzakendi grain-liquor perfumed the air. A potboy bumped into me and dashed on without spilling a drop or apologizing. Near the window, a singer roared out a tale of a young wife who coupled in a tree while assuring her old husband that she was only shaking down the fruit. It sounded hazardous to me, but the audience seemed to love it. After the first drink, so did I. Even Firousi would have had to admit that the jest was appropriate to the audience. A few looked at me curiously, but they kept their questions to themselves.

Time to leave while they still held back. One of them

looked vaguely familiar, too. Would it matter if I were recognized by one of the Tzakendi who'd joined Mother Rissa's caravan? I decided not to find out.

Torches lighted the tavern-front; more torches showed the beginning of the Nadarine Stairs. Their flickering light was worse than darkness in my eyes. Above them the roofs of Tzakende rose in imitation of the stairs.

Ah, that was better! This was a dance that I knew. I made my way uphill by whatever route amused me, not hemmed in by walls or tripped by cobbles. My long cloak, belted, made a handy pocket for my shoes.

Pity, pity that I'd no good way to peddle stolen goods here! I saw a lady's dressing-chamber with jewels lying discarded on her table that I would certainly never have tossed down so carelessly, and in another house they'd actually left a writing-desk standing open with a pile of coins lying on it. Now, that tempted me! There'd be no need to peddle that. But I heard a step within the house, and scampered gracefully over to a nearby house with a fine tall tree sheltering its wall.

I didn't really know these streets, and thieving in strange places can be the last mistake a thief makes. I knew I'd yield to the next temptation. I slithered down and away from it.

The cobbles were unkinder to my cold toes than the tiles had been. It was time to resume my shoes and cloak. The wind had come up again, or perhaps it was worse down here where the streets tried to control it.

Watch yourself, thief, said the wind. It gave me a little push in the back. I stumbled over something, tripped and spun round with my cloak wrapped around me like a shroud. Its folds kept me from seeing, but not from hearing the footsteps that came up the narrow street. I found a wall and leaned against it, motionless, hoping I was in shadow. Two sets of footsteps, a long stride and a short scampering one, approached—someone had a torchbearer. *Kossinli*—the cloak made speech impossible, even if I hadn't needed to be as quiet as possible. *Kossinli, help me out of this unless you want to find another thief you can trust!*

Here was a wall at right angles; I pressed along it, hoping to scrape the damned cloak back from around me as I went. I wriggled free of it just as the footsteps passed. By the time I could see, only a tall shadow and a short one were disappearing into the fog. The torch sputtered and hissed as they went.

"Kossinli, I hope this is You," I said as I hurried up the stairs. The wind laughed in my ear.

Kossinli, or some other Great One? It seemed—I leaped over a basket set rolling uphill by the wind—like Her style.

The fog had iced the courtyard wall by the time I got there. I clambered uphill to where the garden wall met the cliff. Honestly, how did Arakante keep anything of value? That wall was pretty, but a determined child could have found a way around it.

I must think of some way of warning him without revealing that I'd been out that night. Men worry so. No, there was no point in worrying about that. I'd wished for something serious enough to make Firousi take my voices seriously, and I'd got it! I'd have to tell the truth to them both.

The room where we often ate breakfast was shuttered, but the catch was nothing my smallest dagger couldn't lift. Silent as a mongoose, I slipped upstairs through winding halls. I must warn them. I could have taken half what they had in this house. Well, not half, perhaps; those silver urns were too heavy for me.

I had stopped to think. Had I lost my wits? I could think back in my own room; I must get back there before anyone saw me.

There was one problem with that; my feet wouldn't move. Nor would my arms, nor any part of me except my eyes, my lungs and my heart. That heart moved all too well, and had climbed up into my throat.

A hand grasped my shoulder; a lamp burned just at the edge of my vision. "Layla?" said a voice in a soft, incredulous whisper. Arakante moved around to where I could see him.

His grip was stronger than I would have expected. He must have dissolved whatever spell held me motionless, for I found I could turn away from his stare.

"Let's go into my study and talk about this. Please don't try to run."

Very polite, with a grip like a Questioner's on my shoulder. In his study, he courteously offered me tea from a small pot warming over a candle. He said nothing until I'd taken a long swallow of the strange brew, flower-scented yet faintly bitter.

"Was it you I heard creeping around downstairs, or are there two intruders in the house?"

"It was me. Though you could've had half a dozen, no better than you guard your windows!"

"Most people know better than to break in here." His voice was low and even. I decided to say nothing. The charcoal settled in its brazier.

"Why, Layla?"

"I wanted to go out for awhile, that's all. I'm sorry I alarmed you coming back in; I hadn't thought anyone would still be awake."

"I often read late. Layla, you tripped a snare that will only work if someone is thinking of doing harm to me or mine."

"But I wasn't! Or—not really—" I felt tears prickling. Damn him, I would not cry. I gulped some more tea instead. "I was thinking how easy it would be to steal from this house. That doesn't mean I was going to do it! I was thinking how to warn you. I'm a thief, Lord Arakante, and you knew that from the start, but I don't steal from friends." Especially wizardly ones. Gods, what was he doing telling fortunes if he was powerful enough to set a spell spinning and leave it?

He ran one hand through his hair, the red-brown curls catching at his fingers. "You'll only sneak out of a friend's house like an escaping prisoner."

"Since when do I have to ask permission to leave?"

"Who said you did? Merciful whispering gods, Layla, do you enjoy scrambling around over rocks in the rain?" He rose and paced twice between his chair and the west window. "Layla, you're neither my child nor my prisoner. You're my guest, and my guests come and go through doors, not windows. If it's late they bid the gatekeeper open it for them." He kept his back turned. I wished that I could see his face and know how angry he was; his voice told me so little.

He turned, and his eyes were very bright. "Do you hate it here so much?"

Perhaps it would have been easier to talk to his back. "No," I said. My voice sounded sullen in my own ears. "No, I don't hate it at all. It's beautiful here, and you're very kind." There, that was better. It was also at least partly true. I rose from my chair as gracefully as if I'd been using them all my life. "I promise to use the door the next time."

He drew a much deeper breath than was needed for saying, "Thank you." Though I waited, he said nothing more.

Firousi's face went blank when I told her what had happened. She wouldn't tell me what she was thinking. She didn't pick at every small fault of my recital, either. The lessons went better that day even though I'd had no more sleep than a quick nap before breakfast. I mastered the rhyme scheme appropriate for capping a pun concerning flowers, and Firousi actually laughed. She must have been pleased, for she stopped the lesson there. When I left, she remained, silent and intent. I refused to worry about it.

13

*F*irousi came through the door of Arakante's study with no flourish of shawls. She sat with no arrangement of her skirts, which pooled all to one side.

"Can you scry what a Goddess may think?"

"Sometimes," answered Arakante. "If the wind and the moon are in the right quarters, and if the Goddess wishes it." He waited, courteous and quiet, for the rest of the question.

"She's angry. She's angry, but I can't tell why." Now Firousi tugged her skirts into a more graceful fall. There was a long silence. Finally she looked up again. "You always did know how to wait! Arakante, I've done all I know to do, brought Her chosen helper into my—our—own house, tried the best I know to teach her to control her gift. Kossinli's begun to play tricks on me now."

Arakante touched her hand. "Firousi, cousin, are you sure this is anger? She's ever-changeful, your Lady."

"Yet She's always been kind to me." She thrust her hand into her hair; a braid popped loose from the intricate pattern. "Yesterday, when I was wishing for peace and quiet, I went deaf for the rest of the morning. Layla's hearing things! I didn't wish for Layla to hear the Powers, I wished it for myself, only of course I said 'Your servant.' When did my Lady become a lawyer?"

Arakante smiled. "I have known some excellent people who were lawyers. Kind and clever both, with a sense of humor that might please Kossinli herself."

"I'm sorry, I'm sorry! Don't you be angry with me."

"I'm not. But Firi, this isn't like you. Come, you know

Kossinli needs you."

"I know no such thing. Arakante, stop questioning me and tell me! Can you find the cause of Her anger?"

"Truly, I can't tell until I try." His voice was only just loud enough for her to hear. "And I will try, but not now. I spoke plain truth to you, cousin, friend of my youth. And I don't know yet what the proper wind and moon-phase are for this endeavor. Do me a favor."

Firousi stiffened.

"Tell the doorkeeper I'll see no one after Lord Prahin. No, he's here already, I can't turn him away! But Mikante should send to the others and say that I've seen mud clouding the waters; I can do no scrying till it clears. And he should admit no chance comers, no matter what bribes they offer. I'll discover when I can discover."

She'd hoped for better than this when she forced herself to seek help. Firousi rose silently, nodded, and left for her own part of the house.

High up on the southern corner, she had a room made mostly of windows. It was chilly in the weak afternoon sun, but she welcomed that as she began to dance.

Firousi danced in silence. She had known Kossinli's steps for too long to need flute and rebec; besides, without them she'd hear more easily if Kossinli did choose to answer her questions.

Kossinli might be speaking to Layla and not to her only for amusement; her Lady's humor was harsh sometimes. Or it might be that Kossinli was angry at how long it was taking to find the remaining pieces of her statue. Why didn't She tell Layla where to find them, if that was so? Unless She herself didn't know...or unless it had not been She who spoke to Layla.

This part of the dance was a spiral of step-turns, the wild whirl held just in balance so that the pattern was preserved. The spiral and the turns went in opposite directions; Firousi smiled as it all spun smoothly within the limits of the windowed room. She would find the answers she needed.

Then she gasped as her left ankle wobbled out of line. She hauled herself back on balance without actually stumbling, but the rest of the dance was soulless.

Firousi sat on a cushioned bench, rubbing her ankle. "What do you want of me? Do you punish me now for taking joy in your dances?"

She was so tired of not knowing. A priestess and a mage in one house, and they were as helpless as any merchant family who'd lost some bauble to a thief like Layla. Why, why was Kossinli talking to her without really telling her anything?

Layla was getting impatient, and who could blame her? Until a few days ago Firousi would have said that the lessons were helping Layla to control her contact with Kossinli. It had been hard to keep her disappointment to herself.

And yet, was it so bad? Layla had been alone when Kossinli spoke to her, if it was Kossinli. The warning could have been caused by genuine concern for Layla. Yes, and it could have been mockery from some malicious spirit.

She shivered. Now that she was sitting still, the room was chilly. Impatiently, she shrugged her outer robes on over her sweated tunic and pants. The incense that she threw on the coals of the brazier nearly smothered them before the rising cloud of scent made Firousi sneeze.

Well, perhaps that was a fitting sacrifice. Firousi managed to find a clean corner on that day's handkerchief and mopped streaming eyes and nose. "Lady Kossinli," she said softly, refusing to sneeze again. "Was it You who spoke to Layla?"

The incense swirled, though the door-curtain hung motionless. Firousi sat equally still, trying to frame the proper questions in the appropriate modes. There were too many questions.

"Lady of Mirth, my need is too great for my artistry. I may not be a wonderful priestess, I know I'm not half as good as Mother was, but I'm all You have!" Silence. "Are you angry? Why will You speak clearly to that little thief and not to me? Never mind that, I'm sorry I said it. You chose her for Your servant in this. Yet thanks to You, I'm responsible for her, Kossinli, and if she's in danger from someone in Your sphere, I need to know."

There was no answer, only the sense of anger and fruitless struggle. Was that from Kossinli, or only her own soul? Ah, how lucky her mother had been to live in the days when the Lady of Laughter still spoke clearly!

Fragments of speech came to her, like someone shouting from behind heavy curtains. Find the pieces, find the pieces—well, didn't she know that? Make the girl be quiet. What girl? Layla? Where were the pieces? Mother have mercy, Kossinli must not know herself.

"Of course I know," said a muffled voice full of laughter. "They're in Tzakende, but not where they were."

In the silence, Firousi picked up her lap-harp. She played awhile in the Yllurran mode of the Southern Isles, with its odd breaks in the intervals. There were no glad songs in that mode, and many claimed its only value was its surprises.

"The wreath would be a pleasure to me, but get my heart out of this box. I'll help you so far as I can—"

The rings of the door-curtain rattled without warning. The noise stopped almost as soon as it started, but it was enough to silence the voice. Not now, oh plague and pestilence, not now! Not when for once she'd been certain of what she Heard. Really, she'd been sure she had even the kitchen-maids trained never to interrupt Arakante in his study or her in the temple.

"How dare you, you mannerless untrained—" Firousi stopped abruptly. Arakante was standing just within the room. He still clutched the door-curtain, and his eyebrows nearly met.

He tugged the heavy weaving into place behind him. "I'm sorry. From what I was hearing, I expected to find you suffering a seizure."

Hearing? Ah yes, of course. Normal worship wouldn't distract him, but this kind of thrashing around would. He had meant well. "No, I'm well enough. I'm sorry I disturbed you, but Ari, I wish you hadn't come in just then." She paced over to the nearest window.

Instead of leaving politely, he sat down on the bench that circled the room. "Firousi, what is your Lady doing? From the knot of energies that I felt just before I came down here, I truly did expect to find you in convulsions." He touched the back of her hand gently, quickly. "Cousin, I don't want to intrude on your concerns, but I'm worried for you, and for our guest. Much of what I Heard just now wasn't your voice."

"Whose voice was it? Was there more than one?" The question escaped before she considered that Arakante probably wouldn't know. His work seldom brought him into contact with the greater Powers, and Firousi thought that he preferred it that way.

He sat silent for several breaths before he replied. "Only one, though it changed. Was it your Lady? One of the goddesses, certainly, and who else should it be?"

Firousi let herself relax onto the cushioned bench. The winds were all male except for the south wind, and she was never found in Tzakende this time of year. Arakante might never have heard Kossinli before, but no one else she'd ever met had as acute an ear for pitch and texture as he did.

"Yes, at least we have only Kossinli to deal with," Arakante said. "I think that She will be enough."

"Yes," said Firousi. "More than enough."

14

*E*nough to deal with, indeed. Arakante sighed as he poured the water from the silver bowl, surely the most likely way to discover the will of so mutable a Goddess as Kossinli. He had chosen his time carefully. The day swung rapidly from sun to cloud and back again. The week was just at its balance-point.

It should have worked, but it hadn't. He hadn't found a sign of the wreath. Worse, the Heart gave only a flickering heat-lightning. Was it so weak, or was it somehow shielded? He'd been able to sense it before, though never to tell where it was. Now he could barely tell that it existed.

He suspected he and Firousi both already knew why Kossinli was angry. It wasn't fair of Her to be angry with Her priestess, but then, the Deities were not obliged to be fair. He feared that Kossinli Herself was frightened.

The rattle of the rain on the shutters became sharper. He'd chosen this room for light, not warmth; he shrugged and shut the remaining shutters. The sky gave so little light that it darkened the room only a little. He indulged himself by lighting his scholar's lamp with magic instead of hunting for the flint and steel. Unnecessary use of magic was not elegant, but this was not an elegant day.

He'd best go find Firousi and tell her the bad news. That would be better than waiting for her to come asking, as she surely would soon. She was quite clever enough, and knowledgeable enough about his arts, to know he'd try today.

If he went to Firousi, then he could choose when to end

the conversation. Yes, and then he could spend some time with his scroll of Musa's Art of Geloscopy. It had taken him three months to find the work, and he'd barely had time to open it. Even the best-written book was no substitute for actually meeting the magician, of course, but since Musa'd been dead twenty years, a book would have to do. Necromancy simply wasn't worth the risks.

Too late. Firousi swept in with a flurry of shawls and trailing sleeves. Seeing his frown, she asked, "Are you expecting a Seeker, Ari?"

He ducked his head once. "No, not this late. The Nadarine stairs will be solid ice before dinner."

Firousi looked at him sharply, but to his relief she held back from pointing out that the rain-awning was still not up. The menservants were his responsibility; since they'd have to put up the rain-awning, that was his responsibility too. Well, he'd had other things on his mind.

He repressed a shiver. Firousi felt the cold more than he did; with a little self-control he could tell her and get her out of his study before it got cold enough that he had to call the boy to bring in a brazier.

"Arakante?" Firousi was coming as close to staring as she ever did.

"Sorry, my mind was wandering." He set the lamp aside a little and nodded at Firousi. "I tried, Firousi. Nothing worked."

She was silent for one long breath. "I feared it was so. Arakante, this is driving me mad. I am doing everything I can think of to do. Layla's clearly wondering why she's still here, and sometimes I do, too. Just today I used the *Story of the Kumquats* to illustrate a point, and all the damn girl did was gape at me! Nobody has ever failed to see the humor in the *Story of the Kumquats* before. I wish I had other pupils—it would be less work! Almost anyone from here would understand better."

"Careful, cousin."

"What, of wishes? Why? Kossinli's granting that thief's

wishes, not mine."

"Well, why did you choose her if she's so unsuitable?"

"I didn't." Firousi stopped abruptly, blushing.

Arakante leaned forward. "Really? You mean even without Her statue as focus—"

"Even so. Oh, I was doing all I could to discover exactly where the Eye was, and I certainly hope our little group of devotees provided something of a beacon for Kossinli. I think the lack of a focus may be why She chose such a strange beneficiary—though not so strange, perhaps, if She knew She needed something stolen. And, Ari, you should have seen the temple soldiery pouring out in all directions, and our Layla strolling by in women's garb with her water pitcher, trying to blend in with the walls and just about doing it. It was all I could do not to laugh and applaud her performance! She didn't even jump more than a little bit when I spoke to her. Now, if she's bright enough to pull that off, why can't she understand that she's got to learn how things work before she can control them?"

"Because she doesn't have to. I'll be studying divination all my life, and I'll probably never fully understand all the ways of piercing the veil between us and tomorrow, but what of it? And speaking of study, dear cousin, I've some words here that may cast light on another way..."

Firousi rose with a theatrical sigh. "Why didn't you say so, instead of sitting here while the room got cold as a pawnbroker's heart? I was just ready to call the boy for fire myself, since you didn't seem to notice. Shall I do it for you as I go?"

"Yes, please. Tell him to bring more oil for the lamps, too." He bent his head closer to the page.

He had days to enjoy it. The rain was followed by fog so thick that it kept all but the desperate indoors. The loss of a few fees wouldn't pinch too hard. He could blame no one but himself for his lack of concentration.

Silent and tense, Layla slipped in and out of rooms as if she expected to be thrown out if anyone saw her. He asked her once if she was feeling well; her hasty assurance that it was only the weather sounded as thin as she looked.

Thin though she was, she'd none of the angularity that thin women usually did. He wondered if she was using magic without knowing it when she passed for a boy. He'd certainly had no difficulty telling the difference! Best not to think on those lines, though, not if he was to continue Seeing for her.

15

*I*n the courtyard below, a half-dozen men were hauling out poles, ropes, and a long dark bundle that turned out to be a sort of awning. Made of heavy oiled canvas, painted in a complicated interlace of at least a dozen colors, it had little metal troughs at the edges to carry water away. After much clattering and confusion in the courtyard, the oldest of the slaves—no, servants, I must remember that—stamped away from the rest and hurried upstairs to where I was trying to listen to Firousi.

"Please, may we borrow the Lady's donkey? Masun has sprained his shoulder, the clumsy fool."

"What is it you want Imchi to do?" I asked.

The man smiled reassuringly. "Only to pull a rope a little ways, to help us raise the awning. Truly, nothing beyond his strength."

"He's not the most biddable beast, though. I'd better help you manage him. No, no, I insist! I'd never forgive myself if he injured one of my host's men by kicking or biting."

I don't think I fooled Firousi, but she's much too polite to call me a liar, especially in front of a servant. "Take one of the heavy cloaks," was all she said.

So away we went, the old man explaining how never, never in all his days had he seen such unrelenting rain! Why, even in the days of the old Empress, when so much rain fell that the Wastes themselves bloomed, there had been little times between storms when men could hurry out and do the needful outdoor tasks without getting soaked. But now, everything was awry, even the weather. The Immortals were angry about something, that was sure. Lord Arakante said otherwise, but that was just his kind heart, trying to spare an old man worry. My Lord was worried about something, though, he could tell.

Imchi did try to bite the groom. Ears back, teeth bared, he brayed and kicked out until I made the man retreat to a bench near the door. "Not fitting," he grumbled quietly as I proved I hadn't forgotten how to harness a donkey. Poor Imchi, I think he thought it meant we were leaving. He certainly cooperated readily enough until I made him stop in the courtyard.

We had just finished getting the awning in place when a sedan chair arrived. Steam rose from the bearers as they waited to be dismissed.

The chair's occupant was evidently above noticing the raw weather. He stood, tall and thin as a human temple column, nodding approvingly. Had I seen him before? I couldn't remember a time or place, but he looked vaguely familiar. He gave no sign that he'd ever seen me before.

"It's good to see at least one establishment hasn't let this year's heavy rains be an excuse for not putting up the rainshield," he commented to no one in particular. "And what a splendid beast you have there!"

"It's the Lady's donkey, my lord," the porter told him.

"Ah? There's something quite unusual about him. Might I ask where he was bred?"

I believe I would have felt more comfortable answering his question if he hadn't smiled.

"Charransar," I told him. Why not? There are many donkeys in my former husband's city. "Thank you for the compliment, but aside from being a good bit larger than many donkeys, he's nothing extraordinary." Imchi kicked out at me, and the man laughed.

"It would seem he doesn't agree. Charransar, eh? Well, that's a bit far to go for a donkey. Pity, I was minded to have one like him. Would you be interested in putting him with some of my jennies, if you'll still be here in their season?"

Since I didn't know when donkeys mate, or whether I'd be here whenever it was, I murmured something politely agreeable and sneaked a frantic look at Arakante's porter. May his tips be enough to buy him a safe old age, he immediately gave a most contrived-sounding cough.

The client blinked. "Well, but I mustn't be late for my appointment, must I? Our Seer is hard enough to see, this time of year." As he snapped his fingers to dismiss the poor soaked bearers, I could see a bracelet of Sarinsat around his right wrist.

I was still shaking when I returned to what Firousi called her solar. Well, at least it did imply that we might have some sun again sometime.

"I told you you should have worn a heavier cloak!" she cried.

"I did. Anyway, I'm not cold, I'm angry. Why didn't anyone warn me there was a Priest of Sarinsat dropping by today? He's seen me, he's seen Imchi—"

"Layla, he's seen a woman and a donkey. Why should he connect those with a theft on the other side of the Wastes? Perhaps he raises donkeys as a hobby; I could well believe that of a Priest of Sarinsat."

I couldn't think of any reason except, "He said there was something extraordinary about Imchi. You don't suppose he could tell where Imchi really came from?"

"Imchi is extraordinary. He's even more obstreperous than most donkeys, and half again as large. Now, to return to our studies. We were discussing—"

"Firousi. Just how many of Sarinsat's people visit your cousin, as a rule?"

"Really, how should I know? Arakante's clients are Arakante's concern; you surely don't suppose he discusses them with me!" She pushed her long, gold-sewn scarf back from her face and turned towards a draft as if she actually welcomed it.

"He looks familiar to me, but I can't think where I would have seen him. He's Sarinsat's man. Firousi, what if he knows about the theft?"

"What if he does? He has no reason to connect you with it, especially since the last I heard the Emperor's men and Sarinsat's were looking for a young man."

"I'll ask Arakante myself, then." I rose to go.

"Layla, no!" Firousi actually took hold of my arm. "Ask him later, if you must. Never interrupt a seeing, even if it doesn't involve someone you claim to fear!" She hadn't raised her voice. Why should she? She didn't even call me a fool, perhaps seeing no need for that either. I nodded mutely; she let go of my arm.

"One of the duties of the gods," she continued as if the interruption had never occurred.

"But how can the gods have duties, Firousi?"

She frowned. She hated to be interrupted, and I tried hard not to do it, but really! Anyway, she was already mad at me.

"Who could they have duties to?"

She laughed. "I thought you didn't want to go into all the theology, little sister? There are higher powers yet, whose presence we could not bear. We live between gods and demons as we live between the two seas, and we are ill-advised to venture too far out of sight of land! As I was saying," she paused here to give me a silencing look, "One of the few duties common to all the gods, and a good deed which even the grimmest of them do for us, is to remind mortals that they are indeed mortals—that there are indeed limits to their understanding and their control which they will never understand."

"You've never spent much time in the poor quarters, have you? We don't need gods to remind us." She sighed. Then a thought occurred to me, one too funny to hold until whenever I next saw Arakante.

"Do you suppose I've been serving some divine purpose all along, Firousi? A thief certainly reminds people of how quickly wealth can disappear!"

Firousi turned an alarming shade of purplish-red, then laughed out loud hard enough to make the lamp-flame jump. When she'd caught her breath, she gave me a long considering look. "So that's why She chose you—it wasn't just convenience and make-do. That's a very interesting insight, Layla."

She smiled meditatively. In the silence that followed, I heard the front door open and close. When I rose to go, she made no objection.

Arakante looked alarmed when he saw me. "Layla? What's wrong?"

Courteous of him to ask, rather than just find out. I dragged a footstool over to the brazier and seated myself cross-legged. No point in having cold toes while I got through this.

"That man who just left is one of Sarinsat's priests."

He sighed, very gently. "Yes, he is. That has nothing to do with why he came here to me, and that has nothing to do with you."

"Well, pardon me my Lord! Have you forgotten just why I was even in this soggy excuse for a city when you and Firousi wanted something stolen? I made a long, hard journey across the Wastes in order to escape Sarinsat's priests and their spies. Now one of those people shows up in the very house I'm staying in, and neither you nor your cousin can understand why I'm upset? Maybe I can't see above this low-class boring earthly plane, but I can damn well tell when I'm in danger!"

Now he stood up, doing his best to tower over me. "It would seem you can't. That man is no danger to you; he came only to consult me, as a Seer, Layla! The nested spheres of fate do not revolve around you, there are hours and days at a time when neither god nor goddess is paying you the slightest attention, and a longtime client of mine is now almost at the door." He stopped for breath.

"I wish Kossinli would stop paying attention to me!"

Arakante made a sign that began as the sign of aversion that I use myself, but went on to something that flickered in the air like daytime flame. "Don't wish that, Layla. Why do you think Sarinsat's men haven't found you?"

There was a thought to ease my mind! "I unsay it! Lady of Mirth, don't forget me." I hoped that tone of voice didn't matter too much. "But, Arakante, Her gifts drove me from my home and my friends. And now my enemy appears and casts a knowing eye at one of Kossinli's gifts, starts asking questions, and you think I'm just—just—giving myself airs like some pampered child of—of a Lady, I suppose!" I shut up before the stammer got any worse. Here was something else I thought I'd conquered years ago, returned to plague me.

I was looking down at my hands where they lay clenched together in my lap. Mustn't do that either, bad for the fingers and I needed my fingers quick and deft, when I felt an arm go around my shoulders.

"Take care, Layla." Ah yes, his client was no doubt here by now. It must be useful to know when someone's coming after you!

The following days were a wonderful time for anyone wanting to inquire secretly about the future. Between the curtains of the sedan chairs, the rain-flap, and the huge cloaks that the visitors wore, I couldn't have told you whether most of them were male or female. Only the Sarinsat priests's height was unmistakable in any weather.

Arakante would say nothing of any of them. Oh, once he did comment that working in a house well away from the markets didn't seem to have discouraged people with trivial questions, but that was all. There were times, though, when he looked worried more than he looked tired. I smothered my questions; it was no business of mine.

There was no more divine laughter.

Then one morning I woke to near-silence, and a hard white light slicing between the shutters. When I climbed up on the blanket chest to open them, I saw that everything outside was white. All the walls seemed several inches taller. I could see a corner of the garden when I stood on tip-toe; this morning it looked as if it was full of small white yurts. Those were the bushes, I supposed. Early as it was, something had stitched a line of tracks between the bushes; I was suddenly very glad to be leading an honest life most of the time. Imagine leaving that sort of trail behind you!

Would Imchi be warm enough in his stall? He wasn't used to this any more than I was. Turning back inside, dazzled by the light, I almost fell from the chest and landed with a slap that stung the soles of my feet.

The floors were even colder than they'd been before, and I'd've sworn that wasn't possible. I hopped on my stinging, freezing feet to retrieve the slippers I'd politely accepted a week ago and tucked away under the bed. It had seemed faintly insulting to wear shoes indoors, even shoes that were never worn outside of the house; it was like saying that the house was so dirty that I needed to protect my feet. Either that, or it was an insult to me, an implication that as a foreigner I couldn't endure the Tzakendi winter. I wondered if the second might be true. Even with my old shirt on under my boys' clothes, I shivered when I went out into the hall.

The house slippers were evidently no insult to anyone. Arakante entered the central room wearing a high felt pair of slippers like a nomad's boots, and two more layers of tunics peeking out in layers from under his usual loose shirt. Firousi followed soon after, wearing a startling pair of scarlet slippers, and a quilted caftan embroidered in fine-spun upland wool. She laughed when Arakante complained of the early snow.

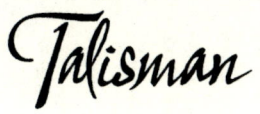

"It's wonderful! I feel as if I'm fully awake for the first time in months. No lessons today, Layla; I'm going over to Lady Raina's. Would you care to come along? We'll probably go up to see what the Ice-Wizard's carved this year. Ari?"

Arakante saw my alarmed expression. "It's a frozen waterfall," he explained. Well, how was I to tell when this precious pair meant real magic?

"Its spirit does write some of what the coming year holds, but I've found I can do at least as well with a bowl of clear water in a warm, comfortable room," he continued. Oh. Real magic after all.

"You could take Imchi, if sedan chairs still bother you," Firousi pursued.

"Take poor little Imchi up through this? He'd freeze his feet!"

"Poor little Imchi has a pelt like a Rabissinian ram, and feet big enough for a dray-horse," scoffed Firousi. While we quarreled, Arakante quietly left the room. As soon as Firousi left, I slipped out to visit Imchi.

I choose that word carefully. Tzakende boasts that it has fewer outright thieves than any other city between the two seas. Tzakendis attribute this to the holiness of their city. Myself, I think it's because the winters kill off any but the nimblest.

Imchi was well, half-asleep in the warm dimness of the stables. He tried to eat my collar while Arakante's groom assured me nervously that the donkey had had nearly as much to eat as a full-sized horse. I could well believe it, whatever the grooms gave him. He's as good a thief in his way as I am in mine.

Outside, it was gray again. Trickles of water flowed across the path that led back to the house, yet the breeze off the duckpond was as sharp as ever. I hurried on towards the house. There was a wonderful smell of mutton stew in the air.

Thinking of mutton stew, I let myself walk normally instead of with the stiff-legged gait that snow and ice require. Both feet slid out from under me.

All my old skill at roof-running worked against me. There was no firm purchase here, and the thick soles of my boots kept me from knowing anything about the treacherous stuff underfoot. I bounced off a stone bench and continued sliding towards the stable.

Suddenly, someone caught me. Arakante? Who would have thought he was that strong?

Both of my husband's senior wives had warned me about the perils of believing romantic songs. They must have been right. For now, as I turned my face upwards to thank my rescuer in the traditional manner, I found myself set firmly back on my feet.

"Are you well?" His voice was perfectly even and controlled, the beautiful cool tone of someone whose voice is one of the tools of the trade.

"Oh, a few bruises, but nothing worse thanks to you." Plagues and pestilence, was I never to chose a man for myself?

We were nearly the same height. I tried leaning yieldingly against him. Cold-weather clothes are a real problem when you're trying to press enticingly against someone.

"Layla!" He took several steps back. "You're a guest in my house. What sort of degenerate do you take me for?"

Degenerate? "Isn't that supposed to be my verse? I'm not that kind of a girl? Sorry if I offended you, I don't usually have quite that effect on men!"

He went on as if I hadn't spoken. "What do you think, because I couldn't keep my family together I just don't care where or how I scatter my seed? I take as good care of my children as my wife will allow—but I mustn't call her that. Not now."

"What children? What wife?" He wasn't listening.

"You're forbidden to me anyway, Layla. Even if I'm a miserable failure as a husband and father, I can be a decent—" He stood quietly as a mouse that's scented the cat. Then, very softly, "You didn't know."

"No." In fact, I still didn't really understand, except that I was evidently not the only one with a past that wouldn't stand too

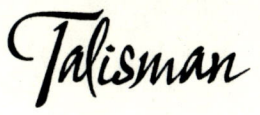

much examination.

"And I call myself a Seer. The water's always silty when you try to see your own life, but this—this was pure mud." I have heard long curses that sounded less obscene than that "mud."

He turned and strode back towards the house as easily as if the path were clean and dry. "Wait! Arakante, please—" Trying to follow his example, I stepped where he had and discovered that footprints in snow are even slicker than the untrodden path. Only grabbing some bush with thorns saved me from landing hard. Like an old woman with bone-bind I hobbled cautiously the rest of the way. He was long gone by the time I reached the house.

That was when I began to wonder how he'd come to be just where he needed to be to rescue me from broken bones. For if I'd continued on downhill, bouncing off garden furnishings as I went, I would surely have broken something.

16

*A*rakante flung himself into a chair and sat staring through the tiny panes of his study window. The distorted pieces of garden visible through them were more clear than the vision he'd gained of his own future. He hadn't talked to himself since early in his apprenticeship, but a wordless groan escaped him. What was the point of all his training if he couldn't use it to keep from making a complete fool of himself?

He could, of course, go to one of the other Seers and ask them to do a divination for him. He had done that service for two of them, but the thought of going to either one made him cringe. Ixta had too many lovers to understand what the fuss was about, and Mikante was still mourning his wife. Nor was Arakante eager to give some less-known mage that much knowledge of his own life.

Very well, then; he would go on alone as before. He had probably solved the problem of Layla anyway. What woman would want a man whose wife had left him? Best to get on with finding the missing pieces of Kossinli's statue; then Layla could go whatever way she chose.

It took three repetitions of the breathing exercises to bring him enough calm that he could look into the silver bowl and see anything but the bottom of the bowl. Changing the color of the cloth beneath it seemed to have helped; at least there were images this time.

The wreath and the heart were somewhere in Tzakende; he had managed to learn that much with the casting-sticks. But where?

Images splintered, blurred into nothingness, or turned dark. He grimaced when the last happened and hastily emptied the bowl. No, this time no actual tarnish marred its surface. That was a mercy; he had no apprentice just then, and doing kitchenmaid duties was a cruel waste of his time.

He allowed himself one Seeing that was purely for his own desires. The images formed easily and quickly this time. He'd warned his former wife that he claimed the right to look in on his daughters whenever he chose, and he'd done so often enough that the link was strong and sure. The girls were playing some game with dice and markers beside a fireplace in the tall fortified manor where his former wife now lived with her parents in a tangle of cousins and family connections. Marissa and little Firousi looked well and happy, as they usually did. They didn't look as if they felt the lack of anything—a father, for instance. Well, surely he wouldn't wish them to be unhappy?

A scratching at the door warned him that more time had passed than he'd thought. "Assure Lord Prahin that I'll join him soon, and make sure he has refreshment," Arakante called out.

"Yes, Lord." Quick soft footsteps faded away as the servant hastened back to the waiting room.

17

I was developing a taste for rose-hip tea, though I still wanted a large dollop of honey in mine. Firousi and I were sharing a pot of it and enjoying a rare sunny moment when Arakante came into the solar. "Forgive me if I'm interrupting."

"Not at all," said Firousi, then chuckled as she saw us both realize how thoroughly ambiguous that was.

"An ice storm's coming. Do either of you know of anything you need to get before we're housebound?"

"Completely?" My voice squeaked.

"Yes, completely. I trust you'll be able to endure this hovel; the ice won't last long this time." He left the room while I was still trying to assure him that I meant no disrespect. I did wonder about that convenient ice-storm. Wizards may foresee storms; they may also call them. I'd do no night-wandering with ice glazing every tile and cobble. With only the Sacred Dances for exercise, I was getting positively feeble.

By Tzakendi standards, the storm was a short one. On the third morning, the sun made blinding rainbows with the ice as it melted. We had no formal lessons, and went marveling from window to window instead. I hope I can amass enough wealth for at least one glass window when I'm living alone again.

I was just thinking of lunch when I heard voices at the front door. Curiosity being even stronger than hunger, I went to see who it was.

Two young girls, barely old enough to be out without Mother or Auntie, and almost too shy to speak, were standing at the door when I got there. A middle-aged woman, plainly clothed, stood behind them. It took several tries for the braver of the two girls to make it clear to the gatekeeper that they were seeking, not Arakante, but Firousi.

"She knows about the Lady of Mirth, doesn't she?" the girl asked in a soft, worried voice. The doorkeeper assured her that it was indeed so, and sent another servant hurrying off to Firousi. Arakante strolled down the stairs with a casualness that might have deceived someone who'd not spent years learning to tell who's paying attention and who is not. Perhaps he felt that his prestige and dignity would survive his answering his own door better than his being discovered lurking on his own stairway. Firousi arrived only a moment later; had she too been lurking on the stair?

"Oh, good." Both girls sighed with relief at Firousi's arrival, then giggled at having spoken in chorus. The braver one continued, "It came to Ariana in a dream that we should find you, but we have been trying for ages to find out where you were, and we couldn't go out looking because the streets were so icy and our families were just certain we'd break both our legs, and they even said we mustn't risk the slaves' legs either by taking a chair, but imagine! Ariana's Auntie Timra, who never ever laughs herself ever since her husband lost all his money in the wars, she used to dance for Kossinli, (it's awfully hard to imagine her dancing either, but she did) and she told us to try here, and it's barely a dozen steps from my house, so they had to let us come."

"And I am so glad that they did," said Firousi. "Would you like to come up to my solar? We can discuss things comfortably there."

"You mean, right now?" breathed one of the girls, softly.

"No, next Thaw!" the more talkative girl hissed. "Come on."

"Whose dream was it, anyway, Mirantha?" Ariana asked. "I'm sorry, Lady Firousi. I just was surprised that you had time to talk to us right away, I mean, I...I expected you'd be busy..I'm really glad you're not." Her eyes slid sideways to where I stood.

Firousi looked at me consideringly. "Layla's been studying with me for awhile now, but perhaps—"

Oh, no! Keep her busy, you two. I announced sweetly, "I've taken far too much of your time recently, Lady Firousi; today I'll leave you free to assist these ladies." I was out the door almost before I'd finished speaking, snagging a hooded cloak from the drying-rack as I went. It turned out not to be mine, but I only discovered that when I was half-way down the hill.

Clouds again hung in the sky, dripping like freshly washed fleeces, but I didn't care. There hadn't even been the excitement of one of Kossinli's peculiar jests to enliven my days.

Had there been a way of leaving Tzakende—but there wasn't. There were less painful ways of committing suicide than by traveling the Wastes in winter. Besides, it had been weeks since Kossinli granted a wish of mine. It would be foolish to leave just as I started to make progress. To be sure, I hadn't wished very hard for anything lately, except an end to lessons—oh. I stood motionless for long enough to have drawn shouts of annoyance anywhere else, but this was Tzakende. Everyone edged around me, ho-hum, another mystic in a trance, wish they'd learn to get off the street first, but what can you expect? At least this one's quiet. Someone did laugh, just loudly enough to get me moving. Surely, surely, it was only some person who'd gone on her way before I could spot her. Besides, even if it was Kossinli, it meant I'd put her in a good mood. If I must be in contact with a goddess, I'd rather have her happy.

Well, for whatever cause, I had some time to myself. I set off downhill, into the old city with its crowded streets and teahouses of dubious reputation.

The gray light glinted on wet walls, on stair-edges and on the earrings of a man buying roasted nuts from a street vendor. I stopped to buy some, too, and got a better look at two fine small sapphires on a silver chain, looped back and caught at the top of the ear with a smaller diamond that could have been better set. A

dangerous man to cross, or so he wished to be thought, with his
jewelry caught neatly back out of the way. In practice, that loop
of chain can be snagged and used to pull a man's head away from
the real fight, and his attention with it. A good sharp tug may pull
it loose and leave the victim too blinded with pain to pursue. Were
I not so near to home...no, probably not even then. That kind of
thievery's such a messy business. Oh, I've done it, in desperation
or in revenge, but I was well-fed now and the man was a stranger.

Then the stranger straightened and turned to go. He stood
a head taller than anyone else; it would've been hard to get those
sapphires. And I had seen him before, at the villa.

Now the gods be thanked for thick crowds with many tall
people in them! I developed a sudden interest in the pickled
melon-rind stall across the street.

I'm not actually fond of the stuff. Moments later, feeling
foolish, I resumed my perfectly respectable stroll. Why should I
fear the man, simply because he served a god whose temple I'd
robbed? That was in another city. Still, why did the man keep
crossing my path? Arakante might be able to tell me...no. I'd not
be spoken to like a child with bad dreams again.

The nuts had an odd sweet taste and a mealy texture; I gave
all but one to an enterprising child trying to sell live lizards to the
crowd. He assured me the lizards would keep all bugs from my
house forever, but I refused; they looked about half dead. He also
assured me that they'd liven up when they were warm again, but I
had my doubts.

The winter light began to go long before I was ready to
climb back up the Nadarine Stairs. Someone with a voice like
Isslarantan silk was singing a satire. I followed the sound to a
singing-house tucked into the sharp corner of three streets and
found an empty bench near the door. All the beauty that singer had
was in his voice; I don't think he could ever have had eyes, though
it was hard to tell. I bought a dish of fried chick-peas and onions
to pay for my seat, and a mug of the inn's thick beer, a safer choice

than wine in such a place. The one pitcher of tea looked even murkier than the beer. The singer went on shredding reputations. To guess by the songs, he'd met many people who'd forgotten that a blind man can still hear.

Firousi wrinkled her nose at me when I came back in the dark. "And how we shall get the smell out of the cloak, I don't know! It wasn't even yours, you know. I had to send Mirantha home with one of mine."

"She could've had mine," I offered. "It would have been closer to the right length."

Firousi only sighed. "You've missed dinner, too."

"'Sall right. I'm full of chickpeas. And onions."

"So I noticed."

Bed seemed like a good idea. I was tired, and in much too good a mood to argue with anyone. As I slogged up yet more stairs, I thought I heard a giggle behind me, but when I turned around there was only Firousi, looking superior.

The two featherheads were not the last seekers after Kossinli to arrive on our doorstep. While Firousi organized them into groups and reveled in their awestruck questions, I was able to wander the city often. Several times I saw Sarinsat's priest, always before he saw me.

I'd thought I was really beginning to learn a few things. Then the little surprises started up again, including a complete consort of Charransar's curved, capped-reed flutes that appeared one afternoon after I wished that Tzakende had a few more loud instruments for times when we had large numbers of worshipers all chattering at once instead of listening. Did I mention that a complete consort has thirty-six instruments, the largest of which has to be played by a musician standing on a small stepladder? Firousi laughed and said that she supposed we were lucky that Kossinli hadn't sent us the musicians, too; that might have strained the house's hospitality at this time of year.

Even Imchi got some good of the changes. Arakante's

grooms had been caring for him well enough, but they were all too afraid of him to give him more exercise than he could get in the little paddock between the grapevines and the cliff. They claimed he bit. It suited us all for me to take him out to help the housekeeper get the villa's supplies replenished. It seems that people who worship Mirth also admire food and drink. Some of the foodsellers were bigger thieves than I am; it gave me some pleasure to defeat them.

Imchi still hated stairs, so it was usually simpler to take the long way 'round for any market. Once you come down off the heights, Tzakende does not divide neatly into rich and poor; we sometimes passed through neighborhoods where I had to keep a sharp eye on the bread-rolls. I was doing just that one afternoon when Imchi yanked his lead rein out of my hand and trotted briskly up a street I'd never followed before.

It was narrow, and so winding that even the winter rains hadn't swept it clean. A skinny girl-child grabbed a roll as Imchi trotted by. I'd no time to chase her, and besides, I've been hungry myself. There were others watching who worried me much more. Scowling like a woman who just might be willing to use her Virtue Dagger, I hurried after Imchi. Don't ask me why I was so determined not to lose an animal who'd been nothing but grief all along.

He stopped beside a hole in the wall. Fragments of a wooden door-frame showed under rough smears of Tzakdendi plaster. By the smell, there was food and drink of sorts for sale within.

I yanked on his halter. He snorted impatiently and thrust his nose through the door.

"Here, now, we ain't the fanciest place in town, but we don't serve asses!" The voice came from a cocoon of rags that hid all but one rheumy eye of the person who spoke.

"Demons you don't." This was definitely a woman, but with shoulders a professional fighter might envy. "Ass don't smell any worse than some 'f the reg'lars."

"This is a respectable place!" objected the ancient. That provoked loud laughter from the others in the place. Now that my eyes were dark-adapted, I could see that several people were sitting in the shadows. All but the broad-shouldered woman had managed to sit backed against a wall.

I wanted to force Imchi out of there right then. I'd avoided places this dismal even during my worst times, if only because there was seldom anything in them to be sold or stolen. There was a good chance of being robbed myself, or raped. Yet I peered into the gloom, convinced that there was something important here.

I'd felt like that before, and I knew where. Well enough, Lady of Mirth; we'll see how long they tolerate us. I let Imchi pull me a little farther in.

"Here, now, does that great ass want some ale?" the brawny woman asked. "It's been called horse piss a few times."

More laughter, and the scrawniest barmaid I'd ever seen thrust a pitcher towards Imchi. He backed up snorting loudly, which caused yet more laughter. Some had grown mellow enough, or desperately thirsty enough, to demand refills. The ancient tottered round with another pitcher.

The barmaid's birdnest hair had something metal in it, something that glittered even in this dim light and trembled as she turned. She saw me staring and gave me a gap-toothed grin. "Like it? I won it off Osralde there last night at draughts." She pushed the headdress up a little and smirked at the brawny woman.

How had such a thing come here? The soft metal had bent out of shape and some of the clusters were missing, but that was a trembling-wreath headdress. It didn't tremble much now, but I knew how to rewind the wires that held those carnelian flowers, those jade leaves. Dirt had dulled the stones...I forced myself to shrug. "Aye, it's pretty."

"I might sell..." The barmaid put her head to one side; the wreath slid over one ear. She mashed it back. Kossinli's headdress

or no, I had to rescue the poor thing.

Osralde swung around to half-face us both. "Damn it, you owe me a chance to win it back! Didn't I damn near get killed getting it?"

"Nay, you waited till they's both dead, killed each other, the soldier and the thief," croaked the ancient. "Sure you want it, Missy? She took it off a dead man." The wrinkles distorted into a toothless grin.

"Hmmm. Maybe not," I said thoughtfully. Well, it made a bargaining point. Cursed goods ought to go cheaper.

The barmaid wanted cash, and wanted it too badly to be a good bargainer. I pointed out the missing clusters and the dirt, and told her the stones were but polished pebbles; she tried to argue but caved in fast when I turned to the door. In less time than I'd needed to buy the bread rolls, I had the wreath. It cost very little more than they had. There are more ways than one of stealing!

I do hate hauling out money in such tight quarters, but there was no help for it. That done, Imchi and I set out for the villa. Even he seemed to understand that we'd better get out of there fast. To make my joy complete, fog was drifting through the streets.

Sure enough, we'd gotten only a few turns of the alley when I heard heavy steps behind us. "If you were a proper magic beast, I could just tie the wreath on you and tell you to go home," I muttered. He wouldn't even get in front of me. Ah well, Osralde would have to get past him to get to me. With his panniers, Imchi blocked most of the narrow passage. I snugged my sash tighter; better to bend the wreath than lose it.

Ahead lay a tangle of street-crossings; the third from the right would lead us back to the Nadarine Stairs. Imchi chose to get stubborn again. In that open space, Osralde darted around him and slashed at my middle. She was fast for someone that big.

Not as fast as I, though. Her knife went over my head as I crouched and thrust upwards. "Shit!" Actually it was mostly fog-water on the cobbles, but it was slick enough to send one foot out from under me.

I fell almost under Imchi's hooves. They looked much larger than before, seen from the street. He cast a wild eye at me, dancing sideways. I lay still and hoped Kossinli wasn't in one of her nasty moods.

Suddenly Imchi leaped forward, nearly planting his back hooves on me. I scrambled away, hoping I hadn't just pulverized Kossinli's jewelry.

I had just gotten back on my feet when I heard Imchi scream. Damn it, if that female ox had hurt him I'd kill her!

Imchi was rearing like a warhorse. His hooves gleamed as he struck out. Osralde fell and rose swearing and clutching her shoulder; Imchi reared and struck again.

The load of bread rolls was never meant to stand that sort of jostling. The cloths over both panniers gave way at once.

Bread rolls bounced off the walls and rolled down the street; I'd've sworn I hadn't bought half so many. Laughing children emerged from who-knows-where, and a few grown folk as well, gleefully scooping up slightly used bread. I threw the last few rolls into the mob and ran for it, with Imchi cooperating for once. I could hear Osralde cursing behind us most of the way to the Nadarine Stairs.

Once we got there I slowed to a fast walk. This was the sort of crowd that might well interfere if they saw murder being done—or if they saw what they saw was a fleeing thief. Would Arakante's bribes hold if someone was obliged to take official notice of me? I drew some suspicious stares for my dirt and dishevelment, as though any thief who wanted to keep both hands would go through the streets so conspicuously! Imchi laughed when I said so.

That drew even more attention, for Tzakendi donkeys are quiet little creatures. We were nearly back to the villa by then, and of course one of Firousi's friends was out enjoying a rare rainless moment.

Lady Mirrim was small and plump, which didn't stop her from piling on layers of long, brightly-colored tunics. She always brought sweet buns when she visited Firousi, well-buttered with a rich assortment of gossip. She chattered like one of Firousi's little feather-headed pupils, but the gossip was usually true. I didn't want her wondering about me just now.

"No, no, I'm all right. It looks much worse than it is."

Lady Mirrim tucked her sleeves briskly back into their embroidered bands and took my arm. "Oh, nonsense, Layla! Poor girl, I only hope you haven't broken a rib! Don't be silly now, I can see by the way you hold yourself you're in pain."

Having a large metal wreath of leaves and flowers pressed against your side will do that. Ah well, I now had an impeccably respectable escort.

Such cries of dismay when we reached the villa! Someone must have had sense enough to send for the stable-boy, who bravely led Imchi away. "And give him a carrot!" I shouted over the general babble.

The helpful Lady Mirrim gave me one really bad moment when she tried to accompany me to the bath. "Nonsense, it's not a trouble. I'm counted a fair healer, I'll have you know, and I want a look at that rib. Firousi, do you have that bonewort salve still? You did keep it from the light, didn't you?"

I had to smile at the look on Firousi's face. Maybe she'd remember this the next time she was lecturing me. I regretted my snide thoughts almost immediately, for Firousi rescued me. "Layla's a little shy, Mirrim. I'll help her; she's used to me." She gestured to her little serving girl, who trotted off in the direction of the baths.

"Ah, well then! That will be a custom of your homeland, no doubt. I'd love to hear of it sometime; I've never had the opportunity to travel to such exotic places as Firousi has. Seven children keep a woman busy!" She was gone then in a flurry of draperies.

I ached in too many places to count, but especially on my left shoulder where one of Imchi's hooves had struck me when he leaped to my defense. Would the stableboy have rubbed him down properly and given him his carrot? Most of them were afraid of him, and almost all of them resented being made to care for a lowly donkey. I expected an argument from Firousi when I went to make certain of his care, but she only warned me that the rains had washed mud over part of the path. I refused her offer of escort. I was only going to the end of the garden!

By the time I got there I wondered if I had been wise, for my bruises felt no better for cooling. I found Imchi dry and blanketed. "I gave him his carrot, Lady Layla, and the head groom says he's only tired and a little strained, for all he's so quiet!"

"Well, he's had a strenuous day," I said, and told the boy of the attack without mentioning what led up to it. Delighted at being the first to know something, he gave Imchi another carrot.

"Are you injured?" asked Firousi when I returned. She looked genuinely worried. Though she was too polite to touch me unasked, she stayed close enough to catch me if I stumbled.

"Only a few bruises. The bath will be welcome; I've grown used to smelling good!" Not that I usually smelled quite this ripe even during my first days of working alone. Some kind and cleanly soul had endowed one night each week at the public baths of Charransar's east quarter for poor but honest women. Well, I was certainly poor.

Firousi laughed when I told her about that, but stayed close. The serving-girl had thought to bring the bonewort salve and plenty of towels, including old ones in case there should be blood. She clearly thought it was poor repayment to be sent away without a chance to find out what happened.

Finally, I could pull the wreath out from under my overrobe. Even half-crushed and filthy, it showed what it could be. Firousi was actually speechless for several breaths.

"Oh, Layla. Oh, may I?" She was asking me? I handed the wreath to her.

"Careful, it's broken in places."

"Yes, yes I see. But this—Layla, how did you find it?" She was turning it gently in her hands, gazing at it with tears in her eyes. "I was beginning to think we'd never get the rest of the things back. This was made by Kossinli's own daughter as they went gathering flowers one spring. Layla, where was it?"

"I'm not sure you want to know." Did she honestly believe that some girl-goddess made the wreath? It was good work, but I'd done nearly as well myself before Father married me off. Marriage to a noble put an end to such humble work.

"I can tell it wasn't properly cherished! Come, tell me." She stopped short. "I'm sorry! Injured or no, you must want that bath! Here, let me help you."

I daresay I could have managed alone, but the help was welcome. She shed her own top layers to keep them out of the way. I settled into the hot pool with a sigh of pleasure.

"Hiastha Herblady have mercy, those bruises look painful!" Firousi shed the last layer and came in with me. While she added oils to the water and helped me wash, I told her my story.

The telling of it helped cover my confusion. By the time I was done, sharing a bath with Firousi felt like sharing with my sister. Naghwa had bathed some of my scrapes and bruises, too. She never sang, though.

There in the baths, naked, Firousi sang a praise-song, altering the lyrics as she went along. It was a simple enough song that even I could join the refrain. Gray light from the high windows shimmered on the water like laughter.

18

The gardener's shed was chilly after the baths, but far enough from the house that the stink of ammonia wouldn't bother anyone there. It was also well enough ventilated that the fumes wouldn't bother me too much. The brazier for warming the mixture would take the chill off so small a place. There are stronger cleaning solutions than the soap, borax and ammonia mix I'd prepared, but they may damage soft stones. They may also take all the skin off your hands.

The wreath was filthy. No one who wore it seemed to have believed in washing her hair; I decided not to think about how some of the sticky grime had gotten onto the wires, or even what it might be. Soak and brush; rinse. Pry small bits of grime out of tight corners. Repeat. Slowly it began to come clean.

I doubt the jeweler was divine, but whoever made the wreath was more careful than most of us mortals. No one who wasn't cleaning the wreath would ever have noticed a rough job on the wiring of the lower rank of leaves, hidden as they were by lapis and carnelian flowers, but the wire ends were smoothed flat as the ones that showed. The only rough joins were where some fool had blobbed on solder trying to fix a break. I was cursing one of those when a choking sound behind me broke my concentration.

Arakante stood behind me. "Sorry," he said hoarsely. "Have I hurt anything?"

Only my composure, by getting so close to me without my knowing it. It was well for Tzakende that he was an honest wizard!

"No, whoever did make this had the best-beaten wire I've

ever seen. See how fine it is, and still not work-brittle?"

He flinched back almost before he'd had a closer look. "I haven't smelled anything like that since I was a boy studying spells! And we were trying to summon demons, my cousin and I!"

"Did you ever?" Well, if he didn't want me to ask, he shouldn't have spoken of it.

"Only once. We wanted one to torment the examining master, but the only demon we could force out of the mists turned out to be his servant already."

"How'd you escape? Oh, sorry, is that something secret?" He'd tensed up again.

"No, it's just embarrassing. We howled for the examining master, who in his mercy banished his servant while we still had all our appendages."

"Sounds like you showed good sense. It's hard to imagine you howling for help, though."

"Oh, only as a very young and foolish boy!" he laughed, then coughed violently. It must have gotten thicker in here than I realized. Arakante fled, apologizing, and I went back to cleaning the necklace.

Dirt must have been all that was holding it together. I came to be glad of Tzakende's flat, cloudy light; under it I could go on with the detailed work for much longer than I could have under a brighter sun. Clusters of carnelian and lapis, and the fine pale jade whose source no one between the two seas knows, lay spread out on the workbench. Many had been mashed flat into the underlying wreath, or stuck back on with something that dissolved immediately in the ammonia. I hoped I wouldn't need some sort of special sacred wire to repair the breaks.

Out of courtesy to Firousi and Arakante I ate alone that evening. Not all the scented oils in the storehouses of Nahouendar could have gotten the smell of ammonia completely from my skin. Growing up, I'd thought all men smelled of it; Father always did underneath whatever scent he used. Father would have loved the ointment Firousi handed me at arm's length. I smelled like a very well-fertilized rose garden after using it, and my hands felt much better.

Next morning I went early to breakfast to thank Firousi, and to ask her about repair materials. If we needed some sort of goddess-spun wire, I hoped she knew where to find it.

"I think regular wire will do," she said as she placed a spoonful of jelly carefully in the middle of a roll.

She didn't know? She was the teacher, she must know.

"No, I don't know!"

"I didn't say anything!"

"No, I know you didn't." She folded her hands loosely before her, arms held in the graceful curve that a Lady learns before her first blood. "Layla, I've had to tell you before that there's much that I don't know. Perhaps I should have warned you at the beginning, but I feared you'd hold all my knowledge worthless, and you truly did need some of it! Now I need your knowledge. And, Layla–whatever happens, I pray you, remember that Kossinli Herself chose you."

Meaning, don't blame me. Well, at least she'd finally come around to the notion that being tied to her precious Lady wasn't entirely a wonderful thing! I nodded. Words seemed too dangerous. What should I have said? That's perfectly all right, I've been submitting myself to you for weeks now thinking that you did know it all, but never mind? I may have just spent a winter putting myself through all sorts of ridiculous exercises that may not even have worked, but never mind, we got another bit of your goddess back. I sat there struggling not to hate Firousi, not to ill-wish her. I didn't want any goddess to hand me vengeance in some artistic form. If any harm came to Firousi, I wanted to do it myself.

Firousi was still looking away from me. "You'll know, not just the techniques for mending the wreath, but the proper mindfulness to have while you're doing it. Poor though my own knowledge is, yet I know that much. For both our sakes, I wish that I knew more."

I smothered an exclamation. Really, was this the time for false humility? She'd never bothered with that before. She poured us both more tea and continued.

"We were invaded the year I would normally have started my secret studies," Firousi said quietly. "No one had much use for the Lady of Mirth just then, even my own family, which had served Her for ten generations. Anyone with wealth fled to the hills or the river villages, even to Nahouendar. We scattered, and when my Aunt Naraya fell ill with the shivering sickness there was no one near who knew the right chants. It may be that they would never have worked against that foreign disease. Well!" She shook her head so hard her earrings jingled. "This is probably not of interest to you; forgive me."

"I wasn't bored. I just didn't know what to say." Had she said a few moments ago that she needed my knowledge? Not just a skill, like thievery, but knowledge? She must need it badly, to admit her own ignorance. I was curious, too; whatever happened to her own mother? Where were all those people who'd fled— even to Nahouendar? I was annoyed about that. My home city is not exactly a village! And of course I wondered whether my husband had been one of those refugees. Probably not, though he might have been merrier before he spent twenty years trying and failing to get a son.

"So I've rendered you speechless? That is an accomplishment!"

I had to laugh. "Treasure the occasion!"

19

*F*inally, it was done. I had raw patches on my fingers from cleaning solutions, a nasty cut where a wire I'd been winding had snapped, and a feeling of satisfaction even greater than when I'd stolen the first emerald.

Strange, how skills so long unused can come back so quickly. Why did the Tzakendi have to be so stupid about letting foreigners move in? There'd be no need here to hide behind a man's name if I went to lawful business. I could get someone else to do the drudgery of selling, and spend my days making beautiful things.

Well, the Tzakendi were unlikely to change for my sweet sake. At least I had re-made this, and been content for a time. Goddess' daughter or no, whoever made it first would surely have been pleased to see it now. The jade and malachite leaves swung freely on chains that only looked too delicate to be secure. The last spiral of wire was clean and shining; the last cluster of gem-petals polished or replaced. The breeze of the workroom door opening set them trembling.

"It's beautiful," said Firousi. "It is absolutely beautiful. Ah, Layla, how much I wish we could give it openly!"

"Why not?" That question had been puzzling me for some time. So had the fact that I'd never actually seen this statue whose Goddess had complicated my life so much.

"I don't dare. Sarinsat's people are powerful and devious; if they know we have this much of Kossinli's statue back together, they'll make certain we don't get Her heart."

"You're sure they have it?"

Firousi laughed. "Sure? We're dealing with the Goddess of Mirth, and with a wizard who's got a reputation for giving riddling answers even among other wizards. We're also dealing with Sarinsat's people. No, I'm not sure, but I'm confident enough to act on it."

I said nothing.

"Once we find that heart, and retrieve it," Firousi continued, "Once our whimsical Lady is whole again, She can defend Herself, and us. For now, the best I can do is to let you see what you've been working on." Firousi smiled her superior smile and sent for Arakante.

Well, it was about time! I wondered who they'd gotten to set the eyes back in, and hoped they'd done a good job. Such fabulous stones! I asked who'd done the work as we walked up stairs steep as the hills outside.

"An old Dancer I knew, who had great skill in such things. You'll see, he did no damage," Firousi said. It seemed that this expert would not be with us, though. "He died shortly afterwards, happy to see so much accomplished. Oh, Layla, relax!" A command that always sets me on tip-toe, watching. "He just died, that's all! He was an old man; he went to sleep and never woke again."

Mm-hmm. Well, it might be so. I'd just have to hope it was; the time for running was long past.

Up here at the top of the house, the walls wandered with even less pattern than they did below. Doorways of all heights gave glimpses of rooms of all sizes; the hall was princely in some places and so narrow that we had to walk single file in others. We stopped at one of the narrow spots, and both Firousi and Arakante smiled.

What was the joke? Firousi raised one finger to her lips. Very well, I'd let them show me. Arakante's rings flashed in the lamplight as he made a complicated sign.

A few handspans of the wall in front of him shivered and dissolved. We slipped through the opening and stood before

Kossinli's statue. It gleamed golden in the lamplight, taller than any
of us and so massive that I wondered how they'd gotten it up all
those stairs and narrow passages. No doubt it helps to have a
wizard helping you move household goods and gods. It wore a
golden caftan, stiff with embroidery and gems, divided into
shimmering panels to allow for movement. The upraised arm
balanced the leg outflung in a dancing step; it would not have been
surprising to see the statue continue the dance. The oval emerald
eyes had been set in at angles that made it look as though the
statue laughed.

"Lady of Mirth, I wish that we could do this openly!"

Firousi lifted the wreath carefully, letting the clusters of
gemflowers hang free. Above the wreath's formal border of
overlapping jade leaves, six-petaled carnelian flowers and
four-petaled lapis ones trembled on their tight spirals of near-
invisible wire. However carefully she moved, they quivered with
each step. Yet the wreath was strongly made, and had endured its
long travels among hired swords and slatterns with remarkably
few breaks.

"When we have the heart back," Arakante said. So, it was
still "when." He watched quietly with a gentle smile on his face as
Firousi continued down the narrow room.

I moved with her, softly as if I stalked someone I planned
to rob. I would do nothing that might interfere, but I meant to see
this clearly. There was room enough for that if I went carefully.
Little puffs of stone-dust came up from all our feet; I could see
Firousi's nose twitch as she struggled not to sneeze.

She paused for several breaths and then turned to me.
"Here." She held the wreath out to me. "Here, take it and give it
to Her. You found it, you worked your hands raw restoring it."

My own hands shook as I took it from her. The silver
bell-flowers chimed. I felt suddenly shy. "I don't know the
proper words, the ritual!" Had Firousi told me during one of the
times when my mind wandered? *Oh, Kossinli, I don't want to*

mess this up!

"There are no established rituals for returning the stolen property of a Goddess. Besides, Kossinli loves improvisation."

I have seldom wished to be taller, but I did now. The statue was made even taller by standing on a raised platform that was the closest they could come to a proper dais.

There I stood with my mouth wide open. Yes, yes, I'd been envying Firousi and wishing I could give Kossinli the wreath myself. Firousi has a dancer's grace and of course knows how it all should be done, but that was my work she was carrying! Oh yes, someone else did the original, but restoring something that delicate and that abused is at least as hard as doing it from the beginning. Well, once again I had my wish.

Now I had to take this masterwork of mine and place it on the head of a statue taller than I. Why had they felt they had to put it on a platform?

A platform, stupid. Would Kossinli mind if I borrowed a bit of it? I certainly hoped not.

I'd borrow as little as I might. Step up on one corner, raise up as if about to dance or to grasp the edge of a roof, and settle the wreath gently on the statue's black earth-glass hair. "Kossinli, I return Your own to You." Trust me, that position's not one to encourage long speeches. The edge of one curl nicked my hand as I stepped back down.

20

The presentation must have been acceptable. Aside from an occasional scent of flowers in the house, we heard nothing from the Lady of Mirth: no jokes, no mysterious appearances, and no hints of where the heart was. None at all, though I knew that both Arakante and Firousi were trying everything they knew.

Firousi and I continued my studies, spending more time dancing now that there were other students to fill out the patterns of the dance. There were times when it actually made sense to me. There were other times when I nobly offered to go hunting through food-stalls for something beyond lentils and root vegetables to feed the growing numbers of dancers.

It didn't always work. "No, thank you, Layla. We need you more here," Firousi said one dark afternoon.

There were so many people trying to dance there that the room was warm in spite of all its windows. Water ran down the glass and puddled onto the floor, adding to the charm of the event.

"Firousi, wouldn't you like—"

"To complete this figure? It will strengthen the Laughing One, who finds as little to amuse Her in this dank weather as we do. Come, Layla, the old name for this one was *How Kossinli Stole Back the Sun*. As they tell the tale in Issrandar, the sun had been hid near Charransar, which is why it's still always hot there." She smiled sweetly, but the cords on her neck stood out.

I danced. It wouldn't be my fault if the Laughing One, or Her devotees, found Her food-offerings small and boring.

The next day began with Firousi scolding the boy who ran the cook's errands. "No more excuses, Mika! I know what time of year it is as well as you do. I'm not asking for berries in fresh cream, but there must be dried apples for sale somewhere in this city. You will find them. Go now, and tell cook I must see him."

Mika darted back down the wide passage to the kitchens as I came through from the outer hall.

Firousi never fidgets, but there was a tension in her poised stillness that made me very glad that I was not responsible to her. As she turned to see who had entered the room, the pull of her skirts against the raffia mat showed her thinner than before.

"Lady Firousi, are you well?"

"Well enough, thank you, Layla. Only a little weary of trying to get ready for tomorrow's gathering. Even during Graymonth in Tzakende, people expect to be offered more than a cup of herb tea! We seem somehow to have run out of dried apples." Her look said she suspected me.

"Not guilty this time, my Lady!" Nor was I. Dried apricots, now... "If there's anything you want me to stay away from, better tell me. Or should I just stay out of the kitchens?" Her color was bad, too. This couldn't all be because of kitchen problems! I decided not to ask again what troubled her; if it was Kossinli, I wasn't at all sure that I wanted to know about it.

She laughed. "Oh, we won't demand that much of you! Just do please consult with cook. You don't have this problem in Charransar, I know. I managed to get quite pleasingly plump the one winter I spent there, before I realized there'd be fruit and fresh meat all winter long."

It was hard to imagine her plump. She touched my cheek, a quick touch almost too quick to feel. "It's kind of you to ask, but don't worry. I grow bored with the same food again and again, and can't eat what we have. Kossinli witness, they tried hard enough to cure me of it when I was a girl!"

Well, I could certainly understand her being weary with the

chickpea-cakes we had again that night. "You know, these wouldn't be bad with some chilis," I commented. I'd eaten six myself, but poverty teaches you not to be picky about food.

Arakante poked at the remaining cakes. "Chilis? Ah, now I can really tell you're from Charransar! They'd put chilis in almond pudding, I think."

"No, though there's a really good stuffed pastry they call 'first love,' made with mangos and honey and chili, mmm..." Neither Firousi nor Arakante looked too impressed. "Surely you'll admit they'd liven this up?"

"Maybe."

"If we could get chilis."

"You can't get chilis?" What kind of a place was this? Cold as it was, why hadn't someone imported a little dinner-time heat?

"Oh, I'm sure—"

"Somewhere in Tzakende—"

"They're not all that well-thought-of here, so not many shopkeepers bother—"

Well, Arakante didn't sound sure. Firousi clearly had no idea where chilis might be found in Tzakende. Come spring, whether I'd restored all of Kossinli's statue or not, whether I'd snapped the bond between me and that whimsical goddess or not, I was going home. I might not like the rules there, but I knew what they were, and I could at least eat well all the year round.

Loud voices woke me the next morning. "In my kitchen!" That was the cook.

"Esran, calm yourself!" That was Arakante. The tapestries hung in every doorway against drafts were muffling their voices. I had to know what was happening. Had someone besides me made a midnight raid on the kitchen? I padded down the stairs.

"Piles and heaps of these foreign hell-plants, all over my kitchen! If it please my lord to have such crude things on his table, well and good! I know my duty, I will prepare them! But what, my Lord, have I done to deserve having all my arrangements ignored,

my skills at finding even the most obscure spice disregarded, and huge piles of ugly red withered things strewn on every surface?"

Oh, Kossinli. So much for all my diligent study! Or was this caused by my studies? That dance had been supposed to strengthen and amuse Kossinli. Everything I did seemed to make matters worse.

Arakante was still soothing the cook. "Nothing at all, Esran. I am as angry as you at this. I'll tell Hinante to send you two of the sweepers. And perhaps you could turn your skills to creating something of a sauce from these mysterious vegetables? You've done wonders with the few things you have to work with in winter; perhaps it would amuse you to invent something new."

The cook gave a gratified grumble of agreement.

21

*T*hose chilis worried me, much though I enjoyed them. I had tried, truly I had, but Kossinli's gifts still arrived. True, bushels of dried chilis are somewhat more manageable than a live donkey. It's also true—and fortunate—that Firousi and Arakante take things calmly that would send most people screaming into the street.

When I left, I was going to have to go back to living alone. Yes, and somehow I was going to have to do better than one rented room. When a Goddess might drop in at any moment you don't want anyone else in the room, or even neighbors just the other side of a wall. It didn't look as if I was ever going to be free of the link with Kossinli, so I'd just have to live with it.

That all seemed clear enough to me. Firousi found it otherwise when I sought her out in the solar. It was a gloomy place again that afternoon, with fog swirling outside and water trickling down all its windows. Only the music of Firousi's lap-harp gave any cheer.

I stopped that. She heard me out, then set the instrument carefully back in its case before she spoke.

"Why set yourself a limit like that, Layla? Once spring has come, you can move back into an inn if you find living here so tedious."

"There has to be some sort of a limit. I can't go on living here, hiding out each winter, until I'm too old to get the heart even if we ever find out where it is. Spring makes sense. I can travel with

a caravan leader I already know." Or so I hoped. If Issimante still carried a grudge, it might be better to find another caravan. "I'd make the journey to Charransar before the heat of the summer begins."

"And go back to petty theft?"

"Oh, I think I can do better than that now." I smiled, and let her wonder what I meant by that. Truth to tell, I wasn't sure myself.

"Layla, don't stop just when you're making progress. If you'll just persevere—"

"Oh, right, the chilis all over the kitchen really show how much progress I've made! It wasn't even that big a wish."

Firousi chuckled. "She chooses what She'll grant. And really, Layla, what would you have Her do? Leave a note on your pillow? I thought Esran's reaction was amusing."

"Well, I hope you still think so when you get your dinner! He won't take even a hint from me, so taste things carefully." I wondered what Esran would do in his zeal to be inventive with a crude foreign seasoning, and shuddered. "Anyway, my point is that I haven't snapped the link, I'm not likely to snap it until we find the heart, and so far nothing's found it. Not Arakante's seeking, not your meditations, not my snooping. Come spring, I'm leaving."

She said nothing.

"I don't mean to insult your hospitality," I said. "You've been more than generous to me. I know I won't be able to live nearly so well once I leave." Yes, and that was another argument for leaving before I lost my edge completely.

"Layla," Firousi said, and then stopped. She opened her mouth to speak, then shook her head and said nothing.

I waited until the silence got too tense. "What?"

"Layla, please promise me that you'll not leave if we're in the middle of something. I'm not demanding this of you. I'm asking it as a kindness and for your own good."

There was that phrase again. "Firousi, how can I promise

that? We're in the middle of something now; we have been for half a year and it shows no sign of ending. Don't ask me that!"

Firousi rose and crossed to the doorway. "Layla, I'm not just trying to control you."

"Then please get out of the door."

"Just give me a few breaths more of your valuable time! Layla, you're linked to the Laughing One. What happens to one of you affects the other. Please–"

"Trust me, I'll do my best to keep from getting myself hurt!" She was still blocking the doorway. It would be unforgivable to wrestle with her in her own home. Didn't she have better sense than to trap me like this?

"Layla, I don't know how much danger you may be in. There's the truth. Something has changed since we met in Charransar, and I can't find out what because part of what's changed is that the Laughing One doesn't speak to me as clearly as once She did."

Firousi was actually trembling. That was frightening, in one so self-controlled. She still stood between me and the door.

"Firousi, either tell me what the danger is or let me go. I'm not talking about leaving tonight, after all. We'll still have time to fix things."

Firousi laughed, a little too high and too loudly. "May it be so." Softly, half to herself, she continued, "The dances may be enough. The Lady seems stronger. I may not compel." Then, louder, "I worry too much, Layla, but if I warn you of some danger, please consider that I may be right." She went back to her seat and took up her lap-harp again. The soft sounds of a meditation-song followed me as I went downstairs, feeling like an ungrateful, stubborn bitch.

I don't know what Esran's first attempt with chilis was like. I was in lower Tzakende, listening to a singer who should've retired already murder the *Lament for Lost Ryalla*. Dinner was various fried lumps that probably used to be pickled vegetables, and a pile

of lentils. I didn't have anyone looking reproachfully or worriedly at me, though. In fact, my table-companions largely ignored me. It was peaceful.

It was almost like my old life. Had I lost my edge to soft living and lofty theories? If I really did mean to leave in the spring, then I'd better find out. It was time for more roof-running, and this time I'd also try my thieving skills. One way or another, finding the heart or finding a living, I was going to need them.

Clothes would be a problem; my Tzakendi tunic was less entangling than Charransar's robes, but not the best choice for roof-running. It would have to do. If I went all the way back to the villa to change clothes, I'd a feeling I'd never make myself go out into the cold darkness again that night.

I waited until the singer had finished her crime. To leave in mid-song would attract attention even in a humble place like this one. There was quite a rush for the door when she did finish.

The roofs of Tzakende rose like uneven stairs under a thieves' moon. Not quite half-full, and half-veiled by clouds, it gave just enough light to cast confusing shadows. In one pool of darkness, I stopped to belt my tunic up high enough to free my legs. The cloak would have to go; I hoped it would still be piled under the stallholder's awning when I got back. Even Tzakende's damp night air was sweet as I slipped away from the crowd, up the wall by way of the remains of a shed, and onto the first roof.

The first three places I tried had all their upper windows well-shuttered against the winter. One more try, and I'd admit that this was foolish and slink away back to the villa.

Sure I would. Two houses later, I made a bad landing and lay shivering on the tiles while I flexed my right ankle carefully. I hadn't sprained it—quite. I'd come to another singing-house, this one with a better singer. Below me, a shutter banged in the wind.

I scrambled up the roof into its neighbor's shadow, ankle or no. I waited; yes, there went the same noise. Someone next door hadn't fastened a latch quite securely enough.

Carefully, now, over to the roof's edge; oh Kossinli! The shutter was on one of the little windows that poke out halfway up the roofs. There'd probably be no great wealth in the room beyond, but that wasn't the point.

The point was that even in a city so unlike Charransar, I could still use my skills. Jumping down is harder than climbing up, but I landed well this time and danced across the slippery tiles to the window. It was dark inside, and smelled moldy. The moon had gone behind a cloud again. I shuffled forward, wishing for more light.

Some of us are slow to learn.

The lamp flame showed through the opening door a moment before the man holding the lamp came in. That would have given me time to get to the window, had it not been for the cat that came in with him. The cat raced for the open window; I tripped over the cat; it yowled; I swore, and the man holding the lamp laughed loudly enough to be heard over all the confusion. He grabbed for me and caught my sleeve.

"I was feeling lonely tonight! Starting a new business, my enterprising friend? Not robbing me, I hope. Maybe home comfort?"

He wasn't much bigger than I am, but I was having trouble keeping him at arm's length. One good swift kick took care of that. Not to leave empty-handed, I pulled the pendant from his greasy neck as he doubled over. I was out of the window before he'd caught breath enough to shout. As I fled away over the roofs, I could hear the yowling of cats. There were shouts later, and footsteps running this way and that.

Before I got back to the villa's gate, I did what I could to look normal. The left shoulder seam of my tunic had popped, but if I hunched a little and walked quickly past the gatekeeper it wouldn't show. At least the cloak I'd lost was plain enough to give no clue who'd left it there. The real trick was keeping from shivering. The gatekeeper let me in without comment.

I thought I'd gotten away with it, I really did. The entire

place was dark, even the windows of Arakante's study. My heart must have been pure enough that I didn't trip any of his alarms as I stepped softly through the halls by touch and memory. I reached my own quarters and decided to see just what prize I'd claimed.

It was better than I'd expected. In that part of town people mostly wear fakes or pretty pebbles, but this—well, it was hard to tell by lamplight. I'd have to look at it again tomorrow, but it might be a ruby.

A ruby? Whose ruby? I was going to have to show this to Firousi. That was going to be awkward.

Someone was coming up the hall. I thrust the pendant back into my clothes and turned to face my door.

Firousi swept in. "What in the name of the Good Goddess have you been doing?"

When I didn't answer immediately, she came closer, peering at me by the light of both our lamps. "Are you hurt, Layla?"

"No, not really. Sorry. I'll look respectable again by morning, I promise."

"Yes, you probably will. I don't know how you do it." She surprised me then by gently brushing some of my hair back from my forehead. "That bump's going to give you a challenge, though." She settled down onto some of my cushions without spilling a drop of lamp oil. The look on her face said that she was prepared to stay as long as needed.

"I'm not just being nosy," Firousi continued. "I have been having the most bizarre dreams about you all night. I assume you didn't really ride through the city on a gigantic cat?"

I shook my head.

"Yet something extraordinary has happened. I asked Kossinli about it, but She'd only laugh. She speaks so seldom now!"

She said it as casually as if she'd been telling of a quarrel with a friend, instead of being out of favor with a Goddess. I was too tired, suddenly, to wrestle with all of this. She wanted to know; very well, I told her the whole story, not prettying anything up for my audience.

"Show me!" Firousi cradled the pendant a moment, not even looking at it, before giving a long sigh. "Odd. It isn't hers, yet it has something to do with her. Was it once owned by someone who worshiped her, I wonder? Guard it well, Layla." She handed it back.

"I've failed to explain something to you," she added.

Quite a few things, I thought, though not for lack of trying.

"I asked you not to steal anything except what I asked you to take. I thought you agreed."

"I never said that." Nor had I, in so many words.

"Layla, didn't you understand? Every time you steal now, it strengthens your ties with Kossinli! She's a wild spirit, my Lady, and She loves tricks. You're no cutpurse, no clumsy breaker of pates and doors; you plot and plan—though not so much tonight, it seems. Your thieving makes Her laugh, Layla, and that puts you in harmony with Her."

"Harmony. That's what you were talking about, with all those speeches about harmony and resonance? I can certainly see why you couldn't have told me this earlier. Why are you telling me now? I stole two emeralds for her, what did that do? I cheated so much getting that wreath it was like stealing! What happens if I ever get a chance to steal that heart?" She had been lying all this time. So had Arakante.

"Layla, no, it doesn't work like that. Those are things She commands you to do, so there's no amusement or tricksiness in them."

"I hate you and your Lady!" And I hated Arakante. If Firousi had run, or tried to come closer to me—but she didn't. She remained still as a statue herself. I wanted to hurt someone, something, but I'd learned long ago to leash that beast. Firousi was too wise to strain its tether again.

Firousi said softly, "I'm sorry. I never meant to be obscure. It's how I myself was taught. I did not always like it, but I know it

works, even when the pupil is unwilling."

"So I wasn't the first victim, I mean *student*."

She shook her head. "Layla, I was the unwilling one. The High Priestess of Laughter doesn't get to do much laughing herself, even in times of peace. After the barbarians conquered, we had to try to keep the Lady of Laughter's ways even though there was little cause for laughter. We also had to try to gather Her statue together again. I was not fond of travel or intrigue; I was the only one with power enough to do the job, that's all." She rose to her feet. "Do you want me to send a maid up with some hot water?"

She hadn't wanted the job. She looked as if she enjoyed running things, but why would she lie about that? It might explain some of those moods.

Oh, she'd asked about water. "They're probably awake by now, aren't they? Yes, thank you. Firousi, I...I'm sorry I lost my temper, but tonight's the first time I've gone thieving since I came here. Why is the link still so strong? And does this mean I'll never be able to go back to my old life?" Granted, it had been a lot less fun tonight than I remembered.

Firousi smiled. "Could you have, anyway?" She left without answering my other question.

22

"She's determined to leave in the spring."

Arakante looked up from the Issrandarian pre-Conquest epic he'd been reading. Issrandar had great wizards once. Where had their knowledge gone? The epics were maddeningly vague on details.

"What? And don't sigh at me, Firousi. I was attempting to concentrate on my studies." Of all people, Firousi ought to know that one couldn't necessarily leap back into the daily world.

Firousi seemed to think so too; she didn't apologize, but she didn't sigh either. "Layla has determined that she will leave when the spring caravans arrive, whether or not we've broken her link with Kossinli and whether or not we've found the heart."

She and Arakante stared at each other in silence. Arakante laid a ribbon on his scroll to mark where he'd stopped and removed the weights that held the parchment flat.

"What's left to try?" He'd tried by water and by flame, both several times.

Firousi did sigh this time. "I hope you can think of something. I can't even tell whether Kossinli doesn't know, or can't or won't tell me. Surely She would if She could." She didn't sound sure. "It doesn't matter, does it? I'd hoped as Layla got farther in her studies that Kossinli'd speak more clearly to her, but that hasn't happened."

Arakante was almost glad of that. Firousi would do whatever she must to recreate her goddess' statue, but she

wouldn't enjoy getting communications from her Lady through the mouth of a thief who'd reject that divine favor if she could. He wouldn't enjoy sharing a house with the two of them, either. It crossed his mind that for a man no longer married, he had a great many domestic problems. He put that thought from him as useless and irrelevant.

"I've one thing left that I could try," he said.

"Not the blood—"

"I'm not a fool, Firousi. I know better than to use that method for your Lady of Mirth. It isn't one I use often or eagerly in any case."

Firousi murmured what might have been an apology.

"No, what I mean to do is clean enough. I'll try a map-seeking. It isn't always dependable, and it is going to be a lot of work for all three of us, but it may give us some hint. Can you explain to Layla that it isn't black magic?"

"Surely, if she seems alarmed. She may not; I'm still surprised at what bothers her and what doesn't. She seems to have lived her whole life without ever considering what she does believe."

Arakante smiled. "Most people don't, you know. We're the odd ones, you and I."

There was a silence in the room. Neither cousin needed to mention those who were missing, and neither cared to mention the sometimes-wish that they were not cousins. Tzakende was lax about many things, but not the kinship laws.

Then, "Well, I suppose I'd best find Layla," said Firousi. "If you propose to do this now?"

"Yes, if we may use your solar? Ideally I'd do this out of doors, but not at this time of year!"

Firousi laughed and agreed.

The sun was touching the towers of the Western Gate before Layla was found. The doorkeeper sent the courtyard sweeper running to find either Arakante or Firousi; when he returned with both, Layla retreated until there was no one between her and the door. Imchi put himself between her and everyone else; Arakante could see the fringe of Firousi's shawl quiver with smothered laughter.

"What's wrong?" Layla looked at Arakante and Firousi, but Arakante saw the quick sideways glances she gave at the gate.

"Leave it," he said when the doorkeeper went to shut it. "Nothing's wrong, Layla," he continued. "We do need your help, though, and no one knew you'd gone out."

She moved away from the gate. "My poor abilities are always at your service."

Arakante repressed a sigh. If the doorkeeper listened any harder he'd flap his ears in truth, and a boy who'd come forward to lead Imchi to the stable was making a great production of coaxing him slowly away. "Your talents grace and inspire our efforts," he replied with equal formality. He added the slight turn of wrist with which a polite host invites a guest to precede him. Layla made an equally elegant bow of assent—where had she learned that?—and strolled into the house. Arakante nodded to the doorkeeper to shut the gate. Firousi followed Arakante into the house in a ripple of pleats and fringes, laughing openly now. To Arakante's relief, Layla ignored her.

Only after honeyed rose-hip tea and sweet biscuits had been brought, and door shut behind the slowly-departing servant, did Arakante explain what was needed.

"You're going to make a map?" Layla sounded more puzzled than shocked.

It took longer than he would have thought possible, and was even vaguer than he'd feared. There were parts of the city that none of them knew well; he hoped that the heart wasn't in the tanneries. Layla knew a surprisingly large area, but only in terms of how long it took to get from one place to another. Firousi knew some places in exquisite detail, with areas between them left almost totally blank.

For days they walked out as far and as long as the weather

would allow, and mapped as long as Arakante's eyes would focus. It was Firousi who finally rebelled.

"Ari, I hope that map is finished, because I certainly am. My feet ache all the time, and my friends are ready to call in a Healer for me whether I wish it or no."

"Lady Mirrim's convinced it's my fault," added Layla.

"It needs to be as precise as we can make it," Arakante objected. "Look, there are still places where we don't have any streets at all. For the scrying to work, it has to have something to work from." Why was it so hard to explain? Any child knew that like called to like.

"Ari, we can't map every street in the city! If it points to a blank spot, then we can go and explore that place."

He shook his head. "I can't See clearly by wood, water or fire. Now you want me to use this half-finished tool to try to find my way past the barriers someone's set up. Whoever it was is sophisticated and strong."

Firousi looked at him straight: he could hear the unspoken thought, the nerve of the man, to lecture her on affinities as if she were some ignorant girl! Firousi leaned forward. "I want to do something this year! Before she leaves," she waved one hand at Layla, "And my Lady is angrier than ever, or weaker. Before I have to begin yet again trying to restore Her. Do you think laughter just happens? Nothing's free, Arakante."

Layla gave her a strange look, but spoke to Arakante. "It took over a year for them to map Nahouendar. I will be gone before then."

"Out, both of you. Leave me in peace until dusk. We'll try then." And much good may we have from it, Arakante thought. Ah well, Kossinli notoriously worked by contraries.

23

*W*ho on earth counts the number of steps it takes to get from here to there? What does it matter how far it is from here to the singing-house or the bakery? What matters is how long it takes, and that question isn't answered by a line on a map. Is the street well-laid cobbles, or a mud track? Is it crowded with pilgrims and sellers of roasted nuts, or swept clean by the devotees of order? By the time we were done puzzling out our map, I had completely lost my fear of the things.

So many sheets of parchment, scattered across the floor! Arakante'd reused old ones for our first attempts, but it still made me wince to see that much money flung around. He'd refused to use wax tablets, though, and after a moment's thought I understood. Melt the map, and what happens to the original?

Maybe that was what happened to Nahouendar. My father and brothers and their friends all said that the walls could never have fallen so quickly without sorcery. Woe to Nahouendar and its prince, that he'd let foreigners talk him into mapping it. They said it would let him rule and order it more easily. Well, it certainly let someone do so.

The map looked nothing like a town to me. It was just a tangle of lines like a skein of silks that a cat had found. Arakante and Firousi both assured me that it was a good map. I think that may be what Firousi calls a contradiction in terms.

I'd given up protesting against making it. It made a weird sort of sense when I thought about it. Having a picture to look at

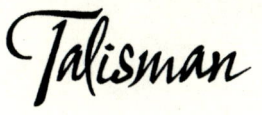

might help Arakante to See.

At dusk, we three came to Firousi's solar. Firousi handed Arakante a silver chain, and a silver needle. I brought the ruby, dark as blood, that I'd stolen in the town below. "Will these do?"

Arakante smiled and nodded. "Oh yes. Yes, indeed." He took the silver needle and sang over it while he threaded the fine chain through its eye. The chant shifted its pattern to one that barely changed pitch at all. He held the ruby and silver cradled in one hand, with the other hand arched protectively over them.

Arakante lifted the chain from his cupped hand, and the ruby clung to the needle's point. I'd seen tricks like that in every market big enough to have entertainers, but I could tell how those were done. Here was no scent of resin, no telltale dark glint that means there's a bit of iron in the chain and the setting. Here was what the bazaar performers had been imitating. His voice was beautiful and steady as ever, but I could see the faint shine of sweat on his forehead.

The needle wavered as he held it over the map.

"Shall I?" asked Firousi.

"Yes."

She sang in her turn, but I could understand her words. It was a praise-song to Kossinli, full of tricky rhythms and surprising skips in pitch. The needle steadied into a spiral path.

It covered the entire city, though! From the look on Arakante's face I didn't think I was missing some arcane significance. This was useless.

He made gestures over the map and needle both at once. The spiral reversed itself and then jerked aside. Arakante grinned. "No, continue," he murmured when Firousi stopped singing. He repeated the gestures, and each time the needle came near one part of the map it hopped away.

Ting! And Arakante was holding nothing but the fine silver chain. "It didn't hit either of you?" he asked.

Firousi sat silent with tears on her face. She'd been on the other side of the room! How could she have been hit? She shook her head at me when I rose and came closer. Very well, then. I turned and looked where I thought I'd heard something strike the wall.

"The needle's here by the window—the pieces of it are," I answered. It had flown so fast that it had chipped the plaster. "So's the ruby. That's a strong stone!" It was undamaged by its rough treatment. I watched carefully, but the two halves of the needle lay quiet as in a sewing kit while Arakante came and picked up both halves and the ruby.

"Odd. If our map is true, the heart is very near here."

"It is," said Firousi.

Arakante sat back in his chair with a thump. We both stared at her. I was ready to strangle her with her own gold-fringed scarf. If she'd known that all along and let us stew over the scrying, I would strangle her.

"Had I known earlier, I would have spoken earlier," Firousi said. She smiled. "Kossinli spoke to me just now. She spoke to me clearly again!"

Arakante brought her a cup of tea from the brazier's pot; she drank it in one gulp. "I'll tell you now that I still don't know exactly where it is, only that it's near here. The map was needed, Arakante. Someone had to put strength into keeping you from scrying out the heart, and that meant that Kossinli could elude the..." she paused, searching for words, "I don't quite know. Something binds Her, something almost silences Her, but She's getting stronger."

Gods, but I wanted to find that heart! My leavetaking in the spring would be easier, my journeys afterwards so much simpler. Besides, though I'd no intention of telling Firousi or Arakante so, I'd come to like this tricksy goddess.

"Well, did Kossinli manage to tell you how close is close? I mean, a goddess might have different ideas about that than we do."

Firousi smiled her most infuriating half-smile. "How far

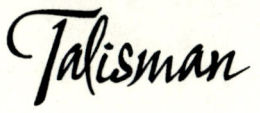

can it be and still be within the walls?"

Arakante added, "It's within our quarter, or why else did the needle swerve from it so?" He sighed. "It flinched from such a large area, though! Layla, I'm sorry; your task is still very hard, but we've learned a little more."

He leaned back in his chair, and I didn't think it was the waning light that pulled all the copper from that bronze skin of his. This time I poured him a cup of the tea, wishing that there were something stronger nearby. Even so, Arakante looked a little less gray after drinking it.

"If it were any stronger, you'd have to carve chunks out of it," he said as he set the cup back down. I decided not to mention that I hadn't actually spoken.

24

*M*y task was still hard, Arakante had said. So far as I could see, my task was still impossible. What I had told Firousi before I got lured into this project was still true. Did Firousi think she'd changed me so completely that I couldn't go back? I went out into the fogs of Tzakende and stole from two more houses, each far from the others, just to prove that I could. How could I be more closely bound to Kossinli than I was?

After my first clumsy attempt, I needed proof. In spite of all that dancing, I'd grown slow. My left shoulder ached for a week afterwards. The tree branch I used to reach the first roof was slippery with half-frozen rain. Why hadn't I foreseen that? Yes, and why hadn't I heard the slave coming upstairs to find something for her mistress? She took long enough about it! I had to crouch clinging underneath a window ledge for so long that my toes were completely numb. Was it the wind or Kossinli that made the sound that startled her into going back downstairs?

Fortunately, the second try went more smoothly. My only peril was an owl that caught its mouse about a handsbreadth from me as I slithered out an attic window. In both houses I took only coin, lovely anonymous easily-carried coin. There was just about enough for dinner at the Singing Shepherd and a few coins for the singers. Even Tzakendi aren't foolish enough to leave really large piles of money lying around.

I heard what were probably some excellent satires at the Singing Shepherd (I still couldn't follow Tzakendi politics, mixed

as they were with magic) but no mention of gems or strange
pendants. Finally I stumbled home. If there'd been any sun it
would have been dawn.

I wasn't the only one coming home as the cook-fires were
lit for the day. There in the doorway stood another female figure,
taller than most, in a rain-soaked hooded street-caftan. Firousi
looked over her shoulder and laughed softly.

I followed her into the house, leaving the gatekeeper
muttering fiercely behind us. She hung the dripping cloak on one
of the stands by the door. I opened my mouth to say—what?

"Nay, Layla, do I ask where you've been?" Firousi purred.

"I didn't ask," I said quietly. She was right. I headed for
the kitchen to feed the one hunger I could satisfy just then. There
I surprised two very athletic scullions and fled upstairs to my bed.
My cold, single bed. Why was I the only one to lie alone? The
Gods all knew, I'd been plagued enough with lustful men when I
didn't want them!

The clouds were nearly white when I woke; I breakfasted
alone also, on boiled-down tea and too-crusty rolls. In this
wealthy house we never went hungry. Even the servants, by the
look of them, got enough food. Even Imchi! If this was what
we were eating, though, I thought I knew why Tzakende refused
most foreigners lodging over the winter. It had nothing to do
with mysticism.

Speaking of mystics, where was Arakante? Even if he
wouldn't be my lover, maybe he'd be my way out of here.

I went up to the public area of his rooms, but the only
creature there was his cat. It was fishing delicately at the latch of
the shutter, the tip of its tail quivering. Well, why shouldn't one of
us be happy? I opened the shutters for it. It sneezed as a raindrop
landed on its nose and meowed at me accusingly. "It isn't my
fault!" The cat gave me one more dirty look and retreated to
Arakante's desk.

There was a step in the hall outside and Arakante came in.

That was courteous of him, to make a noise.

"Hello, Layla." That was all. No questions about my being in his rooms, and no expression of pleasure either. Couldn't I even get him to smile?

"Hello." Brilliant. "Have you found out anything more about the heart?" Even more brilliant, remind the man of his failure. What else could I ask, whether he gave houseguests a discount on fortune-telling?

"Nothing beyond what we discovered the other night. If I learn more, trust me, I won't keep it to myself!"

He looked puzzled. Damn damn damn, I should've paid more attention to women's gossip. Those honorable married ladies in Charransar had certainly talked enough of the arts of seduction at the weddings and welcoming ceremonies for the babies that followed, especially when the baby was a large and healthy seven-months child. All I could remember was the way they'd made fun of those who failed to win a lover.

He would be a lover worth the winning, I thought. I wasn't likely to get a better chance than this. One more try, then I really would put the idea from my mind. "Sorry for the silly question. I keep being afraid it'll turn out to be on one of the Pearl Islands or something." And though I'd no intention of going on a sea voyage, I'd had no intention of studying priestess-lore either.

I sat down on a nice wide bench. "So, what do we do now?" I knew what I'd like to do, but getting there was going to be a challenge. Arakante looked mildly uncomfortable and did not come sit beside me. I began to have some small sympathy for a few of the men who'd tried to get me into bed.

He talked in a vague way of how my own efforts might turn up something and gave even vaguer hints as to how he could pursue more specific knowledge. Suddenly I thought I understood.

"Arakante, do you have to save all your energies for this kind of Seeing?"

He blushed, bronze turning to copper. "Layla! No, it isn't

that. It's just that—as I explained—"

"You were married once, you said. I'm sorry, I just don't understand. You don't seem to dislike me."

I got up; he backed away. I sat back down demurely. He pushed his hair back from his forehead, not that it stayed.

He sighed determinedly. "My wife is a mage herself, well able to look after her own interests. Magic does have this much to do with it: all magicians, those of us who work within the protections that balance gives, accept some limitations. I swore never to force a woman unwilling," he raised his pointing finger as I drew breath to speak, and I kept silence. "Or to take anyone living as a dependent under my roof. Yes, even the servants. It is too easy for a trained mage to turn someone's thoughts so that, unknowing, they do what they wouldn't do if left alone."

I rose and came over to him, putting an oh-so-gentle hand on his shoulder. "Arakante, I'm not unwilling! How direct must I be? As for living as your dependent, I'm Firousi's dependent, if I'm anyone's. I'm not helpless here. I know a few places now where I could live unremarked if I chose to." Well, I was pretty sure of that.

Arakante stared at me, stone-faced. "Gods, Layla, not you too!"

Me, too? Was I just one of many pests, then?

"Are you after the Love Secrets of the Wizards? There aren't any, not if the wizard has any scruples about using his magic rightly."

What was it going to take? I could hardly get him drunk at this hour of the day. Besides, that's as likely to unman as to provoke. "That isn't it. Even if you don't want me, you don't have to be insulting. Just help me get the stupid heart and I'll go away; we'll both be happier."

"Ah, Layla..." At least he sounded sad. That was better than embarrassed.

I put my head a little to one side and smiled. He wasn't so

much taller than I that I could gaze adoringly up at him, and that might very well make him laugh if I did.

"It might, indeed," he said.

"Oh. Oh, forget I spoke! Forget my thoughts, even more! You won't have sex with me, but you'll come into my mind any time you chose? Where's the honor in that, my sweet Lord?"

He glared at me in silence. Suddenly he seized my arm with most unloving force and pulled me towards the door. "I wasn't in your mind! You shout, Layla, before all the gods, I can hardly keep your thoughts from my mind! I don't invade peoples' minds, that's disgusting and dishonorable."

"Don't haul at me that way! I'm leaving, I'm perfectly, absolutely delighted to be leaving. I only wish I was leaving your entire city."

And so it would have ended, but for a wrinkle in the topmost of his fine upland rugs. Truly, I did not mean to crash into him when I tripped. He nearly fell himself, but he's stronger than he looks. I was back on my own two feet, and he was several feet away from me, before I was well aware of what was happening. He gave me a dagger-glare.

"You wish me to be your path out of Tzakende? Then stop trying to seduce me. Have you never wondered why some unfortunate wizard didn't foresee his own danger? We can't. And if I lie with you, Layla, if we become one flesh, I can't see for you either." He grimaced. "Find someone else, Layla."

"I'm a thief, not a whore! I'll warrant I sleep alone more than most fine ladies do—for one thing, it isn't safe to fall asleep after bedding most of the men I meet." I'd had to learn that one the hard way—twice, more shame to me. The second time I'd been lucky not to lose my life as well as my money. "I don't much like the ones that run away as soon as—" I went on, then saw the smile flicker across his face.

"You've done it again, haven't you?" I was at the door when his voice stopped me.

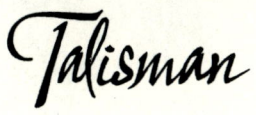

"Layla, I meant no insult. I've just trusted you with more than my body. Not many know for certain that our power is limited in that way."

"I know how to keep quiet," I assured him. Then, very quietly, I left his rooms.

The next three days were a torment. Arakante spent most of his time alone in his study, putting off all but a few clients. I know, from an argument I overheard, that he refused to do any spell-castings even for them. Then he sent me a message that while the stars were propitious he'd seek again for Kossinli's heart. He knew how much I wanted to be free of all that.

Yes, Kossinli, I know. Time after time I'd wished I could find a man with a conscience.

25

*L*ittle of the winter light still fell into the narrow courtyard, and almost none into Arakante's seeing-room. The window's well-oiled parchment mirrored the two men who sat by the lamp's flames. Arakante shifted his chair to put their flickering behind him. He could do nothing about the smell of burning that filled the tightly-closed room. Scented oils were worse.

Prahin leaned forward, his hands propped against each other, fingertips to fingertips. "Can you see no more than this, Lord Arakante? Only that I must be more watchful than ever this spring? I had known that already, with my wife so near her time. There must be nothing to startle or alarm her."

Arakante shook his head, and regretted it instantly as the pain behind his right eye went from a dull ache to a stab so sharp that he saw a flash of light.

It had been a long day. Not one vision had come easily or clearly, and he knew why. Briefly, he wondered if he had been a fool to refuse Layla. He'd at least have had the pleasure before the pain.

"My Lord, I assure you that I've done what I can. The danger does not involve your wife; everything I see for her is happy. I did warn you that priests, especially powerful ones, are often difficult to scry for."

Prahin's thin mouth twitched into a smile. "Lord Arakante, I know you never descend to flattery, or I would suspect you of it! I suppose it's something to know where the threat does not lie."

Arakante smiled in return. "And to know that your wife is

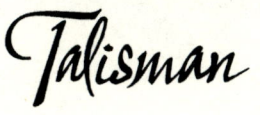

safe. I would that I could do more for you, my Lord; you always pose such interesting questions." Interesting indeed, when one of the chief priests of the unofficial Imperial religion came calling about some serious but unspecified threat to his plans for the new year. Even more interesting when he let fall some of what those plans were. Arakante would never have expected anyone to link the two emerald thefts, separated by time and distance as well as by the type of place from which they were taken. It was lucky that Prahin and his fellow priests assumed that the thief had left when the city closed to almost all foreigners. Lucky, too, that he believed the thief to be a man!

"I know I can always rely on your expertise, and your discretion," Prahin replied.

Arakante murmured the proper reassurances, and his client left. "I will see no one else this afternoon," Arakante instructed his doorkeeper. "And tell Cook to send up some goatberry tisane."

There were exercises that would clear those blinding headaches, of course. A little of the right tea, and awhile alone in quiet to charm the blood to calmness, and he could go on answering questions for clients. His remedies would work that afternoon as they always had.

However, before he answered any more of other people's questions he had a question to answer for himself. His discretion was more than stock-in-trade; it was one of the chief tenets of his training. Never, never might he reveal to one person what he had seen in a scrying for another, or what that other had confided as part of the question.

What was he to do with the knowledge that the search for the emerald thief of Charransar had spread to Tzakende?

He had assured Layla that Prahin's visits had nothing to do with her, and in a sense he was still convinced of that. Prahin had too little imagination to guess that the thief might be a woman; that much was clear from what little he'd said about the search for the thief. He came to inquire of his future as some people visited a healer from time to time, even when their general health was good.

Could he somehow warn Layla without revealing how he knew that she was in danger? She still had a certain awe of his skill at entering the other world. He hoped she still felt some of that awe now, after he'd told her why he had to refuse her.

Maybe he could be essentially true both to her and to his other promises. She already kept out of sight whenever she knew that Lord Prahin would be around. If he could just make sure she understood how important that was without letting her know any of the details, it would at least be a lesser betrayal.

Yes, and so perhaps there would be only a lesser penalty. There had been few absolute prohibitions in his training. Some things were considered ill-advised, like necromancy, but even that was allowable at great need. One simply needed to be extremely careful.

Older students had told him that the visions would stop if he revealed one person's fortune to another. Later, he realized their teachers had allowed that false rumor to live as a way of keeping some vain young fool from bringing them all into scandal, and possible danger, by boasting. The real danger was that the visions would continue, growing stronger and less controllable.

Yet not to warn Layla would be to betray her, and possibly Firousi as well. Also—a selfish thought, this, but he'd never claimed to be Purified—he'd no wish to attract Kossinli's wrath.

"Shit," he muttered.

If the servant who brought the tea heard that, he gave no sign. Arakante sat drinking his tea, grimacing at the bitter taste, and forcing his thoughts into the familiar sequence of meditation. Perhaps he'd be able to see a way out when the pain was gone.

The pounding in his ears quieted as it always did. He heard the door open before the servant spoke. "Does my lord wish us to wait dinner, or does he wish to dine in his room?"

So late as that! "No, thank you. Run tell the rest to begin without me; I'll join them soon."

"Y-yes, my lord." The boy sounded dubious. He was new; Firousi must have decided they could afford to replace that boy who'd run away. At least that one had run before anyone had spent much time training him in the etiquette of a wizard's house.

"Go, say as I told you! However it's done in other houses, no one goes hungry here for the master's absent mindedness." The boy bowed, grinning behind his hand, and ran out.

The hall lamps danced in front of their silvered reflectors as Arakante walked through the twisting hallways. Here in the chill between-rooms, he could feel the faint warmth of each flame. His winter slippers slapped the age-polished stones as he picked up his pace. He would have been willing enough to linger and delay this meal.

There was no way to avoid betrayal. He'd told Layla to stop worrying, and she might actually believe him. She'd as good as said that she thought most Seers were frauds, but she did believe him. He'd have to warn Firousi also. Was there any point at all in trying to conceal from them just how he'd come by his knowledge?

Did it count, Arakante wondered, to make an effort you knew would not succeed?

No, there was no way he could warn Layla without betraying all his knowledge and the teachers from whom he'd learned it. She was discreet enough already, and Prahin visited seldom enough that the danger should be slight. He would keep silent and be watchful.

A whiff of garlic and Layla's beloved chilis told him that chickpeas were a large part of the menu again. Firousi had decreed that anything that added interest to chickpeas was a benefit, no matter how outlandish Cook thought it; Cook limited himself to grumbling, and beating any kitchen boy who neglected the pot-scouring afterwards.

Recklessly, Arakante took a large helping of the dish. Maybe its fire would give him strength! "Please excuse my lateness," he said to both the women. "My last client's visit was difficult."

Both women murmured polite acceptance.

Layla stared at him as she ate, but for once he could not tell what she was thinking. Neither Layla nor Firousi gave any sign that she noticed his silence. It was good to be allowed to eat his meal in peace, and yet—but that was childish, to wish that one of them would notice that he was not his usual entertaining self.

Layla began recounting, with vivid imitations, last nights's satiric singer at the Chorus of Frogs singing-house. Considering her limited singing ability, the imitations were surprisingly good. It seemed that Lissandra was still delaying going to serve the Huntress.

Layla fell silent. Firousi recounted how the dignified Lady Mirrim had roared with laughter on finding her niece standing on one leg to appreciate the Divine Balance. The tale merited more laughter than it received.

Silence settled again over the table. Arakante watched the two women, trying to think how to begin what he had to say. It was a relief and an aggravation when Layla spoke first. "This living as an honest woman is dulling my edge. I'm going to have to practice again before I try to steal any other bits and pieces of your Laughing Lady."

"Layla, no. Not now, not for all the rubies between the two seas." He hadn't meant to say that, and he couldn't blame his lapse on the returning headache. If Layla didn't leave soon, he'd have no control left. He was beginning to understand the ascetics who avoided women altogether. Why couldn't Firousi get Kossinli to tell her where the heart was?

Layla and Firousi both stared at him. Firousi set down her goblet. "Oh? And why not now?"

His control-breath might sound like a sigh, at least to Layla. "Because the gates are still shut to all except a few cattle-herders whose families have lived just outside them since the waters receded. Because if anything much goes missing, it will be

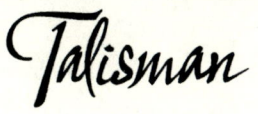

easiest to blame one of the few outsiders known to be here. The fact that it's true will make it harder for me to misdirect attention."

"Are you claiming that none of the Tzakendi rob?" Layla laughed. "My friend, no place is free of thieves! One of the nimblest thieves I ever knew was a boy sold young to a monastery of the Thinkers. The best part, he told me, was that no one ever dared report the thefts of trivial worldly baubles that they weren't supposed to have."

Firousi laughed. "Yes, I can see their difficulty. Still, Layla, perhaps it would be better not to steal anything just now. We may not be free of thieves, but few steal in the winter unless they're actually starving."

Layla raised one eyebrow. "You know a lot about it, for an honest woman."

"We honest women take a deep interest in people who might walk off with what's ours."

"What of the ruby I stole? That turned out to be useful, didn't it? And none of us got into trouble for it. Kossinli was happy about it, you said so yourself, Firousi."

"That was then." Firousi sat straight and still as a statue herself; Layla had turned a little from the table, one hand out of sight beneath it. Both women stole quick sideways glances at Arakante. Neither looked friendly. "And it was not the stealing that amused her," Firousi added.

Arakante seriously considered pleading the return of his headache and fleeing. Instead, he let the argument flow around him. Maybe Firousi would convince Layla, or at least wear her down. Gods have pity, he thought. I made that decision once already. It was hard enough the first time.

Layla's sharp-edged voice cut through his thoughts. "What are you going to do, my Lady Firousi? Lock me up? I doubt Kossinli would approve."

"Even the Great Ones bow to necessity, Layla. If She needs you kept safe—"

Layla rose then. She was out of the room before either Arakante or Firousi could react; the next thing they heard was the doorkeeper's agitated voice, followed by the slam of the door. She had vanished by the time they reached the courtyard.

"Were you trying to make her leave?" Arakante turned and strode back into the house. One house slipper, never designed for such vigorous use, flew off and tangled in Firousi's skirts. "Tell your Goddess of Mirth to stay out of this," he added.

The doorkeeper retreated into his cubbyhole and pulled the latticed windscreen discreetly across its door.

Firousi handed him his slipper. Grimacing, he wiggled his toes back into it.

"She has nothing to do with your clumsiness. Curse you, Arakante, that mud won't come out of silk!" Then, "Never mind the silk. Ari, I've no idea where she'll go. Can you Find her, or is your headache too bad?"

"I can try." Arakante's soggy slippers made faint squishing noises as he and Firousi traveled the stairs and corridors to his study. So, she'd noticed his abstraction after all.

Wooden poles scraped on tiles as Firousi set up the heavy silk screen to block any drafts that made it past the shutters. Even so, the water shimmered in the silver bowl as Arakante stared into it. Layla. An image half-formed, then dissolved in ripples. The surface stilled, but though he sat with as still a mind as he could manage, the image did not return. He raised his eyes to Firousi. "Have you something of hers, something she wears often?"

"I'll find something," Firousi said. Arakante knew that she knew that this was student-level work; no mage of his experience should need a talisman to find someone who was not a mage, and could not be very far away. Should, would, could. Never mind.

As he waited, Arakante did the breathing exercises for calm and concentration. It seemed long until he heard the rustle of Firousi's skirts, but the oil in the lamp had barely sunk when she handed him an indigo wool scarf.

"She wears it often, even in the house."

Holding the scarf, he tried again. Nothing came but the points of light that meant he was trying too hard. He was acutely aware of Firousi watching him. Damn it, he wanted to shout, why did you have to threaten her? Have you no sense at all of what she's like? You couldn't have chosen a worse time. He forced himself to stay silent.

"I'm going to ask Kossinli to help us find her," Firousi said quietly. "She won't be best-pleased with me just now, but I think She'll do it. She's fond of that little thief."

"Thank you. Maybe you can get the job done."

"Oh, Ari—I don't blame you." She touched his arm lightly. Then she was gone; he could hear her rapid steps on the stairs to her rooms.

Arakante leaned over the bowl again. This time the image formed, and though it warped when a strong gust forced its way past shutters and screen alike, it held together.

A small figure slid from shadow to shadow, working its way along the side of the hills of Upper Tzakende. It stopped and started with no pattern that he could see, but the direction was always much the same. She was going to rob someone. He knew whose house lay in that direction.

Firousi was tight-lipped when she returned, smelling faintly of sandalwood. "I'm not sure how much help the Mirthful One will be. She's amused, all right, but I'd almost rather She weren't. I'm coming with you. Don't argue with me, Ari! I'm going to have to apologize."

"She'll not let you get close enough to do it," Arakante predicted. "Stay here, Firousi. Please."

"Do you See this, or guess it?"

"Come then, if you must! I haven't time to argue." He took the scarf with him.

A wind full of half-frozen rain played tag with them all along the way. On Scarfsellers Bridge a gust pulled Layla's scarf out of Arakante's hand; Firousi grabbed it in midair. She thrust it back at him without a word. Layla was not in either of the two singing-houses they'd heard her mention. They went on, choosing their turns by the flip of a medal of Kossinli.

Finally they stood where two narrow alleys joined the cart road that led to the northern gate. They were only a short walk from Lord Prahin's house, but Arakante felt certain that they wouldn't find Layla there.

"We've passed her," Arakante said, and coughed. "All she has to do to elude us is to keep moving. I never cared to study the arts of compulsion, so I can't force her to wait while I find her."

Firousi peeled her wet skirts away from her legs. "We're never going to catch her if she doesn't want us to," she pointed out. "She's a thief. Arakante, why's it so important to find her tonight? Why are we standing out here risking consumption?"

"I asked you to stay home." He was not going to go through that explanation twice.

"I'm the one that sent her screaming into the night," Firousi answered. It might have been the wind and rain that made her voice so hoarse.

"Come, let's start back," said Arakante. "Layla's probably found somewhere warm and dry to wait out the weather. I hope so. And I hope she's had the sense not to steal in this neighborhood."

"We're not so near to home as all that," Firousi said as she turned to go.

"No, but—oh, please Firousi! Let it wait until we're out of the weather."

"Then don't drop mysterious hints."

The argument continued as they picked their way over increasingly slippery streets, stubbing half-frozen toes on lumps of unidentified, ice-hardened debris. Being able to see even in this dim light was slight help to Arakante. He did manage to keep Firousi from stumbling over a series of dark lumps encrusted in ice.

"Thank you," she muttered.

"Just let her be when she does come back," Arakante said.

"Have no fear! And you do the same," Firousi snapped.

The street-walls gave some support against the sideways slope of the street itself. Unfortunately, they also gave cover to the boy who stepped nimbly out of an alley. Firousi flinched aside, but not quickly enough.

Arakante heard Firousi swear; she sounded more angry than hurt. He saved his own breath for summoning fire. A globe of flame appeared and grew to light the street; he plucked a smaller ball of fire from it, turned to throw it—and threw it to the ground, where it hissed its way through ice and mud to sputter in its crater.

Layla stood motionless in the flaring light, one hand extended towards Firousi. Firousi reached out and took her necklace from it.

"She/I was giving it back," said both women in near-unison.

"If I'd known who it was I wouldn't have thrown fire to begin with," Arakante snapped.

"I thought you would know," Layla replied.

He was glad of the darkness that hid them from each other again. He should have known. Even so, she had no right to sound so disappointed.

"And I suppose you always think it through carefully before you draw steel?"

The rain had dwindled to a mist; he could hear her gasp. There were those who claimed that love sapped a wizard's powers; he was beginning to be sure that it weakened his wits.

Firousi's voice, shaky with cold, cut into his mood. "Really, Layla, we dealt with the necessity of matching jest and setting harmoniously weeks ago."

"A jest? Believe me, Lady Teacher, I didn't run out into this weather as a jest," said Layla.

"Nor did I think she was jesting," added Arakante. "If she

was, she's earned the wrath of a wizard."

"Not at the beginning, but surely that flourish at the end was a jest? Had you been following us for long?"

"No, not long," Layla replied.

Firousi sneezed. "My friends, might we discuss all this someplace warmer? If I spoke amiss, I'm sorry for it." She turned, paused to free her feet from her trailing skirts again, and muttered, "Had I known I was going for a walk in the spring rain, I'd have worn less elegant robes."

The laughter that followed was more than the jest deserved. No one spoke during their slog home except to warn of ice-slick puddles. The storm had blown out most of the lanterns people normally kept lit before their gates. Once they passed a woman carrying a midwife's satchel, but otherwise Tzakende slept.

The gatekeeper had their gates open when they were still three houses away. Firousi's maid Roshana had set clothes warming by the brazier in her room, and seen to it that the same was done for Arakante and Layla.

The mulled wine had been ready so long that it had cooked down into a concentrated slurry of spices and honey; Firousi poured a generous measure of Tzakendi Rain into each cup. She drank her own down in three swallows, grimacing slightly.

"Layla, I'm sorry," she said.

Layla stared at her warily.

"No, I mean it. I had no right to order you to stay within doors."

"And no right at all to threaten to keep me here," Layla replied.

Arakante said nothing. Being a wizard, he could disappear simply by not moving. It worked especially well when no one was paying much attention in the first place.

"No," Firousi said. "No right at all."

26

"Well, I did steal something, and we're all three alive and well. Reasonably well," I added as Firousi sneezed.

"Layla, stealing from us and then giving it back doesn't count as far as the city authorities are concerned," she said as soon as she could speak. I had to admit that she was right. Still, the look on their faces when they realized who it was that stole Firousi's necklace! I was a little disappointed at how easy it was to fool them. To be fair, they weren't used to this sort of adventure.

Neither was I anymore. The warmed clothes sat well on sore cold muscles; the mulled wine eased aches, especially after Firousi added that Tzakendi Rain.

I should have known better than to try that sort of jest with a wizard. Of course, most wizards make damn sure that you know how awesome they are every minute that they're around. Arakante just went around quietly in house slippers, letting other people do most of the talking. How could I remember that he was dangerous when he ran from my advances like a gently-raised maiden? Since that day when we'd nearly made love on the rugs, he'd taken good care that he and I were never alone.

He certainly didn't look dangerous at the moment; in fact, he looked as if he might be sickening with something. Could wizards catch cold?

"Layla," he said. I waited. "Layla, I'm relieved that you've done your theft and no harm was done. But please, now that you have done that, stay out of sight. Do it just for a little while, until the gates open."

"The gates are open now," I pointed out, and for once I was not being a smart-mouthed brat. I was truly puzzled. The gates opened most days, unless the weather was horrible. Charcoal sellers came in regularly, and ice-fishers with their catch. Firousi was glaring at me again; the woman was going to wear out her face muscles and wind up blank-faced as a dzian addict.

Arakante sighed. "When foreigners are admitted again. We haven't long to wait now."

"Why, Arakante? What's wrong?" Let it stand to my credit that I kept my voice soft and melodious. Firousi must have noticed; she leaned forward and smiled.

"Layla, is it so awful here? I'll show you how to craft your tales of Charransar into finished form; some of them are nearly fine enough for a recital as they stand, and by the time the gates are open you'll be ready. I think you must have been Kossinli's all along!"

"I am mine, mine alone!" Was I supposed to be flattered at the notion that I'd been wandering around all my life, just waiting until this goddess needed me? Were those weary years of barren marriage some bizarre jest of Hers also? "And I will know why I'm suddenly the crazy auntie in the attic of this house."

"Yes, you will." That was Arakante, cutting in before Firousi could "help" again. "It isn't necessary for you to stay within doors all the time; in fact, it might be better if you didn't. Just—no thefts. No practice runs. Someone has linked the emerald theft in Charransar with Lissandra's loss."

Now the latch lifted! "I knew it. That damn client of yours is watching me, isn't he? What good will it do me to hole up here with him in and out? I told you something was wrong, and you laughed at me, poor simple swell-headed woman who saw ghosts in every windblown scarf! Where was your scrying, Lord Arakante?"

"I can't see everywhere at once, not magically any more than physically," he said.

Firousi touched my arm again. I twitched away, but she spoke anyway. "He's given you the warning now, and at some cost to himself."

I turned to Arakante, puzzled. He hesitated, and when he did speak it was to the wine-pot in the center of the table, not to Firousi or me.

"All who study with my teachers take an oath never to reveal to one person what we scried for another, or what any person told us who came to us for advice." His voice was dead flat.

"What will happen to you?" I half-rose from my seat, then sank back as he flinched away. Who could blame him? I'd nearly made him break a vow before, and now I'd done it. I hadn't meant it! He was Wise, didn't he understand that I hadn't meant to do it?

"I don't know," he admitted. "I've never heard of anyone breaking that particular oath. It may be nothing at all, since I didn't act out of fear or greed." He didn't sound too sure of that.

I felt for my knife.

"Layla, relax. You don't have to defend him," said Firousi.

No, I couldn't defend him from whatever enemies he'd made by warning me. I didn't believe there wouldn't be any.

"Thank you for the warning," I said. There was absolutely no way that I could ever balance the obligation he'd just put me under; I could at least thank him.

He shook his head. "It was necessary, Layla. I'd told you that you were safe. How could I let you go on thinking so when I discovered otherwise? I'll admit, I hoped you wouldn't guess whose questions told me that; you're discreet enough that it wouldn't have been necessary to tell you."

"Discreet! Yes, you can count on a sneak-thief to be discreet!"

Laughter eased us past the rest of dinner, what there was of it. Lentils and rice, a little pickled something-or-other; I could have been in Charransar during a lean week. It felt comforting, in a way.

Would that it had comforted Arakante. He said almost nothing for the rest of dinner. For once he evidently couldn't hear my thoughts. Either that, or he was ignoring what I was thinking of that might take his mind off his troubles. He left us soon and went silently to his rooms.

There was one thing I could do to try to help Arakante. Up in my room that night I lit the lamp, congratulating myself on having convinced Firousi and the servants that I slept better alone. It's true; the hardest part of the journey to Tzakende had been sharing sleeping-space with so many people. It's also convenient. I had been thinking of night-walking when I insisted on sleeping without attendants in the room. This night I was trying to steal ahead in my studies. I did wish I knew what gods Arakante prayed to, or would it be goddesses? A classical education is never wasted, my former husband's first wife had insisted; I remembered some of the old formal words.

I settled comfortably onto my bed, sitting on top of the blankets to avoid getting too comfortable. Then I began Firousi's meditation exercises. They were surprisingly like some of what I did to ready myself for a particularly challenging theft: relax, focus, breathe easily and smoothly, banish the thought that this might not work.

But it wasn't working. I stared at the lamp flame until I saw two of it, breathed until my throat went dry, and it wasn't working. One foot cramped.

Cursing, I rose and did the stretches I'd learned early in my thieving career. The foot uncramped; in spite of the chill of the room I felt warmer than I had on the bed. Maybe if I added the two exercises they'd work?

I moved slowly, trying different combinations. The shadows of the room grew, surrounding the lamp flame. It may be that Firousi could put words to the feeling that told me that things were changing; I can only say that I knew.

"Lady of Mirth," I said, "Lady of Laughter, I hope you can help me with a serious problem. Lady of Jests, please tell Arakante's deities that when he broke his oath it was for me. Ask

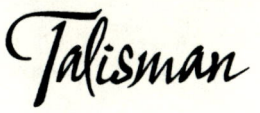

them, for me, to be kind to him."

That was as far as I was going to go. Damn him, it wasn't fair! Why should I have to take this chance? I'd been trying to get free of Kossinli for months, and here I was courting Her attention. Firousi had warned me before I even started studying that close ties between mortals and the Powers were dangerous, and I was already in plenty of trouble. Who knew what the Lady of Mirth would find amusing? How could Arakante put me under this heavy obligation?

The flame returned to normal size; the shadows were only the usual shadows of any room on a winter night. I was sorely tempted to give up, but as I turned to go back to bed I stepped on a thick piece of metal.

"I thought goddesses were supposed to be subtle," I muttered as I picked the heavy Charransar silver from between my toes. Did I need reminding of how this all had started? Was the coin to remind me of just who was in control? To tell me that Arakante hadn't even been consulted before he was dragged into this tangle? Well, neither had I. That was a Charransar coin, and he'd never been in Charransar. Or so I thought. Of course, that might not matter when dealing with a wizard. He hadn't really had to tell me as much as he did. He hadn't had to give me a reason for asking me to live strictly. It was his cursed sense of honor that pushed him into it.

Thieves do have honor, or at least some of us do, which is all you can say for any group of people. I do not rob my friends.

The exercises worked faster this time. The flame leaped, and I stood dazzled by it. A voice said softly, *Were you saving up wishes all this time, then? How thrifty! What I can, I will. Look now, my thief. You'll know what to do.* For the space of a breath, there was absolute silence.

Walls of scrolls towered around me. Each scroll had a ribbon binding it, and each ribbon had writing on it. They lay in heaps in long scalloped shelves. In my left hand, I held a golden dagger with a star sapphire set in the hilt. A soft rustling sound filled the air.

I'd know what to do, would I? Well, I hoped I wasn't supposed to kill anyone with that dagger. Whoever made it had forgotten the purpose of daggers. They're supposed to have at least one edge. This gorgeous toy might cut a scroll-ribbon, but not more than one.

Ah. Yes, I understood. I stepped silently to a gap in the scroll-wall and peered out. As I'd feared, there were many more like it. I couldn't see far, but the ones near me ran in neat straight lines for about a tall man's height, then met others that did the same, but at an angle. Against the far wall, I could see more scribes than I could count, all sitting cross-legged with their writing-boards across their knees. That damned rustling sound made it impossible to hear whether anyone was creeping up on me. Someone must pile up those scrolls. When would they come?

The rustling had changed to a fluttering noise that seemed to come from above. Above? I flinched back under the puny overhang of scrolls and peered up. A moment later, I was curled up on the floor, but not in fear. I was smothering my laughter with both hands, while over my head a bird flew past carrying a scroll. "A little bird told me," my mother would say, when I wondered how she knew some secret of mine.

"Thank you, Kossinli," I murmured.

Well, I couldn't sit here forever. Or maybe I could—I wasn't at all sure what the rules were here—but I didn't want to. I looked again at the dagger. Perhaps it would give me some sign of what direction to go? I tried turning in a circle, but the dagger remained as it was. I looked down at myself. Perhaps Kossinli had made me look like a scribe? Not that I could see.

The righthand direction being lucky, I turned that way. I'd gone halfway down that narrow passage when someone entered the other end. There was absolutely nowhere to hide. My legs wanted to run, but to where? Better hide the dagger in my sleeve.

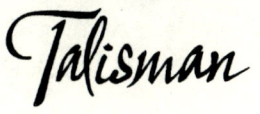

I walked on between the scrolls as if I had every right to be there and knew exactly where I was going.

The other woman reached out her hand to me. Oh Kossinli. She looked straight at me. "Excuse me, but do you know where the Aritran Archives are?"

"No, I'm sorry," I said as I kept walking. One of the hanging lamps flickered and went out; I made an annoyed sound and headed that direction.

Hum-ti-tum, just a scholar in the Otherworld. Don't mind me. How did scholars act, anyhow? I hadn't met many in my line of work, since they hardly ever have anything worth stealing. The dagger was making my arm sore, wedged in bare like that. I pulled the silly toy out and looked at it again. Here in the dimmer light I could see that the sapphire glowed faintly.

I think I walked miles down those rows of scrolls. The sapphire's glow waxed and waned. Now and then I saw another person, though mercifully not often; all the time the birds flew back and forth. I saw no sign of droppings, but then these were celestial birds.

Just as I had that brilliant insight, the star in the sapphire blazed into light. Now all I had to do was find one scroll in this stack. There are so many names that begin with the bird-in-flight!

By the time I found Arakante's name, I had renewed respect for the keepers of records. The dangling ribbons that bore his name were, of course, at the very top of a stack. The support poles looked up to my weight.

Yes, this was fun. Scramble up like a monkey and sit, clinging like a tailless monkey with my thighs, lean out almost too far for balance and hook the bundle with the tip of that silly dagger. Indeed. I stretched out as far as I could, and leaned a little farther yet, hooked the bundle and lost it twice, and finally knocked it to the floor. Oh well, it got the job done. I slithered down and landed with a disgraceful thump.

Now, should I take the whole thing? It was a small bundle

of separate leaves. Did each misdeed get recorded separately? Arakante must not have broken his vows very many times. Maybe it would be better to take just the one that I needed and put the rest back. They'd probably never notice that anything had been taken.

The tip of the dagger came in handy again, this time for prying apart the knot in the ribbon that bound them together. I tried to look only for some mention of telling, but I did notice that my name came up several times.

Ah, here it was. I read it again to be certain. Scrambling back up the pole with the re-tied bundle wasn't quite so much fun as it had been the first time. I wondered if Firousi or Arakante would have a premonition that the bath should be heated.

"Boy, what do you think you're doing?" A man stood just below me, scowling fiercely. He was tall and thin, and yes, I recognized him.

"Have I seen you here before? Surely you know it's forbidden to climb up like that; call an attendant if you can't reach something. Boy, come down from there at once!"

Not a chance. He'd know me if he got a better look at me. I inched higher on the pole.

"Don't be ridiculous! I'm not going to beat you, not unless you damage the scrolls with this nonsense. Now come down, boy, and I'll help you find your master. He'd no business bringing you here at all—it's a waste and a danger."

Gods, what else was I going to do but come down? There wasn't another support-pole near enough to do me any good. Unless the birds carried me away in their little beaks, I was doomed. I tried waving the scroll at the next one to fly by, but it ignored me. Maybe Lord Earrings wouldn't know that a grubby boy and the proper young woman he'd seen at Arakante's were the same person.

Very well. I slid down as fast as I could and let myself land hard. When Lord Earrings tried to help me to rise, I crumpled pitifully back to the ground.

"There now, you see why you're not supposed to climb up

those posts?"

I nodded humbly, looking at the floor.

"Well, where's your master?"

I pointed in the direction of the rows of scribes.

"Are you mute? I need more than hand-waving!"

That muteness seemed like a good idea. I made a strangled sound in the back of my throat. No point in giving him a voice to recognize too.

A hand seized my face and turned it up to him. Eerie cloud-colored eyes stared straight into mine. His eyes narrowed. "Yes, I think I'd best find this master of yours. And what in the name of the inventor of writing are you doing carrying a scroll stuffed into your tunic?"

He might not know me yet, but he soon would. His narrow mind just hadn't quite figured it out. I lashed out with the "injured" foot and hooked his feet out from under him. He toppled over backwards, bringing a row of scrolls down with him.

That had done it. His cries and the crackling of the scrolls were soon drowned out by the pounding of feet running towards us. I ran towards the scribes. No one, I hoped, would expect that.

The worst thing about the whole expedition, and the one thing I'd been resolutely not thinking about, was that I had no idea at all how I was to get out again. *Kossinli, come on, you tricksy goddess, or I'll never be able to get Your heart.*

No one was chasing me yet; it sounded as if they hadn't yet located Lord Earrings. I forced myself to slow to a purposeful walk. I was getting close enough to the scribes that they'd notice me soon. I could see them clearly now, silhouetted by the light behind them.

There were windows behind the scribes! Well, of course there would be. Even celestial scribes must have light. Windows have often served me well.

Still walking as if I had every right to be there, I strode between two scribes and looked out the window. "Get out of the light," one scribe snapped.

I have a good head for heights. The drop from that window, though, made my head swim. There were lines that might be ledges, or not.

"You're in my light!"

I had to get out of there. The wind through the window was cold, so very cold, and the drop was horrible, but what choice had I?

There was a three-colored cat strolling nonchalantly along the ledge below. I need little more room than a cat does. Hadn't Firousi said that cats were Kossinli's?

Carefully, moving only one hand or foot at a time, I followed the cat. It waited for me now and then, meowing loudly as if to bid me hurry. Well, I was willing enough to do that!

"Layla," said the cat. A talking cat? Well, why not?

"I'm coming as fast as I can, cat," I explained. "I'm not so graceful as you."

"No one is," said the cat. She reached out a paw and tapped my foot.

Then I was lying on my bed at the villa. Firousi sat beside me; Arakante was carrying over a sack of warmed sand.

"I brought it back," I told them. "Damn! I had the scroll, and a beautiful dagger, I worked so hard for that scroll and it's gone!"

"What scroll, Layla?" Firousi stroked the hair back from my forehead.

"The scroll with—" I began. I sniffed back tears.

"Don't answer," said Arakante.

He sat there silent and still. By now I knew better than to question him, or Firousi for that matter, when they had that look of being asleep with their eyes open. It was no great hardship to keep silent myself. I wasn't sure I could tell anyone what had just happened. I wasn't at all sure that I wanted Firousi to know.

Finally he came back to us. "I can guess some of what you

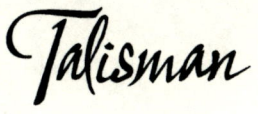

started to say. No, don't tell me, Layla! If you do, and the hole in my memory is mended, it will mean your work has been for nothing. I would not have you waste the risks you took."

"That's fine with me," I answered. "I'm not sure I could tell it all even if you wanted me to." I certainly wasn't eager to try the trick again.

27

Soon I would be able to leave. I could go back to Charransar, back to warmth and my own scruffy freedom; not so scruffy now, even after I paid my way with Mother Rissa. A few determined pilgrims had already arrived; surely her caravan would be among the first of the traders. With a little careful buying of jewels before I left, I'd have stock of unquestionable origin to start that shop I'd dreamed of starting some distant day. I hadn't thought to make that change quite so soon. I might linger awhile in Issrandar, buying lapis; I might head for home as fast as the caravan's pace would allow. I might set up shop somewhere well away from Old Parata.

I would carry the link to Kossinli with me. Would I have been able to snap it, if Firousi or Arakante had been able to find the ruby heart for me to steal? No matter. They hadn't, and I had learned to live with the problem. Perhaps Her new devotees would give the Lady of Mirth enough amusement without me, especially if I did stop roof-running.

I would leave behind Arakante. That did matter; it was better so. Living so close to each other without having each other was driving me half-mad. I couldn't tell what he was feeling. Perhaps nothing. Were there anti-love potions? Spells of indifference?

A girl was selling cloudberries where the roasted-nut seller had had his stand. As she was scooping a couple of handfuls into a rush basket for me, a man pushed through the waiting crowd. "The big basket. Five dinats."

It was the priest with the sapphire earrings again, Arakante's client. He was wearing amethysts today, rather better-cut than the sapphires had been. No one openly protested his cutting in, nor did the girl haggle over the meager price; maybe he was as dangerous as he tried to appear.

Those amethysts were really quite fine. What did he have at home, kept for more formal occasions? He'd be heading home at this hour, and it was probably close to this stall where I'd seen him twice. Why not? The gates were open now; my promise to Arakante was done. I deserved one win out of this bungled year. The fact that he was already looking for the emerald thief without having any idea that I was that thief added to the fun.

This was a dance I knew well. Weaving in and out among the bright-robed Tzakendi as they enjoyed this fine spring evening, I followed Lord Earrings up a hill and down under an archway crowned with the booths of sellers of ribbons and scarves. The cobbles were slick with moss from the stream that had flowed under the arch only a week ago. He grew nervous then; confined passages will do that to some. Up the narrow stairs, then, to buy myself some gold-bordered ribbon, and to get a good look at where he was going. The wind that set the ribbons and scarves dancing ensured me a good view as I strolled across the bridge.

Neither water stains nor bare bricks marred the bone-white walls of the house he entered. Even the gutter in front of it held only a few dead leaves. The wind must have brought them from the square, for neither tree nor vine had been allowed to grow nearby. Worst of all, someone had smoothed away all the helpful irregularities of the usual Tzakendi wall.

There would surely be easier houses to rob, yet that house drew me. If I couldn't go over the wall, could I somehow slip through the gate?

I had felt this way twice before. Lady of Mirth, I thought, this had better not be a joke.

What a suspicious mind!

A person could fall off the bridge! I nearly had, too. This was Tzakende; people simply moved away a little. The scarf-seller nearest me edged her table over to where the bridge was more even. It seemed like a good time for me to come down to the street.

There was a teahouse just at the foot of the bridge. I took the drafty seat near the door that no one wants. *Why didn't You just tell me this before? .*

I did, but you didn't hear me at first. You've made tremendous progress, Layla. And your jests have given Me more strength to reach you. She laughed then. Being a goddess, She undoubtedly knew how I felt about getting better at being in contact with one of the Powers.

Might as well get some good out of it. *What am I supposed to get from that house? And how?*

Oh, really, Layla! You take all the fun out of it. Can't you guess?

Your heart. An easy guess. What else could it be? I was so tired of jests and games. Why had I let anyone convince me that I couldn't simply leave?

Yes. And hurry, my clever thief. Didn't your teacher warn you that what happens to Me happens to you? Even with all of your jests and my Firousi's works, I must have My heart out of the house of My enemy. There are some things even I can't endure.

There was a peculiar feeling, like the whuff of air that you feel when someone slams a door in a small room. What happened to Kossinli happened to me. I shivered. That couldn't be completely true; I couldn't have lived for very long with my heart outside of my body. Men who'd been condemned to the Traitor's Death did live a little while thus, if the executioner had been skillful enough to avoid nicking the great veins. There was a pleasant thought! Kossinli had lived decades without Hers, and gone on making silly jokes. Goddesses must be even more different from us mortals than I'd been taught!

If the Heart were given to someone else then would that

be like the executioner cutting that last connection? I didn't think I'd actually die myself if Kossinli did—would I?

I'd better find that heart. Then I wouldn't have to find out.

The houses of the poor are easy to burgle, assuming you've any reason to bother with the houses of the poor. The houses of princes are easier than the princes would care to believe; with all those servants, supplicants and court sycophants around, there's usually enough of a crowd to hide one person who doesn't belong there. Stay modest in your takings, and you can take quite a lot before anyone notices that there've been an awful lot of things gone missing.

This was the house of a prosperous townsman. Unlike the houses of the poor, it had sturdy walls and locks that worked; unlike the houses of princes, it had no crowds. Lord Earrings hadn't the look of a man who threw riotous parties, either. No, but I knew someone who might know how to find out when he'd be gone from his house. There was someone else who had better be able to tell me how much danger I was in.

The flame flickered under the samovar as a stocky man dressed in stonemason's gray dragged the teahouse door open, followed closely by two more. Outside, the light was fading. When the teahouse boy asked pointedly if I wanted anything more, I paid and left.

There were fresh herbs in that night's dinner, and tiny sweet flowers scattered as garnish over them. Flowers seemed more like Imchi's dinner than mine, but they did taste good. I paid the delicacy less attention than it deserved as I tried to decide just how to say what I needed to say.

"I think I may know where Kossinli's heart is," I said, breaking into some conversation between my two companions. "I think I'll need some help from Arakante in getting it."

Arakante frowned. "Layla, I don't know..."

I hurried on. "It's in that awfully tidy house just down from the Scarfseller's Bridge. The place will be hard to break into—there's no cover near the courtyard wall, and they've smoothed that wall 'till it nearly shines. I think I can slip in through the gate if you," I nodded to Arakante, "can tell me when there'll be the fewest people in the house."

"The man has come to me for readings. To use what I know of him..." Arakante looked puzzled.

I was fairly sure that I knew what puzzled him, and it worried me. If we pressed him on this, would it bring back his memory of when he'd warned me about this same Lord?

Firousi broke the silence. "Arakante, it's no such thing. She's given you the location! Take bowl and water and scry as if you'd never seen the man."

"I can't divide it that cleanly," Arakante replied.

She drew in a long breath and let it out silently. "Arakante. No one is asking you to use the man's secrets against him. If we must do without your help, we can probably find out what we need by watching the house. It will take longer and it will be less certain. In any case, why is it worse than when we sent Layla to steal Kossinli's second eye? Plenty of the women there had been to see you."

Had they, now? And paid in what coin?

"I wasn't entirely happy about that."

"Wouldn't most of the people who seek your readings be better off if the Lady of Mirth had Her old strength back? Wouldn't we all?"

He shook his head. "That isn't the point."

Firousi leaned forward and touched his hand. "Kossinli will help you, you know."

I wondered again how much she'd heard of my conversation with Kossinli.

"She's stronger now," Firousi continued, "and with Her heart She'll be Herself again. You've helped Her greatly, and She will remember that."

"There are things that I may not discuss even with you,

Firousi, perhaps especially with you. I cannot do as you ask! It's even less likely to work now than before the mapmaking. Do you think I put us all through that for the theoretical challenge? Go and gossip with Lady Mirrim. I don't doubt she can tell you details about any upper-class household in Tzakende." He didn't say, including this one. He didn't need to.

Firousi turned her shoulder to him, whether because she was angry or to spare his feelings I don't know. "Layla, are you sure where it is?"

"Yes."

Firousi gave me a long, intense look. "She's spoken to you again, hasn't She?"

I nodded. Firousi'd shown jealousy of my connection with Kossinli before.

"You weren't in a trance or meditating? Good, She's growing stronger." She smiled at me. "Ah, Layla, were you afraid—forgive me, concerned—that I'd be angry? This is wonderful. I thought She was stronger when last I communed with Her, but then, I wanted to think that!"

I shifted uneasily. This wasn't a good subject to argue with Firousi, but I needed to get the heart, and I was pretty sure I needed Arakante's help to dot it. That was going to take some argument.

"Kossinli may be stronger. I think She's...worried (better not say frightened, not of a Goddess) though. So am I. She must need help badly to speak to me like that, and didn't you tell me that your Lady of Mirth and I were more closely linked than ever? She said She needed Her Heart. What happens if She doesn't get it? What happens to Her happens to me, you said."

Firousi shook her head. "She can't die. She's a Goddess, an Immortal, and by definition She can't die. Therefore you aren't in mortal danger." She hesitated a moment, clearly not done speaking. "I'm not sure beyond that."

Arakante looked skeptical, but kept his silence. He could

have reminded Firousi of some of her own earlier arguments about the fate of the world if Kossinli's statue didn't get restored. Firousi sat even straighter than was usual for her, the picture of haughty conviction.

It was some help to be told that I wouldn't actually die. Yet, "Kossinli said there were some things even She couldn't endure," I told Firousi.

She bit her lip. "That's bad. She might withdraw from us completely. Surely, even the Twilight Lands couldn't hold Her forever." Firousi didn't sound sure.

Arakante touched her hand, but looked at me. "It can't be good in any case. Very well. I'll give what help I can."

Firousi and I both thanked him at once. He smiled a thin smile. "There may be practical limits to that! Don't thank me until we've done it."

Firousi smiled at him. "My cautious cousin! We'll have cause to thank you. Now, Layla, how are we going to get that heart?"

We? I tried to picture Firousi climbing through a window. Even though my worries were still gnawing at me, I had to laugh.

"I'm not proposing to scramble in through a window," she said. "Don't look at me like that; it was an obvious jest. However, I could call on the house and see to it that the gate wasn't fastened behind me. It's hard enough to get servants to remember their duties; I'm sure I could distract the gatekeeper."

"Yes, I'm sure you could! Only, I work alone."

Arakante looked up from the almonds he'd been shelling. "Layla, you're already not working alone."

Reasonable men are dangerous. Would this turn out as well as the last time he'd persuaded me to do something I thought unwise? I turned to Firousi. "Well, my Lady, I hope you can run if you have to!"

"Layla, if I can do the *Dance of Rejoicing*, all five segments

including the elaborations introduced by Mayaranda the Jester, I can certainly run if I need to. Besides, shouldn't the Priestess of Mirth be able to play a few tricks?"

That, too, seemed reasonable. Mind you, the last year or so had changed my notions of what was reasonable.

Tzakende in winter is a small place, but I managed a little prying of my own. No one seemed surprised that I'd be tired of my studies now, with spring coming on. I wandered the city for several days, taking care not to concentrate on Lord Earrings' quarter. Firousi visited, and invited visitors. Cook alternately sang and roared, and fed me lopsided tarts and slightly overbrowned cakes until even I'd had plenty. Finally Firousi and I gathered to pool information.

Firousi began. "They keep shockingly few slaves or servants—everybody knows how much their people complain. The kitchen staff stays largely in the kitchen; they should be no trouble. Their one gatekeeper's an old man with poor eyesight; rumor has it that the Lady's too softhearted to sell him and Lord Prahin's too cheap to give him a home without some service."

I added, "Our friend with the fancy earrings spends little time at home, especially late in the day. He's important in the governing of the city and the organization of Sarinsat's temple. Perhaps we should wait a week or so; in better weather he often visits the family's estates in the Isslarantan hills. Unfortunately, his wife is heavily pregnant and spends most of her time in her rooms on the first floor."

"How is that unfortunate?" Firousi asked. "When I inquire there for news of my young cousin Raouf, who ran off declaring that he would seek spiritual growth in the simple life of an Isslarantan shepherd, naturally I'll speak with the Lady of the house. If she's been housebound for weeks, she'll be delighted to offer me mint tea and conversation."

"While I find the heart?"

She smiled smugly and nodded.

"Firousi, you will make an excellent accomplice!" She had the nerve to do what she said, and I was certain she could stretch the conversation out for as long as I'd need.

28

At least this time there was no need to wait. We had a fine fog the next morning, so fine that I asked Arakante if he'd caused it.

"Fog is common in the spring," he answered, and laughed when I told him he just enjoyed being mysterious. He was certainly enjoying something.

In this thin daylight I could wear boy's clothing so long as no one got a close look at me. While Arakante wouldn't admit to causing the fog, he did say that it wouldn't lift before late afternoon. Firousi had put on a widow's gray robe and long, snugly-draped headscarf. She'd never mentioned being married, but I decided not to ask about it just then. The change in clothes certainly changed her appearance. In fact, it almost made her invisible. Fog-colored in the fog, she was also a modestly-cowled widow at whom no one would look directly even if someone did notice her.

Someone was whistling as Firousi and I walked downhill. It was one of the songs we used for Kossinli's celebrations. "That's you whistling!"

"You needn't sound so surprised," Firousi answered. My apology collapsed when she laughed. "It's all right! I know you've found my lessons tedious, but Layla, did you think I could serve Kossinli all my life and not know a few unladylike things?"

If she felt any unease, she hid it well. I forced myself to think only of the words to the tune she whistled. Thinking can make it so. Worry that a theft may fail, or go into it thinking about how desperately you need for it to succeed, and you've cast a curse on your efforts that your enemies would envy.

Yes, and was that why Kossinli had spoken so vaguely of danger, that day on Scarfsellers' Bridge? If mortal thoughts could make something so, what would those of a goddess do?

That was more than enough of such thoughts. Firousi and I let the day's crowd fill in between us as we went down the street. The fog was actually thickening. Once I'd've thought that reasonable, since fogs often do lie longer in low places; now I wondered. In any case, it was helpful. By the time Firousi reached the house, the fog hid me well as I slipped past while Firousi explained her visit to the wizened gatekeeper. Softly, softly on the other side of Firousi from the old man, I crept into the house with her. I could see her shoulders shaking with smothered laughter. A moment's lurking in the hall that probably led off to a storeroom, and I was free to hurry up the stairs. As a door-curtain swung shut I caught a glimpse of the green and blue hangings thought lucky for a pregnant woman.

May the gods help anyone who wants private conversation in a Tzakendi house. The hallways are more like tunnels; the sound flows along them like water. As I slipped away on my nefarious purpose, I could hear Firousi beginning her story. The wife sounded interested; good.

Another reason Tzakende has so few thieves is the mazes the Tzakendi live in. Even this house, so plain outside, had far more halls and alcoves than it needed. At least they'd kept them well swept. I do like a clean, smooth floor with nothing to make noise or show footprints.

It wasn't in the room that looked like a study, and a very promising coffer in the alcove nearby held nothing but papers. Where next? Well, I knew who'd know. I might not ever learn to meditate properly, but I seemed to be rather good at reaching Kossinli. I made as sure as I could that I was alone, and tried to concentrate on Her while keeping aware of any nearby noises.

All I could hear was Firousi's bright social voice.

You don't have to shout!

I couldn't believe no one else had heard that. *I'm sorry. Please remember I'm new at this.*

I'm not likely to forget. I was starting to wonder how long it would take you to ask Me! We haven't much time. Even Firousi's having trouble drawing out a conversation with that Sarinsat-lover downstairs.

That reminder dried up any other questions I'd had. *Where do I find this heart?*

Up above you—turn left—no, not here. I can see it so clearly, but you have to go around all these walls.

I'm good, but I am mortal.

Never mind, I'll guide you. A breeze sprang up in the airless room and pushed against my right side. It guided me up a flight of wear-rounded stairs, through one room and into another, around several corners, and up again to a locked door.

A woman's long hair makes such a good hiding-place for lock picks, especially when the hair's braided tightly so that it stays put under a boy's cap. This householder wasn't going to rely on the famous mystic ability of Tzakende to repel thieves.

That lock was a wonder. Three times I thought I had it open; twice I was wrong. Once I failed only because some stray house-noise sent me dodging back from the light. The next try worked.

There the Heart was, in a windowless room so small that I could have touched any two walls at once with my outstretched hands. It gleamed even in the dim light from the door, gold wires holding rubies in the shape of a darkly glittering heart. Another net of gold and ebony held it suspended before a statue of Sarinsat. Ah, Kossinli, getting that home safely is going to be hard!

"Surprise!" cried a woman's voice, and I cracked my elbow on the edge of the door. "Husband, what a pleasure! My dear?" Now I could hear footsteps, street-boots coming rapidly up the stairs.

I grasped the heart gently to pull it from its nest, and only barely managed not to cry out. Pain like fire ants ran up my hand. I wrapped it in my cap and tried again; this time my arm went numb up to the shoulder.

Damn Arakante! Why hadn't he warned me about this sort of trap? Did I have to think of everything? I'd ask him that if I managed to get back to the villa.

My own heart hurt as I turned from the heart of gold and rubies. This corridor was a dead end. I hurried noiselessly back along it, hoping for an unlocked door. The footsteps were coming closer, pursued by a woman's agitated voice demanding to know what was wrong. I ran on, up three stairs, down two, around corners. The corridor wound without ever a cross-hall or an open door. It's surprisingly hard to run with one arm dangling uselessly.

Here was one door standing open just a hair. I ducked in and stood among racks of woolens, struggling not to sneeze as the footsteps pounded past. "Later!" shouted a man's voice that I recognized from Arakante's villa.

This place was going to be at least as hard to get out of as it was to get into. Nothing grew near the house or its outer wall; the few trees in the garden had been pruned into grotesque balls and triangles. The courtyard was covered in gravel raked into smoothly curving lines; any footsteps would be obvious to a blind person. What did that matter? I couldn't see any way of climbing down to the courtyard. Well for me that most householders weren't this careful! The back gate was too far away to see clearly, but that dark patch was probably a lock. In this household, they probably used it in spite of the inconvenience.

The perfectly-swept floors gave me no clues as to which rooms were used and which kept in reserve. At least I had left no trail of footprints. I could probably lurk here undiscovered for hours.

A woman's voice, not Firousi's, spoke. "Husband, I

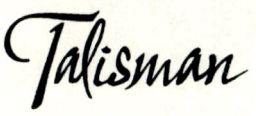

demand to know what's happening! Why are you dashing through the house like a madman?"

Oh ye demons of sour water. They had to be almost outside this door.

"Compose yourself; this disturbance is bad for you and the child. I've had warning concerning the enemies of Sarinsat."

Warning from what source? Surely not Arakante! No, Arakante'd helped us with the fog. He might not use his knowledge of this Lord against him, but surely Arakante wouldn't work against us. He wouldn't be my lover, but he didn't hate me. He'd continue to shelter me; that finely-polished honor of his would demand it.

The precise voice continued. "Now, if you'll rejoin your guest, I'll protect our interests. Who is she, by the way?"

"Oh, what is her name? I only just met her today, Prahin, don't glare at me like that! Someone told her we hold land in Isslaranta, and she's seeking news of her brother who may be herding sheep—Prahin, what's wrong?"

Oh, Firousi, I hope you've had the sense to run for it while you had the chance. I heard a door slam, a lock click, and I knew which ones they were. Booted footsteps went back down the hall, followed by the shuffle of slippers. I tiptoed to the door and risked opening it a crack for a look.

They were just disappearing into the stairwell. Their footsteps continued on down, Prahin's boots thudding as he took the stairs two at a time. As soon as they'd gone a little farther, I could risk a bolt for the front door. Would Firousi have had the sense to run? I certainly hoped so. It was going to be tricky enough getting myself out. I tried moving my arm. It prickled like nettles, but it did move. That helped.

I'd leave without the heart. All this risk, all this work, and I still didn't have the one thing that would free me completely. What would become of Kossinli now, and of me? If I thought much about that, I'd get too sad and angry to move, so I wouldn't think about it.

No, I'd focus on edging along the wall, silently keeping well behind those hurrying footsteps. It was easy enough to hear them, but hard to judge how far away they were. Their argument echoed up the tunnel-like stairs; she was demanding to know what was happening, he was ordering her to let him deal with his own concerns, and she was refusing to be treated like a slave in her own house.

Her voice broke off in mid-argument with a cry. I could hear her falling against the wall twice. Prahin must have caught her, for I heard him grunt loudly. Then I could hear only his footsteps, landing more heavily than before.

Here was my chance. He and his household would all be too busy taking care of the lady of the house to watch properly for a fugitive. With any luck, Firousi had created more confusion for me with her departure.

I took a moment to slip my larger knife free. It is a point of pride with me not to use a knife; a good thief should be quick and clever enough to be gone before the former owner knows he's been robbed. Yes, and it was a point of pride to leave with what I came for. Right now I'd do well to leave with my life. Even if it turned out to be short, I wanted more of it.

Should I try for the front door, or the back? The back would be less guarded, but I had no idea how to get to it. Besides, I'd have to get across all that open gravel before I could get to the back gate, which might well be locked.

As I picked at this tangled question, I ran silently down the stairs. They'd send for a midwife, surely—people would be coming and going—yes, the front door. I need only (only!) keep out of sight as I worked my way through rooms that opened into halls, stairs up and stairs down as I went from one room to another, ah yes, I could see the blue-green hangings billowing out into the hall. Poor lady, to give birth in winter! The shutters must be opened, of course, all bindings must be loosed, but that wind was cold. *And thank You, Lady, for this well-timed labor.*

The sounds from the room would cover any noise I might make. That was good. You simply can't knock a man unconscious, even a scrawny one like the house-slave who tried to stop me, without making some noise.

I made more noise by yanking the door open so hard that it hit the wall. This was disgusting. Yes, and dangerous. For as I dashed through the open door I nearly ran into a man in the courtyard.

Lord Earrings, who really should have been hovering over his wife or running for the midwife, stared at me with his mouth open. "I know you, boy."

Good honest folk, never say that to someone who's not good and honest. Besides that, he was between me and the gate. It was still open, though. Curse this stingy little courtyard! The gatekeeper lay still—Firousi, what did you do? Other footsteps were coming. Damn the man, I hate killing.

He reached for the gate. Oh no, my Lord! I darted by and sliced at his belly. He'd good reflexes for a man of his years, and far too many layers of clothing, but his yell told me I'd drawn blood. All was confusion then, as he tried to grab me and I tried to get to the door. Here's another piece of advice: if intruders are trying to leave, let them! Gods, I was willing to let the fool live if he'd just get out of the way. I hacked at his wrist, a crude blow, but it got the job done. He grabbed his arm to stop the bleeding; I ran past the still-motionless gatekeeper and into the fog-blurred streets.

Fog, wonderful fog, I'd never complain about it again. Lord Earrings' downhill neighbor had let trees grow up past his wall; one hanging branch looked low enough—yes. A quick spring, whip around with the speed that had given me, and I was up on top of the wall. Leaves fallen from the same tree mostly cushioned me against the broken pots embedded in the plaster.

As I lay there, listening to Lord Earrings' slaves shout and run uphill and down, I wondered what else was going to go wrong with this day. The broken pots were digging into my skin. I breathed slowly, concentrating on one of Firousi's meditations, and the pain grew less. Now, *there* was a jest to share when I returned.

That was going to be a challenge. In the breeze, I could feel a sticky tightness where some of Lord Earrings' blood had stained the sleeve of my coat. A breeze. Yes, the fog was shredding. Lord Earrings' slaves hadn't yet given up the search, but with luck I might slip by them. The fog thickened again, and I slithered down to the street.

Of course someone saw me. I ran ahead of my pursuers for a little while, blessing the winding streets with their sudden flights of stairs. I blessed Kossinli's dances, too; in spite of my weeks of living honestly, I wasn't yet breathing hard.

Not so my pursuers, but they were still able to call out "Stop, thief!" That was unfair. I hadn't actually been able to steal anything. One stallholder nearly caught me by thrusting out the long pole he used to fetch down robes from the ridgepole, but I leaped it in time. I pulled his awning down for him in payment, and got well ahead in the confusion that followed.

The fog moved faster than any other that I'd seen or heard of. At times it swirled around me so thickly that I could barely see my feet; at other times it scattered like the crowd at the end of a street-singer's performance. Once it disappeared entirely just as I was about to help myself to a mutton pie. Well, it had been a long time since breakfast, and there the pie lay on a platter with many others all perfuming the moist air.

"That one," I said, and pulled out a coin. My smile was not returned. The old woman tending the brazier squinted suspiciously at me, and bit the coin before she'd hand over the pie. "Wizard weather," she muttered. "Can't they leave us poor folk out of their battles? Twice already someone's taken pies when the dratted wizard-fog came down." She glared at me.

Lord Earrings' men plodded up the street, arguing over

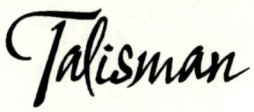

whether they could safely go home. The pie-woman's stare might as well have been a beacon. I was out in plain sight, and they saw me.

Once again I raced through narrow streets, up stairs and down crooked alleys. *Oh, Arakante, where was my fog?* My pursuers were tiring, but so was I. My belly cramped around the half a pie I'd eaten. Twice I felt the cold tingle of fog forming; twice it evaporated even though the cobbles were slick with dampness. I could still hear footsteps following me, though the slaves had given up yelling. The streets were steep here.

When the fog did reappear, it swirled and seized the smoke from a nut-seller's fire to form an evil-smelling blanket that hid me well. It also hid the world from me. Fog and smoke struggled with each other. I walked into a wall once, and dared not curse.

Finally I saw a gap between two buildings. There was barely room enough to squeeze between them, and the blank wall of a third building closed the passage. It was perfect.

There is no magic in going up a smooth wall if there's another smooth wall close enough that you can brace yourself between them. All that you need is strength and nerve. Hearing an angry mob close behind helps supply the nerve.

One alert fellow saw the hidey-hole and investigated it, but of course he never looked up. It's as well for my modesty that he didn't. My trousers hadn't been cut for this kind of acrobatics.

He shrugged and trotted off to rejoin the chase. Inching down was harder than climbing up; it always is. Once down, I began to fear that I'd have to walk bent like a pot-hanger for the rest of my life. I couldn't be getting old already! Nothing prepares you for wall climbing except wall climbing, my teacher always said. I hadn't done this in a long time. That was all that caused my stiffness. That, and the fog that had managed to reform. The night didn't feel like spring any more.

Shifting breezes were pushing remnants of fog this way and that in the dusk as I reached the villa. Firousi herself opened the door for me. Behind her, I could see Arakante shuffle down the stairs.

"I failed." Best to get it said. Firousi pulled me nearer to the entryway lamp.

"Where are you hurt?" She ran her hands lightly over my tunic. "This is all dry..."

"Oh, it isn't mine."

Her hands dropped; she drew back a step. "Layla—you haven't—"

"Killed anyone? No. I cut Lord Earrings, but he'll not die of it. That midwife can stop the blood."

I should have asked how Firousi was, I suppose. She looked well enough, warm in her layers of house-robes. "Can we talk about it tomorrow? I'm tired."

"Oh, Layla, I'm sorry! Of course you are!"

"You're both well, then," said Arakante. He was leaning against the wall; his skin had a grayish cast.

"Are you?" He looked as he'd been running the Tzakendi streets.

Firousi stroked his hair. "Go to bed, Ari; you're exhausted. Shall I send Roshana with a posset?"

Arakante shuddered and refused the offer. After he'd rounded the first bend in the stairs, I could hear him bringing both feet onto each step before going on to the next. Step step pause, step step pause.

"Arakante! Thank you!" I called up after him.

"It was little enough," he said.

When I would have protested, Firousi shook her head at me.

She went with me to the bath herself and tended my scrapes and bruises. I don't suppose she wanted any servant seeing the houseguest with blood on her embroidery. Scented steam rose thickly from the already-hot water. Firousi always thought she knew what was best for people; sometimes she was right.

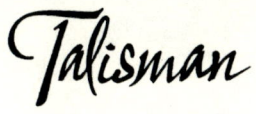

29

*I*n spite of two braziers in my room, in spite of the soft bed and the feather-filled coverlet, my bruises stiffened overnight. Pain and the remembrance of my failure hit as soon as I woke. I groaned aloud, forgetting the little servant girl Firousi had insisted on posting in my room for the night. It took some doing to keep the little fool from running for Firousi, and in the end Firousi came anyway, alerted by the sound of our arguing.

Even that lark's morning sunniness had failed this time. She checked to be sure that none of my injuries were worse than they'd looked last night, then said, "Come down to breakfast now, since you're awake. I don't imagine any of us wants to go through this more than once."

Gods, did they mean to throw me out? Perhaps they should. Perhaps I should leave even if they didn't. If Lord Earrings ever figured out that the boy he'd seen was a woman, then he'd know where to look for me. That would be bad for all of us. He'd had an awfully good look at me yesterday.

And I had failed. I'd had Kossinli's help in finding the heart, Firousi's help within the house and Arakante's wizardly help outside it, and I had failed. I wasn't sure just what Lord Earrings would do with the heart now, but he'd certainly see to it that his wife didn't admit any more strangers.

Arakante was already at the table, staring gloomily at a cup filled with egg posset. He poked it with one finger.

"It works better taken internally," Firousi said. His glare would have silenced many people, but not Firousi. Gently, softly, she added, "You need to eat, cousin."

"It won't do me any good to eat if I throw it right back up." That did silence her. Arakante went back to staring at the posset.

There were no eggs in any of the dishes that the kitchen boy brought in for Firousi and me. Hens seemed to dislike winter almost as much as I do. Ah well, even I didn't have much appetite this morning.

We traded stories. I took first turn, getting through the sad tale as quickly as I could. The silence afterwards almost made me wish I'd embellished it.

Firousi tired of the silence first. She had left her hair loose and unveiled; now she let it swing forward. I'd used that trick myself, when younger.

"Well, my tale is less heroic. When Lord Prahin came in, I couldn't think what to do beyond hauling my widow's veil over my hair and down past my nose to keep him from recognizing me. Fortunately, Lord Prahin barely glanced in my direction before he went tearing upstairs, with Lady Drimma behind him as fast as she could move. Layla, I abandoned you then. I'd no idea where you were, or how to help you. Only later did I think that I could have created a distraction and still escaped. A scream and an overturned brazier would have done it, I imagine."

Neither Arakante nor I spoke, though she was silent then for several breaths.

Firousi managed a smile. "I got past the gatekeeper by hitting him with the torch from the doorway sconce. Oh, Layla, if you could see your face! It was really very satisfying. He wasn't expecting it, of course. I wanted to run, but I thought that everyone would stare and wonder, so I walked away up the street. I heard shouting, and feared they'd found you. I needed to get away from there, but I needed to know what was happening even more! I was just uphill, near the bridge where the scarf-sellers are; I bought three scarves that were not appropriate for a widow while

I tried to decide what to do next. Hearing more noise and confusion from Lord Prahin's decided the question for me; I made my way home and found Arakante sitting shivering beside a brazier of ashes by a silver bowl with ice forming on the water." She shivered a little herself.

I patted her hand. "You did the right thing," I assured her. I'd wanted to see her humbled often enough, but not like this! She looked ashamed.

"Firousi, I can't tell you how glad I was to find you gone when I reached the ground floor. We'd both have been taken if you'd waited. And you did help me, you know. I doubt I could have escaped if the gatekeeper had been awake." She didn't look much comforted.

Arakante pushed away his teacup and the remains of the posset. "Well, I was of little enough use."

"Ari, that's nonsense!" Firousi cried.

"Without the fog—" I added, but he wouldn't let me say more. I felt no magic in the compulsion, only the force of his weary glare.

"No. It is not nonsense. The fog kept dispersing; it was like the nightmares I used to have before trials of strength in my student days, except that this time two lives depended on my winning the contest against some unfamiliar mage. Tzakende has many, to be sure, and we are often solitary folk; still, I would have thought I would have known someone that strong. It would have helped to know who I fought. I think it was the same one who cast the glamour over Lord Prahin's house; I certainly hope so. One such enemy is sufficient!"

He looked at us both in an odd, measuring way. "As you left, I regretted my decision to be a mage. I watched you two women walk to a great test, laughing and whistling, and I sat here, waiting and watching. There are tales of heroic battles between mages, where awe-full voices fill the air until the air itself bursts into flames, but Layla, neither I nor any of my teachers have ever seen such. Struggle between mages is subtle, and always at a distance."

"I understand," I said. He smiled as if he only half-believed me, but I did. He went on in a more normal voice.

"Possibly, my own workings alerted the other mage. I could tell something was going wrong, but not what it was or how to fight it. I lost sight of you both long before you could have reached Lord Prahin's house; there was nothing to do but hold the fog in Tzakende and hope you'd return soon.

"Of course, since I wished to be undisturbed, there were clients at the door. More than once someone tried to argue with the doorkeeper. Hinante's a marvel; he managed to turn away Lord Prahin himself! By the by, Firousi, I've given Hinante fifty sekals in thanks."

She nodded approvingly. I resolved to find some way to thank Hinante myself. He could scowl at me all he liked from now on; I wouldn't mind.

"I waited, and I struggled. I couldn't risk another scrying to see how you did; taking any of my strength from the fog would have let our enemy scatter it. Once Firousi was home I could tell where Layla was by how strong the attacks on my concealment were."

"We didn't know where you were, or even if you lived. No, cousin, that's no accusation! Layla says you'd both have been captured had you stayed, and I bow to her knowledge of such things. Firousi, I hope you know that I went apart only to work my spells the better."

She nodded.

"When it was strong enough, the fog knew where Layla was. When it was that strong, though, I found it harder to coerce into places where it had no wish to be. So I sat in the room as it grew colder and darker, feeding the fog enough but not too much, wrestling with it and warding off someone's efforts to destroy it or drive it forth. Hardest to fight were the other wizard's efforts to feed the fog well enough to turn it to rain; the mists reached out

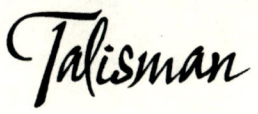

for that hungrily."

Firousi touched his wrist gently. He must have sat silent for long enough to worry her.

He spoke again. "Nightfall helped me, for fog is naturally heavier then. It also worked against me. I was growing weary, finding it harder and harder to concentrate. Layla, I fear I was less than welcoming when you did arrive. Please believe that seeing you made me feel as if a mountain had been lifted from my shoulders."

I assured him that I hadn't thought he was rude. "I know when someone's dog-tired."

All three of us sat silent, drinking tea and eating stodgy winter porridge, or at least Firousi and I did. Arakante kept taking small bites of his posset, which seemed to have set up like a pudding, and grimacing.

30

*N*one of us knew what to do next. We knew where the heart was now, but we had no hope of getting it. Kossinli spoke neither to Firousi nor to me. I wondered whether She could.

Tzakende's spring continued to flirt with us. When the sun shone and the breezes were gentle (the air is never still in Tzakende) we had floods of visitors. I almost came to welcome grey days. On those, we could brood in peace.

Some wanted Firousi to go on with the dances and lessons, which they were still sure we'd need sometime soon. Why should they doubt? None of them knew of our failure; few even knew of our search. Firousi managed; watching her teach, I'd never have guessed how many hours she spent staring silently at the heartless statue.

Some wanted Arakante to tell them what next week's weather would bring; he angered those by telling them, truthfully, that no one can tell that for certain. Then there were all the others with their worries over lovers and money. Arakante told me once that what he did was often not so much magic as listening until the questioner saw the answer that had been there all along.

I went back to my workshop in the garden on days that were warm enough. It was thought to be an eccentric hobby for a Lady, but then, I was known to be a foreigner. I ruined a few stones relearning my old skills at polishing and setting, but it calmed my mind in ways that meditation never could. I did wonder, as I stared at the shards of what had been a good turquoise, if Kossinli had guided my hands on Her wreath. I wondered if the link had

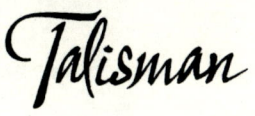

finally broken. I hoped it had. If my head ached, if I slipped on a worn stair, I couldn't help wondering if it was because Kossinli was weakening.

The day after the turquoise disaster, I managed to turn an irregular chunk of malachite into the central pendant of a Breaking Wave necklace. That seemed to call for some celebration, or at least a good lunch. Well for me that neither Firousi not Arakante was near to be shocked by what I said when the muddy path seized one of my shoes!

Yes, and well for me that it did. It meant that I heard the voice in the courtyard as it bounced off the kitchen garden wall.

"Yes, I understand that I'll have to wait," the deep voice said. "Pray tell Master Arakante that I will wait upon his convenience, and that I apologize for any trouble I give him."

Lord Earrings, here again? I stood with one foot in the air while he was ushered into the house. "Kossinli," I muttered, "If You're watching this I hope You're amused enough to help me. Just a little help, Lady of Laughter, so that I can sneak up the back stairs."

How could one shoe make so much noise? Such a rude noise, too! Never mind; I had it back on my foot and the worst of the mud scraped off. I took it back off again as soon as I reached the kitchen. For once, I wasn't hungry.

The back stairs wound all the way up to Firousi's solar. I met no one as I went stocking-footed up the uneven stones; finding Firousi alone would have been too much good luck.

"Layla, my dear, your poor toes must be frozen!" cried Lady Mirrim. That woman has had entirely too many children. She bustled me into a chair with my toes—which weren't actually all that cold—roasting near a brazier. "You'll be ill if you aren't careful. Firousi, look at your friend. Doesn't she have a very poor color?"

Firousi agreed. "In fact, Lady Mirrim, could you send us some of that honeyflower syrup of yours?"

"Why, certainly my dear! I'll go home now and send Ninta with it. Oh, I don't give anyone else the key to my simples room! Well, my dear Firousi, you know as well as I how dangerous some of those healing herbs can be. No, it's no trouble! You can't think how flattering it is to have the cousin of a mage like Arakante ask for my simple remedies. I should have left before this in any case, but I was enjoying our chat so much." She was wreathing her cloudfleece shawl around her shoulders as she spoke. Good, she'd really leave.

"Well-made simple remedies are often best." Firousi followed her downstairs to assist her with her outer wrap.

I waited upstairs toasting my toes. What I'd give to know what was going on between Arakante and Lord Earrings! He'd been consulting a rival of Arakante's ever since Hinante turned him away on the day of the failed burglary. Even I'd never had the nerve to ask if Arakante had truly not foreseen any of that danger, or had simply kept quiet. What was Lord Earrings doing here now, besides keeping me from my lunch? The remains of the ladies' basket of spiced chickpea cakes, pickled kumquats and honeyfritters simply didn't make an adequate substitute.

Finally I heard Firousi returning. Firousi, and who else? The second set of footsteps landed heavily. I'd been so sure that I'd be safe here that I'd come to a room with only one entrance. Only a few of the windows actually opened, and they were all at the top of its arched roof. I'd no reason to think those heavy footsteps meant danger, but I'd've felt much better with a way out or a place to hide.

There were only useless flickers of shadow in the room. I padded over to stand at one side of the doorway hanging. Here in the villa, I'd stopped carrying even one of my knives. Whoever it was would be dazzled by the solar's light after the darkness of the stairs; that might help enough.

A large hand swept the hanging aside with a rattle of rings, and one of the kitchen staff bore in a tray loaded with covered

dishes. I tried to look as if I'd only come over to the doorway to be hospitable, or gracious, or some such thing. Firousi did not look convinced.

She waited quietly for the servant to leave. "Did Lord Prahin see you at all? The one you call Lord Earrings."

I nodded "No," wordlessly, my mouth being full of hot rosemary-bread. Winterberry tea helped clear my mouth. "No, I heard him talking to the gatekeeper and sneaked up to you. He saw me at his house, though, good and clear. Have you found out why he's here?"

She shrugged. "No, but he must have some pressing reason. Ari's kept him waiting this whole time and he's still there."

31

*T*he sharp scent of cleansing herbs hung in the air as Arakante surveyed his consulting room. Even though Lord Prahin had never shown the slightest sign of awareness of psychic residues, it was best to clear the traces of so discouraging a scrying as this last one. Arakante had placed every lamp, every bowl or ewer precisely where it needed to be. Every charm against disaster was renewed. It was a pity that he had to invite Lord Prahin into the room and disturb its stillness.

Arakante sighed and rang the silver bell. He could hear the murmur of the boy inviting Lord Prahin to enter, and the rustle of layers of robes being shaken smooth.

The man himself swept in, barely giving the boy time to slide the heavy tapestry out of his way. He was even thinner than before, and his eyes were shadowed, but he smiled. "My friend, I have a request which I hope you won't take as an insult," he said.

"I always try not to take offense where none was offered." Both men waited while the boy poured out tea and then left. Arakante waited also to discover what had caused his client's strange mix of moods. It had been no surprise when Lord Prahin stopped coming for Seeings; he no doubt felt that a competent soothsayer, let alone a mage, should have foreseen the attempted burglary and warned him. Why was he back now?

"I need an additional charm against theft for my home. I'd normally not ask it of someone of your standing, but all the ones that I already have seem to have been ineffective. I hoped you might know of something different."

Arakante was glad that he could allow his distress to show. "You understand, this isn't normally my work." To be asked for a charm, like some temple-rat! He wanted to laugh as well at being asked for a charm against theft by the man he'd tried to help rob, but he smothered that. Some of this had to be Kossinli's fine work.

"My Lord, I trust you didn't lose anything of great value? I saw no hint of such a thing." Yes, and that should have warned him, when Layla and Firousi came to him asking help with their scheme. Never mind his agonizing over ethical issues; right or wrong, the effort had been doomed.

Lord Prahin smiled graciously. "No, in fact I lost nothing. Your predictions were accurate as always, though I wish I had known that I was to have such an exciting time of it! Some woman took advantage of my wife's trusting nature to slip a thieving boy into my house. Well, they got past the charms that should have kept them out, but in doing so they tangled themselves in a bell-cord they didn't know was there!

"I've seen that boy before, if that was a boy. My eyes are not what they once were, but as he was escaping I almost managed to catch him. I met him once in the Great Library, of all places! Boy or girl, there's powerful protection keeping me from ever seeing...him?...clearly."

"Have you anything of his, My Lord?" Say no, Arakante thought. Please say no.

"No, not so much as a scrap of clothing! Whoever—oh, I'll go on saying 'he'—whoever he is, he got something of mine! I bled on him after he knifed me getting away."

Arakante made a small worried sound.

"Oh, the cut was shallow and it heals well. My mage tells me there's no trace of my blood to be found in the city, so I don't concern myself over that. What worries me, my friend, is that they clearly knew what they were seeking. I don't live lavishly, but there are a number of things that were worth a thief's attention. The boy went past them to try for another treasure, one that I keep well-hidden. In a month's time I will have presented it to Sarinsat, but until then I need it better guarded than it has been. The Emperor's half-brother himself will honor us with his presence, so if I fail I shall have both divine and earthly anger to face."

A mage learns early to control his heart, or he fails early as a mage. Arakante pushed his despair and anger away to be attended to later. Firmly, he closed the lid on that box and turned the iron key.

"For so short a time, would you consider merely hiring some extra guards? At this end of winter, the men who live outside the gates always want work."

Lord Prahin shook his head. "I will not have strangers disturbing the quiet my wife and son need. He's a strong child, for all he came early, and my Lady tolerates no disturbance of his sleep once he finally does sleep."

Arakante accepted his fate. He would have to give Prahin a charm, and it would have to work: the man clearly had used some other mage, and Arakante had no doubt that anything he gave Lord Prahin would be checked by that unknown person.

"Who did the charms you have?" Whoever had done the cloaking spell had been hidden by it; Arakante would find it most helpful to know who opposed him. At the very least, he'd need to be careful adding charms to a household where magic already existed.

"I regret, but the mage has required to remain unknown."

Bad, thought Arakante. Not even a hint as to whether the unknown was man or woman. It was one thing to be reclusive, but this degree of secrecy argued that whoever it was used practices that were dangerous, or questionable, or both. He tried again.

"Well, Lord Prahin, I can give you a general protection charm. I can't give you anything really powerful."

"Why not?"

"Because some charms are like oil and fire: Both are excellent apart, and even together under certain circumstances with the right barriers between or around them, but disastrous if flung together." And may that answer satisfy you, my Lord, Arakante thought. It's as much as you're going to get unless you give me more.

Lord Prahin seemed to realize this. He'd had the wit to bring dust from his doorstep; Arakante was able to prepare the charm that day and send it back before evening. It would probably neither help nor hurt. The charms in place were much stronger, guessing from the little that Lord Prahin had been willing to say; their power would overshadow this trinket. It was fortunate that his reputation rested on solving riddles and seeing the future, rather than protecting houses.

Arakante saw one more client, a middle-aged busines woman seeking foresight of how good this spring's supply of salad greens would be, and ordered the gatekeeper to admit no more chance-comers. He'd a few questions of his own to ask. It wasn't precisely forbidden to ask questions for one's self. Perhaps, since he had refused Layla, he would be allowed some leeway in this. With bowl and water, with an uncovered lamp flame, with casting of hinta-wood sticks, he tried to see the future for himself, and for Firousi and Layla. He knew already that he and Layla had no future; he had made certain of that himself.

The flame told him nothing at all. The water seemed to show him the figure of an unfamiliar man, but the surface shivered and the image dispersed before he could see it clearly. He grunted in disgust. All that he needed now was for the image to reappear as a tall dark stranger!

In the end it was the sticks, those vague and ambiguous guides, that told him anything. Several of them refused to fall at all, but stood almost upright in the midst of the tangle. Those that did fall showed only that some great event would affect the three of them just after the turn of the season. Because of the symmetry of the tangle, Arakante could not tell whether this was auspicious or not.

So, that rule held. It was folly to try to see one's own

future. It might be that including Firousi and Layla in his seeking had given him the little that he got. He'd had to know something, though, and he certainly wasn't about to risk having someone else try for him. Not when he still didn't know who Lord Prahin was dealing with.

The significant event had to be the Viceroy's entry into the city. Though he'd heard vague rumors that some Imperial delegation would come this spring, he'd paid them little mind. Such rumors were common at the end of winter. Neither he nor any other mage he knew had ever been able to get a good definite Seeing of yes or no to one. Gossip among mages said that this was because the Emperor always had at least three plans in view for any one time; less discreet gossip had it that he enjoyed keeping people guessing.

Arakante groaned. Now all he had to do was persuade Layla and Firousi to attend a festival for a ruler they all disliked, where they might see the triumph of a god that both women despised. Yet they would have to be there to have any chance of stopping that triumph; he knew that without water, fire or hinta-wood sticks. And they had to stop it.

32

I sat silently on a wall seat in the eating room, letting Firousi and Arakante argue while I decided what I thought.

"You want me to go to what?" Firousi's voice was more like sword striking sword than bells. "Arakante, I am known. I am known as the Priestess of the Lady of Laughter. Never mind the insult to me; what of the insult to Her if I go to this grand presentation of Her heart to that joyless—" she stopped herself and made signs to divert heavenly attention.

"Firousi—" Arakante protested.

She continued without noticing. "I can't watch while Her heart is given to Her enemy. If anything can kill one of the Immortals, this will. How can you ask such a thing? I have to stop this murder." She swept over to the eastern windows and stood staring out into the darkening sky.

Arakante seized his chance. "I'm not asking you to stand idly by, Firousi. I'm asking you to help bring your Lady's help to us as we all try to get Her heart back. This will be the last chance."

It sounded like a very slight one. Yet if I were there, I might see some way. There would be guards aplenty during the ceremony, but even Duty's guards might celebrate over-well once the presentation was done. Seeing the heart presented might give me some idea of how to take it away again. No, I'd better stop it from happening at all. Even Firousi was beginning to wonder if her Lady could die.

The theft would be thrilling. It would be talked of throughout the empire. And so would I! Fame isn't such a good thing for a thief. Even if I managed the trick and survived, could Kossinli's statue ever be displayed in public with those doubly-claimed jewels in it? What had been stolen once could be stolen again. A ring of armed guards to discourage thieves like me would discourage Her would-be worshipers, too. Yes, and there were some other problems.

"Arakante, you do remember who I stole that first eye from?"

Firousi laughed. Arakante ignored her. "Of course I remember. You'll be one of a huge crowd, Layla; I know how well you can disappear into crowds."

"Why should I get anywhere near a mob of worshipers of the god I robbed? It's crazy! I don't think anyone will recognize me. I'm good at what I do, Arakante! No one gets a good look at me when I'm working." He raised one eyebrow, doubtless remembering the failed burglary. I ignored him. "But if Kossinli's aware of me, why wouldn't Sarinsat be? What can I possibly get from going there that's worth the risk?" Did I really want the answer to that second question?

He sighed. Much more of that dreadfully patient sigh could do a lot to cure me of wanting him. "You're not stupid, Layla. You know the risks of not going. Trust me, I wouldn't ask."

"Trust you? Plague take you, I thought at least you were one man I'd never hear that line from! You're such a great mage, such a skilled Seer, and you can't do any better than 'trust me'?"

He sat so still that neither of us moved. "I have never boasted of my powers. Left to myself, I would be content to study the eternal realms without trying to influence them, but I never am left to myself."

He rose. By the doorway, he turned. "Ask Kossinli then, both of you, and see what you can learn." He was gone as suddenly as if he could vanish like the mages in children's stories. Perhaps he could.

Firousi and I studied our teacups for a time. Just as I was

about to make some excuse for leaving, Firousi said, "I need to meditate on this. We must do something, but I'm not sure Arakante's idea is our only choice, or the one that the Lady of Mirth would choose. There may be some way that doesn't require either of us to be present."

"I'll leave you in peace, then." And I did.

In the stable, I slipped Imchi's halter over his head and set out, letting him choose where we went. The outer gates were open now; like a sensible beast he made for the scent of fresh new grass beyond them. Mother Rissa's caravan would return soon. I wondered whether they'd get to Tzakende before the Emperor's half brother did.

The caravan appeared. For a moment I thought I'd somehow summoned them, that I had acquired some powers simply by living in the same house with a wizard. That was nonsense, surely; I'd spent so much time near the gates lately that it would have been surprising if I hadn't seen Mother Rissa's caravan arrive. You couldn't catch magic, like a cold. Or could you? Divining by donkey, a whole new method of discovering what actions to take.

They came through the gate in a tumble of beasts and children. Mother Rissa's fringed sleeve floated on the breeze as she flourished her token at the Guardian; that stone-faced functionary could not quite keep from smiling as he handed it back. He tried, of course.

Imchi brayed and pulled hard on the lead; he remembered those fringes. Yes, and Mother Rissa remembered that bray.

"Layla!" She was much too discreet to say much of her surprise at finding me still here. "Come, you and your djinn-donkey, join us at the caravanserai and we'll trade stories."

I accepted with thanks. In the course of telling stories, we'd both be able to find out if my traveling with Mother Rissa's clan again would really be a good idea. It might not even be possible. If Kossinli died...I turned away from that dark alley.

Issimante had seen me, and was staring at me with grim concentration. He handed his donkey's lead to a half-grown boy and joined us.

"Is she to travel with us again, after all the trouble she brought?"

Mother Rissa stared at him, and her stare beat his down. "I don't remember that she brought trouble."

"Mysterious strangers added to our party at midnight, Layla herself making the guards at Issrandar so suspicious that we barely got out—"

"What?" I cut in. "There was no such—"

"Indeed there was not. Layla, I will see you at the caravanserai. We will discuss travel plans there." Mother Rissa turned and gave a piercing whistle; half a dozen sheep turned away from a vegetable stall.

"Issimante, I never meant to insult you," I began. Then I stopped, working in silence to hold my temper. He was looking me up and down as if he'd found me leaning in a doorway down on Purse Lane.

"You're looking well," he said. "Got a fine lover, up in the high town?"

"No." He waited for the rest of the speech, but there wasn't any. I certainly wasn't going to tell him that it wasn't for lack of trying. I let Imchi push a way to one side of the crowd for us both. Did Issimante call my name as I left? Never mind. Issimante couldn't keep me from joining the caravan, but he could make it an uncomfortable trip. I wasn't eager to start again with some unknown leader, though. At least with Mother Rissa I knew I'd neither be sold into slavery if I traveled as a humble widow, nor murdered for my gold if I traveled as a rich one.

For the moment, I'd enjoy the rare Tzakendi sunlight shining on Mother Rissa's clan. There was a whole herd of multi-colored sheep with them this time, the sheep looking more prosperous than the people. Zada looked much too thin for a

woman feeding a baby. She had a new one, carried in a sling of striped cloth.

"No, all's well with us," she said when I asked. "This is what it's like for us in early spring. My daughter's the only plump one here. The sheep are lean, too. You just can't tell it under all that wool!"

There was a sudden tug on the lead, and Imchi was gone. Several travelers laughed merrily to see me pursue him through the crowd.

"Like old times, yes?" That was Mayra. I laughed as I ran.

Imchi was happily renewing his acquaintance with Issimante's donkey. They made a comical pair, the rangy, unburdened Imchi sniffing noses with tiny Khamsin, who was almost hidden under his load of leather-clad bottles.

Issimante himself laughed at the sight, though he managed to frown again as soon as he looked at me. "Layla! Your daft donkey's bigger than ever and twice as pushy."

"Nonsense, you're just used to that midget. Imchi's being very polite, for Imchi." To be polite myself, I added, "Your daughter's beautiful."

He smiled at me at last. "Yes, and you should hear her voice! She'll be a great singer, as her grandmother was, I'm sure. She's my first daughter, you know." I hadn't known, but I made an agreeable noise.

We walked on together for awhile. Issimante kept looking sideways at me; finally he said, "You'll leave no broken hearts behind? Sweet Layla, I find that hard to believe."

"Believe it," I assured him. Taking hints really wasn't his style, was it? Was I going to have to tell him not to ask about my love life again? He took my hand then, so that I turned to look at him.

"Ah, Layla," he said sadly. I heard someone giggle. I twisted my hand loose with an old thief's wriggle, but he showed no shock at my knowledge. "Such skills as you have. Maybe you'll share some of them on our long travels." He pretended to cower as I stepped toward him. "Nay, Layla, a man can hope!"

"You certainly will." Oh Kossinli, I know I wanted him friendly. Did I ask for this much friendliness? Lady of Mirth, if I somehow got Your heart, would You leave mine alone?

Children old enough to have made a little money were gleefully buying out the berry-sellers and the bakers; one of Zada's children brought back some for her. She walked along with berries in one hand and a honey fritter in the other; the baby found her breast without help.

Over Mother Rissa's token objections, I bought a large basket of honey-fritters to share. I could see her wondering how I'd got so prosperous, but she respects privacy where money's concerned if nowhere else.

At the caravanserai, Mother Rissa settled into a nest of cushions on the lowest rooftop and beckoned me to sit by her. "You're looking well. Have you finished your mysterious business?"

The woman really needed to do something about her subtle, devious nature. "Not really," I had to admit.

She snorted. "Well, if you manage it in the next moon, you might want to come with us at least as far as Issrandar. The lapis sellers will be in from the Land of Warriors by then, and rumor says there's been an earthquake up there that shook some fine pieces loose."

This was very obliging of her. I thanked her. "But I don't know yet just what my plans are."

She snorted again. "Girl, you mean you don't have any plans!"

Ouch. It wasn't quite true, but close enough to feel the thrown blade's breeze. "I will know before the next new moon." And so I would. I hoped I'd still need a way out of town.

Mother Rissa smiled. "There now, you needn't take that tone with me! You fitted in well, for a city girl, so I speak to you as I would to one of my own."

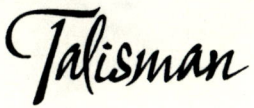

What is it about me that brings out the urge to serve as father or mother? Do I look so helpless? Maybe it's being short and slight. Old Parata, Mother Rissa, Firousi...not Arakante. He at least was willing to let me walk over a cliff if that was what I really wanted to do. I was going to miss that man.

Had Firousi come up with any answers while I lingered here? I made my excuses, towed Imchi away from his friend, and hastened back.

33

*D*inner was brief; Esran claimed half of it had burned while we were up in the solar and, he said with a poisonous glare, wandering about at an hour when sensible folk were at table. Neither Arakante nor Firousi seemed to notice the scanty portions, even when I consoled myself by eating far more than my share of the fried lentils with chilis. Well, there was enough food for me to go to bed with a full belly, and no threat from those who shared it. Hadn't I been glad enough of that, not so long ago?

In my room, I dropped a pinch of dried rose petals in front of the small carving of Kossinli. I wished I had refused outright to ask Her for a sign. Who knew what kind of sign She'd send? She seemed to think we'd failed deliberately. Maybe Arakante's coldness to me was another of Her jests. Yes, there was some humor in seeing someone who'd complained bitterly of men's attentions trying and failing to seduce one.

Ah well, the bed might be empty, but it was warm and clean. I had walked miles that day, and run between laughter and fear, anger and contentment, several times. For all my sorrows, I was soon asleep.

I had my old dream again, and knew it to be a dream, of gathering jewels and silks by a gently-flowing stream. Imchi was with me this time, grazing on grasses that reached to his belly. I climbed the stream's willows to gather flowers made of rubies and sapphires. There were so many, I might just need Imchi!

I certainly would if I tried to bring back many of the thick twists of silk that wound around the trees like vines. Their colors

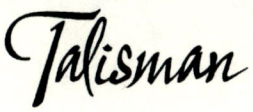

seemed to ripple in the light. It would be no waste of time, surely, to gather some of them as well as the jewels. A good, deep-dyed skein of silk could cost twice its own weight in silver.

A breeze rippled through the meadow, swaying some of those iridescent silks nearer to my hand. I laughed; it was as if they wanted to be gathered.

Below me, Imchi brayed. Stupid animal, why couldn't he enjoy his meal? There was nothing to threaten him in the meadow. I reached back towards the skeins of silk nearest me, and pulled my hand back so fast that I nearly lost my balance.

A snake's head swayed all too near me, tasting the air with its tongue. The hissing of the leaves in the wind became louder, and the silk-vines began to crawl upwards.

A jewel fell sparkling from the sackful I'd gathered and stung my hand when I reached out for it. That felt real! Was this really a dream?

If this wasn't a dream, those might be real snakes. How was I to get down out of this tree past them as they wound around its trunk and branches? They were coming closer.

Fortunately I have never had the fear some women have of snakes. Many garden snakes make good neighbors, eating mice and other pests. These were not that kind of snake. I refused to panic. Fear solved nothing, and I, Layla, did not give way to it.

The snake nearest me was swaying side-to-side. Gods, but he was beautiful! This, surely, was the kind of snake that dancers' bracelets are modeled on. His scales were golden and his eyes, bright green. Light rippled along his scales as he swayed. Rabbits are lulled to their deaths by such swaying. Whatever clever thing I was going to do, I'd better do it soon.

Soon and quickly. There was only one thing to do, since I'd been fool enough to come here unarmed. A slim chance was better than none at all. As he swayed to one side and tasted my scent in the air, I grabbed him just behind his spearpoint-shaped head.

He writhed in my hand, growing stronger and colder as I held him. His scales were cutting my hand so that the blood ran down. I tightened my grip.

Then I clutched a gold and emerald snake. I stared at it for several breaths before I dared relax my grip, still holding it at arm's length. It made no move. Below me, the vines were only vines.

I shouted in triumph and woke myself. I woke half the house as well. The first to arrive was Firousi, slipperless on the cold stone floors. She curled her toes gratefully into the rug by the bed even as she demanded to know what had happened.

Arakante was next. He stood half-in, half-out the door, averting his eyes from me as soon as he saw I wasn't injured. He saw a good bit more than that: I'd flung off most of the bedclothes in my flight from the snake, and I've never cared for night-robes tangling round my ankles. I tried to pull my undertunic down at the same time as I pulled the blankets up. It didn't work. Firousi laughed and tossed the covers over me.

"Well, you told us to ask for signs," Firousi said over her shoulder. "I too have had strange dreams. Shall we wake Cook and tell our stories over breakfast?"

34

*W*hen Firousi came into the common room, she had put on warm house slippers and a long quilted tunic in shades of cinnamon and cream. Her hair was neatly tied back; she'd not taken time for her usual elaborate arrangement of braids. No one said much until the kitchen-maid had handed round the tea and last night's warmed-up bread, with a little honey-preserved fruit. Once she had left, Arakante cast lots. Firousi drew the first telling.

She looked at Arakante and Layla in turn, intensely and without regard for politeness. "She did not speak to me directly. She has not done so since we failed to rescue Her heart. She did send a dream, though, and I doubt Arakante will have any trouble interpreting it.

"Here is how it happened in my dream," she said. "I'll tell it all just as if it made sense, for it did when I dreamed it.

"I was playing the lap-harp, or trying to do so. The new string would not stay tuned. I tightened it again, cautiously, forcing myself to pretend patience. There was no time to play the music itself with all this constant twiddling of pegs. It was almost lunchtime, but I contented myself with a few bites of the chile-spiced lentil crisps Layla had taught Esran to make.

"I'd just have to try the crocodile that lay curled in my harp-case. 'Pestilence!' The creature had bitten me. It was newly hatched and likely to bite at anything available. 'No, no, you're supposed to bite the string and hang on,' I muttered as I detached it from my hand. At least it had nipped the side rather than one of my fingertips. Holding the crocodile more carefully, I jiggled the end of the new string in front of it.

"This time it went as it should; the crocodile clung securely to the string with its paws folded tightly in against its body. Its slight weight helped keep the new string taut. Yes, that was better.

"I played on for a time, that imperceptible time free of demands or reminders of time's passing that only comes in dreams. The crocodile ended that when it began to squirm. 'Not yet,' I told it, for I'd almost mastered a tricky shift in mode.

"Just as I'd done the passage once and had begun the second time that proves the first time wasn't just luck, the crocodile climbed up the end of the string and bit me again.

" 'You are a horrible little beast!' I shouted, and flung it to the floor. It crouched there and looked up at me with tears falling from its glittering red eyes. The tears turned to pearls and rolled away.

"I set the lap harp aside so that I could gather them up; as I did, the new string broke. I cursed the string, the crocodile and the pearls; I cursed my own stupidity. I should have eased the string and fed the crocodile long ago. The crocodile waddled away, still weeping, and disappeared under a chest.

"Perhaps I could have Layla make the pearls into something for Kossinli. First I'd have to get them! They slipped away from my hand as I crouched on the carpet. Although a steady stream of them rolled out from under the chest, none of them rolled near me. My solar was filling up with pearls. It was getting hard to wade through them, but when I tried to pick one up they were all too far away.

"Why did the stupid crocodile hide in the dark, weeping? The chest was too heavy to move. I thrust my hand under the chest, hoping I wouldn't be bitten again.

"That hope was doomed. Sharp teeth seized me and pulled; I suddenly found myself trapped underneath the chest with a red-eyed crocodile. I couldn't free my hand. Only a thin line of light showed between the chest and the floor. It was getting hard

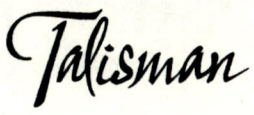

to breathe. I could grasp the crocodile's snout with my free hand, but my knuckles scraped the bottom of the chest when I tried to pry the beast's jaws loose. All the time, more pearls rolled from its eyes. I felt almost sorry for the creature, huddled into a cold dark place when I knew it craved light and warmth. I'd gladly give it both if it would only let loose!

"I kicked out in my anger. The chest rocked from side to side; a plate slid and fell. My hand was free! The crocodile waddled rapidly towards the lentil crisps.

"I wriggled out from under the chest, scraping my hair and my clothes into complete disarray. As I emerged, I saw the room as a very small child might, with the chairs and the chest towering over me. Then I blinked and the sizes were normal.

"The crocodile hissed and started back for the chest. Oh, no, not that again! I lit a stick of incense and waved it slowly back and forth as if I were playing with a cat.

"The incense stick was half-burned when the crocodile rushed forward and clamped its jaws around it. It ate the remainder of the stick eagerly, not minding the coal at one end at all. Its eyes glowed brighter. Snorting like a tiny dragon, it waddled over to an oil lamp and curled up to sleep.

"The pearls were vanishing as it settled into sleep. I'd pushed one into a corner with my efforts to grasp it; now it had no place to roll away from me. I picked it up and dropped it again immediately. My fingers where I'd touched it were burned as with acid. To my surprise, that was the only mark on either hand. Layla's shriek woke me before I could decide what to do next. Not a subtle dream, was it? Perhaps that very fact is another hint."

Arakante raised his left eyebrow. "How do you mean, not subtle?"

"Since you ask—I was doing something dangerous, and using something which I dislike. It worked for a time, but I overdid it. It seems I must be brave, but not too brave; persistent but not stubborn. I must know when to loosen the tension on a new string, though I must say, Layla doesn't look at all likely to snap. Sometimes it takes more than one try to accomplish a task; we all know what task is meant. I must beware hypocrites— crocodile tears, indeed! Lastly, I must do something dangerous that I don't want to do: I don't need you to tell me what it is, Arakante."

35

Arakante smiled, looking down into his teacup. "Layla? What of your dream?"

She told it quickly, finishing up by saying, "So you see, it was much like Firousi's."

Arakante leaned towards Layla. "May I?" he said as he reached for her hands. She smiled wryly and held them both out to him, palms up. Several red lines scored her right palm.

The skin wasn't actually broken. "Is it painful?" he asked.

"No, just a little sore. Does this mean it was a true dream?"

Many would have been frightened. Layla looked curious and almost eager. He wouldn't have expected that from someone who'd gone to the lengths that she had to escape divine involvement.

Firousi coughed gently. He let the silence go a moment longer, then answered. "Yes, it's a true dream. A first year student could read it: you will get a chance at great gain, which you must be quick to use or you will lose the chance and more. There will be pain."

Layla shrugged. No doubt she'd had to endure plenty of that in her life. "Will I succeed?"

"It's incomplete, but yes, the dream would seem to say so. Remember, though—"

"Dreams tell only what may be, not what must be." Layla and Firousi said in chorus.

Arakante made himself laugh. No, there probably hadn't been any need for him to remind them of that. It would be pleasant to get a little respect at home, just now and then. He didn't think it would go to his head too much. In fact, he was pretty sure he was in no danger of getting too high an opinion of himself.

"It's a pity there are only two of you. There's something missing here—"

Layla cut in with, "A nice straightforward instruction?"

Arakante continued, "And a third account traditionally finishes the tale. It's no good my asking for a dreamsending; my talent simply doesn't work that way. If I can't find the answer waking, it will not come to me in dreams."

Layla laughed. "Can you understand the speech of animals? You only need to interview Imchi to get three out of three."

It was tempting. "I do, a little. I wonder...I wonder if he did dream. Do donkeys dream?" Maybe he'd have the leisure to pursue that someday. He hoped that would be a happy circumstance. Could Firousi actually believe her own reasoning?

Firousi laughed. "If you do interview Imchi, I want to be there!" He was relieved to hear her so amused; for all her silence, he'd been well-aware of her gloom. It argued that she had doubts she wouldn't express.

"Why not? We'll all go." And so they and the gatekeeper's boy, laden with an old rug and several cushions, went up the path to where Imchi stood in the paddock. He was stretching as far as he could to bite the opening leaves of a lilac. At least the blossom buds were mostly out of his reach. Firousi's horses trotted over hopefully; Firousi pulled a napkin out from her layers of clothing and gave each one a fruit wafer.

Firousi gestured to the gatekeeper's boy to put the rug over on the flagstones and arranged cushions herself. Arakante strove for patience as she set them in order. "I see no point in being any more uncomfortable than I must," she said, half-apologetically. "No, we need nothing more," she said to the stableboy who'd come over to stand, leaning on his pitchfork and staring at them.

He went back into the stable, looking back only once.

"Imchi, do you have dreams?" Arakante began. The donkey swivelled his ears forward, but made no sound. "Pictures when you sleep?" Imchi snorted.

"Did you have a dream last night?" Another snort. Arakante sighed. If only donkeys didn't have such limited vocabularies! Slowly, working mostly with yes-or-no questions, he worked his way through what Layla had told him of her dream. Imchi grew more talkative as they went on. It might be, Arakante thought, that he would be more eager to talk if he knew there would be someone who understood him. Another interesting question.

He had paused too long; both women were staring at him, and the donkey turned back to nibble at the lilac. "Were you there when Layla climbed the tree?"

Imchi whuffled, and gave a short and quiet (for him) bray. Yes, there had been good grass, tall and juicy.

Layla chuckled at Arakante's translation. "That animal eats even in his sleep!"

Imchi made a very rude noise that needed no translation. Then, "Snakes!" Imchi continued in a high-pitched whinny. "She yelled me, warner!" Arakante did not translate all of that.

Imchi brayed imperiously, bracing his legs. "Run?" Arakante asked. Imchi brayed again, louder, emphasizing the trill that followed the main bray. "Not run," Arakante amended. "Layla must not run?" Imchi whuffled.

"Not run? That's what's saved my life every time in this weird year!" Layla scowled. "I've been thieving for years now, Arakante. I don't need advice on that, particularly from an ass."

Imchi turned as sharply as a large donkey could, and trotted to the other side of the paddock. Firousi's horses looked at each other and slowly walked away.

"I guess that tells me," commented Layla. Clouds were rolling in again; assisted by the stableboy, the three questioners of donkeys got themselves and their gear inside the house before it rained.

There was hot bread now, and yet more tea. Arakante waited until both the others had their mouths full before he spoke. "Shall I assume that you also don't need me to advise you on what the dreams say you should do?" Both women swallowed hastily; Firousi gave him a glare that said she knew what he'd done.

"You may assume that, cousin," Firousi said. She had assumed her Lady face; a slight smile curved her lips, but her eyes told nothing at all. Layla looked thoughtful.

"I'm sorry," he said gently.

"Sorry to have won? Why?" Firousi took a long swallow of tea.

"It wasn't about my winning or losing. It was about keeping you, and you, and the Goddess herself safe." By all the gods that were or would be, he'd be glad when this was over. Had he ever asked to be involved in this struggle? Had he ever claimed to be an intimate of the Gods? One asked, politely and with the proper ritual, for certain insights and sometimes They granted the request. The skill lay in reading the answers. Let those who enjoyed pushing storms around have their fun, so long as they did no great harm.

Ah well, it would be over soon one way or another. There was still a chance that they would all survive. The balance of the hinta-wood sticks lay trembling under their breathing. If they did, then Layla would leave, Layla with her own strange sense of humor that made her such a perfect conduit for Kossinli. He doubted she'd ever shake free of that connection. Layla with such long legs for such a small person...and maybe, when she was gone, she'd also stop troubling his dreams. It might be so. It would be so. Thinking could make things so; he would think that they'd manage somehow.

He could, of course, ban her from his dreams; he knew the warding perfectly. It required no elaborate rituals or exotica. It did require that he truly want to do so.

It was a relief to see the doorkeeper hovering just inside the room, to be reminded discreetly that there were clients waiting. Some nice, boring, everyday questions about finding an auspicious day for a marriage or scrying out where to build a house would be a welcome change.

Firousi wished him good fortune with his Seeing; he thanked her and escaped. She frightened him when she was so carefully polite; he remembered easier times when her temper had escaped those courtesies.

At first the practice of his art eased his mind, just as he'd hoped it would. Then several clients in a row asked him to discover a good day for a marriage for them, or for their children. This hardly demanded the skills of a mage; any of the minor magic workers who'd piled their mud walls against the temples' stones could have done it. When he'd first begun selling his talents, he'd tried to refuse such work; now he wished he'd stood by that.

It was cruel irony to have to arrange the marriage-dates of other people when he slept alone himself. Oh, there were women enough who'd oblige him, but he didn't much care for that kind of arrangement. Gods, but he was going to miss Layla! The only thing worse than seeing her without being able to touch her would be not seeing her at all. Which he certainly hoped he wouldn't, if— no. They would retrieve the Heart.

Marriages. Suddenly he smiled. Marriages, properly done, could provide some level of protection for mages who married and for those who married them. He was almost surely done with need to See for Layla. How on earth had he not thought of this before? She'd never have to leave. She could go on making lovely things in her workshop, and he could go on practicing his magic arts; they could meet for dinner with none of the rivalry that had always lain between his wife and himself.

Arakante saw the one client who was actually on the doorstep, and sent two servants running to cancel his other appointments for the day. Before he had put away his instruments, a Seeing came to him unbidden. Layla was outside the city walls, and she was troubled by things seen and unseen.

36

*F*og clung to the grass; the hems of my skirts were soaked in minutes. The mist settled gently on my face. Coolness came with it, but no longer the icy chill that there had been even a few days ago. I wished I could leave now, set off with Imchi and Mother Rissa's clan while Tzakende disappeared into the soft fog.

Unfortunately, it had already disappeared. I actually felt frightened for a moment. That was foolish. I'm a fast walker, but I couldn't have wandered far from the walls. All I had to do was walk back downhill and I'd find some part of them. The Charransar road gleamed wetly through gaps in the fog. Above it, a white shrine appeared and disappeared.

Now if only I could disappear! I'd had no trouble escaping Firousi's guidance; she herself had left the house soon after Arakante returned to his clients.

It was uncomfortable, being able to see that distant road and not the nearby walls. Was Someone trying to tell me something? I couldn't imagine what. No, I'd just lived too long with a mage and a priestess.

There were several groups of travelers on the road. Brave folk, to travel when surely they could barely see their nearest companions. Perhaps they knew how close they were to the city and its comforts.

And perhaps they had little to fear from fog or anything that it might hide. As the mists shifted in a breeze that didn't reach to where I was, I saw that it was not several groups. Sunlight pale as moonlight glinted off link-coats. Cart after mule-drawn baggage cart stretched out the line. The emperor's half brother would be in Tzakende sooner than anyone thought.

Much sooner than we'd thought, anyway. The cold, heavy wetness of my skirts seemed to spread through the rest of my body. Would the presentation ceremony take place sooner, then? How much time did we have to plan? Surely even Sarinsat's people would need a few days? Maybe not. They had magical help, too, that much was clear; someone in that glittering parade might be able to do a Sending. I needed to get back to the villa. I could only hope that Firousi and Arakante would both be there. This was one theft that must not fail.

I turned to make my way back towards where the walls had to be. After this last year I'd gotten fairly well used to walking on paths I couldn't see.

I walked slowly, but still stumbled in the fog. Surely, even at this slow progress, I should have encountered the walls by now? I'd stubbed my toes on enough other stones.

Well, it was hard to tell how long anything took when there were no shadows to show the sun's movement. I just had to be sure to keep walking downhill. That shouldn't be too hard, fog or no fog. I walked on, tripping now and then over the ropy roots of shrubs that were trying to cling to the mountainside. I lost the beaded tassel from my left shoe to one such tangle.

It took tripping over the same root three times before I realized that I was getting nowhere. On the third time, the beads from my other shoe came loose and soared high enough for me to see their cheerful colors. It made me want to cry. If I ever got back safely home to Charransar, I was going to stay there for the rest of my life. In Charransar I'd never had to deal with sandstorms, or fog, or wizards.

It was better to think about finding my way out of this fog. I was getting very hungry, and yes, afraid. Had I wandered into another battle between wizards? If so, I hoped Arakante was one of them. He'd surely See that I was in the middle of this mess

and shield me.

I wanted to sit down, but everything out here was as wet as I was. I kicked at the root and regretted it as my toe found the rock it was wrapped around. The silent laughter that followed made me bite back my curse. The deities are thick as thieves; however much they fight among themselves, they don't want outsiders making remarks.

"I'm sorry," I muttered. "Believe me, I'll get you that heart if I can, whatever I must do. Lady of Mirth, help me to help you!" There was no answer.

I turned and began walking again, trying for what felt like downhill. What was the point of having the attention of a Goddess if all She did was laugh at my plight and send me gifts I didn't want? I'd been perfectly content to put the proper pinch of incense on the proper altars in the proper season and hope that none of the Immortals bothered themselves with one small thief, but no! Now I must fear a different death than thieves face. I was not going to contemplate what that might be.

I tripped again and fell full-length. This time I did curse, Divine Presence or no. I reached out to find some bush or rock to help me get up; there was nothing there, not even the rocky ground. Keeping my body as still as I could, I swept my arm out in front of me. There was a drop-off just beyond my elbow; when I edged over and felt along the side I couldn't feel the bottom. Mist lay thick below me. Deep enough, then, to injure if not to kill.

"Thank you, Lady of Laughter," I said. "Would it be terribly ungrateful to ask that You find some gentler method of keeping me from falling off the edge of the earth? You used to speak to me." There was a chuckle, but no words. Ah well, at least She'd gotten over Her anger enough to keep me from being badly injured. I shuffled carefully away.

"Layla?" Arakante's voice no longer startled me, even coming unexpectedly out of the fog. I wondered if the rest of him was here, too. It always had been before, but that doesn't necessarily mean much when you're dealing with a mage.

Either Arakante materialized, or he came close enough to be seen even in this fog. He was courteous enough to let me ask my question before he answered it.

"Has anything more gone wrong?"

"No, nothing at all." Arakante was smiling as I'd never seen—no, wait. He'd smiled like that the first time we met, like someone with a delicious secret. He didn't ask why I was out here; I suspect he knew that as he knew so many other things. I did wonder what was causing that smile.

"Did you see the Viceroy's caravan?" I asked.

"Ah, is that what it was? No, I saw something, but the vision was unclear." He laughed. "All that hesitation that Seers do isn't an act, you know!"

"I do now. It's been a very educational year, all 'round." Whatever his secret was, I decided I could wait to hear it next to a fire. "Perhaps we should go back and tell Firousi that the ceremony's likely to happen sooner than we thought?"

"Not just yet." He took my hand. "Layla, forgive my keeping you out here in the wet and the cold, but once we're back home I'll have to cast a spell of avoidance to get any time alone with you."

Did he want to tumble out here in the mists, on the rocks? "Arakante, I do know places in town..." I didn't think about refusing until after I'd made the offer. Where was my pride? Something had made him change his mind about having me, and here he was, just assuming I'd be willing whenever he was. And I was going along. If we failed I might be dead before much longer. What use was pride in the grave?

"No, Layla, it isn't that! Or, not quite." Arakante guided me gently though the fog to a stone ledge. I'd never actually seen a man cast his cloak onto the ground to cushion a woman, unless they were about to have sex, but what happens in love poems can happen in fact. Warily, I hitched myself up onto the ledge.

He stood below me silently. I began to wonder what he could have to say that required such secrecy and caused such hesitation.

"Layla, we've grown fond of each other during this strange year. I've only just now come to know that I..." he hesitated again, "I love you. Layla, will you marry me?"

Oh, ye demons of sour water. What could I say to that? There is no good way to tell a man that you won't marry him.

"Arakante, I can't."

"Why not? Are you still angry with me for refusing you? I had no choice, Layla, and if you knew how difficult it was—"

"No, it isn't that. I'm very fond of you, Arakante—I think I may love you," I heard myself say. I hadn't been able to guard my tongue against what I hadn't even known until I said it.

"Then stay with me! You're known as a jeweler here a little already, to some of Firousi's friends. Once we get Kossinli's Heart back you could stay here, practicing your art while I practice mine."

"Arakante, I've been married. I didn't like it and I wasn't good at it. My husband wasn't happy either. I can't put it plainer than that." It had been a mistake to admit that I loved him. If this was what love felt like, this miserable mix of joy and fear, I wished I'd gone on not knowing.

He turned his back on me and walked away a few steps. When he spoke his voice was flat. "So, I'm good enough to bed but not to wed?"

"No! Gods, Arakante, if anyone would be marrying down it'd be you, not me! I'd marry you if I thought I could marry anyone and not make him miserable. I can't even live with other people very well."

He came back then. "Do you mean that?"

"What, the living with other people? Look at this last year."

Arakante laughed softly and shook his head. Drops of water flew from his hair. "Tell me," he urged. "If you won't marry me, tell me why."

I told him then about my married years. He remained quiet throughout the story, and for several breaths after I'd done. Then, "Does it make no difference at all for me to point out that I'm not him? That I offer you a life with freedom—"

"There's no freedom in marriage! If I survive all this I'll be free of Kossinli soon one way or another, and then—oh, Arakante, if I could marry anyone I'd marry you. I can't." And I may be twelve kinds of a fool for not doing it, too.

In all our encounters I'd never looked directly into his eyes before. I did so now. We stayed thus for several heartbeats while he stared back, looking at me as if I were one of his precious scrolls. I felt as easily read; maybe more so. I hated this, I hated leaving myself undefended, but I had to let him know! How long could I stand this?

He looked away and I could breathe again. He touched my hair very gently and caught the water that dropped from it.

"Let's go back and tell Firousi that the Viceroy's coming," he said softly.

We walked back towards the city together, rags of fog trailing across our feet. "Are wizards fighting again?" I pointed to the changing mists around us.

Arakante nodded. "No, but someone has been using the weather. I wonder why? I can't see that they gained much from such a great effort."

We found out why soon enough. The fog grew denser as we approached the town's western gate, but Arakante led me to it easily. "A first-year student's skill," he laughed. That would be a useful thing to learn. I wondered...no, I'd had more than enough of meddling with the supernatural. And Arakante was hardly likely to give me lessons in anything now.

I am not used to feeling clumsy. In the short time it took us to get back I must have wished for light a dozen times, without caring what Kossinli did about it. She chose to do nothing at all.

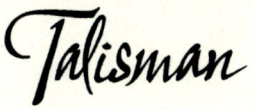

The streets of Tzakende were crowded, even in this fog. After a winter here, I didn't even wonder at it; if Tzakendi waited for fine weather they'd have to hibernate like bears.

A trumpet sounded behind us, and the fog scattered like a band of thieves at sunrise. The Viceroy, half-brother to the Emperor, rode glittering into town. Even his baggage-carts shone with bright paint and jingling ornaments.

"Very nice," murmured Arakante.

37

*T*hat was not Firousi's reaction. Only a lifelong training as Priestess kept her from cursing her own Goddess for letting that show happen.

"Why, Lady?" Firousi cried aloud. She paced the halls of the villa, knowing without caring that servants were ducking into rooms and down staircases like coneys in a boulder-field to avoid her.

"Why did You let that upstart stage a show like that? He's so fond of the Servants of Duty, well, let him come in calmly and soberly."

She stopped abruptly. Had Kossinli been so weakened— no, that was nonsense. Kossinli could surely have made the fog disperse or persist had She wished to summon one of Her servants to do so. Why, Firousi herself could have found Arakante and persuaded him to help. Even without Her Heart, Kossinli could do that much.

Roshana was waiting for Firousi when she returned to her room, hoping for some time for quiet meditation. The maid clucked at Firousi, ignoring her frown. "No, my Lady, what's this? It was a fine-enough court robe, before it got pulled half-apart and flung down on the floor." She held out a long tangle of fabric that hung stiff with gold embroidery.

"Right you are, Roshana. It was a court robe. Now it's a too-large court robe, and I'll be fried in yak-fat if I'll force-feed myself to put on enough flesh to look like a woman in it rather than a walking clothes rack. There won't be time enough before this

hideous ceremony anyway, not now."

"Fried in yak fat? My Lady! Where did you learn that expression?" Her face said that she thought she knew.

Firousi laughed. "No, that wouldn't help, would it? Perhaps we could get Arakante to discover Layla's secret. She never has this problem."

"That greedy brat! You look as a Lady should, my Lady. And you eat as a Lady should, enjoying your food without bolting it as if someone might steal it from you." Roshana gave the robe a good shake. "Now, you let me take this up into the solar where there's light, and I'll have it fitting again in no time. Bless you, do you think I can't rearrange those folds to suit you better? The cloth's too fine to throw away, but I never did think the cut was right for you."

"That isn't fit work for you, Roshana. We'll call Lady Mirrim's seamstress in."

"No need, my Lady, though it's kind of you. I can still see well enough to do simple stitching! Just you be kind again and come up to your solar soon, before the light goes." Roshana bore the robe away.

Firousi did as she was asked. Meditation wouldn't interfere with having the robe fitted; far from it. She could easily leave one part of her mind in charge of responding to requests to "Turn a little this way, Mistress," and let the rest of her mind seek some communion with Kossinli. Her dream had been intriguing, but it hadn't really told her what to do.

How was she to plan without knowledge? There was nothing in the lore that spoke of anything like this. There were dirges of sacrifice that sang of dying gods, but they had nothing to do with Kossinli.

The enforced stillness of the fitting helped her concentrate. Yet Kossinli's answer, when she had it, was more baffling than the dream had been. *Bring Arakante's cat? Lady of Mirth, do I understand you correctly?*

There was a chuckle. *You understand. And you will know what else to do when the time comes.*

Firousi was glad not to find Arakante when she made her way to his study the next day. Dancer, his cat, was dozing in the morning sunlight. The cat seemed to have less confidence in her than Kossinli did. It leaped quickly to the top of the scroll-rack and squinted down at her and at the covered basket she carried.

"Silly cat! I can't take you anywhere yet." She'd thought to entice Dancer into the basket with some of their precious remaining dried fish, just to get her used to the experience of being carried in it. Dancer showed no interest in the fish, or the feather that Firousi waved.

"Where are you proposing to take Dancer?" Arakante stood in the doorway, staring at her. Dancer meowed loudly as if to second the question.

"Ari!"

"And when were you going to ask me about it? Please don't try using childhood names when you answer."

"Just as soon as I could find you!" Firousi set down the basket. "Arakante, Kossinli wants Dancer to be at the presentation."

"What? Why? Dancer will be terrified. You know how she hates to leave her home." They'd tried it once, to introduce Dancer to a fine white long-haired tomcat that a client had imported from the northern mountains. Arakante had spent one whole day and considerable energy healing the tomcat.

"I don't know why. And I've never seen that cat terrified of anything, ever." Firousi forced herself to lower her voice. "Arakante, you know Kossinli doesn't give explanations. Can't you make Dancer come with us? I truly don't think she'll be in danger. Kossinli likes cats." She put the basket down on his desk.

He laughed. "Command a cat? Ah, cousin, you've never shown so high an opinion of my abilities before."

Dancer meowed, and yawned halfway through it. Both

people laughed. "You see? She's not impressed," said Arakante.

"That's one reason Kossinli likes cats. Arakante, She was most specific about it. We need Dancer."

"Why not Imchi, too?"

"Oh, Arakante, don't be silly. Imchi's much too large to be smuggled into the Hall of Ceremonies." Firousi giggled nervously. "It would be amusing if we could do it...no. Just Dancer."

The cat began purring loudly. Arakante turned quickly to stare at her. "So, Dancer, what do you think?" He took a quill from his desk and waved it just below where Dancer lurked. One white paw batted at it. "Do you want to help rescue a Goddess, hmm?"

The cat jumped down onto his shoulder. It looked to Firousi as if Dancer were whispering in his ear, and maybe it was so. Firousi had never seen signs that Dancer was his familiar, or anything but an ordinary cat, but after watching the interview with Imchi she'd no trouble believing that Arakante could understand Dancer's speech.

He raised his head and gave Firousi a wizard's stare. He and Dancer looked at her in so much the same way that she would have laughed at any other time.

"If any harm comes to her, Firousi..."

She darted over to him. "There's no need for threats, Arakante. She's safe. She will be well." Dancer abandoned Arakante's shoulder for his desk. Firousi stroked his hair; her hand lingered on his neck where the curls tapered off.

"Cousin," he said.

"Yes," she answered, and let her hand fall. Behind them, Dancer tapped at the basket, watching with her head to one side as it rocked back and forth. It took only a few taps to send it, and several scrolls, to the floor.

On the morning of the ceremony, Dancer was nowhere to be found. Nothing could lure her from wherever she was, not even catnip. Arakante took precious time doing a reading using two lost whiskers and a tuft of hair combed from her favorite cushion, but could see only that the cat was well.

"You're sure she's well, and unconfined?" Firousi was fond of the little beast. She had found her one cold morning, yowling like a djinn in the street, and carried her back to food and warmth. The ungrateful kitten had promptly declared herself Arakante's cat.

"I'm sure of that much. I hope your Lady can manage without her, cousin; she's not anywhere that I can find."

Firousi bit back a comment about his skill at finding anything. She could tell from his face that he heard it anyway. "I don't know, Arakante. The Lady of Laughter never told me why Dancer should be there." She drew a deep breath. "We'll just have to cope. I ought to be used to that by now."

"She really didn't like that basket," Arakante said.

How was she supposed to get the cat across town, put her in harness like Imchi? There was no time to argue and no point in trying. "I'll go see how Layla's doing," she said.

Layla had put on her underrobe. The pair of high-raised pattens that Firousi had been sure would fit her lay against one wall, and Layla had dug out a beaded pair of street slippers instead. She had also strapped a small knife in a soft leather scabbard to the inside of her upper arm. It looked an uncomfortable place to carry a weapon, but that was beside the point.

"Layla, that's got to go," she said. Experience said there was no point in being subtle about this.

"Why? They won't search us, surely?"

"They'll know. There'll be scores of wizards there, with no duties beyond scanning the crowd to detect any weapon bigger than a cloak clasp. They'll overlook ill intent unless someone's thinking specific plans of harm."

"It'd be a thin crowd otherwise," Layla commented. She made no move to take off the knife. Firousi stared at her.

"Will they really know, however skillfully I hide them? Ah

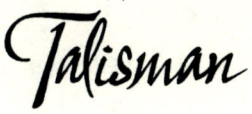

well, you've spent much more time around magic than I have."
Layla discarded the knife, two small disks whose edges glinted
wickedly, and a lockpick. "Suppose I could keep this? No?" She set
it aside with the rest, shaking her head.

Layla turned to the chest that held her warm-weather
clothes and a few valuables. She'd lodged the main part of her
business stock in Arakante's safe room. "Ah, that will do." She
slipped on three silver bangles and an inlaid copper one, all
decorated with rather gaudy-looking raised bosses and ropework.
"A Lady must have her jewelry, must she not?" Layla grinned.

"Indeed she must." Firousi smiled. It probably wasn't
necessary, but it clearly made Layla feel better. It certainly was
clever. She hoped it would be unnecessary for Layla to hit anyone
with those bangles.

38

*T*here were three lines of guards around the Hall of Ceremonies that day. We passed the first line easily; only street-dwellers and branded criminals were denied entry to the first courtyard. We were stopped briefly at the second line while a guard looked us over.

We waited long enough at the third line to worry me. What if we were stuck here while the ceremony took place? Death by waiting in line, what an ignominious way to go.

These were most elegant guards, gleaming in overlapping scale armor like walking snakes. To calm myself I tried to figure the worth of such a suit of armor, assuming I could get it away from its owner, and came up with a figure that would keep both me and Imchi in comfort for well over a year. I was definitely not comfortable just then; people were treading on our heels. Something pulled at my skirts, but when I looked around I saw nothing. They must have snagged against someone else's holiday clothes. There were rich takings here, but little chance of getting away safely with anything. I hoped there weren't any stupid pickpockets among us.

"Can't you just spell us through?" I said in Arakante's ear. He winced. I was sorry I'd had to be so loud, but I couldn't tell him that without shouting in his ear again.

"No, Layla. Their own wizards have thrown up layers of wards that make the guards look like toy soldiers. They dare not risk some rogue wizard finding a way to do mischief."

On the other side of a line of guards, a man in turquoise

brocade looked over his shoulder at us. He had the long white hair and beard of a wizard in a fairy tale, and he leaned on a staff. "Master Arakante! How good to see you!" His voice carried easily over the buzz and bustle.

We were soon passed through with apologies for the delay. The Great Wizard ignored Firousi and me; that rankled after the usual Tzakendi courtesy. "You haven't come to our studies in so long, Master Arakante! No, you were always too modest. I know you've a household to support, but tear yourself away from the work for hire betimes and join us. You might hear much that's of interest to you."

It may be that Arakante's own brocade kept him from bowing with his usual suppleness. "I still hold that you honor me more than I deserve, Lord Nayan. I shall come when I have something to contribute to the feast of knowledge. I would not be a beggar."

"Never that! Well, I hope to see you later." The wizard disappeared into the rest of the dazzle. The Hall of Ceremonies was enough to give a poor thief a headache on that day, glittering on all sides with gold and silver, gems and silks.

"Speaking of rogue wizards," muttered Firousi. Arakante glared; she smiled but said no more.

One of Tzakende's three-colored cats had slipped somehow into this august gathering. She looked nervous, that cat; she held her tail half-up to keep it out of reach of all those feet, and her ears flicked back and forth constantly. She saw the broad gap in the crowd, kept open by lines of priests for the procession, and made for it. I admired her technique. Hardly anyone in that close-packed hall knew she'd slipped by them. I squinted, trying to see her better, but she disappeared behind a young man in green brocade with the latest trailing sleeves. She swatted the point of one neatly as she wriggled through the crowd.

If Firousi had been a cat, her ears would have been up and forward. She stretched to her tallest, poised on her tall shoes, peering over the heads of the crowd. "Layla," she hissed in my ear, "that cat—"

The great doors at the far end of the hall were swung open, and the High Priests of Sarinsat came in. The hall seemed to shake with the sound of voices, cymbals and sistrums. The aisle narrowed as even the burly young priests couldn't completely resist the push from the crowd. Devoted or curious, everyone wanted to see Sarinsat's birthday present.

I wanted a better look at it myself, but being short all I could see was the wide expanse of beaded silk covering the back of the woman in front of me. I imitated the cat. Behind me, either Firousi or Arakante plucked at the side of my caftan, but I was gone.

Incense rose in clouds from plain golden censers swung by young boys. The rubies of the Heart glittered through its fog. It took all the self-discipline I had learned as thief or Goddess-chosen to keep from sneezing.

The cat had found the aisle and sat down to wash herself. A gust of incense made her sneeze; she rose, shaking her head and batting at her nose. Then she saw the steady advance of the procession and ran for the open doors, snaking along between the procession and the edge of the crowd.

I knew that cat! What was Dancer doing here? Someone's jeweled sandal came into view; the cat avoided the kick neatly. She darted straight into the path of the High Priest.

He was gazing forward raptly at the gleaming, sparkling heart he carried. He tripped, slid, tried and failed to recover; as he flailed his arms for balance on the slick marble, the heart flew into the air.

I dodged, I slid under arms and once between the legs of a very tall man. I tapped this one on the shoulder to make him turn away from me, and tugged that one's belt purse to make her step aside in alarm. It takes far longer to tell than it took to wriggle my way to the opening in the crowd. The guard who might have barred my way had stepped forward to help the priest. I leaped into

the air and caught the heart just before it could hit the floor. What now? There was no escaping this crowd; I had acted without asking what my next move should be.

Sarinsat's High Priest scrambled to his feet and came towards me. I'd no chance of escaping, and for once I didn't want to. I turned in place and held the heart up so that the Viceroy could see it.

The crowd fell back as the Emperor's half-brother came down from his throne, halfway down the steps. His eyes were black as earth-glass, and as hard. The entire hall fell silent as he stared at me with those strange eyes that seemed to have no pupils. That was a pity; the pupils of people's eyes will often tell you their mood.

"Majesty." It was Firousi's priestess-voice, pitched to carry without shouting. "Majesty, I crave permission to remind you of a promise made to us by the Emperor."

He turned one hand upwards with a graceful turn of the wrist.

"He swore to me, through his governor in Charransar, that if the jeweled heart of Kossinli, Lady of Laughter, could be found it would be restored to Her. Majesty, I tell you that it has been found."

In all the room, only one person moved. A gray-haired man in Rememberer's green edged his way out of the crowd on the lower steps of the dais. Then he, too, was still. His eyes stared straight ahead, past the Heart and its claimants.

"Majesty!" The High Priest rushed forward. Two of the Imperial guard stepped forward smartly, scimitars unsheathed. At a gesture from the Viceroy they fell back, but only half a step. "Majesty, that heart belongs by right of conquest to Sarinsat. His soldiers it was who came to the front of the battle, time and again. His priests still ride many weary miles keeping the Empire's cities informed of the Emperor's will, and the Emperor informed of the actions of His subjects."

Firousi laughed, a bright bronze knife of a laugh. "Right

of conquest? Majesty, can you explain to me why one of the triumphs of your family's reign has been hidden away for all these years? If it is rightfully theirs," she glanced at the Priests of Sarinsat, "Why has it not been displayed before now? Were they waiting for the worshipers of the Lady of Laughter to become so poor and so few that we could make no protest?"

The Viceroy gestured for silence. At a snap of the royal fingers, the Rememberer came forward. "Was there such a promise?"

"Majesty, there was."

"And is this the Heart?"

"Majesty, it is as it was described to your august brother's governor by a woman who much resembled this one." The Viceroy nodded; the Rememberer bowed and stepped back into the crowd.

Lord Prahin had not given up. "Majesty, this man had never seen the Heart. With all due respect, how can he know that it is the one mentioned in a promise given so many years ago? Why—"

The Viceroy opened his mouth, and Lord Prahin fell silent. "Why has it been hidden so long?"

"Majesty, such was the advice of Sarinsat, who seldom explains His reasons to His servants. Majesty, do not punish the most dedicated followers of Your family—" He fell silent again at a glare from the Viceroy.

The Hall was silent now, or as close to it as a room that large can be when filled with people. Firousi had moved to stand as close to me as the guards would allow. Though I couldn't see Arakante, I could hear him murmuring the same words over and over. He was staring intently at the white-bearded mage we'd seen earlier. His fine beard and mustache concealed his mouth, but I'd bet he was saying something. My skin shivered like Imchi's. Wards or no, some battle was being fought. As Arakante had said, there were no fireballs or lightning. There was only a shivering like heat over stones at midsummer.

The heart trembled in my hands. I cupped it carefully,

feeling it shift and strain. Didn't Arakante or his opponent understand that you can't bend metal forever without snapping it? My own heart was beating as if I'd just scaled a city wall. His Majesty had better decide soon.

There are songs of the burdens of rulers. I had never much believed them before this afternoon, when I stood waiting for one man to decide whether to honor a promise (thus offending the most powerful supporters of his brother and Lord) or publicly wriggle out of doing so (thus calling into question the value of the Royal Word). The Rememberer's answer had been carefully given, but what he had said was clear. The hall was so quiet that I could hear the wind outside singing among the arched roofs. A shaft of light found its way down from the center of the largest dome through incense and dust to glitter in the Heart.

The Viceroy raised his hands together in front of his face, then swept them out shoulder-high, palms out. "The Emperor has given his word, and that word must never be broken. The Heart goes to the Lady of Laughter."

"No!" The young priest with the censer charged toward me, swinging its heated weight. Sparks flew; the crowd tumbled back, slapping at scorched brocades and stinging skin. The air was full of shrieks and incense. "Sarinsat!"

"Timur, no!" That was Lord Earrings. His acolyte ignored him.

The crowd was packed too thickly for me to find shelter among them. The guards were running towards us, but I doubted they'd get there in time. The helpful cat had long since vanished. Firousi stood exactly where she had been, now at the edge of our half of the crowd. Arakante? I couldn't see him at all. Surely he hadn't run?

There was another shiver in the air. The sound of the crowd deepened; what words I could hear sounded slurred. The censer-swinger ran with a weird dreamlike slowness. Someone was giving me a chance. Arakante or Kossinli? I'd worry about all that later. What a useful magic this would be for a thief, if I could find a magician who'd work it!

"Firousi," I called. She came towards me with the same weird slowness. Some of the gold wires bent as I thrust the heart into her grasp. She winced, but kept a firm hold.

Timur had swerved towards us. Now I ran, but not into the crowd. I ran under the ponderous arc of the censer's chain, shifting my fine silver bangle forward on my hand. That bit of jewelry's half a handspan wide, and decorated with raised bosses. Firousi calls it barbaric, and she's right. When I hit Timur on the underside of his beautifully chiseled chin, he dropped at once. The censer fell also, opening as it landed, strewing coals and incense across the marble floor.

Then time returned to its normal pace, and I could do nothing but gasp for breath while guards bound the acolyte and Lord Earrings himself tidied up the censer's mess. I coughed as the last of the smoke burned my lungs. Maybe it wouldn't be such a useful magic after all, if you had to stagger around gasping like this afterwards.

Far away, some pompous ass was shouting, but my coughing was all that concerned me. Imps of sour water, was I going to faint now?

Firousi's voice in my ear. "Layla, here, drink this." A cool silver flask pushed against my mouth; reluctantly I drank. The water had a faint metallic tang that might have come from the flask.

Arakante stood with us now, smiling faintly. "That was nimbly done," he murmured.

"I had help."

"So did I."

Firousi laughed softly. "Oh, we all did," she said, and held the heart so that it caught what light there was. No one stood within arm's length of the three of us, not even the guards. As I stared at the heart of gold and rubies, my own heart's beat slowed. I drew a deep breath.

A loud crash drew people's attention from us, much to my relief. Lord Earrings had cast himself, jewelry, charcoal smudges and all, at the feet of the Viceroy.

"Lord, I pray you, let us take this youth and deal with him." Lord Earrings' voice was muffled by his position, but the Viceroy could hear well enough.

"He has done violence in Our presence," he said.

"Excellency, he is our disgrace. Please allow us to discipline him."

Neither of them looked at the unfortunate Timur. The Viceroy would probably have him executed in some spectacular way; Lord Earrings would—what? Timur didn't look at all comforted by his superior's efforts to get him out of Imperial hands.

"My dread Lord, I assure you that this wretched man will never offend you again. I pray you, Excellency, grant us this one favor."

The Viceroy frowned, doubtless remembering the favor he'd had to deny. "Very well. He's yours."

39

"Two jars of pickled lemons." I thumped one of them to show how full it was. Yellow as the lemons they held, their smooth sides rose as high as my knee.

"Layla, that's fantastic. You're fantastic. I won't ask how you got them; the servants haven't been able to find any, even in the Strangers' Quarter." Firousi hugged me hard, and then came out into the kitchen yard to give Imchi some slices of dried apple. He well deserved it after hauling those two enormous jars all the way up from Sarinsat's temple. Well, they weren't going to be celebrating anything, were they? Besides, it would teach them to treat their slaves better. Until I came by, the poor fellows shifting their kitchen supplies back into the storage shed hadn't even had enough coppers for beer to quench their thirst.

It was warm enough for Imchi to stay in the paddock, and for me to wander over by the pond where Firousi had begun my lessons. The ice was gone, and the pavilion had been swept clean of winter's dead leaves and the dirt snow leaves behind. I'd miss these gardens, fine though the public gardens of Charransar were. I'd even miss Firousi. As for Arakante...

As if my thoughts had summoned him, I heard his step on the stone path. "Layla, well met."

We hadn't met much since regaining the heart. I'd been enjoying myself, obtaining supplies by devious means that Firousi couldn't employ and telling our story again and again to the followers and curiosity-seekers who dropped by. Arakante had been in his study. I knew he hadn't been seeing clients, but that was all

I knew.

He sighed and stretched. "Well, it's done! Firousi may think Kossinli doesn't need any help now, but a good protective net of wards won't do any harm." He looked at me sideways. "Someone tested them last night, just after moonrise. I had enough done that I was warned."

"Not me! I go in and out by the door now, just like a respectable woman. Actually, I was downright stodgy last night, asleep before the moon was one-quarter up the sky."

He touched my shoulder gently. "I wasn't accusing you, Layla. And I can't imagine you ever being stodgy. "

That was a relief. What was he so edgy about, though? If Arakante didn't really have anything to say he usually kept silence.

I felt edgy myself when he did stay quiet. One of us had to say something, so I did. "It's so good to see the sun again! How do you stand it, winter after cold damp winter? You should come to Charransar sometime."

"Are you returning to your home city, then?" Without discussing it, we began walking toward the pavilion. I suspected I knew what this was about! After all, Arakante didn't need to be able to See for me any more, did he? And we'd already dealt with the question of marriage.

"I'll leave with Mother Rissa's caravan after the celebration," I answered. "I'm not sure exactly how soon—" I didn't want to sound as if I were fishing for an invitation to stay with them, particularly if Arakante did want to be my lover. I've been bought and sold—what else was my marriage? I'll not live that way again.

"Layla, I'm not rushing you! We've grown close this year. It will seem very strange not to have you here." Arakante shifted away from me on the bench and took my hand. "Layla, if you're considering staying..."

I smiled. "Hmm?"

"Would you reconsider becoming my wife? I promise you,

it would be quite different from your first marriage."

I could well believe that. Even so, "No. No, I'm truly sorry."

"Even if," he hesitated a moment, then continued. "Even if the man your father married you to hasn't divorced you, and I can find that out readily enough if you'll just tell me a little more, you can divorce him. I won't ask you how long it's been, but surely it's been long enough for that to be easy."

"Arakante, have mercy! I'm hurting you, and of all people I don't want to hurt you. I'd stay here awhile as your lover, but Firousi tells me the law's clear—"

"You discussed this with Firousi?" He dropped my hand so abruptly that it struck the bench.

"Oh, not you and me! Not that, Arakante!" I must not laugh. The pain in my hand helped keep me from unseemly mirth. "Just whether I could stay here past summer's end. But she says that I'm too public now for bribes to make anyone overlook me, and I won't live here on sufferance as somebody's wife, even yours. What happens if we stop loving each other?"

"That isn't going to happen."

"Really? Your magic has told you that? You said you couldn't See for yourself." That kept him silent for several breaths. He went so pale that I began to fear that I'd finally managed to enrage him beyond his wizardly self-control. Tzakendi winters were bad enough as a person; I really didn't want to spend one as a frog.

Finally he spoke. "I'd like to strangle that first husband of yours! What did he do to you to make you so fearful of marriage? So you've been married before. So was I, don't forget. You had no choice at all, and I—well, no amount of magic will keep you from making mistakes. Others took the omens for us, and found them favorable. So much for wise and careful choices!"

"So you admit I'm not a wise or careful choice."

He shook his head like a dog coming out of the water. "Firousi should never have taught you formal argument. But this is supposed to be a marriage proposal, not a debate! Layla."

So, he didn't like my using formal argument? I knew another sort. I kissed him, no more than that. He kissed back, enjoying it but still thinking. I can tell when a man's still thinking. I sat back a little, trying not to be angry again.

Then he moved toward me, with a small laugh. Was I amusing, then? He shook his head. "Not you, Layla. Me." For once I didn't resent his being able to hear my unspoken thoughts. Would he go on doing that while we made love, though? And did that thought excite me or frighten me?

"Let's find out," he said.

At first it did both; after awhile there were too few real thoughts for it to matter. He certainly didn't seem to be offended by any of the thoughts that he caught. There was no need to say, "Touch me there, no there." He knew. Did I borrow some of his magic? Few men have complained of me, but I've never before had such a talent for pleasing us both.

I hope no servant was working in that part of the grounds. When I'm happy, the world knows it. Arakante cried out only once.

Wide though the bench was, we couldn't quite lie side by side on it when we were done. Besides, evenings were still chilly. We sorted out our clothing, laughing at how it had become tangled together. He helped me into the long Tzakendi overrobe; I helped him wind his wide sash properly once we'd untangled it from my own sash and its tassels.

We cuddled together on the bench that had suddenly become much colder and harder. Neither of us wanted to go in yet. It was as if we were invisible out here. Once we returned to the house, we'd be visible again.

He began to speak, but I stopped him with a kiss. "Don't, love." This time I knew what he was going to say. Arrogant of me? Maybe, but I was right.

"So, I wasn't as persuasive as I'd hoped?"

"Oh, is that what all that was about? Well...you could

always try again to convince me." I giggled at the look on his face. Even a Wizard may be afraid of the Insatiable Female. "That's appetite, Arakante, not hunger." Even a wizard may get that funny smirk that men do when they've made you happy.

40

*L*amp-flames flickered in their fretwork holders, and laughter filled the room. The incense smoke rose, thinned, braided itself into an elaborate interlace, then scattered in the half-seen carvings of the gilded ceiling. It left behind a half-covered tang of sweat from our dances.

It was time. Firousi glided over to me, smiling calmly. Well might she look calm! The next responsibility was mine.

The heart lay nested in gold-shot silk in a box of sandalwood. I lifted it carefully, lightly as if I were trying to take it from someone's pocket. Most gems will catch light. Those of good quality seem to have their own. This one seemed to create light, for it sparkled like a fire; I stood still for several heartbeats watching it.

Firousi unhooked the fastenings of the statue's woven-gold caftan and turned the stiff folds aside. A high-raised band almost like a sword-harness ran over the statue's left shoulder, between the breasts and down to the right hip; no doubt it continued across Kossinli's back. Just to one side of the left breast, slightly higher than the human heart lies, was a niche only slightly larger than the heart itself.

I would have words for Firousi later. In all those lessons, why had she never mentioned that I'd be obliged to insert a delicately-made heart of rubies and gold wire into such a small niche? Actually, I could answer that. Oh yes, and I'd have to do it in public, with lots of worshipers to rip my own heart out if I fumbled the job and let the heart fall to its ruin on the marble floor.

My hands were shaking. I, who had never trembled even on my first solo theft, was shivering like a virgin bride.

The musicians had done the same repeat twice now, and were looking sideways at Firousi as they neared the end of it. She must have signaled them somehow, for they went into a song from our early lessons.

It was almost insulting, but it worked. My hands steadied enough that I dared lift the heart up, one hand under it and the other guiding it gently, smoothly, into the niche in Kossinli's chest.

Now it glowed even brighter, dazzling my eyes with the light from the rubies and the gold behind them. I could almost believe that I saw it beat. Perhaps I did.

The dances began again, led by three dancers so old that it was hard to tell who was a man and who a woman. They mimicked my own hesitation with a broad exaggeration that would normally have infuriated me. Now I was too relieved to have done it all correctly to care. A minor goddess, a goddess of tricks and laughter, is still a goddess.

Firousi stood with her head thrown back and her arms curved, palms forward. The grin on her face was nothing like the rapt look that visionaries are supposed to have. Someone giggled; someone else whimpered.

Something was happening beyond the room, a dance or a song, but I couldn't quite tell what it was. If I came a little closer, could I see?

Whispers from the crowd behind me drew my attention. They were afraid, and why not? None of this was part of the ceremony, and from where they stood they couldn't see Firousi's smile. Kossinli's worship had lain quiet for a generation. What if Firousi had misinterpreted Kossinli's will or misremembered some of what she'd learned as a young child?

The late afternoon sun made the eyes of Kossinli glow. It looked to me like happiness rather than anger. If Firousi wasn't frightened, why should I be? I had a question to ask, and surely

Kossinli was in the best mood she was ever likely to be. *Will You release me now?*

Will you release me?

If She was happier than before, I couldn't tell it by the divine Voice. Strange; I'd always thought a goddess' voice would be perfect.

Please don't make fun of me! No doubt I should have been more respectful, but even when dealing with a goddess I couldn't make myself pretend not to mind.

I'm not mocking you. Did you think this had all been by My choice?

Well, it certainly wasn't by mine! Haven't I been trying for weeks—months—to free myself?

So angry! Laugh a little, my thief. For here's the joke: I couldn't help but listen to you.

Somehow it didn't seem funny. Did she mean She couldn't free me? Or that She had needed me too much to be picky?

I needed a thief. I didn't need to drag one complaining all the way across the Wastes! Was your life so wonderful in Charransar?

It was MY life! It was the life I'd chosen, though it was a hard choice. I had answered to no one. I had needed no one.

And no one needed you.

Unkind, but true; it was also beside the point. I had done my part! This might all be amusing for a goddess with eternity to spend on a jest, but I wanted my freedom more than I wanted anything else in this world or the next. How could I win free if She could hear everything I thought?

I reached delicately for the tricks Firousi'd tried to teach me, going as carefully as if I were sliding through the narrow window of a Lady's cluttered dressing room. There was a way through; I'd glimpsed it from time to time, but never managed the focus to get through. Now I must.

Only a faint reddish sunlight touched the statue now. I must hurry through that crowded room, filled with the dances and stories like a tangle of bright scarves, the rituals and legends like delicate tables of porcelain, never tripping or snagging. There was something here that would free me.

There was a soft whuffle in my ear, and a distinct gust of donkey-breath came to my nose. I had to laugh, and to sneeze. Trust Kossinli not to use the scent of supernatural jasmine! When I opened my eyes I saw the key, balanced in nested lattice-spheres of crystal. Now, here was something much like things I'd long known how to do.

It's something any dancer could easily learn to do. You need only move part of your hand alone, without disturbing the balance at the wrist while two fingers–not the thumb!–slide in among the orbs to take the prize. I'd never done it with a device that had no central pole before. If anything, that made it easier. Just once I brushed against the icy cold of the crystal.

I had the key, and something slid shut like a lock fastening behind me to stop my pursuers. That usually brings a howl of anger. Today it brought a laugh, just barely audible behind the door I'd shut.

I still saw the cluttered dressing room rather than the open temple. Had I locked myself in? Surely not. The trick of getting out of a strange house with a whole skin is to remember exactly what you passed on the way in, and be aware of everything you've moved. That way you don't trip over some heavy treasure you left near the window.

Did I remember well enough? This wasn't quite like a real house. Would it even stay as I'd first imagined it? Well, if it wouldn't I was lost. Maybe Firousi would see to it that my body was cared for until I got back from my trance, if I ever did. At least she wouldn't have to worry that my body would go eat up all the honeyed almonds.

There below me was the many-paned window of the

temple! Silver light shone through the shutters as I picked my way across to it. Yes. Slip the latch of the rough wood, climb through and up to the roof.

I staggered a little as the roof became the temple floor. "If this was mystic journeying, leave me the earthly kind!" I muttered.

Well, wildling, we're free of each other now, said a sweet low voice. The edge was gone from it now, but a slight rasp remained. *But you've amused Me well. If you call upon Me sometime, who can say? I might answer.*

I bowed as Firousi had taught me, the long bow with one foot well behind the other that will topple you on your nose if you don't get it just right. *Be sure, gracious Goddess, that I'll call on You only at great need!*

Don't be so wary. I can refuse now, you know.

Firousi laughed and came out of her tranced pose. "O Lady of Mirth," she said, but nothing more.

Behind us the roomful of people stirred. One couple came timidly to within a yard or so of where we stood. "Is it well? Is She happy?"

"Oh, yes," Firousi said quietly. Then, taking my hand, she came into the center of the room. "The Lady of Mirth laughs again! Join Her!"

She didn't need to urge people twice.

*I*t was time to go. No, it had already been time on the day after the Restoration. Delaying by just two days had only made it harder to leave; it had given me more time to wonder if it would be so very bad to settle into a comfortable, secure life. All I'd have to give up would be my freedom. Arakante wouldn't enforce a husband's right to command, surely. Surely? I was certain that if our love ended, he'd deal with me honorably.

When he asked a third time, though, I found I had to give the same answer. It rains even in the summer in Tzakende, and it was raining that day as we lay curled in our nest of sheets. I kissed him, and he knew it was a good-bye kiss. "I'm sorry. I just can't—"

He cut in. "If it would be such a burden, please forgive me for asking. I should have known better."

Getting back into the intricate layers of Tzakendi clothes, even summer clothes, gave him an excuse not to look at me. My tunics took all too little time; it seemed rude beyond forgiveness to leave while he was still dressing, so I waited and tried not to look nervous.

He dropped a quick kiss on my forehead when he was done. "I should have known better, shouldn't I?" He smiled at me almost shyly. "I know I can't persuade you to stay," he said. "Can I persuade you to return?"

"Yes," I said. "I don't know when, though, Arakante. Don't wait for me."

"Don't ask me to promise that. Don't worry either,

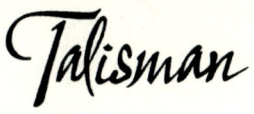

though. Have you any idea how far behind I am in my studies thanks to you and Firousi and the Laughing One? I'll be too busy to be lonely." I hadn't wanted a scene, but this calm acceptance wasn't exactly flattering. Perhaps he was only putting on a brave face? I'd never know.

Certainly he looked composed enough on the morning of my departure as I embraced him and Firousi. She and I had also had our farewells; I think we were both relieved to have this awkward partnership finished.

Besides, she was very busy now. The worship of Kossinli might still be unpopular at court, but Tzakende is a long way from the capitol. She laughed often as she told the old stories to new worshipers, and I began to see how she'd become a Priestess of Kossinli.

She made time for a proper goodbye one afternoon. We sat under the grape arbor along the south wall; without saying why, Firousi had refused to use the little pavilion where we first studied.

"What will you do now?"

"Oh, go with Mother Rissa as far as Issrandar at least. After that, who knows? I'd like to see Charransar again. You'll agree that their winters are more pleasant?"

She laughed. "Oh, no question! But will you be a nomad, like Mother Rissa and her clan?"

"No, though I think I'll find The Wastes easier to endure this time than last. Money does help, especially when you don't have to hide it! But I've never had a choice of where to live before, Firousi. Issrandar was beautiful, too. You needn't worry about me."

"No, I'm sure not." She smiled her closed-mouth smile, and was silent.

There was no point in saying a formal farewell to Kossinli, but I put a branch of Thousand Wonders roses on Her altar. Red, orange and yellow, sometimes all in one blossom, they seemed the right flower for Her. She must have liked them, for I heard soft laughter as I left the temple room. That room was too small for Her worshipers now; the morning air was already full of the noise of the work on her new temple just up the street. They were able to use some of the stones from the old one that had stood there before the earthquake and the Conquest between them tumbled it down.

Imchi stood loaded down with gear for my journey, shifting his feet restlessly. Mother Rissa's caravan waited down in the square, but they wouldn't delay much longer.

We still stood there a moment, until Imchi thrust his whiskery muzzle in between Firousi and me.

She laughed and shoved it back out of her way. "Don't be too long coming back to us."

"Who can say? But I will miss you." I walked down the hill with Imchi pulling at his lead. I forced him to wait long enough for me to look back at the top of the Nadarine stairs. I could just see them both in the arched entrance to the courtyard. One last wave, and I hurried down towards the tumult of the Stranger's Quarter.

Printed in the United States
50653LVS00003B/1-72

9 781932 636208